THE BLUE CASTLE
&
A TANGLED WEB

BY

L. M. MONTGOMERY

Author of
"Anne of Green Gables,"
"Anne of Avonlea,"
"Kilmeny of the Orchard," etc.

British Library Cataloguing-in-Publication Data
A catalogue record for this book is available
from the British Library

CONTENTS

Lucy Maud Montgomery 5
THE BLUE CASTLE 7
A TANGLED WEB 235

Lucy Maud Montgomery

Lucy Maud Montgomery was born on 30th November 1874, on Prince Edward Island, Canada. Her mother, Clara Woolner (Macneil), died before Lucy reached the age of two and so she was raised by her maternal grandparents in a family of wealthy Scottish immigrants. The Family were deeply rooted in the development of the island, having arrived there in the 1770's, and both Lucy's grandfather and great grandfather had been figures in the province's governance.

As a young girl, Montgomery had a very privileged upbringing. Due to the families wealth, she had access to a greater number of books than was usual in this era. These resources, coupled with the family's Scottish traditions of oral storytelling, gave her a taste for literature.

Montgomery took a teacher's degree at Charlottetown's Prince of Wales College before beginning work at a rural school to raise funds for and additional year at Dalhousie University. She continued to teach for a couple of years until her income from writing enabled her to become a full-time author. She then moved back home to live with her grandmother. In 1908, Montgomery produced her first full-length novel, titled *Anne of Green Gables*. It was an instant success and, following it up with several sequels, Montgomery became a regular on the best-seller list and an international household name.

In 1911 she married Ewan Macdonald, a Presbyterian minister, following the death of her grandmother. They had two sons together but the marriage was fraught with difficulties. Ewan had a severe mental disorder that frequently left him incapacitated, seriously hampering his career and eventually forcing him to resign from the ministry in 1935. The couple retired to Toronto and resided there together until Montgomery's death on 24th April 1942.

THE BLUE CASTLE

First published in 1926

CHAPTER I

If it had not rained on a certain May morning Valancy Stirling's whole life would have been entirely different. She would have gone, with the rest of her clan, to Aunt Wellington's engagement picnic and Dr. Trent would have gone to Montreal. But it did rain and you shall hear what happened to her because of it.

Valancy wakened early, in the lifeless, hopeless hour just preceding dawn. She had not slept very well. One does not sleep well, sometimes, when one is twenty-nine on the morrow, and unmarried, in a community and connection where the unmarried are simply those who have failed to get a man.

Deerwood and the Stirlings had long since relegated Valancy to hopeless old maidenhood. But Valancy herself had never quite relinquished a certain pitiful, shamed, little hope that Romance would come her way yet—never, until this wet, horrible morning, when she wakened to the fact that she was twenty-nine and unsought by any man.

Ay, *there* lay the sting. Valancy did not mind so much being an old maid. After all, she thought, being an old maid couldn't possibly be as dreadful as being married to an Uncle Wellington or an Uncle Benjamin, or even an Uncle Herbert. What hurt her was that she had never had a chance to be anything but an old maid. No man had ever desired her.

The tears came into her eyes as she lay there alone in the faintly greying darkness. She dared not let herself cry as hard as she wanted to, for two reasons. She was afraid that crying might bring on another attack of that pain around the heart. She had had a spell of it after she had got into bed—rather worse than any she had had yet. And she was afraid her mother would notice her red eyes at breakfast and keep at her with minute, persistent, mosquito-like questions regarding the cause thereof.

"Suppose," thought Valancy with a ghastly grin, "I answered with the plain truth, 'I am crying because I cannot get married.' How horrified Mother would be—though she is ashamed every day of her life of her old maid daughter."

But of course appearances should be kept up. "It is not," Valancy could hear her mother's prim, dictatorial voice asserting, "it is not *maidenly* to think about *men*."

The thought of her mother's expression made Valancy laugh— for she had a sense of humour nobody in her clan suspected. For that matter, there were a good many things about Valancy that nobody suspected. But her laughter was very superficial and presently she lay there, a huddled, futile little figure, listening to the rain pouring down outside and watching, with a sick distaste, the chill, merciless light creeping into her ugly, sordid room.

She knew the ugliness of that room by heart—knew it and hated it. The yellow-painted floor, with one hideous, "hooked" rug by the bed, with a grotesque, "hooked" dog on it, always grinning at her when she awoke; the faded, dark-red paper; the ceiling discoloured by old leaks and crossed by cracks; the narrow, pinched little washstand; the brown-paper lambrequin with purple roses on it; the spotted old looking-glass with the crack across it, propped up on the inadequate dressing-table; the jar of ancient potpourri made by her mother in her mythical honeymoon; the shell-covered box, with one burst corner, which Cousin Stickles had made in her equally mythical girlhood; the beaded pincushion with half its bead fringe gone; the one stiff, yellow chair; the faded old motto, "Gone but not forgotten," worked in coloured yarns about Great-grandmother Stirling's grim old face; the old photographs of ancient relatives long banished from the rooms below. There were only two pictures that were not of relatives. One, an old chromo of a puppy sitting on a rainy doorstep. That picture always made Valancy unhappy. That forlorn little dog crouched on the doorstep in the driving rain! Why didn't *some one* open the door and let him in? The other picture was a faded, passe-partouted engraving of Queen Louise coming down a stairway, which Aunt Wellington had lavishly given her on her tenth birthday. For nineteen years she had looked at it and hated it, beautiful, smug, self-satisfied Queen Louise. But she never dared destroy it or remove it. Mother and Cousin Stickles would have been aghast, or, as Valancy irreverently expressed it in her thoughts, would have had a fit.

Every room in the house was ugly, of course. But downstairs appearances were kept up somewhat. There was no money for rooms nobody ever saw. Valancy sometimes felt that she could have done something for her room herself, even without money, if she were permitted. But her mother had negatived every timid suggestion and Valancy did not persist. Valancy never persisted. She was afraid to. Her mother could not brook opposition. Mrs. Stirling would sulk for days if offended, with the airs of an insulted duchess.

The only thing Valancy liked about her room was that she could be alone there at night to cry if she wanted to.

But, after all, what did it matter if a room, which you used for nothing except sleeping and dressing in, were ugly? Valancy was never permitted to stay alone in her room for any other purpose. People who wanted to be alone, so Mrs. Frederick Stirling and Cousin Stickles believed, could only want to be alone for some sinister purpose. But her room in the Blue Castle was everything a room should be.

Valancy, so cowed and subdued and overridden and snubbed in real life, was wont to let herself go rather splendidly in her day-dreams. Nobody in the Stirling clan, or its ramifications, suspected this, least of all her mother and Cousin Stickles. They never knew that Valancy had two homes—the ugly red brick box of a home, on Elm Street, and the Blue Castle in Spain. Valancy had lived spiritually in the Blue Castle ever since she could remember. She had been a very tiny child when she found herself possessed of it. Always, when she shut her eyes, she could see it plainly, with its turrets and banners on the pine-clad mountain height, wrapped in its faint, blue loveliness, against the sunset skies of a fair and unknown land. Everything wonderful and beautiful was in that castle. Jewels that queens might have worn; robes of moonlight and fire; couches of roses and gold; long flights of shallow marble steps, with great, white urns, and with slender, mist-clad maidens going up and down them; courts, marble-pillared, where shimmering fountains fell and nightingales sang among the myrtles; halls of mirrors that reflected only handsome knights and lovely women—herself the loveliest of all, for whose glance men died. All that supported her through the boredom of her days was the hope of going on a dream spree at night. Most, if not all, of the Stirlings would have died of horror if they had known half the things Valancy did in her Blue Castle.

For one thing she had quite a few lovers in it. Oh, only one at a time. One who wooed her with all the romantic ardour of the age of chivalry and won her after long devotion and many deeds of derring-do, and was wedded to her with pomp and circumstance in the great, banner-hung chapel of the Blue Castle.

At twelve, this lover was a fair lad with golden curls and heavenly blue eyes. At fifteen, he was tall and dark and pale, but still necessarily handsome. At twenty, he was ascetic, dreamy, spiritual. At twenty-five, he had a clean-cut jaw, slightly grim, and a face strong and rugged rather than handsome. Valancy never grew older than twenty-five in her Blue Castle, but recently—very recently—her hero had had reddish, tawny hair, a twisted smile and a mysterious past.

I don't say Valancy deliberately murdered these lovers as she outgrew them. One simply faded away as another came. Things are very convenient in this respect in Blue Castles.

But, on this morning of her day of fate, Valancy could not find the key of her Blue Castle. Reality pressed on her too hardly, barking at her heels like a maddening little dog. She was twenty-nine, lonely, undesired, ill-favoured—the only homely girl in a handsome clan, with no past and no future. As far as she could look back, life was drab and colourless, with not one single crimson or purple spot anywhere. As far as she could look forward it seemed certain to be just the same until she was nothing but a solitary, little withered leaf clinging to a wintry bough. The moment when a woman realises that she has nothing to live for—neither love, duty, purpose nor hope—holds for her the bitterness of death.

"And I just have to go on living because I can't stop. I may have to live eighty years," thought Valancy, in a kind of panic. "We're all horribly long-lived. It sickens me to think of it."

She was glad it was raining—or rather, she was drearily satisfied that it was raining. There would be no picnic that day. This annual picnic, whereby Aunt and Uncle Wellington—one always thought of them in that succession—inevitably celebrated their engagement at a picnic thirty years before, had been, of late years, a veritable nightmare to Valancy. By an impish coincidence it was the same day as her birthday and, after she had passed twenty-five, nobody let her forget it.

Much as she hated going to the picnic, it would never have occurred to her to rebel against it. There seemed to be nothing of the revolutionary in her nature. And she knew exactly what every one would say to her at the picnic. Uncle Wellington, whom she disliked and despised even though he had fulfilled the highest Stirling aspiration, "marrying money," would say to her in a pig's whisper, "Not thinking of getting married yet, my dear?" and then go off into the bellow of laughter with which he invariably concluded his dull remarks. Aunt Wellington, of whom Valancy stood in abject awe, would tell her about Olive's new chiffon dress and Cecil's last devoted letter. Valancy would have to look as pleased and interested as if the dress and letter had been hers or else Aunt Wellington would be offended. And Valancy had long ago decided that she would rather offend God than Aunt Wellington, because God might forgive her but Aunt Wellington never would.

Aunt Alberta, enormously fat, with an amiable habit of always referring to her husband as "he," as if he were the only male creature in the world, who could never forget that she had been a great beauty in her youth, would condole with Valancy on her sallow skin—

"I don't know why all the girls of today are so sunburned. When I was a girl my skin was roses and cream. I was counted the prettiest girl in Canada, my dear."

Perhaps Uncle Herbert wouldn't say anything—or perhaps he would remark jocularly, "How fat you're getting, Doss!" And then everybody would laugh over the excessively humorous idea of poor, scrawny little Doss getting fat.

Handsome, solemn Uncle James, whom Valancy disliked but respected because he was reputed to be very clever and was therefore the clan oracle—brains being none too plentiful in the Stirling connection—would probably remark with the owl-like sarcasm that had won him his reputation, "I suppose you're busy with your hope-chest these days?"

And Uncle Benjamin would ask some of his abominable conundrums, between wheezy chuckles, and answer them himself.

"What is the difference between Doss and a mouse?

"The mouse wishes to harm the cheese and Doss wishes to charm the he's."

Valancy had heard him ask that riddle fifty times and every time she wanted to throw something at him. But she never did. In the first place, the Stirlings simply did not throw things; in the second place, Uncle Benjamin was a wealthy and childless old widower and Valancy had been brought up in the fear and admonition of his money. If she offended him he would cut her out of his will—supposing she were in it. Valancy did not want to be cut out of Uncle Benjamin's will. She had been poor all her life and knew the galling bitterness of it. So she endured his riddles and even smiled tortured little smiles over him.

Aunt Isabel, downright and disagreeable as an east wind,

would criticise her in some way—Valancy could not predict just how, for Aunt Isabell never repeated a criticism—she found something new with which to jab you every time. Aunt Isabel prided herself on saying what she thought, but didn't like it so well when other people said what *they* thought to *her*. Valancy never said what *she* thought.

Cousin Georgiana—named after her great-great-grandmother, who had been named after George the Fourth—would recount dolorously the names of all relatives and friends who had died since the last picnic and wonder "which of us will be the first to go next."

Oppressively competent, Aunt Mildred would talk endlessly of her husband and her odious prodigies of babies to Valancy, because Valancy would be the only one she could find to put up with it. For the same reason, Cousin Gladys—really First Cousin Gladys once removed, according to the strict way in which the Stirlings tabulated relationship—a tall, thin lady who admitted she had a sensitive disposition, would describe minutely the tortures of her neuritis. And Olive, the wonder girl of the whole Stirling clan, who had everything Valancy had not—beauty, popularity, love—would show off her beauty and presume on her popularity and flaunt her diamond insignia of love in Valancy's dazzled, envious eyes.

There would be none of all this today. And there would be no packing up of teaspoons. The packing up was always left for Valancy and Cousin Stickles. And once, six years ago, a silver teaspoon from Aunt Wellington's wedding set had been lost. Valancy never heard the last of that silver teaspoon. Its ghost appeared Banquo-like at every subsequent family feast.

Oh, yes, Valancy knew exactly what the picnic would be like and she blessed the rain that had saved her from it. There would be no picnic this year. If Aunt Wellington could not celebrate on the sacred day itself she would have no celebration at all. Thank whatever gods there were for that.

Since there would be no picnic, Valancy made up her mind

that, if the rain held up in the afternoon, she would go up to the library and get another of John Foster's books. Valancy was never allowed to read novels, but John Foster's books were not novels. They were "nature books"—so the librarian told Mrs. Frederick Stirling—"all about the woods and birds and bugs and things like that, you know." So Valancy was allowed to read them—under protest, for it was only too evident that she enjoyed them too much. It was permissible, even laudable, to read to improve your mind and your religion, but a book that was enjoyable was dangerous. Valancy did not know whether her mind was being improved or not; but she felt vaguely that if she had come across John Foster's books years ago life might have been a different thing for her. They seemed to her to yield glimpses of a world into which she might once have entered, though the door was forever barred to her now. It was only within the last year that John Foster's books had been in the Deerwood library, though the librarian told Valancy that he had been a well-known writer for several years.

"Where does he live?" Valancy had asked.

"Nobody knows. From his books he must be a Canadian, but no more information can be had. His publishers won't say a word. Quite likely John Foster is a nom de plume. His books are so popular we can't keep them in at all, though I really can't see what people find in them to rave over."

"I think they're wonderful," said Valancy, timidly.

"Oh—well—" Miss Clarkson smiled in a patronising fashion that relegated Valancy's opinions to limbo, "I can't say I care much for bugs myself. But certainly Foster seems to know all there is to know about them."

Valancy didn't know whether she cared much for bugs either. It was not John Foster's uncanny knowledge of wild creatures and insect life that enthralled her. She could hardly say what it was—some tantalising lure of a mystery never revealed—some hint of a great secret just a little further on—some faint, elusive echo of lovely, forgotten things—John Foster's magic was indefinable.

Yes, she would get a new Foster book. It was a month since she had *Thistle Harvest,* so surely Mother could not object. Valancy had read it four times—she knew whole passages off by heart.

And—she almost thought she would go and see Dr. Trent about that queer pain around the heart. It had come rather often lately, and the palpitations were becoming annoying, not to speak of an occassional dizzy moment and a queer shortness of breath. But could she go to him without telling any one? It was a most daring thought. None of the Stirlings ever consulted a doctor without holding a family council and getting Uncle James' approval. *Then,* they went to Dr. Ambrose Marsh of Port Lawrence, who had married Second Cousin Adelaide Stirling.

But Valancy disliked Dr. Ambrose Marsh. And, besides, she could not get to Port Lawrence, fifteen miles away, without being taken there. She did not want any one to know about her heart. There would be such a fuss made and every member of the family would come down and talk it over and advise her and caution her and warn her and tell her horrible tales of great-aunts and cousins forty times removed who had been "just like that and dropped dead without a moment's warning, my dear."

Aunt Isabel would remember that she had always said Doss looked like a girl who would have heart trouble—"so pinched and peaked always"; and Uncle Wellington would take it as a personal insult, when "no Stirling ever had heart disease before"; and Georgiana would forebode in perfectly audible asides that "poor, dear little Doss isn't long for this world, I'm afraid"; and Cousin Gladys would say, "Why, *my* heart has been like that for *years,*" in a tone that implied no one else had any business even to have a heart; and Olive—Olive would merely look beautiful and superior and disgustingly healthy, as if to say, "Why all this fuss over a faded superfluity like Doss when you have *me?*"

Valancy felt that she couldn't tell anybody unless she had to. She felt quite sure there was nothing at all seriously wrong with her heart and no need of all the pother that would ensue if she mentioned it. She would just slip up quietly and see Dr. Trent that very day. As for his bill, she had the two hundred dollars that her father had put in the bank for her the day she was born, but she would secretly take out enough to pay Dr. Trent. She was never allowed to use even the interest of this.

Dr. Trent was a gruff, outspoken, absent-minded old fellow, but he was a recognised authority on heart-disease, even if he were only a general practitioner in out-of-the-world Deerwood. Dr. Trent was over seventy and there had been rumours that he meant to retire soon. None of the Stirling clan had ever gone to him since he had told Cousin Gladys, ten years before, that her neuritis was all imaginary and that she enjoyed it. You couldn't patronise a doctor who insulted your first-cousin-once-removed like that—not to mention that he was a Presbyterian when all the Stirlings went to the Anglican church. But Valancy, between the devil of disloyalty to clan and the deep sea of fuss and clatter and advice, thought she would take a chance with the devil.

CHAPTER II

When cousin Stickles knocked at her door, Valancy knew it was half-past seven and she must get up. As long as she could remember, Cousin Stickles had knocked at her door at half-past seven. Cousin Stickles and Mrs. Frederick Stirling had been up since seven, but Valancy was allowed to lie abed half an hour longer because of a family tradition that she was delicate. Valancy got up, though she hated getting up more this morning than ever she had before. What was there to get up for? Another dreary day like all the days that had preceded it, full of meaningless little tasks, joyless and unimportant, that benefited nobody. But if she did not get up at once she would not be ready for breakfast at eight o'clock. Hard and fast times for meals were the rule in Mrs. Stirling's household. Breakfast at eight, dinner at one, supper at six, year in and year out. No excuses for being late were ever tolerated. So up Valancy got, shivering.

The room was bitterly cold with the raw, penetrating chill of a wet May morning. The house would be cold all day. It was one of Mrs. Frederick's rules that no fires were necessary after the twenty-fourth of May. Meals were cooked on the little oil-stove in the back porch. And though May might be icy and October frost-bitten, no fires were lighted until the twenty-first of October by the calendar. On the twenty-first of October Mrs. Frederick began cooking over the kitchen range and lighted a fire in the sitting-room stove in the evenings. It was whispered about in the connection that the late Frederick Stirling had caught the cold which resulted in his death during Valancy's first year of life because Mrs. Frederick would not have a fire on the twentieth of October. She lighted it the next day—but that was a day too late for Frederick Stirling.

Valancy took off and hung up in the closet her nightdress of coarse, unbleached cotton, with high neck and long, tight sleeves. She put on undergarments of a similar nature, a dress of brown gingham, thick, black stockings and rubber-heeled boots. Of late years she had fallen into the habit of doing her hair with the shade of the window by the looking-glass pulled down. The lines on her face did not show so plainly then. But this morning she jerked the shade to the very top and looked at herself in the leprous mirror with a passionate determination to see herself as the world saw her.

The result was rather dreadful. Even a beauty would have found that harsh, unsoftened side-light trying. Valancy saw straight black hair, short and thin, always lustreless despite the fact that she gave it one hundred strokes of the brush, neither more nor less, every night of her life and faithfully rubbed Redfern's Hair Vigor into the roots, more lustreless than ever in its morning roughness; fine, straight, black brows; a nose she had always felt was much too small even for her small, three-cornered, white face; a small, pale mouth that always fell open a trifle over little, pointed white teeth; a figure thin and flat-breasted, rather below the average height. She had somehow escaped the family high cheek-bones, and her dark-brown eyes, too soft and shadowy to be black, had a slant that was almost Oriental. Apart from her eyes she was neither pretty nor ugly—just insignificant-looking, she concluded bitterly. How plain the lines around her eyes and mouth were in that merciless light! And never had her narrow, white face looked so narrow and so white.

She did her hair in a pompadour. Pompadours had long gone out of fashion, but they had been in when Valancy first put her hair up and Aunt Wellington had decided that she must always wear her hair so.

"It is the *only* way that becomes you. Your face is so small that you *must* add height to it by a pompadour effect," said Aunt Wellington, who always enunciated commonplaces as if uttering profound and important truths.

Valancy had hankered to do her hair pulled low on her forehead, with puffs above the ears, as Olive was wearing hers. But Aunt Wellington's dictum had such an effect on her that she never dared change her style of hairdressing again. But then, there were so many things Valancy never dared do.

All her life she had been afraid of something, she thought bitterly. From the very dawn of recollection, when she had been so horribly afraid of the big black bear that lived, so Cousin Stickles told her, in the closet under the stairs.

"And I always will be—I know it—I can't help it. I don't know what it would be like not to be afraid of something."

Afraid of her mother's sulky fits—afraid of offending Uncle Benjamin—afraid of becoming a target for Aunt Wellington's contempt—afraid of Aunt Isabel's biting comments—afraid of Uncle James' disapproval—afraid of offending the whole clan's opinions and prejudices—afraid of not keeping up appearances— afraid to say what she really thought of anything—afraid of poverty in her old age. Fear—fear—fear—she could never escape from it. It bound her and enmeshed her like a spider's web of steel. Only in her Blue Castle could she find temporary release. And this morning Valancy could not believe she had a Blue Castle. She would never be able to find it again. Twenty-nine, unmarried, undesired—what had she to do with the fairy-like chatelaine of the Blue Castle? She would cut such childish nonsense out of her life forever and face reality unflinchingly.

She turned from her unfriendly mirror and looked out. The ugliness of the view always struck her like a blow; the ragged fence, the tumble-down old carriage-shop in the next lot, plastered with crude, violently coloured advertisements; the grimy railway station beyond, with the awful derelicts that were always hanging around it even at this early hour. In the pouring rain everything looked worse than usual, especially the beastly advertisement, "Keep that schoolgirl complexion." Valancy *had* kept her schoolgirl complexion. That was just the trouble. There was not a gleam of beauty anywhere—"exactly like my life," thought Valancy drearily. Her brief bitterness had passed. She accepted facts as resignedly as she had always accepted them. She was one of the people whom life always passes by. There was no altering that fact.

In this mood Valancy went down to breakfast.

CHAPTER III

Breakfast was always the same. Oatmeal porridge, which Valancy loathed, toast and tea, and one teaspoonful of marmalade. Mrs. Frederick thought two teaspoonfuls extravagant—but that did not matter to Valancy, who hated marmalade, too. The chilly, gloomy little dining-room was chillier and gloomier than usual; the rain streamed down outside the window; departed Stirlings, in atrocious, gilt frames, wider than the pictures, glowered down from the walls. And yet Cousin Stickles wished Valancy many happy returns of the day!

"Sit up straight, Doss," was all her mother said.

Valancy sat up straight. She talked to her mother and Cousin Stickles of the things they always talked of. She never wondered what would happen if she tried to talk of something else. She knew. Therefore she never did it.

Mrs. Frederick was offended with Providence for sending a rainy day when she wanted to go to a picnic, so she ate her breakfast in a sulky silence for which Valancy was rather grateful. But Christine Stickles whined endlessly on as usual, complaining about everything—the weather, the leak in the pantry, the price of oatmeal and butter—Valancy felt at once she had buttered her toast too lavishly—the epidemic of mumps in Deerwood.

"Doss will be sure to ketch them," she foreboded.

"Doss must not go where she is likely to catch mumps," said Mrs. Frederick shortly.

Valancy had never had mumps—or whooping cough—or chicken-pox—or measles—or anything she should have had—nothing but horrible colds every winter. Doss' winter colds were a sort of tradition in the family. Nothing, it seemed, could prevent her from catching them. Mrs. Frederick and Cousin Stickles did

23

their heroic best. One winter they kept Valancy housed up from November to May, in the warm sitting-room. She was not even allowed to go to church. And Valancy took cold after cold and ended up with bronchitis in June.

"None of *my* family were ever like that," said Mrs. Frederick, implying that it must be a Stirling tendency.

"The Stirling's seldom take cold," said Cousin Stickles resentfully. *She* had been a Stirling.

"I think," said Mrs. Frederick, "that if a person makes up her mind *not* to have colds she will not *have* colds."

So that was the trouble. It was all Valancy's own fault.

But on this particular morning Valancy's unbearable grievance was that she was called Doss. She had endured it for twenty-nine years, and all at once she felt she could not endure it any longer. Her full name was Valancy Jane. Valancy Jane was rather terrible, but she liked Valancy, with its odd, out-land tang. It was always a wonder to Valancy that the Stirlings had allowed her to be so christened. She had been told that her maternal grandfather, old Amos Wansbarra, had chosen the name for her. Her father had tacked on the Jane by way of civilising it, and the whole connection got out of the difficulty by nicknaming her Doss. She never got Valancy from any one but outsiders.

"Mother," she said timidly, "would you mind calling me Valancy after this? Doss seems so—so—I don't like it."

Mrs. Frederick looked at her daughter in astonishment. She wore glasses with enormously strong lenses that gave her eyes a peculiarly disagreeable appearance.

"What is the matter with Doss?"

"It—seems so childish," faltered Valancy.

"Oh!" Mrs. Frederick had been a Wansbarra and the Wansbarra smile was not an asset. "I see. Well, it should suit *you* then. You are childish enough in all conscience, my dear child."

"I am twenty-nine," said the dear child desperately.

"I wouldn't proclaim it from the house-tops if I were you, dear," said Mrs. Frederick. "Twenty-nine! *I* had been married nine years when I was twenty-nine."

"*I* was married at seventeen," said Cousin Stickles proudly.

Valancy looked at them furtively. Mrs. Frederick, except for those terrible glasses and the hooked nose that made her look, more like a parrot than a parrot itself could look, was not ill-looking. At twenty she might have been quite pretty. But Cousin Stickles! And yet Christine Stickles had once been desirable in some man's eyes. Valancy felt that Cousin Stickles, with her broad, flat, wrinkled face, a mole right on the end of her dumpy nose, bristling hairs on her chin, wrinkled yellow neck, pale, protruding eyes, and thin, puckered mouth, had yet this advantage over her—this right to look down on her. And even yet Cousin Stickles was necessary to Mrs. Frederick. Valancy wondered pitifully what it would be like to be wanted by some one—needed by some one. No one in the whole world needed her, or would miss anything from life if she dropped suddenly out of it. She was a disappointment to her mother. No one loved her. She had never so much as had a girl friend.

"I haven't even a gift for friendship," she had once admitted to herself pitifully.

"Doss, you haven't eaten your crusts," said Mrs. Frederick rebukingly.

It rained all the forenoon without cessation. Valancy pieced a quilt. Valancy hated piecing quilts. And there was no need of it. The house was full of quilts. There were three big chests, packed with quilts, in the attic. Mrs. Frederick had begun storing away quilts when Valancy was seventeen and she kept on storing them, though it did not seem likely that Valancy would ever need them. But Valancy must be at work and fancy work materials were too expensive. Idleness was a cardinal sin in the Stirling household. When Valancy had been a child she had been made to write down every night, in a small, hated, black notebook, all the minutes she had spent in idleness that day. On Sundays her mother made her tot them up and pray over them.

On this particular forenoon of this day of destiny Valancy

spent only ten minutes in idleness. At least, Mrs. Frederick and Cousin Stickles would have called it idleness. She went to her room to get a better thimble and she opened *Thistle Harvest* guiltily at random.

"The woods are so human," wrote John Foster, "that to know them one must live with them. An occasional saunter through them, keeping to the well-trodden paths, will never admit us to their intimacy. If we wish to be friends we must seek them out and win them by frequent, reverent visits at all hours; by morning, by noon, and by night; and at all seasons, in spring, in summer, in autumn, in winter. Otherwise we can never really know them and any pretence we may make to the contrary will never impose on them. They have their own effective way of keeping aliens at a distance and shutting their hearts to mere casual sightseers. It is of no use to seek the woods from any motive except sheer love of them; they will find us out at once and hide all their sweet, old-world secrets from us. But if they know we come to them because we love them they will be very kind to us and give us such treasures of beauty and delight as are not bought or sold in any market-place. For the woods, when they give at all, give unstintedly and hold nothing back from their true worshippers. We must go to them lovingly, humbly, patiently, watchfully, and we shall learn what poignant loveliness lurks in the wild places and silent intervales, lying under starshine and sunset, what cadences of unearthly music are harped on aged pine boughs or crooned in copses of fir, what delicate savours exhale from mosses and ferns in sunny corners or on damp brooklands, what dreams and myths and legends of an older time haunt them. Then the immortal heart of the woods will beat against ours and its subtle life will steal into our veins and make us its own forever, so that no matter where we go or how widely we wander we shall yet be drawn back to the forest to find our most enduring kinship."

"Doss," called her mother from the hall below, "what are you doing all by yourself in that room?"

Valancy dropped *Thistle Harvest* like a hot coal and fled

downstairs to her patches; but she felt the strange exhilaration of spirit that always came momentarily to her when she dipped into one of John Foster's books. Valancy did not know much about woods—except the haunted groves of oak and pine around her Blue Castle. But she had always secretly hankered after them and a Foster book about woods was the next best thing to the woods themselves.

At noon it stopped raining, but the sun did not come out until three. Then Valancy timidly said she thought she would go uptown.

"What do you want to go uptown for?" demanded her mother.

"I want to get a book from the library."

"You got a book from the library only last week."

"No, it was four weeks."

"Four weeks. Nonsense!"

"Really it was, Mother."

"You are mistaken. It cannot possibly have been more than two weeks. I dislike contradiction. And I do not see what you want to get a book for, anyhow. You waste too much time reading."

"Of what value is my time?" asked Valancy bitterly.

"Doss! Don't speak in that tone to *me*."

"We need some tea," said Cousin Stickles. "She might go and get that if she wants a walk—though this damp weather is bad for colds."

They argued the matter for ten minutes longer and finally Mrs. Frederick agreed rather grudgingly that Valancy might go.

CHAPTER IV

"Got your rubbers on?" called Cousin Stickles, as Valancy left the house.

Christine Stickles had never once forgotten to ask that question when Valancy went out on a damp day.

"Yes."

"Have you got your flannel petticoat on?" asked Mrs. Frederick.

"No."

"Doss, I really do not understand you. Do you want to catch your death of cold *again*?" Her voice implied that Valancy had died of a cold several times already. "Go upstairs this minute and put it on!"

"Mother, I don't *need* a flannel petticoat. My sateen one is warm enough."

"Doss, remember you had bronchitis two years ago. Go and do as you are told!"

Valancy went, though nobody will ever know just how near she came to hurling the rubber-plant into the street before she went. She hated that grey flannel petticoat more than any other garment she owned. Olive never had to wear flannel petticoats. Olive wore ruffled silk and sheer lawn and filmy laced flounces. But Olive's father had "married money" and Olive never had bronchitis. So there you were.

"Are you sure you didn't leave the soap in the water?" demanded Mrs. Frederick. But Valancy was gone. She turned at the corner and looked back down the ugly, prim, respectable street where she lived. The Stirling house was the ugliest on it—more like a red brick box than anything else. Too high for its breadth, and made still higher by a bulbous glass cupola on top. About it was the desolate, barren peace of an old house whose life is lived.

There was a very pretty house, with leaded casements and dubbed gables, just around the corner—a new house, one of those houses you love the minute you see them. Clayton Markley had built it for his bride. He was to be married to Jennie Lloyd in June. The little house, it was said, was furnished from attic to cellar, in complete readiness for its mistress.

"I don't envy Jennie the man," thought Valancy sincerely— Clayton Markley was not one of her many ideals—"but I *do* envy her the house. It's such a nice young house. Oh, if I could only have a house of my own—ever so poor, so tiny—but my own! But then," she added bitterly, "there is no use in yowling for the moon when you can't even get a tallow candle."

In dreamland nothing would do Valancy but a castle of pale sapphire. In real life she would have been fully satisfied with a little house of her own. She envied Jennie Lloyd more fiercely than ever today. Jennie was not so much better looking than she was, and not so very much younger. Yet she was to have this delightful house. And the nicest little Wedgwood teacups— Valancy had seen them; an open fireplace, and monogrammed linen; hemstitched tablecloths, and china-closets. Why did *everything* come to some girls and *nothing* to others? It wasn't fair.

Valancy was once more seething with rebellion as she walked along, a prim, dowdy little figure in her shabby raincoat and three-year-old hat, splashed occasionally by the mud of a passing motor with its insulting shrieks. Motors were still rather a novelty in Deerwood, though they were common in Port Lawrence, and most of the summer residents up at Muskoka had them. In Deerwood only some of the smart set had them; for even Deerwood was divided into sets. There was the smart set—the intellectual set—the old-family set—of which the Stirlings were members—the common run, and a few pariahs. Not one of the Stirling clan had as yet condescended to a motor, though Olive was teasing her father to have one. Valancy had never even been in a motorcar. But she did not hanker after this. In truth, she felt rather afraid of motorcars, especially at night. They seemed to be too much like big purring beasts that might turn and crush you—or make some terrible savage leap somewhere. On the steep mountain trails around her Blue Castle only gaily caparisoned steeds might proudly pace; in real life Valancy would have been quite contented to drive in a buggy behind a nice horse. She got a buggy drive only when some uncle or cousin remembered to fling her "a chance," like a bone to a dog.

CHAPTER V

Of course she must buy the tea in Uncle Benjamin's grocery-store. To buy it anywhere else was unthinkable. Yet Valancy hated to go to Uncle Benjamin's store on her twenty-ninth birthday. There was no hope that he would not remember it.

"Why," demanded Uncle Benjamin, leeringly, as he tied up her tea, "are young ladies like bad grammarians?"

Valancy, with Uncle Benjamin's will in the background of her mind, said meekly, "I don't know. Why?"

"Because," chuckled Uncle Benjamin, "they can't decline matrimony."

The two clerks, Joe Hammond and Claude Bertram, chuckled also, and Valancy disliked them a little more than ever. On the first day Claude Bertram had seen her in the store she had heard him whisper to Joe, "Who is that?" And Joe had said, "Valancy Stirling—one of the Deerwood old maids." "Curable or incurable?" Claude had asked with a snicker, evidently thinking the question very clever. Valancy smarted anew with the sting of that old recollection.

"Twenty-nine," Uncle Benjamin was saying. "Dear me, Doss, you're dangerously near the second corner and not even thinking of getting married yet. Twenty-nine. It seems impossible."

Then Uncle Benjamin said an original thing. Uncle Benjamin said, "How time does fly!"

"I think it *crawls*," said Valancy passionately. Passion was so alien to Uncle Benjamin's conception of Valancy that he didn't know what to make of her. To cover his confusion, he asked another conundrum as he tied up her beans—Cousin Stickles had remembered at the last moment that they must have beans. Beans were cheap and filling.

"What two ages are apt to prove illusory?" asked Uncle Benjamin; and, not waiting for Valancy to "give it up," he added, "Mir-age and marri-age."

"M-i-r-a-g-e is pronounced *mirazh*," said Valancy shortly, picking up her tea and her beans. For the moment she did not care whether Uncle Benjamin cut her out of his will or not. She walked out of the store while Uncle Benjamin stared after her with his mouth open. Then he shook his head.

"Poor Doss is taking it hard," he said.

Valancy was sorry by the time she reached the next crossing. Why had she lost her patience like that? Uncle Benjamin would be annoyed and would likely tell her mother that Doss had been impertinent—"to *me*!"—and her mother would lecture her for a week.

"I've held my tongue for twenty years," thought Valancy. "Why couldn't I have held it once more?"

Yes, it was just twenty, Valancy reflected, since she had first been twitted with her loverless condition. She remembered the bitter moment perfectly. She was just nine years old and she was standing alone on the school playground while the other little girls of her class were playing a game in which you must be chosen by a boy as his partner before you could play. Nobody had chosen Valancy—little, pale, black-haired Valancy, with her prim, long-sleeved apron and odd, slanted eyes.

"Oh," said a pretty little girl to her, "I'm so sorry for you. You haven't got a beau."

Valancy had said defiantly, as she continued to say for twenty years, "I don't *want* a beau." But this afternoon Valancy once and for all stopped saying that.

"I'm going to be honest with myself anyhow," she thought savagely. "Uncle Benjamin's riddles hurt me because they are true. I *do* want to be married. I want a house of my own—I want a husband of my own—I want sweet, little fat *babies* of my own—" Valancy stopped suddenly aghast at her own recklessness. She felt sure that Rev. Dr. Stalling, who passed her at this moment, read her thoughts and disapproved of them thoroughly. Valancy was afraid of Dr. Stalling—had been afraid of him ever since the Sunday, twenty-three years before, when he had first come to St. Albans'. Valancy had been too late for Sunday School that day and she had gone into the church timidly and sat in their pew. No one else was in the church—nobody except the new rector, Dr. Stalling. Dr. Stalling stood up in front of the choir door, beckoned to her, and said sternly, "Little boy, come up here."

Valancy had stared around her. There was no little boy—there was no one in all the huge church but herself. This strange man with the blue glasses couldn't mean her. She was not a boy.

"Little boy," repeated Dr. Stalling, more sternly still, shaking his forefinger fiercely at her, "come up here at once!"

Valancy arose as if hypnotised and walked up the aisle. She was too terrified to do anything else. What dreadful thing was going to happen to her? What *had* happened to her? Had she actually turned into a boy? She came to a stop in front of Dr. Stalling. Dr. Stalling shook his forefinger—such a long, knuckly forefinger—at her and said:

"Little boy, take off your hat."

Valancy took off her hat. She had a scrawny little pigtail hanging down her back, but Dr. Stalling was shortsighted and did not perceive it.

"Little boy, go back to your seat and *always* take off your hat in church. *Remember!*"

Valancy went back to her seat carrying her hat like an automaton. Presently her mother came in.

"Doss," said Mrs. Stirling, "what do you mean by taking off your hat? Put it on instantly!"

Valancy put it on instantly. She was cold with fear lest Dr. Stalling should immediately summon her up front again. She would have to go, of course—it never occurred to her that one could disobey the rector—and the church was full of people now. Oh, what would she do if that horrible, stabbing forefinger were shaken at her again before all those people? Valancy sat through the whole service in an agony of dread and was sick for a week afterwards. Nobody knew why—Mrs. Frederick again bemoaned herself of her delicate child.

Dr. Stalling found out his mistake and laughed over it to Valancy—who did not laugh. She never got over her dread of Dr. Stalling. And now to be caught by him on the street corner, thinking such things!

Valancy got her John Foster book—*Magic of Wings*. "His latest—all about birds," said Miss Clarkson. She had almost decided that she would go home, instead of going to see Dr. Trent. Her courage had failed her. She was afraid of offending Uncle James—afraid of angering her mother—afraid of facing gruff, shaggy-browed old Dr. Trent, who would probably tell her, as he had told Cousin Gladys, that her trouble was entirely imaginary and that she only had it because she liked to have it. No, she would not go; she would get a bottle of Redfern's Purple Pills instead. Redfern's Purple Pills were the standard medicine of the Stirling clan. Had they not cured Second Cousin Geraldine when five doctors had given her up? Valancy always felt very sceptical concerning the virtues of the Purple Pills; but there *might* be something in them; and it was easier to take them than to face Dr. Trent alone. She would glance over the magazines in the reading-room a few minutes and then go home.

Valancy tried to read a story, but it made her furious. On every page was a picture of the heroine surrounded by adoring men. And here was she, Valancy Stirling, who could not get a solitary beau! Valancy slammed the magazine shut; she opened *Magic of Wings*. Her eyes fell on the paragraph that changed her life.

"*Fear is the original sin,*" wrote John Foster. "*Almost all the evil in the world has its origin in the fact that some one is afraid of something. It is a cold, slimy serpent coiling about you. It is horrible to live with fear; and it is of all things degrading.*"

Valancy shut *Magic of Wings* and stood up. She would go and see Dr. Trent.

CHAPTER VI

The ordeal was not so dreadful, after all. Dr. Trent was as gruff and abrupt as usual, but he did not tell her her ailment was imaginary. After he had listened to her symptoms and asked a few questions and made a quick examination, he sat for a moment looking at her quite intently. Valancy thought he looked as if he were sorry for her. She caught her breath for a moment. Was the trouble serious? Oh, it couldn't be, surely—it really hadn't bothered her *much*—only lately it had got a little worse.

Dr. Trent opened his mouth—but before he could speak the telephone at his elbow rang sharply. He picked up the receiver. Valancy, watching him, saw his face change suddenly as he listened, "'Lo—yes—yes—*what?*—yes—yes"—a brief interval—"My God!"

Dr. Trent dropped the receiver, dashed out of the room and upstairs without even a glance at Valancy. She heard him rushing madly about overhead, barking out a few remarks to somebody—presumably his housekeeper. Then he came tearing downstairs with a club bag in his hand, snatched his hat and coat from the rack, jerked open the street door and rushed down the street in the direction of the station.

Valancy sat alone in the little office, feeling more absolutely foolish than she had ever felt before in her life. Foolish—and humiliated. So this was all that had come of her heroic determination to live up to John Foster and cast fear aside. Not only was she a failure as a relative and non-existent as a sweetheart or friend, but she was not even of any importance as a patient. Dr. Trent had forgotten her very presence in his excitement over whatever message had come by the telephone. She had gained nothing by ignoring Uncle James and flying in the face of family tradition.

For a moment she was afraid she was going to cry. It *was* all so—ridiculous. Then she heard Dr. Trent's housekeeper coming down the stairs. Valancy rose and went to the office door.

"The doctor forgot all about me," she said with a twisted smile.

"Well, that's too bad," said Mrs. Patterson sympathetically. "But it wasn't much wonder, poor man. That was a telegram they 'phoned over from the Port. His son has been terribly injured in an auto accident in Montreal. The doctor had just ten minutes to catch the train. I don't know what he'll do if anything happens to Ned—he's just bound up in the boy. You'll have to come again, Miss Stirling. I hope it's nothing serious."

"Oh, no, nothing serious," agreed Valancy. She felt a little less humiliated. It was no wonder poor Dr. Trent had forgotten her at such a moment. Nevertheless, she felt very flat and discouraged as she went down the street.

Valancy went home by the short-cut of Lover's Lane. She did not often go through Lover's Lane—but it was getting near supper-time and it would never do to be late. Lover's Lane wound back of the village, under great elms and maples, and deserved its name. It was hard to go there at any time and not find some canoodling couple—or young girls in pairs, arms intertwined, earnestly talking over their secrets. Valancy didn't know which made her feel more self-conscious and uncomfortable.

This evening she encountered both. She met Connie Hale and Kate Bayley, in new pink organdy dresses with flowers stuck coquettishly in their glossy, bare hair. Valancy had never had a pink dress or worn flowers in her hair. Then she passed a young couple she didn't know, dandering along, oblivious to everything but themselves. The young man's arm was around the girl's waist quite shamelessly. Valancy had never walked with a man's arm about her. She felt that she ought to be shocked—they might leave that sort of thing for the screening twilight, at least—but she wasn't shocked. In another flash of desperate, stark honesty she owned to herself that she was merely envious. When she passed

them she felt quite sure they were laughing at her—pitying her—
"there's that queer little old maid, Valancy Stirling. They say she
never had a beau in her whole life"—Valancy fairly ran to get
out of Lover's Lane. Never had she felt so utterly colourless and
skinny and insignificant.

Just where Lover's Lane debouched on the street, an old car
was parked. Valancy knew that car well—by sound, at least—and
everybody in Deerwood knew it. This was before the phrase "tin
Lizzie" had come into circulation—in Deerwood, at least; but if
it had been known, this car was the tinniest of Lizzies—though
it was not a Ford but an old Grey Slosson. Nothing more battered
and disreputable could be imagined.

It was Barney Snaith's car and Barney himself was just
scrambling up from under it, in overalls plastered with mud.
Valancy gave him a swift, furtive look as she hurried by. This
was only the second time she had ever seen the notorious Barney
Snaith, though she had heard enough about him in the five years
that he had been living "up back" in Muskoka. The first time
had been nearly a year ago, on the Muskoka road. He had been
crawling out from under his car then, too, and he had given her
a cheerful grin as she went by—a little, whimsical grin that gave
him the look of an amused gnome. He didn't look bad—she
didn't believe he was bad, in spite of the wild yarns that were
always being told of him. Of course he went tearing in that
terrible old Grey Slosson through Deerwood at hours when all
decent people were in bed—often with old "Roaring Abel," who
made the night hideous with his howls—"both of them dead
drunk, my dear." And every one knew that he was an escaped
convict and a defaulting bank clerk and a murderer in hiding
and an infidel and an illegitimate son of old Roaring Abel Gay
and the father of Roaring Abel's illegitimate grandchild and a
counterfeiter and a forger and a few other awful things. But still
Valancy didn't believe he was bad. Nobody with a smile like that
could be bad, no matter what he had done.

It was that night the Prince of the Blue Castle changed from a being of grim jaw and hair with a dash of premature grey to a rakish individual with overlong, tawny hair, dashed with red, dark-brown eyes, and ears that stuck out just enough to give him an alert look but not enough to be called flying jibs. But he still retained something a little grim about the jaw.

Barney Snaith looked even more disreputable than usual just now. It was very evident that he hadn't shaved for days, and his hands and arms, bare to the shoulders, were black with grease. But he was whistling gleefully to himself and he seemed so happy that Valancy envied him. She envied him his light-heartedness and his irresponsibility and his mysterious little cabin up on an island in Lake Mistawis—even his rackety old Grey Slosson. Neither he nor his car had to be respectable and live up to traditions. When he rattled past her a few minutes later, bareheaded, leaning back in his Lizzie at a rakish angle, his longish hair blowing in the wind, a villainous-looking old black pipe in his mouth, she envied him again. Men had the best of it, no doubt about that. This outlaw was happy, whatever he was or wasn't. She, Valancy Stirling, respectable, well-behaved to the last degree, was unhappy and had always been unhappy. So there you were.

Valancy was just in time for supper. The sun had clouded over, and a dismal, drizzling rain was falling again. Cousin Stickles had the neuralgia. Valancy had to do the family darning and there was no time for *Magic of Wings*.

"Can't the darning wait till tomorrow?" she pleaded.

"Tomorrow will bring its own duties," said Mrs. Frederick inexorably.

Valancy darned all the evening and listened to Mrs. Frederick and Cousin Stickles talking the eternal, niggling gossip of the clan, as they knitted drearily at interminable black stockings. They discussed Second Cousin Lilian's approaching wedding in all its bearings. On the whole, they approved. Second Cousin Lilian was doing well for herself.

"Though she hasn't hurried," said Cousin Stickles. "She must be twenty-five."

"There have not—fortunately—been many old maids in our connection," said Mrs. Frederick bitterly.

Valancy flinched. She had run the darning needle into her finger.

Third Cousin Aaron Gray had been scratched by a cat and had blood-poisoning in his finger. "Cats are most dangerous animals," said Mrs. Frederick. "I would never have a cat about the house."

She glared significantly at Valancy through her terrible glasses. Once, five years ago, Valancy had asked if she might have a cat. She had never referred to it since, but Mrs. Frederick still suspected her of harbouring the unlawful desire in her heart of hearts.

Once Valancy sneezed. Now, in the Stirling code, it was very bad form to sneeze in public.

"You can always repress a sneeze by pressing your finger on your upper lip" said Mrs. Frederick rebukingly.

Half-past nine o'clock and so, as Mr. Pepys would say, to bed. But First Cousin Stickles' neuralgic back must be rubbed with Redfern's Liniment. Valancy did that. Valancy always had to do it. She hated the smell of Redfern's Liniment—she hated the smug, beaming, portly, be-whiskered, be-spectacled picture of Dr. Redfern on the bottle. Her fingers smelled of the horrible stuff after she got into bed, in spite of all the scrubbing she gave them.

Valancy's day of destiny had come and gone. She ended it as she had begun it, in tears.

CHAPTER VII

There was a rosebush on the little Stirling lawn, growing beside the gate. It was called "Doss's rosebush." Cousin Georgiana had given it to Valancy five years ago and Valancy had planted it joyfully. She loved roses. But—of course—the rosebush never bloomed. That was her luck. Valancy did everything she could think of and took the advice of everybody in the clan, but still the rosebush would not bloom. It throve and grew luxuriantly, with great leafy branches untouched of rust or spider; but not even a bud had ever appeared on it. Valancy, looking at it two days after her birthday, was filled with a sudden, overwhelming hatred for it. The thing wouldn't bloom: very well, then, she would cut it down. She marched to the tool-room in the barn for her garden knife and she went at the rosebush viciously. A few minutes later horrified Mrs. Frederick came out to the verandah and beheld her daughter slashing insanely among the rosebush boughs. Half of them were already strewn on the walk. The bush looked sadly dismantled.

"Doss, what on earth are you doing? Have you gone crazy?"

"No," said Valancy. She meant to say it defiantly, but habit was too strong for her. She said it deprecatingly. "I—I just made up my mind to cut this bush down. It is no good. It never blooms— never will bloom."

"That is no reason for destroying it," said Mrs. Frederick sternly. "It was a beautiful bush and quite ornamental. You have made a sorry-looking thing of it."

"Rose trees should *bloom*," said Valancy a little obstinately.

"Don't argue with *me*, Doss. Clear up that mess and leave the bush alone. I don't know what Georgiana will say when she sees how you have hacked it to pieces. Really, I'm surprised at you.

And to do it without consulting *me!*"

"The bush is mine," muttered Valancy.

"What's that? What did you say, Doss?"

"I only said the bush was mine," repeated Valancy humbly.

Mrs. Frederick turned without a word and marched back into the house. The mischief was done now. Valancy knew she had offended her mother deeply and would not be spoken to or noticed in any way for two or three days. Cousin Stickles would see to Valancy's bringing-up but Mrs. Frederick would preserve the stony silence of outraged majesty.

Valancy sighed and put away her garden knife, hanging it precisely on its precise nail in the tool-shop. She cleared away the several branches and swept up the leaves. Her lips twitched as she looked at the straggling bush. It had an odd resemblance to its shaken, scrawny donor, little Cousin Georgiana herself.

"I certainly have made an awful-looking thing of it," thought Valancy.

But she did not feel repentant—only sorry she had offended her mother. Things would be so uncomfortable until she was forgiven. Mrs. Frederick was one of those women who can make their anger felt all over a house. Walls and doors are no protection from it.

"You'd better go uptown and git the mail," said Cousin Stickles, when Valancy went in. "*I* can't go—I feel all sorter peaky and piny this spring. I want you to stop at the drugstore and git me a bottle of Redfern's Blood Bitters. There's nothing like Redfern's Bitters for building a body up. Cousin James says the Purple Pills are the best, but I know better. My poor dear husband took Redfern's Bitters right up to the day he died. Don't let them charge you more'n ninety cents. I kin git it for that at the Port. And what *have* you been saying to your poor mother? Do you ever stop to think, Doss, that you kin only have one mother?"

"One is enough for me," thought Valancy undutifully, as she went uptown.

She got Cousin Stickles' bottle of bitters and then she went to the post-office and asked for her mail at the General Delivery. Her mother did not have a box. They got too little mail to bother with it. Valancy did not expect any mail, except the *Christian Times,* which was the only paper they took. They hardly ever got any letters. But Valancy rather liked to stand in the office and watch Mr. Carewe, the grey-bearded, Santa-Clausy old clerk, handing out letters to the lucky people who did get them. He did it with such a detached, impersonal, Jove-like air, as if it did not matter in the least to him what supernal joys or shattering horrors might be in those letters for the people to whom they were addressed. Letters had a fascination for Valancy, perhaps because she so seldom got any. In her Blue Castle exciting epistles, bound with silk and sealed with crimson, were always being brought to her by pages in livery of gold and blue, but in real life her only letters were occasional perfunctory notes from relatives or an advertising circular.

Consequently she was immensely surprised when Mr. Carewe, looking even more Jovian than usual, poked a letter out to her. Yes, it was addressed to her plainly, in a fierce, black hand: "Miss Valancy Stirling, Elm Street, Deerwood"—and the postmark was Montreal. Valancy picked it up with a little quickening of her breath. Montreal! It must be from Doctor Trent. He had remembered her, after all.

Valancy met Uncle Benjamin coming in as she was going out and was glad the letter was safely in her bag.

"What," said Uncle Benjamin, "is the difference between a donkey and a postage-stamp?"

"I don't know. What?" answered Valancy dutifully.

"One you lick with a stick and the other you stick with a lick. Ha, ha!"

Uncle Benjamin passed in, tremendously pleased with himself.

Cousin Stickles pounced on the *Times* when Valancy got home, but it did not occur to her to ask if there were any letters. Mrs. Frederick would have asked it, but Mrs. Frederick's lips at present were sealed. Valancy was glad of this. If her mother had asked if there were any letters Valancy would have had to admit there was. Then she would have had to let her mother and Cousin Stickles read the letter and all would be discovered.

Her heart acted strangely on the way upstairs, and she sat down by her window for a few minutes before opening her letter. She felt very guilty and deceitful. She had never before kept a letter secret from her mother. Every letter she had ever written or received had been read by Mrs. Frederick. That had never mattered. Valancy had never had anything to hide. But this *did* matter. She could not have any one see this letter. But her fingers trembled with a consciousness of wickedness and unfilial conduct as she opened it—trembled a little, too, perhaps, with apprehension. She felt quite sure there was nothing seriously wrong with her heart but—one never knew.

Dr. Trent's letter was like himself—blunt, abrupt, concise, wasting no words. Dr. Trent never beat about the bush. "Dear Miss Sterling"—and then a page of black, positive writing. Valancy seemed to read it at a glance; she dropped it on her lap, her face ghost-white.

Dr. Trent told her that she had a very dangerous and fatal form of heart disease—angina pectoris—evidently complicated with an aneurism—whatever that was—and in the last stages. He said, without mincing matters, that nothing could be done for her. If she took great care of herself she might live a year—but she might also die at any moment—Dr. Trent never troubled himself about euphemisms. She must be careful to avoid all excitement and all severe muscular efforts. She must eat and drink moderately, she must never run, she must go upstairs and uphill with great care. Any sudden jolt or shock might be fatal. She was to get the prescription he enclosed filled and carry it with her always, taking a dose whenever her attacks came on. And he was hers truly, H. B. Trent.

Valancy sat for a long while by her window. Outside was a world drowned in the light of a spring afternoon—skies entrancingly blue, winds perfumed and free, lovely, soft, blue hazes at the end of every street. Over at the railway station a group of young girls was waiting for a train; she heard their gay laughter as they chattered and joked. The train roared in and roared out again. But none of these things had any reality. Nothing had any reality except the fact that she had only another year to live.

When she was tired of sitting at the window she went over and lay down on her bed, staring at the cracked, discoloured ceiling. The curious numbness that follows on a staggering blow possessed her. She did not feel anything except a boundless surprise and incredulity—behind which was the conviction that Dr. Trent knew his business and that she, Valancy Stirling, who had never lived, was about to die.

When the gong rang for supper Valancy got up and went downstairs mechanically, from force of habit. She wondered that she had been let alone so long. But of course her mother would not pay any attention to her just now. Valancy was thankful for this. She thought the quarrel over the rose-bush had been really, as Mrs. Frederick herself might have said, Providential. She could not eat anything, but both Mrs. Frederick and Cousin Stickles thought this was because she was deservedly unhappy over her mother's attitude, and her lack of appetite was not commented on. Valancy forced herself to swallow a cup of tea and then sat and watched the others eat, with an odd feeling that years had passed since she had sat with them at the dinner-table. She found herself smiling inwardly to think what a commotion she could make if she chose. Let her merely tell them what was in Dr. Trent's letter and there would be as much fuss made as if—Valancy thought bitterly—they really cared two straws about her.

"Dr. Trent's housekeeper got word from him today," said Cousin Stickles, so suddenly that Valancy jumped guiltily. Was there anything in thought waves? "Mrs. Judd was talking to her uptown. They think his son will recover, but Dr. Trent wrote that if he did he was going to take him abroad as soon as he was able to travel and wouldn't be back here for a year at least."

"That will not matter much to *us*," said Mrs. Frederick majestically. "He is not *our* doctor. I would not"—here she looked or seemed to look accusingly right through Valancy—"have *him* to doctor a sick cat."

"May I go upstairs and lie down?" said Valancy faintly. "I—I have a headache."

"What has given you a headache?" asked Cousin Stickles, since Mrs. Frederick would not. The question has to be asked. Valancy could not be allowed to have headaches without interference.

"You ain't in the habit of having headaches. I hope you're not taking the mumps. Here, try a spoonful of vinegar."

"Piffle!" said Valancy rudely, getting up from the table. She did not care just then if she were rude. She had had to be so polite all her life.

If it had been possible for Cousin Stickles to turn pale she would have. As it was not, she turned yellower.

"Are you sure you ain't feverish, Doss? You sound like it. You go and get right into bed," said Cousin Stickles, thoroughly alarmed, "and I'll come up and rub your forehead and the back of your neck with Redfern's Liniment."

Valancy had reached the door, but she turned. "I won't be rubbed with Redfern's Liniment!" she said.

Cousin Stickles stared and gasped. "What—what do you mean?"

"I said I wouldn't be rubbed with Redfern's Liniment," repeated Valancy. "Horrid, sticky stuff! And it has the vilest smell of any liniment I ever saw. It's no good. I want to be left alone, that's all."

Valancy went out, leaving Cousin Stickles aghast.

"She's feverish—she *must* be feverish," ejaculated Cousin Stickles.

Mrs. Frederick went on eating her supper. It did not matter whether Valancy was or was not feverish. Valancy had been guilty of impertinence to *her*.

45

CHAPTER VIII

Valancy did not sleep that night. She lay awake all through the long dark, hours—thinking—thinking. She made a discovery that surprised her: she, who had been afraid of almost everything in life, was not afraid of death. It did not seem in the least terrible to her. And she need not now be afraid of anything else. Why had she been afraid of things? Because of life. Afraid of Uncle Benjamin because of the menace of poverty in old age. But now she would never be old—neglected—tolerated. Afraid of being an old maid all her life. But now she would not be an old maid very long. Afraid of offending her mother and her clan because she had to live with and among them and couldn't live peaceably if she didn't give in to them. But now she hadn't. Valancy felt a curious freedom.

But she was still horribly afraid of one thing—the fuss the whole jamfry of them would make when she told them. Valancy shuddered at the thought of it. She couldn't endure it. Oh, she knew so well how it would be. First there would be indignation—yes, indignation on the part of Uncle James because she had gone to a doctor—any doctor—without consulting HIM. Indignation on the part of her mother for being so sly and deceitful—"to your own mother, Doss." Indignation on the part of the whole clan because she had not gone to Dr. Marsh.

Then would come the solicitude. She would be taken to Dr. Marsh, and when Dr. Marsh confirmed Dr. Trent's diagnosis she would be taken to specialists in Toronto and Montreal. Uncle Benjamin would foot the bill with a splendid gesture of munificence in thus assisting the widow and orphan, and talk forever after of the shocking fees specialists charged for looking wise and saying they couldn't do anything. And when the specialists could do nothing for her Uncle James would insist on her taking Purple Pills—"I've known them to effect a cure when *all* the doctors had given up"—and her mother would insist on Redfern's Blood Bitters, and Cousin Stickles would insist on rubbing her over the heart every night with Redfern's Liniment on the grounds that it *might* do good and *couldn't* do harm; and everybody else would have some pet dope for her to take. Dr. Stalling would come to her and say solemnly, "You are very ill. Are you prepared for what may be before you?"—almost as if he were going to shake his forefinger at her, the forefinger that had not grown any shorter or less knobbly with age. And she would be watched and checked like a baby and never let do anything or go anywhere alone. Perhaps she would not even be allowed to sleep alone lest she die in her sleep. Cousin Stickles or her mother would insist on sharing her room and bed. Yes, undoubtedly they would.

It was this last thought that really decided Valancy. She could not put up with it and she wouldn't. As the clock in the hall below struck twelve Valancy suddenly and definitely made up her mind that she would not tell anybody. She had always been told, ever since she could remember, that she must hide her feelings. "It is not ladylike to have feelings," Cousin Stickles had once told her disapprovingly. Well, she would hide them with a vengeance.

But though she was not afraid of death she was not indifferent to it. She found that she *resented* it; it was not fair that she should have to die when she had never lived. Rebellion flamed up in her soul as the dark hours passed by—not because she had no future but because she had no past.

"I'm poor—I'm ugly—I'm a failure—and I'm near death," she thought. She could see her own obituary notice in the Deerwood *Weekly Times,* copied into the Port Lawrence *Journal.* "A deep gloom was cast over Deerwood, etc., etc."—"leaves a large circle of friends to mourn, etc., etc., etc."—lies, all lies. Gloom, forsooth! Nobody would miss her. Her death would not matter a straw to anybody. Not even her mother loved her—her mother who had been so disappointed that she was not a boy—or at least, a pretty girl.

Valancy reviewed her whole life between midnight and the early spring dawn. It was a very drab existence, but here and there an incident loomed out with a significance out of all proportion to its real importance. These incidents were all unpleasant in one way or another. Nothing really pleasant had every happened to Valancy.

"I've never had one wholly happy hour in my life—not one," she thought. "I've just been a colourless nonentity. I remember reading somewhere once that there is an hour in which a woman might be happy all her life if she could but find it. I've never found my hour—never, never. And I never will now. If I could only have had that hour I'd be willing to die."

Those significant incidents kept bobbing up in her mind like unbidden ghosts, without any sequence of time or place. For instance, that time when, at sixteen, she had blued a tubful of clothes too deeply. And the time when, at eight, she had "stolen" some raspberry jam from Aunt Wellington's pantry. Valancy never heard the last of those two misdemeanours. At almost every clan gathering they were raked up against her as jokes. Uncle Benjamin hardly ever missed re-telling the raspberry jam incident—he had been the one to catch her, her face all stained and streaked.

"I have really done so few bad things that they have to keep harping on the old ones," thought Valancy. "Why, I've never even had a quarrel with any one. I haven't an enemy. What a spineless thing I must be not to have even one enemy!"

There was that incident of the dust-pile at school when she was seven. Valancy always recalled it when Dr. Stalling referred to the text, "To him that hath shall be given and from him that hath not shall be taken even that which he hath." Other people might puzzle over that text but it never puzzled Valancy. The whole relationship between herself and Olive, dating from the day of the dust-pile, was a commentary on it.

She had been going to school a year, but Olive, who was a year younger, had just begun and had about her all the glamour of "a new girl" and an exceedingly pretty girl at that. It was at recess and all the girls, big and little, were out on the road in front of the school making dust-piles. The aim of each girl was to have the biggest pile. Valancy was good at making dust-piles—there was an art in it—and she had secret hopes of leading. But Olive, working off by herself, was suddenly discovered to have a larger dust-pile than anybody. Valancy felt no jealousy. Her dust-pile was quite big enough to please her. Then one of the older girls had an inspiration.

"Let's put all our dust on Olive's pile and make a tremendous one," she exclaimed.

A frenzy seemed to seize the girls. They swooped down on the dust-piles with pails and shovels and in a few seconds Olive's pile was a veritable pyramid. In vain Valancy, with scrawny, outstretched little arms, tried to protect hers. She was ruthlessly swept aside, her dust-pile scooped up and poured on Olive's. Valancy turned away resolutely and began building another dust-pile. Again a bigger girl pounced on it. Valancy stood before it, flushed, indignant, arms outspread.

"Don't take it," she pleaded. "Please don't take it."

"But *why*?" demanded the older girl. "Why won't you help to build Olives bigger?"

"I want my own little dust-pile," said Valancy piteously.

Her plea went unheeded. While she argued with one girl another scraped up her dust-pile. Valancy turned away, her heart swelling, her eyes full of tears.

"Jealous—you're jealous!" said the girls mockingly.

"You were very selfish," said her mother coldly, when Valancy told her about it at night. That was the first and last time Valancy had ever taken any of her troubles to her mother.

Valancy was neither jealous nor selfish. It was only that she wanted a dust-pile of her own—small or big mattered not. A team of horses came down the street—Olive's dust pile was scattered

49

over the roadway—the bell rang—the girls trooped into school and had forgotten the whole affair before they reached their seats. Valancy never forgot it. To this day she resented it in her secret soul. But was it not symbolical of her life?

"I've never been able to have my own dust-pile," thought Valancy.

The enormous red moon she had seen rising right at the end of the street one autumn evening of her sixth year. She had been sick and cold with the awful, uncanny horror of it. So near to her. So big. She had run in trembling to her mother and her mother had laughed at her. She had gone to bed and hidden her face under the clothes in terror lest she might look at the window and see that horrible moon glaring in at her through it.

The boy who had tried to kiss her at a party when she was fifteen. She had not let him—she had evaded him and run. He was the only boy who had ever tried to kiss her. Now, fourteen years later, Valancy found herself wishing that she had let him.

The time she had been made to apologise to Olive for something she hadn't done. Olive had said that Valancy had pushed her into the mud and spoiled her new shoes *on purpose*. Valancy knew she hadn't. It had been an accident—and even that wasn't her fault—but nobody would believe her. She had to apologise—and kiss Olive to "make up." The injustice of it burned in her soul tonight.

That summer when Olive had the most beautiful hat, trimmed with creamy yellow net, with a wreath of red roses and little ribbon bows under the chin. Valancy had wanted a hat like that more than she had ever wanted anything. She pleaded for one and had been laughed at—all summer she had to wear a horrid little brown sailor with elastic that cut behind her ears. None of the girls would go around with her because she was so shabby—nobody but Olive. People had thought Olive so sweet and unselfish.

"I was an excellent foil for her," thought Valancy. "Even then she knew that."

Valancy had tried to win a prize for attendance in Sunday School once. But Olive won it. There were so many Sundays Valancy had to stay home because she had colds. She had once tried to "say a piece" in school one Friday afternoon and had broken down in it. Olive was a good reciter and never got stuck.

The night she had spent in Port Lawrence with Aunt Isabel when she was ten. Byron Stirling was there; from Montreal, twelve years old, conceited, clever. At family prayers in the morning Byron had reached across and given Valancy's thin arm such a savage pinch that she screamed out with pain. After prayers were over she was summoned to Aunt Isabel's bar of judgment. But when she said Byron had pinched her Byron denied it. He said she cried out because the kitten scratched her. He said she had put the kitten up on her chair and was playing with it when she should have been listening to Uncle David's prayer. He was *believed*. In the Stirling clan the boys were always believed before the girls. Valancy was sent home in disgrace because of her exceeding bad behavior during family prayers and she was not asked to Aunt Isabel's again for many moons.

The time Cousin Betty Stirling was married. Somehow Valancy got wind of the fact that Betty was going to ask her to be one of her bridesmaids. Valancy was secretly uplifted. It would be a delightful thing to be a bridesmaid. And of course she would have to have a new dress for it—a pretty new dress—a pink dress. Betty wanted her bridesmaids to dress in pink.

But Betty had never asked her, after all. Valancy couldn't guess why, but long after her secret tears of disappointment had been dried Olive told her. Betty, after much consultation and reflection, had decided that Valancy was too insignificant—she would "spoil the effect." That was nine years ago. But tonight Valancy caught her breath with the old pain and sting of it.

That day in her eleventh year when her mother had badgered her into confessing something she had never done. Valancy had denied it for a long time but eventually for peace' sake she had given in and pleaded guilty. Mrs. Frederick was always making people lie by pushing them into situations where they *had* to lie. Then her mother had made her kneel down on parlour floor, between herself and Cousin Stickles, and say, "O God, please forgive me for not speaking the truth." Valancy had said it, but as she rose from her knees she muttered, "But O God, *you* know I did speak the truth." Valancy had not then heard of Galileo but her fate was similar to his. She was punished just as severely as if she hadn't confessed and prayed.

The winter she went to dancing-school. Uncle James had decreed she should go and had paid for her lessons. How she had looked forward to it! And how she had hated it! She had never had a voluntary partner. The teacher always had to tell some boy to dance with her, and generally he had been sulky about it. Yet Valancy was a good dancer, as light on her feet as thistledown. Olive, who never lacked eager partners, was heavy.

The affair of the button-string, when she was ten. All the girls in school had button-strings. Olive had a very long one with a great many beautiful buttons. Valancy had one. Most of the buttons on it were very commonplace, but she had six beauties that had come off Grandmother Stirling's wedding-gown—sparkling buttons of gold and glass, much more beautiful than any Olive had. Their possession conferred a certain distinction on Valancy. She knew every little girl in school envied her the exclusive possession of those beautiful buttons. When Olive saw them on the button-string she had looked at them narrowly but said nothing—then. The next day Aunt Wellington had come to Elm Street and told Mrs. Frederick that she thought Olive should have some of those buttons—Grandmother Stirling was just as much Wellington's mother as Frederick's. Mrs. Frederick had agreed amiably. She could not afford to fall out with Aunt Wellington. Moreover, the matter was of no importance whatever. Aunt Wellington carried off four of the buttons, generously leaving two for Valancy. Valancy had torn these from her string and flung them on the floor—she had not yet learned that it was unladylike to have feelings—and had been sent supperless to bed for the exhibition.

The night of Margaret Blunt's party. She had made such pathetic efforts to be pretty that night. Rob Walker was to be there; and two nights before, on the moonlit verandah of Uncle Herbert's cottage at Mistawis, Rob had really seemed attracted to her. At Margaret's party Rob never even asked her to dance—did not notice her at all. She was a wallflower, as usual. That, of course, was years ago. People in Deerwood had long since given up inviting Valancy to dances. But to Valancy its humiliation and disappointment were of the other day. Her face burned in the darkness as she recalled herself, sitting there with her pitifully crimped, thin hair and the cheeks she had pinched for an hour before coming, in an effort to make them red. All that came of it was a wild story that Valancy Stirling was rouged at Margaret Blunt's party. In those days in Deerwood that was enough to wreck your character forever. It did not wreck Valancy's, or even damage it. People knew *she* couldn't be fast if she tried. They only laughed at her.

"I've had nothing but a second-hand existence," decided Valancy. "All the great emotions of life have passed me by. I've never even had a grief. And have I ever really loved anybody? Do I really love Mother? No, I don't. That's the truth, whether it is disgraceful or not. I don't love her—I've never loved her. What's worse, I don't even like her. So I don't know anything about any kind of love. My life has been empty—empty. Nothing is worse than emptiness. Nothing!" Valancy ejaculated the last "nothing" aloud passionately. Then she moaned and stopped thinking about anything for a while. One of her attacks of pain had come on.

When it was over something had happened to Valancy—perhaps the culmination of the process that had been going on in her mind ever since she had read Dr. Trent's letter. It was three o'clock in the morning—the wisest and most accursed hour of the clock. But sometimes it sets us free.

"I've been trying to please other people all my life and failed," she said. "After this I shall please myself. I shall never pretend anything again. I've breathed an atmosphere of fibs and pretences and evasions all my life. What a luxury it will be to tell the truth! I may not be able to do much that I want to do but I won't do another thing that I don't want to do. Mother can pout for weeks—I shan't worry over it. 'Despair is a free man—hope is a slave.'"

Valancy got up and dressed, with a deepening of that curious sense of freedom. When she had finished with her hair she opened the window and hurled the jar of potpourri over into the next lot. It smashed gloriously against the schoolgirl complexion on the old carriage-shop.

"I'm sick of fragrance of dead things," said Valancy.

CHAPTER IX

Uncle Herbert and Aunt Alberta's silver wedding was delicately referred to among the Stirlings during the following weeks as "the time we first noticed poor Valancy was—a little— *you* understand?"

Not for words would any of the Stirlings have said out and out at first that Valancy had gone mildly insane or even that her mind was slightly deranged. Uncle Benjamin was considered to have gone entirely too far when he had ejaculated, "She's dippy—I tell you, she's dippy," and was only excused because of the outrageousness of Valancy's conduct at the aforsaid wedding dinner.

But Mrs. Frederick and Cousin Stickles had noticed a few things that made them uneasy *before* the dinner. It had begun with the rosebush, of course; and Valancy never was really "quite right" again. She did not seem to worry in the least over the fact that her mother was not speaking to her. You would never suppose she noticed it at all. She had flatly refused to take either Purple Pills or Redfern's Bitters. She had announced coolly that she did not intend to answer to the name of "Doss" any longer. She had told Cousin Stickles that she wished she would give up wearing that brooch with Cousin Artemas Stickles' hair in it. She had moved her bed in her room to the opposite corner. She had read *Magic of Wings* Sunday afternoon. When Cousin Stickles had rebuked her Valancy had said indifferently, "Oh, I forgot it was Sunday"—and *had gone on reading it.*

Cousin Stickles had seen a terrible thing—she had caught Valancy sliding down the bannister. Cousin Stickles did not tell Mrs. Frederick this—poor Amelia was worried enough as it was. But it was Valancy's announcement on Saturday night that she was not going to go to the Anglican church any more that broke through Mrs. Frederick's stony silence.

"Not going to church any more! Doss, have you absolutely taken leave—"

"Oh, I'm going to church," said Valancy airily. "I'm going to the Presbyterian church. But to the Anglican church I will not go."

This was even worse. Mrs. Frederick had recourse to tears, having found outraged majesty had ceased to be effective.

"What have you got against the Anglican church?" she sobbed.

"Nothing—only just that you've always made me go there. If you'd made me go to the Presbyterian church I'd want to go to the Anglican."

"Is that a nice thing to say to your mother? Oh, how true it is that it is sharper than a serpent's tooth to have a thankless child."

"Is that a nice thing to say to your daughter?" said unrepentant Valancy.

So Valancy's behaviour at the silver wedding was not quite the surprise to Mrs. Frederick and Christine Stickles that it was to the rest. They were doubtful about the wisdom of taking her, but concluded it would "make talk" if they didn't. Perhaps she would behave herself, and so far no outsider suspected there was anything queer about her. By a special mercy of Providence it had poured torrents Sunday morning, so Valancy had not carried out her hideous threat of going to the Presbyterian church.

Valancy would not have cared in the least if they had left her at home. These family celebrations were all hopelessly dull. But the Stirlings always celebrated everything. It was a long-established custom. Even Mrs. Frederick gave a dinner party on her wedding anniversary and Cousin Stickles had friends in to supper on her birthday. Valancy hated these entertainments because they had to pinch and save and contrive for weeks afterwards to pay for them. But she wanted to go to the silver wedding. It would hurt Uncle Herbert's feelings if she stayed away, and she rather liked Uncle Herbert. Besides, she wanted to look over all her relatives from her new angle. It would be an excellent place to make public her declaration of independence if occasion offered.

"Put on your brown silk dress," said Mrs. Stirling.

As if there were anything else to put on! Valancy had only the one festive dress—that snuffy-brown silk Aunt Isabel had given her. Aunt Isabel had decreed that Valancy should never wear colours. They did not become her. When she was young they allowed her to wear white, but that had been tacitly dropped for some years. Valancy put on the brown silk. It had a high collar and long sleeves. She had never had a dress with low neck and elbow sleeves, although they had been worn, even in Deerwood, for over a year. But she did not do her hair pompadour. She knotted it on her neck and pulled it out over her ears. She thought it became her—only the little knot was so absurdly small. Mrs. Frederick resented the hair but decided it was wisest to say nothing on the eve of the party. It was so important that Valancy should be kept in good humour, if possible, until it was over. Mrs. Frederick did not reflect that this was the first time in her life that she had thought it necessary to consider Valancy's humours. But then Valancy had never been "queer" before.

On their way to Uncle Herbert's—Mrs. Frederick and Cousin Stickles walking in front, Valancy trotting meekly along behind—Roaring Abel drove past them. Drunk as usual but not in the roaring stage. Just drunk enough to be excessively polite. He raised his disreputable old tartan cap with the air of a monarch saluting his subjects and swept them a grand bow, Mrs. Frederick and Cousin Stickles dared not cut Roaring Abel altogether. He was the only person in Deerwood who could be got to do odd jobs of carpentering and repairing when they needed to be done, so it would not do to offend him. But they responded with only the stiffest, slightest of bows. Roaring Abel must be kept in his place.

Valancy, behind them, did a thing they were fortunately spared seeing. She smiled gaily and waved her hand to Roaring Abel. Why not? She had always liked the old sinner. He was such a jolly, picturesque, unashamed reprobate and stood out against the drab respectability of Deerwood and its customs like a flame-red flag of revolt and protest. Only a few nights ago Abel had gone through Deerwood in the wee sma's, shouting oaths at the top of his stentorian voice which could be heard for miles, and lashing his horse into a furious gallop as he tore along prim, proper Elm Street.

"Yelling and blaspheming like a fiend," shuddered Cousin Stickles at the breakfast-table.

"I cannot understand why the judgment of the Lord has not fallen upon that man long ere this," said Mrs. Frederick petulantly, as if she thought Providence was very dilatory and ought to have a gentle reminder.

"He'll be picked up dead some morning—he'll fall under his horse's hoofs and be trampled to death," said Cousin Stickles reassuringly.

Valancy had said nothing, of course; but she wondered to herself if Roaring Abel's periodical sprees were not his futile protest against the poverty and drudgery and monotony of his existence. *She* went on dream sprees in her Blue Castle. Roaring Abel, having no imagination, could not do that. *His* escapes from reality had to be concrete. So she waved at him today with a sudden fellow feeling, and Roaring Abel, not too drunk to be astonished, nearly fell off his seat in his amazement.

By this time they had reached Maple Avenue and Uncle Herbert's house, a large, pretentious structure peppered with meaningless bay windows and excrescent porches. A house that always looked like a stupid, prosperous, self-satisfied man with warts on his face.

"A house like that," said Valancy solemnly, "is a blasphemy."

Mrs. Frederick was shaken to her soul. What had Valancy said? Was it profane? Or only just queer? Mrs. Frederick took off her hat in Aunt Alberta's spare-room with trembling hands. She made one more feeble attempt to avert disaster. She held Valancy back on the landing as Cousin Stickles went downstairs.

"Won't you try to remember you're a lady?" she pleaded.

"Oh, if there were only any hope of being able to forget it!" said Valancy wearily.

Mrs. Frederick felt that she had not deserved this from Providence.

CHAPTER X

"Bless this food to our use and consecrate our lives to Thy service," said Uncle Herbert briskly.

Aunt Wellington frowned. She always considered Herbert's graces entirely too short and "flippant." A grace, to be a grace in Aunt Wellington's eyes, had to be at least three minutes long and uttered in an unearthly tone, between a groan and a chant. As a protest she kept her head bent a perceptible time after all the rest had been lifted. When she permitted herself to sit upright she found Valancy looking at her. Ever afterwards Aunt Wellington averred that she had known from that moment that there was something wrong with Valancy. In those queer, slanted eyes of hers—"we should always have known she was not entirely *right* with eyes like that"—there was an odd gleam of mockery and amusement—as if Valancy were laughing at *her*. Such a thing was unthinkable, of course. Aunt Wellington at once ceased to think it.

Valancy was enjoying herself. She had never enjoyed herself at a "family reunion" before. In social functions, as in childish games, she had only "filled in." Her clan had always considered her very dull. She had no parlour tricks. And she had been in the habit of taking refuge from the boredom of family parties in her Blue Castle, which resulted in an absent-mindedness that increased her reputation for dullness and vacuity.

"She has no social presence whatever," Aunt Wellington had decreed once and for all. Nobody dreamed that Valancy was dumb in their presence merely because she was afraid of them. Now she was no longer afraid of them. The shackles had been stricken off her soul. She was quite prepared to talk if occasion offered. Meanwhile she was giving herself such freedom of thought as she had never dared to take before. She let herself go with a wild, inner exultation, as Uncle Herbert carved the turkey. Uncle Herbert gave Valancy a second look that day. Being a man, he didn't know what she had done to her hair, but he thought surprisedly that Doss was not such a bad-looking girl, after all; and he put an extra piece of white meat on her plate.

"What herb is most injurious to a young lady's beauty?" propounded Uncle Benjamin by way of starting conversation— "loosening things up a bit," as he would have said.

Valancy, whose duty it was to say, "What?" did not say it. Nobody else said it, so Uncle Benjamin, after an expectant pause, had to answer, "Thyme," and felt that his riddle had fallen flat. He looked resentfully at Valancy, who had never failed him before, but Valancy did not seem even to be aware of him. She was gazing around the table, examining relentlessly every one in this depressing assembly of sensible people and watching their little squirms with a detached, amused smile.

So these were the people she had always held in reverence and fear. She seemed to see them with new eyes.

Big, capable, patronising, voluble Aunt Mildred, who thought herself the cleverest woman in the clan, her husband a little lower than the angels and her children wonders. Had not her son, Howard, been all through teething at eleven months? And could she not tell you the best way to do everything, from cooking mushrooms to picking up a snake? What a bore she was! What ugly moles she had on her face!

Cousin Gladys, who was always praising her son, who had died young, and always fighting with her living one. She had neuritis—or what she called neuritis. It jumped about from one part of her body to another. It was a convenient thing. If anybody wanted her to go somewhere she didn't want to go she had neuritis in her legs. And always if any mental effort was required she could have neuritis in her head. You can't *think* with neuritis in your head, my dear.

"What an old humbug you are!" thought Valancy impiously.

Aunt Isabel. Valancy counted her chins. Aunt Isabel was the critic of the clan. She had always gone about squashing people flat. More members of it than Valancy were afraid of her. She had, it was conceded, a biting tongue.

"I wonder what would happen to your face if you ever smiled," speculated Valancy, unblushingly.

Second Cousin Sarah Taylor, with her great, pale, expressionless eyes, who was noted for the variety of her pickle recipes and for nothing else. So afraid of saying something indiscreet that she never said anything worth listening to. So proper that she blushed when she saw the advertisement picture of a corset and had put a dress on her Venus de Milo statuette which made it look "real tasty."

Little Cousin Georgiana. Not such a bad little soul. But dreary—very. Always looking as if she had just been starched and ironed. Always afraid to let herself go. The only thing she really enjoyed was a funeral. You knew where you were with a corpse. Nothing more could happen to *it*. But while there was life there was fear.

Uncle James. Handsome, black, with his sarcastic, trap-like mouth and iron-grey side-burns, whose favourite amusement was to write controversial letters to the *Christian Times,* attacking Modernism. Valancy always wondered if he looked as solemn when he was asleep as he did when awake. No wonder his wife had died young. Valancy remembered her. A pretty, sensitive thing. Uncle James had denied her everything she wanted and showered on her everything she didn't want. He had killed her— quite legally. She had been smothered and starved.

Uncle Benjamin, wheezy, pussy-mouthed. With great pouches under eyes that held nothing in reverence.

Uncle Wellington. Long, pallid face, thin, pale-yellow hair— "one of the fair Stirlings"—thin, stooping body, abominably high forehead with such ugly wrinkles, and "eyes about as intelligent as a fish's," thought Valancy. "Looks like a cartoon of himself."

Aunt Wellington. Named Mary but called by her husband's

name to distinguish her from Great-aunt Mary. A massive, dignified, permanent lady. Splendidly arranged, iron-grey hair. Rich, fashionable beaded dress. Had *her* moles removed by electrolysis—which Aunt Mildred thought was a wicked evasion of the purposes of God.

Uncle Herbert, with his spiky grey hair. Aunt Alberta, who twisted her mouth so unpleasantly in talking and had a great reputation for unselfishness because she was always giving up a lot of things she didn't want. Valancy let them off easily in her judgment because she liked them, even if they were in Milton's expressive phrase, "stupidly good." But she wondered for what inscrutable reason Aunt Alberta had seen fit to tie a black velvet ribbon around each of her chubby arms above the elbow.

Then she looked across the table at Olive. Olive, who had been held up to her as a paragon of beauty, behaviour and success as long as she could remember. "Why can't you hold yourself like Olive, Doss? Why can't you stand correctly like Olive, Doss? Why can't you speak prettily like Olive, Doss? Why can't you make an effort, Doss?"

Valancy's elfin eyes lost their mocking glitter and became pensive and sorrowful. You could not ignore or disdain Olive. It was quite impossible to deny that she was beautiful and effective and sometimes she was a little intelligent. Her mouth might be a trifle heavy—she might show her fine, white, regular teeth rather too lavishly when she smiled. But when all was said and done, Olive justified Uncle Benjamin's summing up—"a stunning girl." Yes, Valancy agreed in her heart, Olive was stunning.

Rich, golden-brown hair, elaborately dressed, with a sparkling bandeau holding its glossy puffs in place; large, brilliant blue eyes and thick silken lashes; face of rose and bare neck of snow, rising above her gown; great pearl bubbles in her ears; the blue-white diamond flame on her long, smooth, waxen finger with its rosy, pointed nail. Arms of marble, gleaming through green chiffon and shadow lace. Valancy felt suddenly thankful that her own scrawny arms were decently swathed in brown silk. Then she resumed her tabulation of Olive's charms.

Tall. Queenly. Confident. Everything that Valancy was *not*. Dimples, too, in cheeks and chin. "A woman with dimples always gets her own way," thought Valancy, in a recurring spasm of bitterness at the fate which had denied her even one dimple.

Olive was only a year younger than Valancy, though a stranger would have thought that there was at least ten years between them. But nobody ever dreaded old maidenhood for her. Olive had been surrounded by a crowd of eager beaus since her early teens, just as her mirror was always surrounded by a fringe of cards, photographs, programmes and invitations. At eighteen, when she had graduated from Havergal College, Olive had been engaged to Will Desmond, lawyer in embryo. Will Desmond had died and Olive had mourned for him properly for two years. When she was twenty-three she had a hectic affair with Donald Jackson. But Aunt and Uncle Wellington disapproved of that and in the end Olive dutifully gave him up. Nobody in the Stirling clan—whatever outsiders might say—hinted that she did so because Donald himself was cooling off. However that might be, Olive's third venture met with everybody's approval. Cecil Price was clever and handsome and "one of the Port Lawrence Prices." Olive had been engaged to him for three years. He had just graduated in civil engineering and they were to be married as soon as he landed a contract. Olive's hope chest was full to overflowing with exquisite things and Olive had already confided to Valancy what her wedding-dress was to be. Ivory silk draped with lace, white satin court train, lined with pale green georgette, heirloom veil of Brussels lace. Valancy knew also—though Olive had not told her—that the bridesmaids were selected and that she was not among them.

Valancy had, after a fashion, always been Olive's confidante— perhaps because she was the only girl in the connection who could not bore Olive with return confidences. Olive always told Valancy all the details of her love affairs, from the days when the little boys in school used to "persecute" her with love letters.

Valancy could not comfort herself by thinking these affairs mythical. Olive really had them. Many men had gone mad over her besides the three fortunate ones.

"I don't know what the poor idiots see in me, that drives them to make such double idiots of themselves," Olive was wont to say. Valancy would have liked to say, "I don't either," but truth and diplomacy both restrained her. She *did* know, perfectly well. Olive Stirling was one of the girls about whom men do go mad just as indubitably as she, Valancy, was one of the girls at whom no man ever looked twice.

"And yet," thought Valancy, summing her up with a new and merciless conclusiveness, "she's like a dewless morning. There's *something* lacking."

CHAPTER XI

Meanwhile the dinner in its earlier stages was dragging its slow length along true to Stirling form. The room was chilly, in spite of the calendar, and Aunt Alberta had the gas-logs lighted. Everybody in the clan envied her those gas-logs except Valancy. Glorious open fires blazed in every room of her Blue Castle when autumnal nights were cool, but she would have frozen to death in it before she would have committed the sacrilege of a gas-log. Uncle Herbert made his hardy perennial joke when he helped Aunt Wellington to the cold meat—"Mary, will you have a little lamb?" Aunt Mildred told the same old story of once finding a lost ring in a turkey's crop. Uncle Benjamin told *his* favourite prosy tale of how he had once chased and punished a now famous man for stealing apples. Second Cousin Jane described all her sufferings with an ulcerating tooth. Aunt Wellington admired the pattern of Aunt Alberta's silver teaspoons and lamented the fact that one of her own had been lost.

"It spoiled the set. I could never get it matched. And it was my wedding-present from dear old Aunt Matilda."

Aunt Isabel thought the seasons were changing and couldn't imagine what had become of our good, old-fashioned springs. Cousin Georgiana, as usual, discussed the last funeral and wondered, audibly, "which of us will be the next to pass away." Cousin Georgiana could never say anything as blunt as "die." Valancy thought she could tell her, but didn't. Cousin Gladys, likewise as usual, had a grievance. Her visiting nephews had nipped all the buds off her house-plants and chivied her brood of fancy chickens—"squeezed some of them actually to death, my dear."

"Boys will be boys," reminded Uncle Herbert tolerantly.

"But they needn't be ramping, rampageous animals," retorted Cousin Gladys, looking round the table for appreciation of her wit. Everybody smiled except Valancy. Cousin Gladys remembered that. A few minutes later, when Ellen Hamilton was being discussed, Cousin Gladys spoke of her as "one of those shy, plain girls who can't get husbands," and glanced significantly at Valancy.

Uncle James thought the conversation was sagging to a rather low plane of personal gossip. He tried to elevate it by starting an abstract discussion on "the greatest happiness." Everybody was asked to state his or her idea of "the greatest happiness."

Aunt Mildred thought the greatest happiness—for a woman—was to be "a loving and beloved wife and mother." Aunt Wellington thought it would be to travel in Europe. Olive thought it would be to be a great singer like Tetrazzini. Cousin Gladys remarked mournfully that *her* greatest happiness would be to be free—absolutely free—from neuritis. Cousin Georgiana's greatest happiness would be "to have her dear, dead brother Richard back." Aunt Alberta remarked vaguely that the greatest happiness was to be found in "the poetry of life" and hastily gave some directions to her maid to prevent any one asking her what she meant. Mrs. Frederick said the greatest happiness was to spend your life in loving service for others, and Cousin Stickles and Aunt Isabel agreed with her—Aunt Isabel with a resentful air, as if she thought Mrs. Frederick had taken the wind out of her sails by saying it first. "We are all too prone," continued Mrs. Frederick, determined not to lose so good an opportunity, "to live in selfishness, worldliness and sin." The other women all felt rebuked for their low ideals, and Uncle James had a conviction that the conversation had been uplifted with a vengeance.

"The greatest happiness," said Valancy suddenly and distinctly, "is to sneeze when you want to."

Everybody stared. Nobody felt it safe to say anything. Was Valancy trying to be funny? It was incredible. Mrs. Frederick, who had been breathing easier since the dinner had progressed so far without any outbreak on the part of Valancy began to tremble again. But she deemed it the part of prudence to say nothing. Uncle Benjamin was not so prudent. He rashly rushed in where Mrs. Frederick feared to tread.

"Doss," he chuckled, "what is the difference between a young girl and an old maid?"

"One is happy and careless and the other is cappy and hairless," said Valancy. "You have asked that riddle at least fifty times in my recollection, Uncle Ben. Why don't you hunt up some new riddles if riddle you *must*? It is such a fatal mistake to try to be funny if you don't succeed."

Uncle Benjamin stared foolishly. Never in his life had he, Benjamin Stirling, of Stirling and Frost, been spoken to so. And by Valancy of all people! He looked feebly around the table to see what the others thought of it. Everybody was looking rather blank. Poor Mrs. Frederick had shut her eyes. And her lips moved tremblingly—as if she were praying. Perhaps she was. The situation was so unprecedented that nobody knew how to meet it. Valancy went on calmly eating her salad as if nothing out of the usual had occurred.

Aunt Alberta, to save her dinner, plunged into an account of how a dog had bitten her recently. Uncle James, to back her up, asked where the dog had bitten her.

"Just a little below the Catholic church," said Aunt Alberta.

At that point Valancy laughed. Nobody else laughed. What was there to laugh at?

"Is that a vital part?" asked Valancy.

"What do you mean?" said bewildered Aunt Alberta, and Mrs. Frederick was almost driven to believe that she had served God all her years for naught.

Aunt Isabel concluded that it was up to her to suppress Valancy.

"Doss, you are horribly thin," she said. "You are *all* corners. Do you *ever* try to fatten up a little?"

"No." Valancy was not asking quarter or giving it. "But I can tell you where you'll find a beauty parlour in Port Lawrence where they can reduce the number of your chins."

"*Val-an-cy!*" The protest was wrung from Mrs. Frederick. She meant her tone to be stately and majestic, as usual, but it sounded more like an imploring whine. And she did not say "Doss."

"She's feverish," said Cousin Stickles to Uncle Benjamin in an agonised whisper. "We've thought she's seemed feverish for several days."

"She's gone dippy, in my opinion," growled Uncle Benjamin. "If not, she ought to be spanked. Yes, spanked."

"You can't spank her." Cousin Stickles was much agitated. "She's twenty-nine years old."

"So there is that advantage, at least, in being twenty-nine," said Valancy, whose ears had caught this aside.

"Doss," said Uncle Benjamin, "when I am dead you may say what you please. As long as I am alive I demand to be treated with respect."

"Oh, but you know we're all dead," said Valancy, "the whole Stirling clan. Some of us are buried and some aren't—yet. That is the only difference."

"Doss," said Uncle Benjamin, thinking it might cow Valancy, "do you remember the time you stole the raspberry jam?"

Valancy flushed scarlet—with suppressed laughter, not shame. She had been sure Uncle Benjamin would drag that jam in somehow.

"Of course I do," she said. "It was good jam. I've always been sorry I hadn't time to eat more of it before you found me. Oh, *look* at Aunt Isabel's profile on the wall. Did you ever see anything so funny?"

Everybody looked, including Aunt Isabel herself which of course, destroyed it. But Uncle Herbert said kindly, "I—I wouldn't eat any more if I were you, Doss. It isn't that I grudge it—but don't you think it would be better for yourself? Your—your stomach seems a little out of order."

"Don't worry about my stomach, old dear," said Valancy. "It is all right. I'm going to keep right on eating. It's so seldom I get the chance of a satisfying meal."

It was the first time any one had been called "old dear" in Deerwood. The Stirlings thought Valancy had invented the phrase and they were afraid of her from that moment. There was something so uncanny about such an expression. But in poor Mrs. Frederick's opinion the reference to a satisfying meal was the worst thing Valancy had said yet. Valancy had always been a disappointment to her. Now she was a disgrace. She thought she would have to get up and go away from the table. Yet she dared not leave Valancy there.

Aunt Alberta's maid came in to remove the salad plates and bring in the dessert. It was a welcome diversion. Everybody brightened up with a determination to ignore Valancy and talk as if she wasn't there. Uncle Wellington mentioned Barney Snaith. Eventually somebody did mention Barney Snaith at every Stirling function, Valancy reflected. Whatever he was, he was an individual that could not be ignored. She resigned herself to listen. There was a subtle fascination in the subject for her, though she had not yet faced this fact. She could feel her pulses beating to her finger-tips.

Of course they abused him. Nobody ever had a good word to say of Barney Snaith. All the old, wild tales were canvassed— the defaulting cashier-counterfeiter-infidel-murderer-in-hiding legends were thrashed out. Uncle Wellington was very indignant that such a creature should be allowed to exist at all in the neighbourhood of Deerwood. He didn't know what the police at Port Lawrence were thinking of. Everybody would be murdered in their beds some night. It was a shame that he should be allowed to be at large after all that he had done.

"What *has* he done?" asked Valancy suddenly.

Uncle Wellington stared at her, forgetting that she was to be ignored.

"Done! Done! He's done *everything*."

"*What* has he done?" repeated Valancy inexorably. "What do

you *know* that he has done? You're always running him down. And what has ever been proved against him?"

"I don't argue with women," said Uncle Wellington. "And I don't need proof. When a man hides himself up there on an island in Muskoka, year in and year out, and nobody can find out where he came from or how he lives, or what he does there, *that's* proof enough. Find a mystery and you find a crime."

"The very idea of a man named Snaith!" said Second Cousin Sarah. "Why, the name itself is enough to condemn him!"

"I wouldn't like to meet him in a dark lane," shivered Cousin Georgiana.

"What do you suppose he would do to you?" asked Valancy.

"Murder me," said Cousin Georgiana solemnly.

"Just for the fun of it?" suggested Valancy.

"Exactly," said Cousin Georgiana unsuspiciously. "When there is so much smoke there must be some fire. I was afraid he was a criminal when he came here first. I *felt* he had something to hide. I am not often mistaken in my intuitions."

"Criminal! Oh course he's a criminal," said Uncle Wellington. "Nobody doubts it"—glaring at Valancy. "Why, they say he served a term in the penitentiary for embezzlement. I don't doubt it. And they say he's in with that gang that are perpetrating all those bank robberies round the country."

"*Who* say?" asked Valancy.

Uncle Wellington knotted his ugly forehead at her. What had got into this confounded girl, anyway? He ignored the question.

"He has the identical look of a jail-bird," snapped Uncle Benjamin. "I noticed it the first time I saw him."

"'A fellow by the hand of nature marked, Quoted and sighed to do a deed of shame'," declaimed Uncle James. He looked enormously pleased over the managing to work that quotation in at last. He had been waiting all his life for the chance.

"One of his eyebrows is an arch and the other is a triangle," said Valancy. "Is *that* why you think him so villainous?"

Uncle James lifted *his* eyebrows. Generally when Uncle

71

James lifted his eyebrows the world came to an end. This time it continued to function.

"How do *you* know his eyebrows so well, Doss?" asked Olive, a trifle maliciously. Such a remark would have covered Valancy with confusion two weeks ago, and Olive knew it.

"Yes, how?" demanded Aunt Wellington.

"I've seen him twice and I looked at him closely," said Valancy composedly. "I thought his face the most interesting one I ever saw."

"There is no doubt there is something fishy in the creature's past life," said Olive, who began to think she was decidedly out of the conversation, which had centred so amazingly around Valancy. "But he can hardly be guilty of *everything* he's accused of, you know."

Valancy felt annoyed with Olive. Why should *she* speak up in even this qualified defence of Barney Snaith? What had she to do with him? For that matter, what had Valancy? But Valancy did not ask herself this question.

"They say he keeps dozens of cats in that hut up back on Mistawis," said Second Cousin Sarah Taylor, by way of appearing not entirely ignorant of him.

Cats. It sounded quite alluring to Valancy, in the plural. She pictured an island in Muskoka haunted by pussies.

"That alone shows there is something wrong with him," decreed Aunt Isabel.

"People who don't like cats," said Valancy, attacking her dessert with a relish, "always seem to think that there is some peculiar virtue in not liking them."

"The man hasn't a friend except Roaring Abel," said Uncle Wellington. "And if Roaring Abel had kept away from him, as everybody else did, it would have been better for—for some members of his family."

Uncle Wellington's rather lame conclusion was due to a marital glance from Aunt Wellington reminding him of what he had almost forgotten—that there were girls at the table.

"If you mean," said Valancy passionately, "that Barney Snaith is the father of Cecily Gay's child, he *isn't*. It's a wicked lie."

In spite of her indignation Valancy was hugely amused at the expression of the faces around that festal table. She had not seen anything like it since the day, seventeen years ago, when at Cousin Gladys' thimble party, they discovered that she had got—SOMETHING—in her head at school. *Lice* in her head! Valancy was done with euphemisms.

Poor Mrs. Frederick was almost in a state of collapse. She had believed—or pretended to believe—the Valancy still supposed that children were found in parsley beds.

"Hush—hush!" implored Cousin Stickles.

"I don't mean to hush," said Valancy perversely. "I've hush-hushed all my life. I'll scream if I want to. Don't make me want to. And stop talking nonsense about Barney Snaith."

Valancy didn't exactly understand her own indignation. What did Barney Snaith's imputed crimes and misdemeanours matter to her? And why, out of them all, did it seem most intolerable that he should have been poor, pitiful little Cecily Gay's false lover? For it *did* seem intolerable to her. She did not mind when they called him a thief and a counterfeiter and jail-bird; but she could not endure to think that he had loved and ruined Cecily Gay. She recalled his face on the two occasions of their chance meetings—his twisted, enigmatic, engaging smile, his twinkle, his thin, sensitive, almost ascetic lips, his general air of frank daredeviltry. A man with such a smile and lips might have murdered or stolen but he could not have betrayed. She suddenly hated every one who said it or believed it of him.

"When *I* was a young girl I never thought or spoke about such matters, Doss," said Aunt Wellington, crushingly.

"But I'm not a young girl," retorted Valancy, uncrushed. "Aren't you always rubbing that into me? And you are all evil-minded, senseless gossips. Can't you leave poor Cissy Gay alone? She's dying. Whatever she did, God or the Devil has punished her enough for it. You needn't take a hand, too. As for Barney Snaith, the only crime he has been guilty of is living to himself and minding his own business. He can, it seems, get along without you. Which *is* an unpardonable sin, of course, in your little snobocracy." Valancy coined that concluding word suddenly and felt that it was an inspiration. That was exactly what they were and not one of them was fit to mend another.

"Valancy, your poor father would turn over in his grave if he could hear you," said Mrs. Frederick.

"I dare say he would like that for a change," said Valancy brazenly.

"Doss," said Uncle James heavily, "the Ten Commandments are fairly up to date still—especially the fifth. Have you forgotten that?"

"No," said Valancy, "but I thought *you* had—especially the ninth. Have you ever thought, Uncle James, how dull life would be without the Ten Commandments? It is only when things are forbidden that they become fascinating."

But her excitement had been too much for her. She knew, by certain unmistakable warnings, that one of her attacks of pain was coming on. It must not find her there. She rose from her chair.

"I am going home now. I only came for the dinner. It was very good, Aunt Alberta, although your salad-dressing is not salt enough and a dash of cayenne would improve it."

None of the flabbergasted silver wedding guests could think of anything to say until the lawn gate clanged behind Valancy in the dusk. Then—

"She's feverish—I've said right along she was feverish," moaned Cousin Stickles.

Uncle Benjamin punished his pudgy left hand fiercely with his pudgy right.

"She's dippy—I tell you she's gone dippy," he snorted angrily. "That's all there is about it. Clean dippy."

"Oh, Benjamin," said Cousin Georgiana soothingly, "don't condemn her too rashly. We *must* remember what dear old

Shakespeare says—that charity thinketh no evil."

"Charity! Poppy-cock!" snorted Uncle Benjamin. "I never heard a young woman talk such stuff in my life as she just did. Talking about things she ought to be ashamed to think of, much less mention. Blaspheming! Insulting *us!* What she wants is a generous dose of spank-weed and I'd like to be the one to administer it. H-uh-h-h-h!" Uncle Benjamin gulped down the half of a scalding cup of coffee.

"Do you suppose that the mumps could work on a person that way?" wailed Cousin Stickles.

"I opened an umbrella in the house yesterday," sniffed Cousin Georgiana. "I *knew* it betokened some misfortune."

"Have you tried to find out if she has a temperature?" asked Cousin Mildred.

"She wouldn't let Amelia put the thermometer under her tongue," whimpered Cousin Stickles.

Mrs. Frederick was openly in tears. All her defences were down.

"I must tell you," she sobbed, "that Valancy has been acting very strangely for over two weeks now. She hasn't been a bit like herself—Christine could tell you. I have hoped against hope that it was only one of her colds coming on. But it is—it must be something worse."

"This is bringing on my neuritis again," said Cousin Gladys, putting her hand to her head.

"Don't cry, Amelia," said Herbert kindly, pulling nervously at his spiky grey hair. He hated "family ructions." Very inconsiderate of Doss to start one at *his* silver wedding. Who could have supposed she had it in her? "You'll have to take her to a doctor. This may be only a—er—a brainstorm. There are such things as brainstorms nowadays, aren't there?"

"I—I suggested consulting a doctor to her yesterday," moaned Mrs. Frederick. "And she said she wouldn't go to a doctor—wouldn't. Oh, surely I have had trouble enough!"

"And she *won't* take Redfern's Bitters," said Cousin Stickles.

"Or *anything*," said Mrs. Frederick. "And she's determined to go to the Presbyterian church," said Cousin Stickles—repressing, however, to her credit be it said, the story of the bannister.

"That proves she's dippy," growled Uncle Benjamin. "I noticed something strange about her the minute she came in today. I noticed it *before* today." (Uncle Benjamin was thinking of "m-i-r-a-z-h.") "Everything she said today showed an unbalanced mind. That question—'Was it a vital part?' Was there any sense at all in that remark? None whatever! There never was anything like that in the Stirlings. It must be from the Wansbarras."

Poor Mrs. Frederick was too crushed to be indignant. "I never heard of anything like that in the Wansbarras," she sobbed,

"Your father was odd enough," said Uncle Benjamin.

"Poor Pa was—peculiar," admitted Mrs. Frederick tearfully, "but his mind was never affected."

"He talked all his life exactly as Valancy did today," retorted Uncle Benjamin. "And he believed he was his own great-great grandfather born over again. I've heard him say it. Don't tell *me* that a man who believed a thing like *that* was ever in his right senses. Come, come, Amelia, stop sniffling. Of course Doss has made a terrible exhibition of herself today, but she's not responsible. Old maids are apt to fly off at a tangent like that. If she had been married when she should have been she wouldn't have got like this."

"Nobody wanted to marry her," said Mrs. Frederick, who felt that, somehow, Uncle Benjamin was blaming her.

"Well, fortunately there's no outsider here," snapped Uncle Benjamin. "We may keep it in the family yet. I'll take her over to see Dr. Marsh tomorrow. *I* know how to deal with pig-headed people. Won't that be best, James?"

"We must have medical advice certainly," agreed Uncle James.

"Well, that's settled. In the meantime, Amelia, act as if nothing had happened and keep an eye on her. Don't let her be alone. Above all, don't let her sleep alone."

Renewed whimpers from Mrs. Frederick.

"I can't help it. Night before last I suggested she'd better have Christine sleep with her. She positively refused—*and locked her door*. Oh, you don't know how she's changed. She won't work. At least, she won't sew. She does her usual housework, of course. But she wouldn't sweep the parlour yesterday morning, though we *always* sweep it on Thursdays. She said she'd wait till it was dirty. 'Would you rather sweep a dirty room than a clean one?' I asked her. She said, 'Of course. I'd see something for my labour then.' Think of it!"

Uncle Benjamin thought of it.

"The jar of potpourri"—Cousin Stickles pronounced it as spelled—"has disappeared from her room. I found the pieces in the next lot. She won't tell us what happened to it."

"I should never have dreamed it of Doss," said Uncle Herbert. "She has always seemed such a quiet, sensible girl. A bit backward—but sensible."

"The only thing you can be sure of in this world is the multiplication table," said Uncle James, feeling cleverer than ever.

"Well, let's cheer up," suggested Uncle Benjamin. "Why are chorus girls like fine stock raisers?"

"Why?" asked Cousin Stickles, since it had to be asked and Valancy wasn't there to ask it.

"Like to exhibit calves," chuckled Uncle Benjamin.

Cousin Stickles thought Uncle Benjamin a little indelicate. Before Olive, too. But then, he was a man.

Uncle Herbert was thinking that things were rather dull now that Doss had gone.

CHAPTER XII

Valancy hurried home through the faint blue twilight—hurried too fast perhaps. The attack she had when she thankfully reached the shelter of her own room was the worst yet. It was really very bad. She might die in one of those spells. It would be dreadful to die in such pain. Perhaps—perhaps this was death. Valancy felt pitifully alone. When she could think at all she wondered what it would be like to have someone with her who could sympathise—someone who really cared—just to hold her hand tight, if nothing else—some one just to say, "Yes, I know. It's dreadful—be brave—you'll soon be better;" not some one merely fussy and alarmed. Not her mother or Cousin Stickles. Why did the thought of Barney Snaith come into her mind? Why did she suddenly feel, in the midst of this hideous loneliness of pain, that *he* would be sympathetic—sorry for any one that was suffering? Why did he seem to her like an old, well-known friend? Was it because she had been defending him—standing up to her family for him?

She was so bad at first that she could not even get herself a dose of Dr. Trent's prescription. But eventually she managed it, and soon after relief came. The pain left her and she lay on her bed, spent, exhausted, in a cold perspiration. Oh, that had been horrible! She could not endure many more attacks like that. One didn't mind dying if death could be instant and painless. But to be hurt so in dying!

Suddenly she found herself laughing. That dinner *had* been fun. And it had all been so simple. She had merely *said* the things she had always *thought*. Their faces! Uncle Benjamin—poor, flabbergasted Uncle Benjamin! Valancy felt quite sure he would make a new will that very night. Olive would get Valancy's share of his fat hoard. Olive had always got Valancy's share of everything. Remember the dust-pile.

To laugh at her clan as she had always wanted to laugh was all the satisfaction she could get out of life now. But she thought it was rather pitiful that it should be so. Might she not pity herself a little when nobody else did?

Valancy got up and went to her window. The moist, beautiful wind blowing across groves of young-leafed wild trees touched her face with the caress of a wise, tender, old friend. The lombardies in Mrs. Tredgold's lawn, off to the left—Valancy could just see them between the stable and the old carriage-shop—were in dark purple silhouette against a clear sky and there was a milk-white, pulsating star just over one of them, like a living pearl on a silver-green lake. Far beyond the station were the shadowy, purple-hooded woods around Lake Mistawis. A white, filmy mist hung over them and just above it was a faint, young crescent. Valancy looked at it over her thin left shoulder.

"I wish," she said whimsically, "that I may have *one* little dust-pile before I die."

CHAPTER XIII

Uncle Benjamin found he had reckoned without his host when he promised so airily to take Valancy to a doctor. Valancy would not go. Valancy laughed in his face.

"Why on earth should I go to Dr. Marsh? There's nothing the matter with my mind. Though you all think I've suddenly gone crazy. Well, I haven't. I've simply grown tired of living to please other people and have decided to please myself. It will give you something to talk about besides my stealing the raspberry jam. So that's that."

"Doss," said Uncle Benjamin, solemnly and helplessly, "you are not—like yourself."

"Who am I like, then?" asked Valancy.

Uncle Benjamin was rather posed.

"Your Grandfather Wansbarra," he answered desperately.

"Thanks." Valancy looked pleased. "That's a real compliment. I remember Grandfather Wansbarra. He was one of the few human beings I *have* known—almost the only one. Now, it is of no use to scold or entreat or command, Uncle Benjamin—or exchange anguished glances with Mother and Cousin Stickles. I am not going to any doctor. And if you bring any doctor here I won't see him. So what are you going to do about it?"

What indeed! It was not seemly—or even possible—to hale Valancy doctorwards by physical force. And in no other way could it be done, seemingly. Her mother's tears and imploring entreaties availed not.

"Don't worry, Mother," said Valancy, lightly but quite respectfully. "It isn't likely I'll do anything very terrible. But I mean to have a little fun."

"Fun!" Mrs. Frederick uttered the word as if Valancy had said she was going to have a little tuberculosis.

Olive, sent by her mother to see if *she* had any influence over Valancy, came away with flushed cheeks and angry eyes. She told her mother that nothing could be done with Valancy. After *she,* Olive, had talked to her just like a sister, tenderly and wisely, all Valancy had said, narrowing her funny eyes to mere slips, was, "*I* don't show my gums when I laugh."

"More as if she were talking to herself than to me. Indeed, Mother, all the time I was talking to her she gave me the impression of not really listening. And that wasn't all. When I finally decided that what I was saying had no influence over her I begged her, when Cecil came next week, not to say anything queer before him, at least. Mother, what do you think she said?"

"I'm sure I can't imagine," groaned Aunt Wellington, prepared for anything.

"She said, 'I'd rather like to shock Cecil. His mouth is too red for a man's.' Mother, I can never feel the same to Valancy again."

"Her mind is affected, Olive," said Aunt Wellington solemnly. "You must not hold her responsibile for what she says."

When Aunt Wellington told Mrs. Frederick what Valancy had said to Olive, Mrs. Frederick wanted Valancy to apoligise.

"You made me apologise to Olive fifteen years ago for something I didn't do," said Valancy. "That old apology will do for now."

Another solemn family conclave was held. They were all there except Cousin Gladys, who had been suffering such tortures of neuritis in her head "ever since poor Doss went queer" that she couldn't undertake any responsibility. They decided—that is, they accepted a fact that was thrust in their faces—that the wisest thing was to leave Valancy alone for a while—"give her her head" as Uncle Benjamin expressed it—"keep a careful eye on her but let her pretty much alone." The term of "watchful waiting" had not been invented then, but that was practically the policy Valancy's distracted relatives decided to follow.

"We must be guided by developments," said Uncle Benjamin.

"It is"—solemnly—"easier to scramble eggs that unscramble them. Of course—if she becomes violent—"

Uncle James consulted Dr. Ambrose Marsh. Dr. Ambrose Marsh approved their decision. He pointed out to irate Uncle James—who would have liked to lock Valancy up somewhere, out of hand—that Valancy had not, as yet, really done or said anything that could be constructed as proof of lunacy—and without proof you cannot lock people up in this degenerate age. Nothing that Uncle James had reported seemed very alarming to Dr. Marsh, who put up his hand to conceal a smile several times. But then he himself was not a Stirling. And he knew very little about the old Valancy. Uncle James stalked out and drove back to Deerwood, thinking that Ambrose Marsh wasn't much of a doctor, after all, and that Adelaide Stirling might have done better for herself.

CHAPTER XIV

Life cannot stop because tragedy enters it. Meals must be made ready though a son dies and porches must be repaired even if your only daughter is going out of her mind. Mrs. Frederick, in her systematic way, had long ago appointed the second week in June for the repairing of the front porch, the roof of which was sagging dangerously. Roaring Abel had been engaged to do it many moons before and Roaring Abel promptly appeared on the morning of the first day of the second week, and fell to work. Of course he was drunk. Roaring Abel was never anything but drunk. But he was only in the first stage, which made him talkative and genial. The odour of whisky on his breath nearly drove Mrs. Frederick and Cousin Stickles wild at dinner. Even Valancy, with all her emancipation, did not like it. But she liked Abel and she liked his vivid, eloquent talk, and after she washed the dinner dishes she went out and sat on the steps and talked to him.

Mrs. Frederick and Cousin Stickles thought it a terrible proceeding, but what could they do? Valancy only smiled mockingly at them when they called her in, and did not go. It was so easy to defy once you got started. The first step was the only one that really counted. They were both afraid to say anything more to her lest she might make a scene before Roaring Abel, who would spread it all over the country with his own characteristic comments and exaggerations. It was too cold a day, in spite of the June sunshine, for Mrs. Frederick to sit at the dining-room window and listen to what was said. She had to shut the window and Valancy and Roaring Abel had their talk to themselves. But if Mrs. Frederick had known what the outcome of that talk was to be she would have prevented it, if the porch was never repaired.

Valancy sat on the steps, defiant of the chill breeze of this cold June which had made Aunt Isabel aver the seasons were changing. She did not care whether she caught a cold or not. It was delightful to sit there in that cold, beautiful, fragrant world and feel free. She filled her lungs with the clean, lovely wind and held out her arms to it and let it tear her hair to pieces while she listening to Roaring Abel, who told her his troubles between intervals of hammering gaily in time to his Scotch songs. Valancy liked to hear him. Every stroke of his hammer fell true to the note.

Old Abel Gay, in spite of his seventy years, was handsome still, in a stately, patriarchal manner. His tremendous beard, falling down over his blue flannel shirt, was still a flaming, untouched red, though his shock of hair was white as snow, and his eyes were a fiery, youthful blue. His enormous, reddish-white eyebrows were more like moustaches than eyebrows. Perhaps this was why he always kept his upper lip scrupulously shaved. His cheeks were red and his nose ought to have been, but wasn't. It was a fine, upstanding, aquiline nose, such as the noblest Roman of them all might have rejoiced in. Abel was six feet two in his stockings, broad-shouldered, lean-hipped. In his youth he had been a famous lover, finding all women too charming to bind himself to one. His years had been a wild, colourful panorama of follies and adventures, gallantries, fortunes and misfortunes. He had been forty-five before he married—a pretty slip of a girl whom his goings-on killed in a few years. Abel was piously drunk at her funeral and insisted on repeating the fifty-fifth chapter of Isaiah—Abel knew most of the Bible and all the Psalms by heart—while the minister, whom he disliked, prayed or tried to pray. Thereafter his house was run by an untidy old cousin who cooked his meals and kept things going after a fashion. In this unpromising environment little Cecilia Gay had grown up.

Valancy had known "Cissy Gay" fairly well in the democracy of the public school, though Cissy had been three years younger than she. After they left school their paths diverged and she had seen nothing of her. Old Abel was a Presbyterian. That is, he got a Presbyterian preacher to marry him, baptise his child and bury his wife; and he knew more about Presbyterian theology than most ministers, which made him a terror to them in arguments. But Roaring Abel never went to church. Every Presbyterian minister who had been in Deerwood had tried his hand—once—at reforming Roaring Abel. But he had not been pestered of late. Rev. Mr. Bently had been in Deerwood for eight years, but he had not sought out Roaring Abel since the first three months of his pastorate. He had called on Roaring Abel then and found him in the theological stage of drunkenness—which always followed the sentimental maudlin one, and preceded the roaring, blasphemous one. The eloquently prayerful one, in which he realised himself temporarily and intensely as a sinner in the hands of an angry God, was the final one. Abel never went beyond it. He generally fell asleep on his knees and awakened sober, but he had never been "dead drunk" in his life. He told Mr. Bently that he was a sound Presbyterian and sure of his election. He had no sins—that he knew of—to repent of.

"Have you never done anything in your life that you are sorry for?" asked Mr. Bently.

Roaring Abel scratched his bushy white head and pretended to reflect.

"Well, yes," he said finally. "There were some women I might have kissed and didn't. I've always been sorry for *that.*"

Mr. Bently went out and went home.

Abel had seen that Cissy was properly baptised—jovially drunk at the same time himself. He made her go to church and Sunday School regularly. The church people took her up and she was in turn a member of the Mission Band, the Girls' Guild and the Young Women's Missionary Society. She was a faithful, unobtrusive, sincere, little worker. Everybody liked Cissy Gay and was sorry for her. She was so modest and sensitive and pretty in that delicate, elusive fashion of beauty which fades so quickly if life is not kept in it by love and tenderness. But then liking and pity did not prevent them from tearing her in pieces like hungry cats when the catastrophe came. Four years previously Cissy Gay had gone up to a Muskoka hotel as a summer waitress. And when she had come back in the fall she was a changed creature. She hid herself away and went nowhere. The reason soon leaked out and scandal raged. That winter Cissy's baby was born. Nobody ever knew who the father was. Cecily kept her poor pale lips tightly locked on her sorry secret. Nobody dared ask Roaring Abel any questions about it. Rumour and surmise laid the guilt at Barney Snaith's door because diligent inquiry among the other maids at the hotel revealed the fact that nobody there had ever seen Cissy Gay "with a fellow." She had "kept herself to herself" they said, rather resentfully. "Too good for *our* dances. And now look!"

The baby had lived for a year. After its death Cissy faded away. Two years ago Dr. Marsh had given her only six months to live— her lungs were hopelessly diseased. But she was still alive. Nobody went to see her. Women would not go to Roaring Abel's house. Mr. Bently had gone once, when he knew Abel was away, but the dreadful old creature who was scrubbing the kitchen floor told him Cissy wouldn't see any one. The old cousin had died and Roaring Abel had had two or three disreputable housekeepers— the only kind who could be prevailed on to go to a house where a girl was dying of consumption. But the last one had left and Roaring Abel had now no one to wait on Cissy and "do" for him. This was the burden of his plaint to Valancy and he condemned the "hypocrites" of Deerwood and its surrounding communities with some rich, meaty oaths that happened to reach Cousin Stickles' ears as she passed through the hall and nearly finished the poor lady. Was Valancy listening to *that?*

Valancy hardly noticed the profanity. Her attention was focussed on the horrible thought of poor, unhappy, disgraced little Cissy Gay, ill and helpless in that forlorn old house out on the Mistawis road, without a soul to help or comfort her. And this in a nominally Christian community in the year of grace nineteen and some odd!

"Do you mean to say that Cissy is all alone there now, with nobody to do anything for her—*nobody*?"

"Oh, she can move about a bit and get a bite and sup when she wants it. But she can't work. It's d——d hard for a man to work hard all day and go home at night tired and hungry and cook his own meals. Sometimes I'm sorry I kicked old Rachel Edwards out." Abel described Rachel picturesquely.

"Her face looked as if it had wore out a hundred bodies. And she moped. Talk about temper! Temper's nothing to moping. She was too slow to catch worms, and dirty—d——d dirty. I ain't unreasonable—I know a man has to eat his peck before he dies— but she went over the limit. What d'ye sp'ose I saw that lady do? She'd made some punkin jam—had it on the table in glass jars with the tops off. The dawg got up on the table and stuck his paw into one of them. What did she do? She jest took holt of the dawg and wrung the syrup off his paw back into the jar! Then screwed the top on and set it in the pantry. I sets open the door and says to her, 'Go!' The dame went, and I fired the jars of punkin after her, two at a time. Thought I'd die laughing to see old Rachel run— with them punkin jars raining after her. She's told everywhere I'm crazy, so nobody'll come for love or money."

"But Cissy *must* have some one to look after her," insisted Valancy, whose mind was centred on this aspect of the case. She did not care whether Roaring Abel had any one to cook for him or not. But her heart was wrung for Cecilia Gay.

"Oh, she gits on. Barney Snaith always drops in when he's passing and does anything she wants done. Brings her oranges and flowers and things. There's a Christian for you. Yet that sanctimonious, snivelling parcel of St. Andrew's people wouldn't be seen on the same side of the road with him. Their dogs'll go to heaven before they do. And their minister—slick as if the cat had licked him!"

"There are plenty of good people, both in St. Andrew's and St. George's, who would be kind to Cissy if *you* would behave yourself," said Valancy severely. "They're afraid to go near your place."

"Because I'm such a sad old dog? But I don't bite—never bit any one in my life. A few loose words spilled around don't hurt any one. And I'm not asking people to come. Don't want 'em poking and prying about. What I want is a housekeeper. If I shaved every Sunday and went to church I'd get all the housekeepers I'd want. I'd be respectable then. But what's the use of going to church when it's all settled by predestination? Tell me that, Miss."

"Is it?" said Valancy.

"Yes. Can't git around it nohow. Wish I could. I don't want either heaven or hell for steady. Wish a man could have 'em mixed in equal proportions."

"Isn't that the way it is in this world?" said Valancy thoughtfully—but rather as if her thought was concerned with something else than theology.

"No, no," boomed Abel, striking a tremendous blow on a stubborn nail. "There's too much hell here—entirely too much hell. That's why I get drunk so often. It sets you free for a little while—free from yourself—yes, by God, free from predestination. Ever try it?"

"No, I've another way of getting free," said Valancy absently. "But about Cissy now. She *must* have some one to look after her—"

"What are you harping on Sis for? Seems to me you ain't bothered much about her up to now. You never even come to see her. And she used to like you so well."

"I should have," said Valancy. "But never mind. You couldn't understand. The point is—you must have a housekeeper."

"Where am I to get one? I can pay decent wages if I could get a decent woman. D'ye think I like old hags?"

"Will I do?" said Valancy.

CHAPTER XV

Let us be calm," said Uncle Benjamin. "Let us be perfectly calm."

"Calm!" Mrs. Frederick wrung her hands. "How can I be calm—how could anybody be calm under such a disgrace as this?"

"Why in the world did you let her go?" asked Uncle James.

"*Let* her! How could I stop her, James? It seems she packed the big valise and sent it away with Roaring Abel when he went home after supper, while Christine and I were out in the kitchen. Then Doss herself came down with her little satchel, dressed in her green serge suit. I felt a terrible premonition. I can't tell you how it was, but I seemed to *know* that Doss was going to do something dreadful."

"It's a pity you couldn't have had your premonition a little sooner," said Uncle Benjamin drily.

"I said, 'Doss, *where are you going*?' and *she* said, I am going to look for my Blue Castle.'"

"Wouldn't you think *that* would convince Marsh that her mind is affected?" interjected Uncle James.

"And *I* said, 'Valancy, what *do* you mean?' And *she* said, 'I am going to keep house for Roaring Abel and nurse Cissy. He will pay me thirty dollars a month.' I wonder I didn't drop dead on the spot."

"You shouldn't have let her go—you shouldn't have let her out of the house," said Uncle James. "You should have locked the door—anything—"

"She was between me and the front door. And you can't realise how determined she was. She was like a rock. That's the strangest thing of all about her. She used to be so good and obedient, and now she's neither to hold nor bind. But I said *everything* I could think of to bring her to her senses. I asked her if she had no regard for her reputation. I said to her solemnly, 'Doss, when a woman's reputation is once smirched nothing can ever make it spotless again. Your character will be gone for ever if you go to Roaring Abel's to wait on a bad girl like Sis Gay. And she said, 'I don't believe Cissy was a bad girl, but I don't care if she was.' Those were her very words, 'I don't care if she was.'"

"She has lost all sense of decency," exploded Uncle Benjamin.

"'Cissy Gay is dying,' she said, 'and it's a shame and disgrace that she is dying in a Christian community with no one to do anything for her. Whatever she's been or done, she's a human being.'"

"Well, you know, when it comes to that, I suppose she is," said Uncle James with the air of one making a splendid concession.

"I asked Doss if she had no regard for appearances. She said, 'I've been keeping up appearances all my life. Now I'm going in for realities. Appearances can go hang!' *Go hang*!"

"An outrageous thing!" said Uncle Benjamin violently. "An outrageous thing!"

Which relieved his feelings, but didn't help any one else.

Mrs. Frederick wept. Cousin Stickles took up the refrain between her moans of despair.

"I told her—we *both* told her—that Roaring Abel had certainly killed his wife in one of his drunken rages and would kill her. She laughed and said, 'I'm not afraid of Roaring Abel. He won't kill *me,* and he's too old for me to be afraid of his gallantries.' What did she mean? What *are* gallantries?"

Mrs. Frederick saw that she must stop crying if she wanted to regain control of the conversation.

"*I* said to her, 'Valancy, if you have no regard for your own reputation and your family's standing, have you none for *my* feelings?' She said, 'None.' Just like that, '*None*!'"

"Insane people never *do* have any regard for other people's feelings," said Uncle Benjamin. "That's one of the symptoms."

"I broke out into tears then, and she said, 'Come now, Mother, be a good sport. I'm going to do an act of Christian charity, and as for the damage it will do my reputation, why, you know I haven't any matrimonial chances anyhow, so what does it matter?' And with that she turned and went out."

"The last words I said to her," said Cousin Stickles pathetically, "were, 'Who will rub my back at nights now?' And she said—she said—but no, I cannot repeat it."

"Nonsense," said Uncle Benjamin. "Out with it. This is no time to be squeamish."

"She said"—Cousin Stickles' voice was little more than a whisper—"she said—'*Oh, darn!*'"

"To think I should have lived to hear my daughter swearing!" sobbed Mrs. Frederick,

"It—it was only imitation swearing," faltered Cousin Stickles, desirous of smoothing things over now that the worst was out. But she had *never* told about the bannister.

"It will be only a step from that to real swearing," said Uncle James sternly.

"The worst of this"—Mrs. Frederick hunted for a dry spot on her handkerchief—"is that every one will know now that she is deranged. We can't keep it a secret any longer. Oh, I cannot bear it!"

"You should have been stricter with her when she was young," said Uncle Benjamin.

"I don't see how I could have been," said Mrs. Frederick—truthfully enough.

"The worst feature of the case is that that Snaith scoundrel is always hanging around Roaring Abel's, said Uncle James. "I shall be thankful if nothing worse comes of this mad freak than a few weeks at Roaring Abel's. Cissy Gay *can't* live much longer."

"And she didn't even take her flannel petticoat!" lamented Cousin Stickles.

"I'll see Ambrose Marsh again about this," said Uncle Benjamin—meaning Valancy, not the flannel petticoat.

91

"I'll see Lawyer Ferguson," said Uncle James.

"Meanwhile," added Uncle Benjamin, "let us be calm."

CHAPTER XVI

Valancy had walked out to Roaring Abel's house on the Mistawis road under a sky of purple and amber, with a queer exhilaration and expectancy in her heart. Back there, behind her, her mother and Cousin Stickles were crying—over themselves, not over her. But here the wind was in her face, soft, dew-wet, cool, blowing along the grassy roads. Oh, she loved the wind! The robins were whistling sleepily in the firs along the way and the moist air was fragrant with the tang of balsam. Big cars went purring past in the violet dusk—the stream of summer tourists to Muskoka had already begun—but Valancy did not envy any of their occupants. Muskoka cottages might be charming, but beyond, in the sunset skies, among the spires of the firs, her Blue Castle towered. She brushed the old years and habits and inhibitions away from her like dead leaves. She would *not* be littered with them.

Roaring Abel's rambling, tumble-down old house was situated about three miles from the village, on the very edge of "up back," as the sparsely settled, hilly, wooded country around Mistawis was called vernacularly. It did not, it must be confessed, look much like a Blue Castle.

It had once been a snug place enough in the days when Abel Gay had been young and prosperous, and the punning, arched sign over the gate—"A. Gay, Carpenter," had been fine and freshly painted. Now it was a faded, dreary old place, with a leprous, patched roof and shutters hanging askew. Abel never seemed to do any carpenter jobs about his own house. It had a listless air, as if tired of life. There was a dwindling grove of ragged, crone-like old spruces behind it. The garden, which Cissy used to keep neat and pretty, had run wild. On two sides of the house were fields full of nothing but mulleins. Behind the house was a long stretch of useless barrens, full of scrub pines and spruces, with here and there a blossoming bit of wild cherry, running back to a belt of timber on the shores of Lake Mistawis, two miles away. A rough, rocky, boulder-strewn lane ran through it to the woods—a lane white with pestiferous, beautiful daisies.

Roaring Abel met Valancy at the door.

"So you've come," he said incredulously. "I never s'posed that ruck of Stirlings would let you."

Valancy showed all her pointed teeth in a grin.

"They couldn't stop me."

"I didn't think you'd so much spunk," said Roaring Abel admiringly. "And look at the nice ankles of her," he added, as he stepped aside to let her in.

If Cousin Stickles had heard this she would have been certain that Valancy's doom, earthly and unearthly, was sealed. But Abel's superannuated gallantry did not worry Valancy. Besides, this was the first compliment she had ever received in her life and she found herself liking it. She sometimes suspected she had nice ankles, but nobody had ever mentioned it before. In the Stirling clan ankles were among the unmentionables.

Roaring Abel took her into the kitchen, where Cissy Gay was lying on the sofa, breathing quickly, with little scarlet spots on her hollow cheeks. Valancy had not seen Cecilia Gay for years. Then she had been such a pretty creature, a slight blossom-like girl, with soft, golden hair, clear-cut, almost waxen features, and large, beautiful blue eyes. She was shocked at the change in her. Could this be sweet Cissy—this pitiful little thing that looked like a tired broken flower? She had wept all the beauty out of her eyes; they looked too big—enormous—in her wasted face. The last time Valancy had seen Cecilia Gay those faded, piteous eyes had been limpid, shadowy blue pools aglow with mirth. The contrast was so terrible that Valancy's own eyes filled with tears. She knelt down by Cissy and put her arms about her.

"Cissy dear, I've come to look after you. I'll stay with you till—

till—as long as you want me."

"Oh!" Cissy put her thin arms about Valancy's neck. "Oh—
will you? It's been so—lonely. I can wait on myself—but it's been
so *lonely*. It—would just be like—heaven—to have some one
here—like you. You were always—so sweet to me—long ago."

Valancy held Cissy close. She was suddenly happy. Here was
some one who needed her—some one she could help. She was no
longer a superfluity. Old things had passed away; everything had
become new.

"Most things are predestinated, but some are just darn sheer
luck," said Roaring Abel, complacently smoking his pipe in the
corner.

CHAPTER XVII

When Valancy had lived for a week at Roaring Abel's she felt as if years had separated her from her old life and all the people she had known in it. They were beginning to seem remote—dream-like—far-away—and as the days went on they seemed still more so, until they ceased to matter altogether.

She was happy. Nobody ever bothered her with conundrums or insisted on giving her Purple Pills. Nobody called her Doss or worried her about catching cold. There were no quilts to piece, no abominable rubber-plant to water, no ice-cold maternal tantrums to endure. She could be alone whenever she liked, go to bed when she liked, sneeze when she liked. In the long, wondrous, northern twilights, when Cissy was asleep and Roaring Abel away, she could sit for hours on the shaky back verandah steps, looking out over the barrens to the hills beyond, covered with their fine, purple bloom, listening to the friendly wind singing wild, sweet melodies in the little spruces, and drinking in the aroma of the sunned grasses, until darkness flowed over the landscape like a cool, welcome wave.

Sometimes of an afternoon, when Cissy was strong enough, the two girls went into the barrens and looked at the wood-flowers. But they did not pick any. Valancy had read to Cissy the gospel thereof according to John Foster: "It is a pity to gather wood-flowers. They lose half their witchery away from the green and the flicker. The way to enjoy wood-flowers is to track them down to their remote haunts—gloat over them—and then leave them with backward glances, taking with us only the beguiling memory of their grace and fragrance."

Valancy was in the midst of realities after a lifetime of unrealities. And busy—very busy. The house had to be cleaned.

Not for nothing had Valancy been brought up in the Stirling habits of neatness and cleanliness. If she found satisfaction in cleaning dirty rooms she got her fill of it there. Roaring Abel thought she was foolish to bother doing so much more than she was asked to do, but he did not interfere with her. He was very well satisfied with his bargain. Valancy was a good cook. Abel said she got a flavour into things. The only fault he found with her was that she did not sing at her work.

"Folk should always sing at their work," he insisted. "Sounds cheerful-like."

"Not always," retorted Valancy. "Fancy a butcher singing at his work. Or an undertaker."

Abel burst into his great broad laugh.

"There's no getting the better of you. You've got an answer every time. I should think the Stirlings would be glad to be rid of you. *They* don't like being sassed back."

During the day Abel was generally away from home—if not working, then shooting or fishing with Barney Snaith. He generally came home at nights—always very late and often very drunk. The first night they heard him come howling into the yard, Cissy had told Valancy not to be afraid.

"Father never does anything—he just makes a noise."

Valancy, lying on the sofa in Cissy's room, where she had elected to sleep, lest Cissy should need attention in the night—Cissy would never have called her—was not at all afraid, and said so. By the time Abel had got his horses put away, the roaring stage had passed and he was in his room at the end of the hall crying and praying. Valancy could still hear his dismal moans when she went calmly to sleep. For the most part, Abel was a good-natured creature, but occasionally he had a temper. Once Valancy asked him coolly:

"What is the use of getting in a rage?"

"It's such a d——d relief," said Abel.

They both burst out laughing together.

"You're a great little sport," said Abel admiringly. "Don't mind my bad French. I don't mean a thing by it. Jest habit. Say, I like a woman that ain't afraid to speak to me. Sis there was always too meek—too meek. That's why she got adrift. I like you."

"All the same," said Valancy determinedly, "there is no use in sending things to hell as you're always doing. And I'm *not* going to have you tracking mud all over a floor I've just scrubbed. You *must* use the scraper whether you consign it to perdition or not."

Cissy loved the cleanness and neatness. She had kept it so, too, until her strength failed. She was very pitifully happy because she had Valancy with her. It had been so terrible—the long, lonely days and nights with no companionship save those dreadful old women who came to work. Cissy had hated and feared them. She clung to Valancy like a child.

There was no doubt that Cissy was dying. Yet at no time did she seem alarmingly ill. She did not even cough a great deal. Most days she was able to get up and dress—sometimes even to work about in the garden or the barrens for an hour or two. For a few weeks after Valancy's coming she seemed so much better that Valancy began to hope she might get well. But Cissy shook her head.

"No, I can't get well. My lungs are almost gone. And I—don't want to. I'm so tired, Valancy. Only dying can rest me. But it's lovely to have you here—you'll never know how much it means to me. But Valancy—you work too hard. You don't need to— Father only wants his meals cooked. I don't think you are strong yourself. You turn so pale sometimes. And those drops you take. *Are* you well, dear?"

"I'm all right," said Valancy lightly. She would not have Cissy worried. "And I'm not working hard. I'm glad to have some work to do—something that really wants to be done."

"Then"—Cissy slipped her hand wistfully into Valancy's— "don't let's talk any more about my being sick. Let's just forget it. Let's pretend I'm a little girl again—and you have come here to play with me. I used to wish that long ago—wish that you could come. I knew you couldn't, of course. But how I did wish it! You always seemed so different from the other girls—so kind and sweet—and as if you had something in yourself nobody knew about—some dear, pretty secret. *Had* you, Valancy?"

"I had my Blue Castle," said Valancy, laughing a little. She was pleased that Cissy had thought of her like this. She had never suspected that anybody liked or admired or wondered about her. She told Cissy all about her Blue Castle. She had never told any one about it before.

"Every one has a Blue Castle, I think," said Cissy softly. "Only every one has a different name for it. *I* had mine—once."

She put her two thin little hands over her face. She did not tell Valancy—then—who had destroyed her Blue Castle. But Valancy knew that, whoever it was, it was not Barney Snaith.

CHAPTER XVIII

Valancy was acquainted with Barney by now—well acquainted, it seemed, though she had spoken to him only a few times. But then she had felt just as well acquainted with him the first time they had met. She had been in the garden at twilight, hunting for a few stalks of white narcissus for Cissy's room when she heard that terrible old Grey Slosson coming down through the woods from Mistawis—one could hear it miles away. Valancy did not look up as it drew near, thumping over the rocks in that crazy lane. She had never looked up, though Barney had gone racketting past every evening since she had been at Roaring Abel's. This time he did not racket past. The old Grey Slosson stopped with even more terrible noises than it made going. Valancy was conscious that Barney had sprung from it and was leaning over the ramshackle gate. She suddenly straightened up and looked into his face. Their eyes met—Valancy was suddenly conscious of a delicious weakness. Was one of her heart attacks coming on?—But this was a new symptom.

His eyes, which she had always thought brown, now seen close, were deep violet—translucent and intense. Neither of his eyebrows looked like the other. He was thin—too thin— she wished she could feed him up a bit—she wished she could sew the buttons on his coat—and make him cut his hair—and shave every day. There was *something* in his face—one hardly knew what it was. Tiredness? Sadness? Disillusionment? He had dimples in his thin cheeks when he smiled. All these thoughts flashed through Valancy's mind in that one moment while his eyes looked into hers.

"Good-evening, Miss Stirling."

Nothing could be more commonplace and conventional. Any

one might have said it. But Barney Snaith had a way of saying things that gave them poignancy. When he said good-evening you felt that it *was* a good evening and that it was partly his doing that it was. Also, you felt that some of the credit was yours. Valancy felt all this vaguely, but she couldn't imagine why she was trembling from head to foot—it *must* be her heart. If only he didn't notice it!

"I'm going over to the Port," Barney was saying. "Can I acquire merit by getting or doing anything there for you or Cissy?"

"Will you get some salt codfish for us?" said Valancy. It was the only thing she could think of. Roaring Abel had expressed a desire that day for a dinner of boiled salt codfish. When her knights came riding to the Blue Castle, Valancy had sent them on many a quest, but she had never asked any of them to get her salt codfish.

"Certainly. You're sure there's nothing else? Lots of room in Lady Jane Grey Slosson. And she always gets back *some* time, does Lady Jane."

"I don't think there's anything more," said Valancy. She knew he would bring oranges for Cissy anyhow—he always did.

Barney did not turn away at once. He was silent for a little. Then he said, slowly and whimsically:

"Miss Stirling, you're a brick! You're a whole cartload of bricks. To come here and look after Cissy—under the circumstances."

"There's nothing so bricky about that," said Valancy. "I'd nothing else to do. And—I like it here. I don't feel as if I'd done anything specially meritorious. Mr. Gay is paying me fair wages. I never earned any money before—and I like it." It seemed so easy to talk to Barney Snaith, someway—this terrible Barney Snaith of the lurid tales and mysterious past—as easy and natural as if talking to herself.

"All the money in the world couldn't buy what you're doing for Cissy Gay," said Barney. "It's splendid and fine of you. And if there's anything I can do to help you in any way, you have only to let me know. If Roaring Abel ever tries to annoy you—"

"He doesn't. He's lovely to me. I like Roaring Abel," said Valancy frankly.

"So do I. But there's one stage of his drunkenness—perhaps you haven't encountered it yet—when he sings ribald songs—"

"Oh, yes. He came home last night like that. Cissy and I just went to our room and shut ourselves in where we couldn't hear him. He apologised this morning. I'm not afraid of any of Roaring Abel's stages."

"Well, I'm sure he'll be decent to you, apart from his inebriated yowls," said Barney. "And I've told him he's got to stop damning things when you're around."

"Why?" asked Valancy slyly, with one of her odd, slanted glances and a sudden flake of pink on each cheek, born of the thought that Barney Snaith had actually done so much for *her*. "I often feel like damning things myself."

For a moment Barney stared. Was this elfin girl the little, old-maidish creature who had stood there two minutes ago? Surely there was magic and devilry going on in that shabby, weedy old garden.

Then he laughed.

"It will be relief to have some one to do it for you, then. So you don't want anything but salt codfish?"

"Not tonight. But I dare say I'll have some errands for you very often when you go to Port Lawrence. I can't trust Mr. Gay to remember to bring all the things I want."

Barney had gone away, then, in his Lady Jane, and Valancy stood in the garden for a long time.

Since then he had called several times, walking down through the barrens, whistling. How that whistle of his echoed through the spruces on those June twilights! Valancy caught herself listening for it every evening—rebuked herself—then let herself go. Why shouldn't she listen for it?

He always brought Cissy fruit and flowers. Once he brought Valancy a box of candy—the first box of candy she had ever been given. It seemed sacrilege to eat it.

She found herself thinking of him in season and out of season. She wanted to know if he ever thought about her when she wasn't before his eyes, and, if so, what. She wanted to see that mysterious house of his back on the Mistawis island. Cissy had never seen it. Cissy, though she talked freely of Barney and had known him for five years, really knew little more of him than Valancy herself.

"But he isn't bad," said Cissy. "Nobody need ever tell me he is. He *can't* have done a thing to be ashamed of."

"Then why does he live as he does?" asked Valancy—to hear somebody defend him.

"I don't know. He's a mystery. And of course there's something behind it, but I *know* it isn't disgrace. Barney Snaith simply couldn't do anything disgraceful, Valancy."

Valancy was not so sure. Barney must have done *something*—sometime. He was a man of education and intelligence. She had soon discovered that, in listening to his conversations and wrangles with Roaring Abel—who was surprisingly well read and could discuss any subject under the sun when sober. Such a man wouldn't bury himself for five years in Muskoka and live and look like a tramp if there were not too good—or bad—a reason for it. But it didn't matter. All that mattered was that she was sure now that he had never been Cissy Gay's lover. There was nothing like *that* between them. Though he was very fond of Cissy and she of him, as any one could see. But it was a fondness that didn't worry Valancy.

"You don't know what Barney has been to me, these past two years," Cissy had said simply. "*Everything* would have been unbearable without him."

"Cissy Gay is the sweetest girl I ever knew—and there's a man somewhere I'd like to shoot if I could find him," Barney had said savagely.

Barney was an interesting talker, with a knack of telling a great deal about his adventures and nothing at all about himself. There was one glorious rainy day when Barney and Abel swapped yarns all the afternoon while Valancy mended tablecloths and listened.

Barney told weird tales of his adventures with "shacks" on trains while hoboing it across the continent. Valancy thought she ought to think his stealing rides quite dreadful, but didn't. The story of his working his way to England on a cattle-ship sounded more legitimate. And his yarns of the Yukon enthralled her— especially the one of the night he was lost on the divide between the Gold Run and Sulphur Valley. He had spent two years out there. Where in all this was there room for the penitentiary and the other things?

If he were telling the truth. But Valancy knew he was.

"Found no gold," he said. "Came away poorer than when I went. But such a place to live! Those silences at the back of the north wind *got* me. I've never belonged to myself since."

Yet he was not a great talker. He told a great deal in a few well-chosen words—how well-chosen Valancy did not realise. And he had a knack of saying things without opening his mouth at all.

"I like a man whose eyes say more than his lips," thought Valancy.

But then she liked everything about him—his tawny hair— his whimsical smiles—the little glints of fun in his eyes—his loyal affection for that unspeakable Lady Jane—his habit of sitting with his hands in his pockets, his chin sunk on his breast, looking up from under his mismated eyebrows. She liked his nice voice which sounded as if it might become caressing or wooing with very little provocation. She was at times almost afraid to let herself think these thoughts. They were so vivid that she felt as if the others *must* know what she was thinking.

"I've been watching a woodpecker all day," he said one evening on the shaky old back verandah. His account of the woodpecker's doings was satisfying. He had often some gay or cunning little anecdote of the wood folk to tell them. And sometimes he and Roaring Abel smoked fiercely the whole evening and never said a word, while Cissy lay in the hammock swung between the verandah posts and Valancy sat idly on the steps, her hands clasped over her knees, and wondered dreamily if she were really

Valancy Stirling and if it were only three weeks since she had left the ugly old house on Elm Street.

The barrens lay before her in a white moon splendour, where dozens of little rabbits frisked. Barney, when he liked, could sit down on the edge of the barrens and lure those rabbits right to him by some mysterious sorcery he possessed. Valancy had once seen a squirrel leap from a scrub pine to his shoulder and sit there chattering to him. It reminded her of John Foster.

It was one of the delights of Valancy's new life that she could read John Foster's books as often and as long as she wanted to. She read them all to Cissy, who loved them. She also tried to read them to Abel and Barney, who did not love them. Abel was bored and Barney politely refused to listen at all.

"Piffle," said Barney.

CHAPTER XIX

Of course, the Stirlings had not left the poor maniac alone all this time or refrained from heroic efforts to rescue her perishing soul and reputation. Uncle James, whose lawyer had helped him as little as his doctor, came one day and, finding Valancy alone in the kitchen, as he supposed, gave her a terrible talking to—told her she was breaking her mother's heart and disgracing her family.

"But *why*?" said Valancy, not ceasing to scour her porridge pot decently. "I'm doing honest work for honest pay. What is there in that that is disgraceful?"

"Don't quibble, Valancy," said Uncle James solemnly. "This is no fit place for you to be, and you know it. Why, I'm told that that jail-bird, Snaith, is hanging around here every evening."

"Not *every* evening," said Valancy reflectively. "No, not quite every evening."

"It's—it's insufferable!" said Uncle James violently. "Valancy, you *must* come home. We won't judge you harshly. I assure you we won't. We will overlook all this."

"Thank you," said Valancy.

"Have you no sense of shame?" demanded Uncle James.

"Oh, yes. But the things *I* am ashamed of are not the things *you* are ashamed of." Valancy proceeded to rinse her dishcloth meticulously.

Still was Uncle James patient. He gripped the sides of his chair and ground his teeth.

"We know your mind isn't just right. We'll make allowances. But you *must* come home. You shall not stay here with that drunken, blasphemous old scoundrel—"

"Were you by any chance referring to *me*, *Mister* Stirling?"

demanded Roaring Abel, suddenly appearing in the doorway of the back verandah where he had been smoking a peaceful pipe and listening to "old Jim Stirling's" tirade with huge enjoyment. His red beard fairly bristled with indignation and his huge eyebrows quivered. But cowardice was not among James Stirling's shortcomings.

"I was. And, furthermore, I want to tell you that you have acted an iniquitous part in luring this weak and unfortunate girl away from her home and friends, and I will have you punished yet for it—"

James Stirling got no further. Roaring Abel crossed the kitchen at a bound, caught him by his collar and his trousers, and hurled him through the doorway and over the garden paling with as little apparent effort as he might have employed in whisking a troublesome kitten out of the way.

"The next time you come back here," he bellowed, "I'll throw you through the window—and all the better if the window is shut! Coming here, thinking yourself God to put the world to rights!"

Valancy candidly and unashamedly owned to herself that she had seen few more satisfying sights than Uncle James' coat-tails flying out into the asparagus bed. She had once been afraid of this man's judgment. Now she saw clearly that he was nothing but a rather stupid little village tin-god.

Roaring Abel turned with his great broad laugh.

"He'll think of that for years when he wakes up in the night. The Almighty made a mistake in making so many Stirlings. But since they are made, we've got to reckon with them. Too many to kill out. But if they come here bothering you I'll shoo 'em off before a cat could lick its ear."

The next time they sent Dr. Stalling. Surely Roaring Abel would not throw him into asparagus beds. Dr. Stalling was not so sure of this and had no great liking for the task. He did not believe Valancy Stirling was out of her mind. She had always been queer. He, Dr. Stalling, had never been able to understand her. Therefore, beyond doubt, she was queer. She was only just a little queerer than usual now. And Dr. Stalling had his own reasons for disliking Roaring Abel. When Dr. Stalling had first come to Deerwood he had had a liking for long hikes around Mistawis and Muskoka. On one of these occasions he had got lost and after much wandering had fallen in with Roaring Abel with his gun over his shoulder.

Dr. Stalling had contrived to ask his question in about the most idiotic manner possible. He said, "Can you tell me where I'm going?"

"How the devil should I know where you're going, gosling?" retorted Abel contemptuously.

Dr. Stalling was so enraged that he could not speak for a moment or two and in that moment Abel had disappeared in the woods. Dr. Stalling had eventually found his way home, but he had never hankered to encounter Abel Gay again.

Nevertheless he came now to do his duty. Valancy greeted him with a sinking heart. She had to own to herself that she was terribly afraid of Dr. Stalling still. She had a miserable conviction that if he shook his long, bony finger at her and told her to go home, she dared not disobey.

"Mr. Gay," said Dr. Stalling politely and condescendingly, "may I see Miss Stirling alone for a few minutes?" Roaring Abel was a little drunk—just drunk enough to be excessively polite and very cunning. He had been on the point of going away when Dr. Stalling arrived, but now he sat down in a corner of the parlour and folded his arms.

"No, no, mister," he said solemnly. "That wouldn't do— wouldn't do at all. I've got the reputation of my household to keep up. I've got to chaperone this young lady. Can't have any sparkin' going on here behind my back."

Outraged Dr. Stalling looked so terrible that Valancy wondered how Abel could endure his aspect. But Abel was not worried at all.

"D'ye know anything about it, anyway?" he asked genially.

"About *what*?"

"Sparking," said Abel coolly.

Poor Dr. Stalling, who had never married because he believed in a celibate clergy, would not notice this ribald remark. He turned his back on Abel and addressed himself to Valancy.

"Miss Stirling, I am here in response to your mother's wishes. She begged me to come. I am charged with some messages from her. Will you"—he wagged his forefinger—"will you hear them?"

"Yes," said Valancy faintly, eyeing the forefinger. It had a hypnotic effect on her.

"The first is this. If you will leave this—this—"

"House," interjected Roaring Abel. "H-o-u-s-e. Troubled with an impediment in your speech, ain't you, Mister?"

"—this *place* and return to your home, Mr. James Stirling will himself pay for a good nurse to come here and wait on Miss Gay."

Back of her terror Valancy smiled in secret. Uncle James must indeed regard the matter as desperate when he would loosen his purse-strings like that. At any rate, her clan no longer despised her or ignored her. She had become important to them.

"That's *my* business, Mister," said Abel. "Miss Stirling can go if she pleases, or stay if she pleases. I made a fair bargain with her, and she's free to conclude it when she likes. She gives me meals that stick to my ribs. She don't forget to put salt in the porridge. She never slams doors, and when she has nothing to say she don't talk. That's uncanny in a woman, you know, Mister. I'm satisfied. If she isn't, she's free to go. But no woman comes here in Jim Stirling's pay. If any one does"—Abel's voice was uncannily bland and polite—"I'll spatter the road with her brains. Tell him that with A. Gay's compliments."

"Dr. Stalling, a nurse is not what Cissy needs," said Valancy earnestly. "She isn't so ill as that, yet. What she wants is companionship—somebody she knows and likes just to live with her. You can understand that, I'm sure."

"I understand that your motive is quite—ahem—commendable." Dr. Stalling felt that he was very broad-minded indeed—especially as in his secret soul he did not believe Valancy's motive *was* commendable. He hadn't the least idea what she was up to, but he was sure her motive was not commendable. When he could not understand a thing he straightway condemned it. Simplicity itself! "But your first duty is to your mother. *She* needs you. She implores you to come home—she will forgive everything if you will only come home."

"That's a pretty little thought," remarked Abel meditatively, as he ground some tobacco up in his hand.

Dr. Stalling ignored him.

"She entreats, but I, Miss Stirling,"—Dr. Stalling remembered that he was an ambassador of Jehovah—"*I command*. As your pastor and spiritual guide, I command you to come home with me—this very day. Get your hat and coat and come *now*."

Dr. Stalling shook his finger at Valancy. Before that pitiless finger she drooped and wilted visibly.

"She's giving in," thought Roaring Abel. "She'll go with him. Beats all, the power these preacher fellows have over women."

Valancy *was* on the point of obeying Dr. Stalling. She must go home with him—and give up. She would lapse back to Doss Stirling again and for her few remaining days or weeks be the cowed, futile creature she had always been. It was her fate— typified by that relentless, uplifted forefinger. She could no more escape from it than Roaring Abel from his predestination. She eyed it as the fascinated bird eyes the snake. Another moment—

"Fear is the original sin," suddenly said a still, small voice away back—back—back of Valancy's consciousness. *"Almost all the evil in the world has its origin in the fact that some one is afraid of something."*

Valancy stood up. She was still in the clutches of fear, but her soul was her own again. She would not be false to that inner voice.

"Dr. Stalling," she said slowly, "I do not at present owe *any* duty to my mother. She is quite well; she has all the assistance and companionship she requires; she does not need me at all. I *am* needed here. I am going to stay here."

"There's spunk for you," said Roaring Abel admiringly.

Dr. Stalling dropped his forefinger. One could not keep on shaking a finger forever.

"Miss Stirling, is there *nothing* that can influence you? Do you remember your childhood days—"

"Perfectly. And hate them."

"Do you realise what people will say? What they *are* saying?"

"I can imagine it," said Valancy, with a shrug of her shoulders. She was suddenly free of fear again. "I haven't listened to the gossip of Deerwood teaparties and sewing circles twenty years for nothing. But, Dr. Stalling, it doesn't matter in the least to me what they say—not in the least."

Dr. Stalling went away then. A girl who cared nothing for public opinion! Over whom sacred family ties had no restraining influence! Who hated her childhood memories!

Then Cousin Georgiana came—on her own initiative, for nobody would have thought it worth while to send her. She found Valancy alone, weeding the little vegetable garden she had planted, and she made all the platitudinous pleas she could think of. Valancy heard her patiently. Cousin Georgiana wasn't such a bad old soul. Then she said:

"And now that you have got all that out of your system, Cousin Georgiana, can you tell me how to make creamed codfish so that it will not be as thick as porridge and as salt as the Dead Sea?"

* * * * * * * *

"We'll just have to *wait*," said Uncle Benjamin. "After all, Cissy Gay can't live long. Dr. Marsh tells me she may drop off any day."

Mrs. Frederick wept. It would really have been so much easier to bear if Valancy had died. She could have worn mourning then.

CHAPTER XX

When Abel gay paid Valancy her first month's wages—which he did promptly, in bills reeking with the odour of tobacco and whiskey—Valancy went into Deerwood and spent every cent of it. She got a pretty green crêpe dress with a girdle of crimson beads, at a bargain sale, a pair of silk stockings, to match, and a little crinkled green hat with a crimson rose in it. She even bought a foolish little beribboned and belaced nightgown.

She passed the house on Elm Street twice—Valancy never even thought about it as "home"—but saw no one. No doubt her mother was sitting in the room this lovely June evening playing solitaire—and cheating. Valancy knew that Mrs. Frederick always cheated. She never lost a game. Most of the people Valancy met looked at her seriously and passed her with a cool nod. Nobody stopped to speak to her.

Valancy put on her green dress when she got home. Then she took it off again. She felt so miserably undressed in its low neck and short sleeves. And that low, crimson girdle around the hips seemed positively indecent. She hung it up in the closet, feeling flatly that she had wasted her money. She would never have the courage to wear that dress. John Foster's arraignment of fear had no power to stiffen her against this. In this one thing habit and custom were still all-powerful. Yet she sighed as she went down to meet Barney Snaith in her old snuff-brown silk. That green thing had been very becoming—she had seen so much in her one ashamed glance. Above it her eyes had looked like odd brown jewels and the girdle had given her flat figure and entirely different appearance. She wished she could have left it on. But there were some things John Foster did not know.

Every Sunday evening Valancy went to the little Free Methodist church in a valley on the edge of "up back"—a spireless little grey building among the pines, with a few sunken graves and mossy gravestones in the small, paling-encircled, grass-grown square beside it. She liked the minister who preached there. He was so simple and sincere. An old man, who lived in Port Lawrence and came out by the lake in a little disappearing propeller boat to give a free service to the people of the small, stony farms back of the hills, who would otherwise never have heard any gospel message. She liked the simple service and the fervent singing. She liked to sit by the open window and look out into the pine woods. The congregation was always small. The Free Methodists were few in number, poor and generally illiterate. But Valancy loved those Sunday evenings. For the first time in her life she liked going to church. The rumour reached Deerwood that she had "turned Free Methodist" and sent Mrs. Frederick to bed for a day. But Valancy had not turned anything. She went to the church because she liked it and because in some inexplicable way it did her good. Old Mr. Towers believed exactly what he preached and somehow it made a tremendous difference.

Oddly enough, Roaring Abel disapproved of her going to the hill church as strongly as Mrs. Frederick herself could have done. He had "no use for Free Methodists. He was a Presbyterian." But Valancy went in spite of him.

"We'll hear something worse than *that* about her soon," Uncle Benjamin predicted gloomily.

They did.

Valancy could not quite explain, even to herself, just why she wanted to go to that party. It was a dance "up back" at Chidley Corners; and dances at Chidley Corners were not, as a rule, the sort of assemblies where well-brought-up young ladies were found. Valancy knew it was coming off, for Roaring Abel had been engaged as one of the fiddlers.

But the idea of going had never occurred to her until Roaring Abel himself broached it at supper.

"You come with me to the dance," he ordered. "It'll do you

good—put some colour in your face. You look peaked—you want something to liven you up."

Valancy found herself suddenly wanting to go. She knew nothing at all of what dances at Chidley Corners were apt to be like. Her idea of dances had been fashioned on the correct affairs that went by that name in Deerwood and Port Lawrence. Of course she knew the Corners' dance wouldn't be just like them. Much more informal, of course. But so much the more interesting. Why shouldn't she go? Cissy was in a week of apparent health and improvement. She wouldn't mind staying alone in the least. She entreated Valancy to go if she wanted to. And Valancy *did* want to go.

She went to her room to dress. A rage against the snuff-brown silk seized her. Wear *that* to a party! Never. She pulled her green crêpe from its hanger and put in on feverishly. It was nonsense to feel so—so—naked—just because her neck and arms were bare. That was just her old maidishness. She would not be ridden by it. On went the dress—the slippers.

It was the first time she had worn a pretty dress since the organdies of her early teens. And *they* had never made her look like this.

If she only had a necklace or something. She wouldn't feel so bare then. She ran down to the garden. There were clovers there—great crimson things growing in the long grass. Valancy gathered handfuls of them and strung them on a cord. Fastened above her neck they gave her the comfortable sensation of a collar and were oddly becoming. Another circlet of them went round her hair, dressed in the low puffs that became her. Excitement brought those faint pink stains to her face. She flung on her coat and pulled the little, twisty hat over her hair.

"You look so nice and—and—different, dear," said Cissy. "Like a green moonbeam with a gleam of red in it, if there could be such a thing."

Valancy stooped to kiss her.

"I don't feel right about leaving you alone, Cissy."

114

"Oh, I'll be all right. I feel better tonight than I have for a long while. I've been feeling badly to see you sticking here so closely on my account. I hope you'll have a nice time. I never was at a party at the Corners, but I used to go sometimes, long ago, to dances up back. We always had good times. And you needn't be afraid of Father being drunk tonight. He never drinks when he engages to play for a party. But—there may be—liquor. What will you do if it gets rough?"

"Nobody would molest me."

"Not seriously, I suppose. Father would see to that. But it *might* be noisy and—and unpleasant."

"I won't mind. I'm only going as a looker-on. I don't expect to dance. I just want to *see* what a party up back is like. I've never seen anything except decorous Deerwood."

Cissy smiled rather dubiously. She knew much better than Valancy what a party "up back" might be like if there should be liquor. But again there mightn't be.

"I hope you'll enjoy it," she repeated.

Valancy enjoyed the drive there. They went early, for it was twelve miles to Chidley Corners, and they had to go in Abel's old, ragged top-buggy. The road was rough and rocky, like most Muskoka roads, but full of the austere charm of northern woods. It wound through beautiful, purring pines that were ranks of enchantment in the June sunset, and over the curious jade-green rivers of Muskoka, fringed by aspens that were always quivering with some supernal joy.

Roaring Abel was excellent company, too. He knew all the stories and legends of the wild, beautiful "up back," and told them to Valancy as they drove along. Valancy had several fits of inward laughter over what Uncle Benjamin and Aunt Wellington, *et al.,* would feel and think and say if they saw her driving with Roaring Abel in that terrible buggy to a dance at Chidley Corners.

At first the dance was quiet enough, and Valancy was amused and entertained. She even danced twice herself, with a couple of nice "up back" boys who danced beautifully and told her she did, too.

Another compliment came her way—not a very subtle one, perhaps, but Valancy had had too few compliments in her life to be over-nice on that point. She overheard two of the "up back" young men talking about her in the dark "lean-to" behind her.

"Know who that girl in green is?"

"Nope. Guess she's from out front. The Port, maybe. Got a stylish look to her."

"No beaut but cute-looking, I'll say. 'Jever see such eyes?"

The big room was decorated with pine and fir boughs, and lighted by Chinese lanterns. The floor was waxed, and Roaring Abel's fiddle, purring under his skilled touch, worked magic. The "up back" girls were pretty and prettily dressed. Valancy thought it the nicest party she had ever attended.

By eleven o'clock she had changed her mind. A new crowd had arrived—a crowd unmistakably drunk. Whiskey began to circulate freely. Very soon almost all the men were partly drunk. Those in the porch and outside around the door began howling "come-all-ye's" and continued to howl them. The room grew noisy and reeking. Quarrels started up here and there. Bad language and obscene songs were heard. The girls, swung rudely in the dances, became dishevelled and tawdry. Valancy, alone in her corner, was feeling disgusted and repentant. Why had she ever come to such a place? Freedom and independence were all very well, but one should not be a little fool. She might have known what it would be like—she might have taken warning from Cissy's guarded sentences. Her head was aching—she was sick of the whole thing. But what could she do? She must stay to the end. Abel could not leave till then. And that would probably be not till three or four in the morning.

The new influx of boys had left the girls far in the minority and partners were scarce. Valancy was pestered with invitations to dance. She refused them all shortly, and some of her refusals were not well taken. There were muttered oaths and sullen looks.

Across the room she saw a group of the strangers talking together and glancing meaningly at her. What were they plotting?

It was at this moment that she saw Barney Snaith looking in over the heads of the crowds at the doorway. Valancy had two distinct convictions—one was that she was quite safe now; the other was that *this* was why she had wanted to come to the dance. It had been such an absurd hope that she had not recognised it before, but now she knew she had come because of the possibility that Barney might be there, too. She thought that perhaps she ought to be ashamed for this, but she wasn't. After her feeling of relief her next feeling was one of annoyance with Barney for coming there unshaved. Surely he might have enough self-respect to groom himself up decently when he went to a party. There he was, bareheaded, bristly-chinned, in his old trousers and his blue homespun shirt. Not even a coat. Valancy could have shaken him in her anger. No wonder people believed everything bad of him.

But she was not afraid any longer. One of the whispering group left his comrades and came across the room to her, through the whirling couples that now filled it uncomfortably. He was a tall, broad-shouldered fellow, not ill-dressed or ill-looking but unmistakably half drunk. He asked Valancy to dance. Valancy declined civilly. His face turned livid. He threw his arm about her and pulled her to him. His hot, whiskied breath burned her face.

"We won't have fine-lady airs here, my girl. If you ain't too good to come here you ain't too good to dance with us. Me and my pals have been watching you. You're got to give us each a turn and a kiss to boot."

Valancy tried desperately and vainly to free herself. She was being dragged out into the maze of shouting, stamping, yelling dancers. The next moment the man who held her went staggering across the room from a neatly planted blow on the jaw, knocking down whirling couples as he went. Valancy felt her arm grasped.

"This way—quick," said Barney Snaith. He swung her out through the open window behind him, vaulted lightly over the sill and caught her hand.

"Quick—we must run for it—they'll be after us."

Valancy ran as she had never run before, clinging tight to Barney's hand, wondering why she did not drop dead in such a mad scamper. Suppose she did! What a scandal it would make for her poor people. For the first time Valancy felt a little sorry for them. Also, she felt glad that she had escaped from that horrible row. Also, glad that she was holding tight to Barney's hand. Her feelings were badly mixed and she had never had so many in such a brief time in her life.

They finally reached a quiet corner in the pine woods. The pursuit had taken a different direction and the whoops and yells behind them were growing faint. Valancy, out of breath, with a crazily beating heart, collapsed on the trunk of a fallen pine.

"Thanks," she gasped.

"What a goose you were to come to such a place!" said Barney.

"I—didn't—know—it—would—be like this," protested Valancy.

"You *should* have known. Chidley Corners!"

"It—was—just—a name—to me."

Valancy knew Barney could not realise how ignorant she was of the regions "up back." She had lived in Deerwood all her life and of course he supposed she knew. He didn't know how she had been brought up. There was no use trying to explain.

"When I drifted in at Abel's this evening and Cissy told me you'd come here I was amazed. And downright scared. Cissy told me she was worried about you but hadn't liked to say anything to dissuade you for fear you'd think she was thinking selfishly about herself. So I came on up here instead of going to Deerwood."

Valancy felt a sudden delightful glow irradiating soul and body under the dark pines. So he had actually come up to look after her.

"As soon as they stop hunting for us we'll sneak around to the Muskoka road. I left Lady Jane down there. I'll take you home. I suppose you've had enough of your party."

118

"Quite," said Valancy meekly. The first half of the way home neither of them said anything. It would not have been much use. Lady Jane made so much noise they could not have heard each other. Anyway, Valancy did not feel conversationally inclined. She was ashamed of the whole affair—ashamed of her folly in going—ashamed of being found in such a place by Barney Snaith. By Barney Snaith, reputed jail-breaker, infidel, forger and defaulter. Valancy's lips twitched in the darkness as she thought of it. But she *was* ashamed.

And yet she was enjoying herself—was full of a strange exultation—bumping over that rough road beside Barney Snaith. The big trees shot by them. The tall mulleins stood up along the road in stiff, orderly ranks like companies of soldiers. The thistles looked like drunken fairies or tipsy elves as their car-lights passed over them. This was the first time she had even been in a car. After all, she liked it. She was not in the least afraid, with Barney at the wheel. Her spirits rose rapidly as they tore along. She ceased to feel ashamed. She ceased to feel anything except that she was part of a comet rushing gloriously through the night of space.

All at once, just where the pine woods frayed out to the scrub barrens, Lady Jane became quiet—too quiet. Lady Jane slowed down quietly—and stopped.

Barney uttered an aghast exclamation. Got out. Investigated. Came apologetically back.

"I'm a doddering idiot. Out of gas. I knew I was short when I left home, but I meant to fill up in Deerwood. Then I forgot all about it in my hurry to get to the Corners."

"What can we do?" asked Valancy coolly.

"I don't know. There's no gas nearer than Deerwood, nine miles away. And I don't dare leave you here alone. There are always tramps on this road—and some of those crazy fools back at the Corners may come straggling along presently. There were boys there from the Port. As far as I can see, the best thing to do is for us just to sit patiently here until some car comes along and lends us enough gas to get to Roaring Abel's with."

"Well, what's the matter with that?" said Valancy.

"We may have to sit here all night," said Barney.

"I don't mind," said Valancy.

Barney gave a short laugh. "If you don't, I needn't. I haven't any reputation to lose."

"Nor I," said Valancy comfortably.

CHAPTER XXI

We'll just sit here," said Barney, "and if we think of anything worth while saying we'll say it. Otherwise, not. Don't imagine you're bound to talk to me."

"John Foster says," quoted Valancy, "'If you can sit in silence with a person for half an hour and yet be entirely comfortable, you and that person can be friends. If you cannot, friends you'll never be and you need not waste time in trying.'"

"Evidently John Foster says a sensible thing once in a while," conceded Barney.

They sat in silence for a long while. Little rabbits hopped across the road. Once or twice an owl laughed out delightfully. The road beyond them was fringed with the woven shadow lace of trees. Away off to the southwest the sky was full of silvery little cirrus clouds above the spot where Barney's island must be.

Valancy was perfectly happy. Some things dawn on you slowly. Some things come by lightning flashes. Valancy had had a lightning flash.

She knew quite well now that she loved Barney. Yesterday she had been all her own. Now she was this man's. Yet he had done nothing—said nothing. He had not even looked at her as a woman. But that didn't matter. Nor did it matter what he was or what he had done. She loved him without any reservations. Everything in her went out wholly to him. She had no wish to stifle or disown her love. She seemed to be his so absolutely that thought apart from him—thought in which he did not predominate—was an impossibility.

She had realised, quite simply and fully, that she loved him, in the moment when he was leaning on the car door, explaining that Lady Jane had no gas. She had looked deep into his eyes in the moonlight and had known. In just that infinitesimal space of time everything was changed. Old things passed away and all things became new.

She was no longer unimportant, little old maid Valancy Stirling. She was a woman, full of love and therefore rich and significant—justified to herself. Life was no longer empty and futile, and death could cheat her of nothing. Love had cast out her last fear.

Love! What a searing, torturing, intolerably sweet thing it was—this possession of body, soul and mind! With something at its core as fine and remote and purely spiritual as the tiny blue spark in the heart of the unbreakable diamond. No dream had ever been like this. She was no longer solitary. She was one of a vast sisterhood—all the women who had ever loved in the world.

Barney need never know it—though she would not in the least have minded his knowing. But *she* knew it and it made a tremendous difference to her. Just to love! She did not ask to be loved. It was rapture enough just to sit there beside him in silence, alone in the summer night in the white splendour of moonshine, with the wind blowing down on them out of the pine woods. She had always envied the wind. So free. Blowing where it listed. Through the hills. Over the lakes. What a tang, what a zip it had! What a magic of adventure! Valancy felt as if she had exchanged her shop-worn soul for a fresh one, fire-new from the workshop of the gods. As far back as she could look, life had been dull—colourless—savourless. Now she had come to a little patch of violets, purple and fragrant—hers for the plucking. No matter who or what had been in Barney's past—no matter who or what might be in his future—no one else could ever have this perfect hour. She surrendered herself utterly to the charm of the moment.

"Ever dream of ballooning?' said Barney suddenly.

"No," said Valancy.

"I do—often. Dream of sailing through the clouds—seeing the glories of sunset—spending hours in the midst of a terrific storm with lightning playing above and below you—skimming above a silver cloud floor under a full moon—wonderful!"

"It does sound so," said Valancy. "I've stayed on earth in my dreams."

She told him about her Blue Castle. It was so easy to tell Barney things. One felt he understood everything—even the things you didn't tell him. And then she told him a little of her existence before she came to Roaring Abel's. She wanted him to see why she had gone to the dance "up back."

"You see—I've never had any real life," she said. "I've just—breathed. Every door has always been shut to me."

"But you're still young," said Barney.

"Oh, I know. Yes, I'm 'still young'—but that's so different from *young*," said Valancy bitterly. For a moment she was tempted to tell Barney why her years had nothing to do with her future; but she did not. She was not going to think of death tonight.

"Though I never was really young," she went on—"until tonight," she added in her heart. "I never had a life like other girls. You couldn't understand. Why,"—she had a desperate desire that Barney should know the worst about her—"I didn't even love my mother. Isn't it awful that I don't love my mother?"

"Rather awful—for her," said Barney drily.

"Oh, she didn't know it. She took my love for granted. And I wasn't any use or comfort to her or anybody. I was just a—a—vegetable. And I got tired of it. That's why I came to keep house for Mr. Gay and look after Cissy."

"And I suppose your people thought you'd gone mad."

"They did—and do—literally," said Valancy. "But it's a comfort to them. They'd rather believe me mad than bad. There's no other alternative. But I've been *living* since I came to Mr. Gay's. It's been a delightful experience. I suppose I'll pay for it when I have to go back—but I'll have *had* it."

"That's true," said Barney. "If you buy your experience it's your own. So it's no matter how much you pay for it. Somebody else's experience can never be yours. Well, it's a funny old world."

123

"Do you think it really is old?" asked Valancy dreamily. "I never believe *that* in June. It seems so young tonight—somehow. In that quivering moonlight—like a young, white girl—waiting."

"Moonlight here on the verge of up back is different from moonlight anywhere else," agreed Barney. "It always makes me feel so clean, somehow—body and soul. And of course the age of gold always comes back in spring."

It was ten o'clock now. A dragon of black cloud ate up the moon. The spring air grew chill—Valancy shivered. Barney reached back into the innards of Lady Jane and clawed up an old, tobacco-scented overcoat.

"Put that on," he ordered.

"Don't you want it yourself?" protested Valancy.

"No. I'm not going to have you catching cold on my hands."

"Oh, I won't catch cold. I haven't had a cold since I came to Mr. Gay's—though I've done the foolishest things. It's funny, too—I used to have them all the time. I feel so selfish taking your coat."

"You've sneezed three times. No use winding up your 'experience' up back with grippe or pneumonia."

He pulled it up tight about her throat and buttoned it on her. Valancy submitted with secret delight. How nice it was to have some one look after you so! She snuggled down into the tobaccoey folds and wished the night could last forever.

Ten minutes later a car swooped down on them from "up back." Barney sprang from Lady Jane and waved his hand. The car came to a stop beside them. Valancy saw Uncle Wellington and Olive gazing at her in horror from it.

So Uncle Wellington had got a car! And he must have been spending the evening up at Mistawis with Cousin Herbert. Valancy almost laughed aloud at the expression on his face as he recognised her. The pompous, be-hiskered old humbug!

"Can you let me have enough gas to take me to Deerwood?" Barney was asking politely. But Uncle Wellington was not attending to him.

"Valancy, how came you *here!*" he said sternly.

"By chance or God's grace," said Valancy.

"With this jail-bird—at ten o'clock at night!" said Uncle Wellington.

Valancy turned to Barney. The moon had escaped from its dragon and in its light her eyes were full of deviltry.

"*Are* you a jail-bird?"

"Does it matter?" said Barney, gleams of fun in *his* eyes.

"Not to me. I only asked out of curiosity," continued Valancy.

"Then I won't tell you. I never satisfy curiosity." He turned to Uncle Wellington and his voice changed subtly.

"Mr. Stirling, I asked you if you could let me have some gas. If you can, well and good. If not, we are only delaying you unnecessarily."

Uncle Wellington was in a horrible dilemma. To give gas to this shameless pair! But not to give it to them! To go away and leave them there in the Mistawis woods—until daylight, likely. It was better to give it to them and let them get out of sight before any one else saw them.

"Got anything to get gas in?" he grunted surlily.

Barney produced a two-gallon measure from Lady Jane. The two men went to the rear of the Stirling car and began manipulating the tap. Valancy stole sly glances at Olive over the collar of Barney's coat. Olive was sitting grimly staring straight ahead with an outraged expression. She did not mean to take any notice of Valancy. Olive had her own secret reasons for feeling outraged. Cecil had been in Deerwood lately and of course had heard all about Valancy. He agreed that her mind was changed and was exceedingly anxious to find out whence the derangement had been inherited. It was a serious thing to have in the family—a very serious thing. One had to think of one's—descendants.

"She got it from the Wansbarras," said Olive positively. "There's nothing like that in the Stirlings—nothing!"

"I hope not—I certainly hope not," Cecil had responded dubiously. "But then—to go out as a servant—for that is what it

125

practically amounts to. Your cousin!"

Poor Olive felt the implication. The Port Lawrence Prices were not accustomed to ally themselves with families whose members "worked out."

Valancy could not resist temptation. She leaned forward.

"Olive, does it hurt?"

Olive bit—stiffly.

"Does *what* hurt?"

"Looking like that."

For a moment Olive resolved she would take no further notice of Valancy. Then duty came uppermost. She must not miss the opportunity.

"Doss," she implored, leaning forward also, "won't you come home—come home tonight?"

Valancy yawned.

"You sound like a revival meeting," she said. "You really do."

"If you will come back—"

"All will be forgiven."

"Yes," said Olive eagerly. Wouldn't it be splendid if *she* could induce the prodigal daughter to return? "We'll never cast it up to you. Doss, there are nights when I cannot sleep for thinking of you."

"And me having the time of my life," said Valancy, laughing.

"Doss, I can't believe you're bad. I've always said you couldn't be bad—"

"I don't believe I can be," said Valancy. "I'm afraid I'm hopelessly proper. I've been sitting here for three hours with Barney Snaith and he hasn't even tried to kiss me. I wouldn't have minded if he had, Olive."

Valancy was still leaning forward. Her little hat with its crimson rose was tilted down over one eyes—Valancy's smile—what had happened to Valancy! She looked—not pretty—Doss couldn't be pretty—but provocative, fascinating—yes, abominably so. Olive drew back. It was beneath her dignity to say more. After all, Valancy must be both mad *and* bad.

"Thanks—that's enough," said Barney behind the car. "Much obliged, Mr. Stirling. Two gallons—seventy cents. Thank you."

Uncle Wellington climbed foolishly and feebly into his car. He wanted to give Snaith a piece of his mind, but dared not. Who knew what the creature might do if provoked? No doubt he carried firearms.

Uncle Wellington looked indecisively at Valancy. But Valancy had turned her back on him and was watching Barney pour the gas into Lady Jane's maw.

"Drive on," said Olive decisively. "There's no use in waiting here. Let me tell you what she said to me."

"The little hussy! The shameless little hussy!" said Uncle Wellington.

CHAPTER XXII

The next thing the Stirlings heard was that Valancy had been seen with Barney Snaith in a movie theatre in Port Lawrence and after it at supper in a Chinese restaurant there. This was quite true—and no one was more surprised at it than Valancy herself. Barney had come along in Lady Jane one dim twilight and told Valancy unceremoniously if she wanted a drive to hop in.

"I'm going to the Port. Will you go there with me?"

His eyes were teasing and there was a bit of defiance in his voice. Valancy, who did not conceal from herself that she would have gone anywhere with him to any place, "hopped in" without more ado. They tore into and through Deerwood. Mrs. Frederick and Cousin Stickles, taking a little air on the verandah, saw them whirl by in a cloud of dust and sought comfort in each other's eye. Valancy, who in some dim pre-existence had been afraid of a car, was hatless and her hair was blowing wildly round her face. She would certainly come down with bronchitis—and die at Roaring Abel's. She wore a low-neck dress and her arms were bare. That Snaith creature was in his shirt-sleeves, smoking a pipe. They were going at the rate of forty miles an hour—sixty, Cousin Stickles averred. Lady Jane could hit the pike when she wanted to. Valancy waved her hand gaily to her relatives. As for Mrs. Frederick, she was wishing she knew how to go into hysterics.

"Was it for this," she demanded in hollow tones, that I suffered the pangs of motherhood?"

"I will *not* believe," said Cousin Stickles solemnly, "that our prayers will not yet be answered."

"Who—*who* will protect that unfortunate girl when I am gone?" moaned Mrs. Frederick.

As for Valancy, she was wondering if it could really be only a few weeks since she had sat there with them on that verandah. Hating the rubberplant. Pestered with teasing questions like black flies. Always thinking of appearances. Cowed because of Aunt Wellington's teaspoons and Uncle Benjamin's money. Poverty-stricken. Afraid of everybody. Envying Olive. A slave to moth-eaten traditions. Nothing to hope for or expect.

And now every day was a gay adventure.

Lady Jane flew over the fifteen miles between Deerwood and the Port—through the Port. The way Barney went past traffic policemen was not holy. The lights were beginning to twinkle out like stars in the clear, lemon-hued twilight air. This was the only time Valancy ever really liked the town, and she was crazy with the delight of speeding. Was it possible she had ever been afraid of a car? She was perfectly happy, riding beside Barney. Not that she deluded herself into thinking it had any significance. She knew quite well that Barney had asked her to go on the impulse of the moment—an impulse born of a feeling of pity for her and her starved little dreams. She was looking tired after a wakeful night with a heart attack, followed by a busy day. She had so little fun. He'd give her an outing for once. Besides, Abel was in the kitchen, at the point of drunkenness where he was declaring he did not believe in God and beginning to sing ribald songs. It was just as well she should be out of the way for a while. Barney knew Roaring Abel's repertoire.

They went to the movie—Valancy had never been to a movie. And then, finding a nice hunger upon them, they went and had fried chicken—unbelievable delicious—in the Chinese restaurant. After which they rattled home again, leaving a devastating trail of scandal behind them. Mrs. Frederick gave up going to church altogether. She could not endure her friends' pitying glances and questions. But Cousin Stickles went every Sunday. She said they had been given a cross to bear.

CHAPTER XXIII

On one of Cissy's wakeful nights, she told Valancy her poor little story. They were sitting by the open window. Cissy could not get her breath lying down that night. An inglorious gibbous moon was hanging over the wooded hills and in its spectral light Cissy looked frail and lovely and incredibly young. A child. It did not seem possible that she could have lived through all the passion and pain and shame of her story.

"He was stopping at the hotel across the lake. He used to come over in his canoe at night—we met in the pines down the shore. He was a young college student—his father was a rich man in Toronto. Oh, Valancy, I didn't mean to be bad—I didn't, indeed. But I loved him so—I love him yet—I'll always love him. And I—didn't know—some things. I didn't understand. Then his father came and took him away. And—after a little—I found out—oh, Valancy,—I was so frightened. I didn't know what to do. I wrote him—and he came. He—he said he would marry me, Valancy."

"And why—and why?—"

"Oh, Valancy, he didn't love me any more. I saw that at a glance. He—he was just offering to marry me because he thought he ought to—because he was sorry for me. He wasn't bad—but he was so young—and what was I that he should keep on loving me?"

"Never mind making excuses for him," said Valancy a bit shortly. "So you wouldn't marry him?"

"I couldn't—not when he didn't love me any more. Somehow—I can't explain—it seemed a worse thing to do than—the other. He—he argued a little—but he went away. Do you think I did right, Valancy?"

"Yes, I do. *You* did right. But he—"

"Don't blame him, dear. Please don't. Let's not talk about him at all. There's no need. I wanted to tell you how it was—I didn't want you to think me bad—"

"I never did think so."

"Yes, I felt that—whenever you came. Oh, Valancy, what you've been to me! I can never tell you—but God will bless you for it. I know He will—'with what measure ye mete.'"

Cissy sobbed for a few minutes in Valancy's arms. Then she wiped her eyes.

"Well, that's almost all. I came home. I wasn't really so very unhappy. I suppose I should have been—but I wasn't. Father wasn't hard on me. And my baby was so sweet, Valancy—with such lovely blue eyes—and little rings of pale gold hair like silk floss—and tiny dimpled hands. I used to bite his satin-smooth little face all over—softly, so as not to hurt him, you know—"

"I know," said Valancy, wincing. "I know—a woman *always* knows—and dreams—"

"And he was *all* mine. Nobody else had any claim on him. When he died, oh, Valancy, I thought I must die too—I didn't see how anybody could endure such anguish and live. To see his dear little eyes and know he would never open them again—to miss his warm little body nestled against mine at night and think of him sleeping alone and cold, his wee face under the hard frozen earth. It was so awful for the first year—after that it was a little easier, one didn't keep thinking 'this day last year'—but I was so glad when I found out I was dying."

"'Who could endure life if it were not for the hope of death?'" murmured Valancy softly—it was of course a quotation from some book of John Foster's.

"I'm glad I've told you all about it," sighed Cissy. "I wanted you to know."

Cissy died a few nights after that. Roaring Abel was away. When Valancy saw the change that had come over Cissy's face she wanted to telephone for the doctor. But Cissy wouldn't let her.

"Valancy, why should you? He can do nothing for me. I've known for several days that—this—was near. Let me die in peace, dear—just holding your hand. Oh, I'm so glad you're here. Tell Father good-bye for me. He's always been as good to me as he knew how—and Barney. Somehow, I think that Barney—"

But a spasm of coughing interrupted and exhausted her. She fell asleep when it was over, still holding to Valancy's hand. Valancy sat there in the silence. She was not frightened—or even sorry. At sunrise Cissy died. She opened her eyes and looked past Valancy at something—something that made her smile suddenly and happily. And, smiling, she died.

Valancy crossed Cissy's hands on her breast and went to the open window. In the eastern sky, amid the fires of sunrise, an old moon was hanging—as slender and lovely as a new moon. Valancy had never seen an old, old moon before. She watched it pale and fade until it paled and faded out of sight in the living rose of day. A little pool in the barrens shone in the sunrise like a great golden lily.

But the world suddenly seemed a colder place to Valancy. Again nobody needed her. She was not in the least sorry Cecilia was dead. She was only sorry for all her suffering in life. But nobody could ever hurt her again. Valancy had always thought death dreadful. But Cissy had died so quietly—so pleasantly. And at the very last—something—had made up to her for everything. She was lying there now, in her white sleep, looking like a child. Beautiful! All the lines of shame and pain gone.

Roaring Abel drove in, justifying his name. Valancy went down and told him. The shock sobered him at once. He slumped down on the seat of his buggy, his great head hanging.

"Cissy dead—Cissy dead," he said vacantly. "I didn't think it would 'a' come so soon. Dead. She used to run down the lane to meet me with a little white rose stuck in her hair. Cissy used to be a pretty little girl. And a good little girl."

"She has always been a good little girl," said Valancy.

CHAPTER XXIV

Valancy herself made Cissy ready for burial. No hands but hers should touch that pitiful, wasted little body. The old house was spotless on the day of burial. Barney Snaith was not there. He had done all he could to help Valancy before it—he had shrouded the pale Cecilia in white roses from the garden—and then had gone back to his island. But everybody else was there. All Deerwood and "up back" came. They forgave Cissy splendidly at last. Mr. Bradly gave a very beautiful funeral address. Valancy had wanted her old Free Methodist man, but Roaring Abel was obdurate. He was a Presbyterian and no one but a Presbyterian minister should bury *his* daughter. Mr. Bradly was very tactful. He avoided all dubious points and it was plain to be seen he hoped for the best. Six reputable citizens of Deerwood bore Cecilia Gay to her grave in decorous Deerwood cemetery. Among them was Uncle Wellington.

The Stirlings all came to the funeral, men and women. They had had a family conclave over it. Surely now that Cissy Gay was dead Valancy would come home. She simply could not stay there with Roaring Abel. That being the case, the wisest course— decreed Uncle James—was to attend the funeral—legitimise the whole thing, so to speak—show Deerwood that Valancy had really done a most creditable deed in going to nurse poor Cecilia Gay and that her family backed her up in it. Death, the miracle worker, suddenly made the thing quite respectable. If Valancy would return to home and decency while public opinion was under its influence all might yet be well. Society was suddenly forgetting all Cecilia's wicked doings and remembering what a pretty, modest little thing she had been—"and motherless, you know—motherless!" It was the psychological moment—said

133

Uncle James.

So the Stirlings went to the funeral. Even Cousin Gladys' neuritis allowed her to come. Cousin Stickles was there, her bonnet dripping all over her face, crying as woefully as if Cissy had been her nearest and dearest. Funerals always brought Cousin Stickles' "own sad bereavement" back.

And Uncle Wellington was a pall-bearer.

Valancy, pale, subdued-looking, her slanted eyes smudged with purple, in her snuff-brown dress, moving quietly about, finding seats for people, consulting in undertones with minister and undertaker, marshalling the "mourners" into the parlour, was so decorous and proper and Stirlingish that her family took heart of grace. This was not—could not be—the girl who had sat all night in the woods with Barney Snaith—who had gone tearing bareheaded through Deerwood and Port Lawrence. This was the Valancy they knew. Really, surprisingly capable and efficient. Perhaps she had always been kept down a bit too much—Amelia really was rather strict—hadn't had a chance to show what was in her. So thought the Stirlings. And Edward Beck, from the Port road, a widower with a large family who was beginning to take notice, took notice of Valancy and thought she might make a mighty fine second wife. No beauty—but a fifty-year-old widower, Mr. Beck told himself very reasonably, couldn't expect everything. Altogether, it seemed that Valancy's matrimonial chances were never so bright as they were at Cecilia Gay's funeral.

What the Stirlings and Edward Beck would have thought had they known the back of Valancy's mind must be left to the imagination. Valancy was hating the funeral—hating the people who came to stare with curiosity at Cecilia's marble-white face—hating the smugness—hating the dragging, melancholy singing—hating Mr. Bradly's cautious platitudes. If she could have had her absurd way, there would have been no funeral at all. She would have covered Cissy over with flowers, shut her away from prying eyes, and buried her beside her nameless little baby in the grassy burying-ground under the pines of the "up back" church, with a bit of kindly prayer from the old Free Methodist minister. She remembered Cissy saying once, "I wish I could be buried deep in the heart of the woods where nobody would ever come to say, 'Cissy Gay is buried here.' and tell over my miserable story."

But this! However, it would soon be over. Valancy knew, if the Stirlings and Edward Beck didn't, exactly what she intended to do then. She had lain awake all the preceding night thinking about it and finally deciding on it.

When the funeral procession had left the house, Mrs. Frederick sought out Valancy in the kitchen.

"My child," she said tremulously, "you'll come home *now?*"

"Home," said Valancy absently. She was getting on an apron and calculating how much tea she must put to steep for supper. There would be several guests from "up back"—distant relatives of the Gays' who had not remembered them for years. And she was so tired she wished she could borrow a pair of legs from the cat.

"Yes, home," said Mrs. Frederick, with a touch of asperity. "I suppose you won't dream of staying here now—alone with Roaring Abel."

"Oh, no, I'm not going to stay *here*," said Valancy. "Of course, I'll have to stay for a day or two, to put the house in order generally. But that will be all. Excuse me, Mother, won't you? I've a frightful lot to do—all those "up back" people will be here to supper."

Mrs. Frederick retreated in considerable relief, and the Stirlings went home with lighter hearts.

"We will just treat her as if nothing had happened when she comes back," decreed Uncle Benjamin. "That will be the best plan. Just as if nothing had happened."

CHAPTER XXV

On the evening of the day after the funeral Roaring Abel went off for a spree. He had been sober for four whole days and could endure it no longer. Before he went, Valancy told him she would be going away the next day. Roaring Abel was sorry, and said so. A distant cousin from "up back" was coming to keep house for him—quite willing to do so now since there was no sick girl to wait on—but Abel was not under any delusions concerning her.

"She won't be like you, my girl. Well, I'm obliged to you. You helped me out of a bad hole and I won't forget it. And I won't forget what you did for Cissy. I'm your friend, and if you ever want any of the Stirlings spanked and sot in a corner send for me. I'm going to wet my whistle. Lord, but I'm dry! Don't reckon I'll be back afore tomorrow night, so if you're going home tomorrow, good-bye now."

"I *may* go home tomorrow," said Valancy, "but I'm not going back to Deerwood."

"Not going—"

"You'll find the key on the woodshed nail," interrupted Valancy, politely and unmistabably. "The dog will be in the barn and the cat in the cellar. Don't forget to feed her till your cousin comes. The pantry is full and I made bread and pies today. Good-bye, Mr. Gay. You have been very kind to me and I appreciate it."

"We've had a d——d decent time of it together, and that's a fact," said Roaring Abel. "You're the best small sport in the world, and your little finger is worth the whole Stirling clan tied together. Good-bye and good-luck."

Valancy went out to the garden. Her legs trembled a little, but otherwise she felt and looked composed. She held something tightly in her hand. The garden was lying in the magic of the warm, odorous July twilight. A few stars were out and the robins were calling through the velvety silences of the barrens. Valancy stood by the gate expectantly. Would he come? If he did not—

He was coming. Valancy heard Lady Jane Grey far back in the woods. Her breath came a little more quickly. Nearer—and nearer—she could see Lady Jane now—bumping down the lane—nearer—nearer—he was there—he had sprung from the car and leaning over the gate, looking at her.

"Going home, Miss Stirling?"

"I don't know—yet," said Valancy slowly. Her mind was made up, with no shadow of turning, but the moment was very tremendous.

"I thought I'd run down and ask if there was anything I could do for you," said Barney.

Valancy took it with a canter.

"Yes, there is something you can do for me," she said, evenly and distinctly. "Will you marry me?"

For a moment Barney was silent. There was no particular expression on his face. Then he gave an odd laugh.

"Come, now! I knew luck was just waiting around the corner for me. All the signs have been pointing that way today."

"Wait." Valancy lifted her hand. "I'm in earnest—but I want to get my breath after that question. Of course, with my bringing up, I realise perfectly well that this is one of the things 'a lady should not do.'"

"But why—why?"

"For two reasons." Valancy was still a little breathless, but she looked Barney straight in the eyes while all the dead Stirlings revolved rapidly in their graves and the living ones did nothing because they did not know that Valancy was at that moment proposing lawful marriage to the notorious Barney Snaith. "The first reason is, I—I—" Valancy tried to say "I love you" but could not. She had to take refuge in a pretended flippancy. "I'm crazy about you. The second is—this."

She handed him Dr. Trent's letter.

Barney opened it with the air of a man thankful to find some safe, sane thing to do. As he read it his face changed. He understood—more perhaps than Valancy wanted him to.

"Are you sure nothing can be done for you?"

Valancy did not misunderstand the question.

"Yes. You know Dr. Trent's reputation in regard to heart disease. I haven't long to live—perhaps only a few months—a few weeks. I want to *live* them. I can't go back to Deerwood—you know what my life was like there. And"—she managed it this time—"I love you. I want to spend the rest of my life with you. That's all."

Barney folded his arms on the gate and looked gravely enough at a white, saucy star that was winking at him just over Roaring Abel's kitchen chimney.

"You don't know anything about me. I may be a—murderer."

"No, I don't. You *may* be something dreadful. Everything they say of you may be true. But it doesn't matter to me."

"You care that much for me, Valancy?" said Barney incredulously, looking away from the star and into her eyes—her strange, mysterious eyes.

"I care—that much," said Valancy in a low voice. She was trembling. He had called her by her name for the first time. It was sweeter than another man's caress could have been just to hear him say her name like that.

"If we are going to get married," said Barney, speaking suddenly in a casual, matter-of-fact voice, "some things must be understood."

"Everything must be understood," said Valancy.

"I have things I want to hide," said Barney coolly "You are not to ask me about them."

"I won't," said Valancy.

"You must never ask to see my mail."

"Never."

"And we are never to pretend anything to each other."

"We won't," said Valancy. "You won't even have to pretend you like me. If you marry me I know you're only doing it out of pity."

"And we'll never tell a lie to each other about anything—a big lie or petty lie."

"Especially a petty lie," agreed Valancy.

"And you'll have to live back on my island. I won't live anywhere else."

"That's partly why I want to marry you," said Valancy.

Barney peered at her.

"I believe you mean it. Well—let's get married, then."

"Thank you," said Valancy, with a sudden return of primness. She would have been much less embarrassed if he had refused her.

"I suppose I haven't any right to make conditions. But I'm going to make one. You are never to refer to my heart or my liability to sudden death. You are never to urge me to be careful. You are to forget—absolutely forget—that I'm not perfectly healthy. I have written a letter to my mother—here it is—you are to keep it. I have explained everything in it. If I drop dead suddenly—as I likely will do—"

"It will exonerate me in the eyes of your kindred from the suspicion of having poisoned you," said Barney with a grin.

"Exactly." Valancy laughed gaily. "Dear me, I'm glad this is over. It has been—a bit of an ordeal. You see, I'm not in the habit of going about asking men to marry me. It is so nice of you not to refuse me—or offer to be a brother!"

"I'll go to the Port tomorrow and get a license. We can be married tomorrow evening. Dr. Stalling, I suppose?"

"Heavens, no." Valancy shuddered. "Besides, he wouldn't do it. He'd shake his forefinger at me and I'd jilt you at the altar. No, I want my old Mr. Towers to marry me."

"Will you marry me as I stand?" demanded Barney. A passing car, full of tourists, honked loudly—it seemed derisively. Valancy looked at him. Blue homespun shirt, nondescript hat, muddy overalls. Unshaved!

"Yes," she said.

Barney put his hands over the gate and took her little, cold ones gently in his.

"Valancy," he said, trying to speak lightly, "of course I'm not in love with you—never thought of such a thing as being in love. But, do you know, I've always thought you were a bit of a dear."

CHAPTER XXVI

The next day passed for Valancy like a dream. She could not make herself or anything she did seem real. She saw nothing of Barney, though she expected he must go rattling past on his way to the Port for a license.

Perhaps he had changed his mind.

But at dusk the lights of Lady Jane suddenly swooped over the crest of the wooded hill beyond the lane. Valancy was waiting at the gate for her bridegroom. She wore her green dress and her green hat because she had nothing else to wear. She did not look or feel at all bride-like—she really looked like a wild elf strayed out of the greenwood. But that did not matter. Nothing at all mattered except that Barney was coming for her.

"Ready?" said Barney, stopping Lady Jane with some new, horrible noises.

"Yes." Valancy stepped in and sat down. Barney was in his blue shirt and overalls. But they were clean overalls. He was smoking a villainous-looking pipe and he was bareheaded. But he had a pair of oddly smart boots on under his shabby overalls. And he was shaved. They clattered into Deerwood and through Deerwood and hit the long, wooded road to the Port.

"Haven't changed your mind?" said Barney.

"No. Have you?"

"No."

That was their whole conversation on the fifteen miles. Everything was more dream-like than ever. Valancy didn't know whether she felt happy. Or terrified. Or just plain fool.

Then the lights of Port Lawrence were about them. Valancy felt as if she were surrounded by the gleaming, hungry eyes of hundreds of great, stealthy panthers. Barney briefly asked where

Mr. Towers lived, and Valancy as briefly told him. They stopped before the shabby little house in an unfashionable street. They went in to the small, shabby parlour. Barney produced his license. So he *had* got it. Also a ring. This thing was real. She, Valancy Stirling, was actually on the point of being married.

They were standing up together before Mr. Towers. Valancy heard Mr. Towers and Barney saying things. She heard some other person saying things. She herself was thinking of the way she had once planned to be married—away back in her early teens when such a thing had not seemed impossible. White silk and tulle veil and orange-blossoms; no bridesmaid. But one flower girl, in a frock of cream shadow lace over pale pink, with a wreath of flowers in her hair, carrying a basket of roses and lilies-of-the-valley. And the groom, a noble-looking creature, irreproachably clad in whatever the fashion of the day decreed. Valancy lifted her eyes and saw herself and Barney in the little slanting, distorting mirror over the mantelpiece. She in her odd, unbridal green hat and dress; Barney in shirt and overalls. But it was Barney. That was all that mattered. No veil—no flowers—no guests—no presents—no wedding-cake—but just Barney. For all the rest of her life there would be Barney.

"Mrs. Snaith, I hope you will be very happy," Mr. Towers was saying.

He had not seemed surprised at their appearance—not even at Barney's overalls. He had seen plenty of queer weddings "up back." He did not know Valancy was one of the Deerwood Stirlings—he did not even know there *were* Deerwood Stirlings. He did not know Barney Snaith was a fugitive from justice. Really, he was an incredibly ignorant old man. Therefore he married them and gave them his blessing very gently and solemnly and prayed for them that night after they had gone away. His conscience did not trouble him at all.

"What a nice way to get married!" Barney was saying as he put Lady Jane in gear. "No fuss and flub-dub. I never supposed it was half so easy."

"For heaven's sake," said Valancy suddenly, "let's forget we *are* married and talk as if we weren't. I can't stand another drive like the one we had coming in."

Barney howled and threw Lady Jane into high with an infernal noise.

"And I thought I was making it easy for you," he said. "You didn't seem to want to talk."

"I didn't. But I wanted you to talk. I don't want you to make love to me, but I want you to act like an ordinary human being. Tell me about this island of yours. What sort of a place is it?"

"The jolliest place in the world. You're going to love it. The first time I saw it I loved it. Old Tom MacMurray owned it then. He built the little shack on it, lived there in winter and rented it to Toronto people in summer. I bought it from him—became by that one simple transaction a landed proprietor owning a house and an island. There is something so satisfying in owning a whole island. And isn't an uninhabited island a charming idea? I'd wanted to own one ever since I'd read *Robinson Crusoe*. It seemed too good to be true. And beauty! Most of the scenery belongs to the government, but they don't tax you for looking at it, and the moon belongs to everybody. You won't find my shack very tidy. I suppose you'll want to make it tidy."

"Yes," said Valancy honestly. "I *have* to be tidy. I don't really *want* to be. But untidiness hurts me. Yes, I'll have to tidy up your shack."

"I was prepared for that," said Barney, with a hollow groan.

"But," continued Valancy relentingly, "I won't insist on your wiping your feet when you come in."

"No, you'll only sweep up after me with the air of a martyr," said Barney. "Well, anyway, you can't tidy the lean-to. You can't even enter it. The door will be locked and I shall keep the key."

"Bluebeard's chamber," said Valancy. "I shan't even think of it. I don't care how many wives you have hanging up in it. So long as they're really dead."

"Dead as door-nails. You can do as you like in the rest of the house. There's not much of it—just one big living-room and one small bedroom. Well built, though. Old Tom loved his job. The beams of our house are cedar and the rafters fir. Our living-room windows face west and east. It's wonderful to have a room where you can see both sunrise and sunset. I have two cats there. Banjo and Good luck. Adorable animals. Banjo is a big, enchanting, grey devil-cat. Striped, of course. I don't care a hang for any cat that hasn't stripes. I never knew a cat who could swear as genteely and effectively as Banjo. His only fault is that he snores horribly when he is asleep. Luck is a dainty little cat. Always looking wistfully at you, as if he wanted to tell you something. Maybe he will pull it off sometime. Once in a thousand years, you know, one cat is allowed to speak. My cats are philosophers—neither of them ever cries over spilt milk.

"Two old crows live in a pine-tree on the point and are reasonably neighbourly. Call 'em Nip and Tuck. And I have a demure little tame owl. Name, Leander. I brought him up from a baby and he lives over on the mainland and chuckles to himself o'nights. And bats—it's a great place for bats at night. Scared of bats?"

"No; I like them."

"So do I. Nice, queer, uncanny, mysterious creatures. Coming from nowhere—going nowhere. Swoop! Banjo likes 'em, too. Eats 'em. I have a canoe and a disappearing propeller boat. Went to the Port in it today to get my license. Quieter than Lady Jane."

"I thought you hadn't gone at all—that you *had* changed your mind," admitted Valancy.

Barney laughed—the laugh Valancy did not like—the little, bitter, cynical laugh.

"I never change my mind," he said shortly. They went back through Deerwood. Up the Muskoka road. Past Roaring Abel's. Over the rocky, daisied lane. The dark pine woods swallowed them up. Through the pine woods, where the air was sweet with the incense of the unseen, fragile bells of the linnaeas that carpeted the banks of the trail. Out to the shore of Mistawis.

Lady Jane must be left here. They got out. Barney led the way down a little path to the edge of the lake.

"There's our island," he said gloatingly.

Valancy looked—and looked—and looked again. There was a diaphanous, lilac mist on the lake, shrouding the island. Through it the two enormous pine-trees that clasped hands over Barney's shack loomed out like dark turrets. Behind them was a sky still rose-hued in the afterlight, and a pale young moon.

Valancy shivered like a tree the wind stirs suddenly. Something seemed to sweep over her soul.

"My Blue Castle!" she said. "Oh, my Blue Castle!"

They got into the canoe and paddled out to it. They left behind the realm of everyday and things known and landed on a realm of mystery and enchantment where anything might happen—anything might be true. Barney lifted Valancy out of the canoe and swung her to a lichen-covered rock under a young pine-tree. His arms were about her and suddenly his lips were on hers. Valancy found herself shivering with the rapture of her first kiss.

"Welcome home, dear," Barney was saying.

CHAPTER XXVII

Cousin Georgiana came down the lane leading up to her little house. She lived half a mile out of Deerwood and she wanted to go in to Amelia's and find out if Doss had come home yet. Cousin Georgiana was anxious to see Doss. She had something very important to tell her. Something, she was sure, Doss would be delighted to hear. Poor Doss! She *had* had rather a dull life of it. Cousin Georgiana owned to herself that *she* would not like to live under Amelia's thumb. But that would be all changed now. Cousin Georgiana felt tremendously important. For the time being, she quite forgot to wonder which of them would go next.

And here was Doss herself, coming along the road from Roaring Abel's in such a queer green dress and hat. Talk about luck. Cousin Georgiana would have a chance to impart her wonderful secret right away, with nobody else about to interrupt. It was, you might say, a Providence.

Valancy, who had been living for four days on her enchanted island, had decided that she might as well go in to Deerwood and tell her relatives that she was married. Otherwise, finding that she had disappeared from Roaring Abel's, they might get out a search warrant for her. Barney had offered to drive her in, but she had preferred to go alone. She smiled very radiantly at Cousin Georgiana, who, she remembered, as of some one known a long time ago, had really been not a bad little creature. Valancy was so happy that she could have smiled at anybody—even Uncle James. She was not averse to Cousin Georgiana's company. Already, since the houses along the road were becoming numerous, she was conscious that curious eyes were looking at her from every window.

"I suppose you're going home, dear Doss?" said Cousin

Georgiana as she shook hands—furtively eyeing Valancy's dress and wondering if she had *any* petticoat on at all.

"Sooner or later," said Valancy cryptically.

"Then I'll go along with you. I've been wanting to see you *very* especially, Doss dear. I've something quite *wonderful* to tell you."

"Yes?" said Valancy absently. What on earth was Cousin Georgiana looking so mysterious and important about? But did it matter? No. Nothing mattered but Barney and the Blue Castle up back in Mistawis.

"Who do you suppose called to see me the other day?" asked Cousin Georgiana archly.

Valancy couldn't guess.

"Edward Beck." Cousin Georgiana lowered her voice almost to a whisper. *"Edward Beck."*

Why the italics? And *was* Cousin Georgiana blushing?

"Who on earth is Edward Beck?" asked Valancy indifferently.

Cousin Georgiana stared.

"Surely you remember Edward Beck," she said reproachfully. "He lives in that lovely house on the Port Lawrence road and he comes to our church—regularly. You *must* remember him."

"Oh, I think I do now," said Valancy, with an effort of memory. "He's that old man with a wen on his forehead and dozens of children, who always sits in the pew by the door, isn't he?"

"Not dozens of children, dear—oh, no, not dozens. Not even *one* dozen. Only nine. At least only nine that count. The rest are dead. He *isn't* old—he's only about forty-eight—the prime of life, Doss—and what does it matter about a wen?"

"Nothing, of course," agreed Valancy quite sincerely. It certainly did not matter to her whether Edward Beck had a wen or a dozen wens or no wen at all. But Valancy was getting vaguely suspicious. There was certainly an air of suppressed triumph about Cousin Georgiana. Could it be possible that Cousin Georgiana was thinking of marrying again? Marrying Edward Beck? Absurd. Cousin Georgiana was sixty-five if she were a day and her little anxious face was as closely covered with fine wrinkles as if she had been a hundred. But still—

"My dear," said Cousin Georgiana, "Edward Beck wants to marry *you*."

Valancy stared at Cousin Georgiana for a moment. Then she wanted to go off into a peal of laughter. But she only said:

"Me?"

"Yes, you. He fell in love with you at the funeral. And he came to consult me about it. I was such a friend of his first wife, you know. He is very much in earnest, Dossie. And its a wonderful chance for you. He's very well off—and you know—you—you—"

"Am not so young as I once was," agreed Valancy. "'To her that hath shall be given.' Do you really think I would make a good stepmother, Cousin Georgiana?"

"I'm sure you would. You were always so fond of children."

"But nine is such a family to start with," objected Valancy gravely.

"The two oldest are grown up and the third almost. That leaves only six that really count. And most of them are boys. So much easier to bring up than girls. There's an excellent book—'Health Care of the Growing Child'—Gladys has a copy, I think. It would be such a help to you. And there are books about morals. You'd manage nicely. Of course I told Mr. Beck that I thought you would—would—"

"Jump at him," supplied Valancy.

"Oh, no, no, dear. I wouldn't use such an indelicate expression. I told him I thought you would consider his proposal favourably. And you will, won't you, dearie?"

"There's only one obstacle," said Valancy dreamily. "You see, I'm married already."

"Married!" Cousin Georgiana stopped stock-still and stared at Valancy. "Married!"

"Yes. I was married to Barney Snaith last Tuesday evening in Port Lawrence."

There was a convenient gate-post hard by. Cousin Georgiana took firm hold of it.

"Doss, dear—I'm an old woman—are you trying to make fun of me?"

"Not at all. I'm only telling you the truth. For heaven's sake, Cousin Georgiana,"—Valancy was alarmed by certain symptoms—"don't go crying here on the public road!"

Cousin Georgiana choked back the tears and gave a little moan of despair instead.

"Oh, Doss, *what* have you done? What *have* you done?"

"I've just been telling you. I've got married," said Valancy, calmly and patiently.

"To that—that—aw—that—*Barney Snaith*. Why, they say he's had a dozen wives already."

"I'm the only one round at present," said Valancy.

"What will your poor mother say?" moaned Cousin Georgiana.

"Come along with me and hear, if you want to know," said Valancy. "I'm on my way to tell her now."

Cousin Georgiana let go the gate-post cautiously and found that she could stand alone. She meekly trotted on beside Valancy—who suddenly seemed quite a different person in her eyes. Cousin Georgiania had a tremendous respect for a married woman. But it was terrible to think of what the poor girl had done. So rash. So reckless. Of course Valancy must be stark mad. But she seemed so happy in her madness that Cousin Georgiana had a momentary conviction that it would be a pity if the clan tried to scold her back to sanity. She had never seen that look in Valancy's eyes before. But what *would* Amelia say? And Ben?

"To marry a man you know nothing about," thought Cousin Georgiana aloud.

"I know more about him than I know of Edward Beck," said Valancy.

"Edward Beck *goes to church*," said Cousin Georgiana. "Does Bar—does your husband?"

"He has promised that he will go with me on fine Sundays," said Valancy.

When they turned in at the Stirling gate Valancy gave an

exclamation of surprise.

"Look at my rosebush! Why, it's blooming!"

It was. Covered with blossoms. Great, crimson, velvety blossoms. Fragrant. Glowing. Wonderful.

"My cutting it to pieces must have done it good," said Valancy, laughing. She gathered a handful of the blossoms—they would look well on the supper-table of the verandah at Mistawis—and went, still laughing, up the walk, conscious that Olive was standing on the steps, Olive, goddess-like in loveliness, looking down with a slight frown on her forehead. Olive, beautiful, insolent. Her full form voluptuous in its swathings of rose silk and lace. Her golden-brown hair curling richly under her big, white-frilled hat. Her colour ripe and melting.

"Beautiful," thought Valancy coolly, "but"—as if she suddenly saw her cousin through new eyes—"without the slightest touch of distinction."

So Valancy had come home, thank goodness, thought Olive. But Valancy was not looking like a repentant, returned prodigal. This was the cause of Olive's frown. She was looking triumphant—graceless! That outlandish dress—that queer hat—those hands full of blood-red roses. Yet there was something about both dress and hat, as Olive instantly felt, that was entirely lacking in her own attire. This deepened the frown. She put out a condescending hand.

"So you're back, Doss? Very warm day, isn't it? Did you walk in?"

"Yes. Coming in?"

"Oh, no. I've just been in. I've come often to comfort poor Aunty. She's been so lonesome. I'm going to Mrs. Bartlett's tea. I have to help pour. She's giving it for her cousin from Toronto. Such a charming girl. You'd have loved meeting her, Doss. I think Mrs. Bartlett did send you a card. Perhaps you'll drop in later on."

"No, I don't think so," said Valancy indifferently. "I'll have to be home to get Barney's supper. We're going for a moonlit canoe ride around Mistawa tonight."

"Barney? Supper?" gasped Olive. "What *do* you mean, Valancy Stirling?"

"Valancy Snaith, by the grace of God."

Valancy flaunted her wedding-ring in Olive's stricken face. Then she nimbly stepped past her and into the house. Cousin Georgiana followed. She would not miss a moment of the great scene, even though Olive did look as if she were going to faint.

Olive did not faint. She went stupidly down the street to Mrs. Bartlett's. *What* did Doss mean? She couldn't have—that ring—oh, what fresh scandal was that wretched girl bringing on her defenceless family now? She should have been—shut up—long ago.

Valancy opened the sitting-room door and stepped unexpectedly right into grim assemblage of Stirlings. They had not come together of malice prepense. Aunt Wellington and Cousin Gladys and Aunt Mildred and Cousin Sarah had just called in on their way home from a meeting of the missionary society. Uncle James had dropped in to give Amelia some information regarding a doubtful investment. Uncle Benjamin had called, apparently, to tell them it was a hot day and ask them what was the difference between a bee and a donkey. Cousin Stickles had been tactless enough to know the answer—"one gets all the honey, the other all the whacks"—and Uncle Benjamin was in a bad humour. In all of their minds, unexpressed, was the idea of finding out if Valancy had yet come home, and, if not, what steps must be taken in the matter.

Well, here was Valancy at last, a poised, confident thing, not humble and deprecating as she should have been. And so oddly, improperly young-looking. She stood in the doorway and looked at them, Cousin Georgiana timorous, expectant, behind her. Valancy was so happy she didn't hate her people any more. She could even see a number of good qualities in them that she had never seen before. And she was sorry for them. Her pity made her quite gentle.

"Well, Mother," she said pleasantly.

"So you've come home at last!" said Mrs. Frederick, getting out a handkerchief. She dared not be outraged, but she did not mean to be cheated of her tears.

"Well, not exactly," said Valancy. She threw her bomb. "I thought I ought to drop in and tell you I was married. Last Tuesday night. To Barney Snaith."

Uncle Benjamin bounced up and sat down again.

"God bless my soul," he said dully. The rest seemed turned to stone. Except Cousin Gladys, who turned faint. Aunt Mildred and Uncle Wellington had to help her out to the kitchen.

"She would have to keep up the Victorian traditions," said Valancy, with a grin. She sat down, uninvited, on a chair. Cousin Stickles had begun to sob.

"Is there *one* day in your life that you haven't cried?" asked Valancy curiously.

"Valancy," said Uncle James, being the first to recover the power of utterance, "did you mean what you said just now?"

"I did."

"Do you mean to say that you have actually gone and married—*married*—that notorious Barney Snaith—that—that—criminal—that—"

"I have."

"Then," said Uncle James violently, "you are a shameless creature, lost to all sense of propriety and virtue, and I wash my hands entirely of you. I do not want ever to see your face again."

"What have you left to say when I commit murder?" asked Valancy.

Uncle Benjamin again appealed to God to bless his soul.

"That drunken outlaw—that—"

A dangerous spark appeared in Valancy's eyes. They might say what they liked to and of her but they should not abuse Barney.

"Say 'damn' and you'll feel better," she suggested.

"I can express my feelings without blasphemy. And I tell you you have covered yourself with eternal disgrace and infamy by marrying that drunkard—"

"*You* would be more endurable if you got drunk occasionally. Barney is *not* a drunkard."

"He was seen drunk in Port Lawrence—pickled to the gills," said Uncle Benjamin.

"If that is true—and I don't believe it—he had a good reason for it. Now I suggest that you all stop looking tragic and accept the situation. I'm married—you can't undo that. And I'm perfectly happy."

"I suppose we ought to be thankful he has really married her," said Cousin Sarah, by way of trying to look on the bright side.

"If he really has," said Uncle James, who had just washed his hands of Valancy. "Who married you?"

"Mr. Towers, of Port Lawrence."

"By a Free Methodist!" groaned Mrs. Frederick—as if to have been married by an imprisoned Methodist would have been a shade less disgraceful. It was the first thing she had said. Mrs. Frederick didn't know *what* to say. The whole thing was too horrible—too horrible—too nightmarish. She was sure she must wake up soon. After all their bright hopes at the funeral!

"It makes me think of those what-d'ye-call-'ems," said Uncle Benjamin helplessly. "Those yarns—you know—of fairies taking babies out of their cradles."

"Valancy could hardly be a changeling at twenty-nine," said Aunt Wellington satirically.

"She was the oddest-looking baby I ever saw, anyway," averted Uncle Benjamin. "I said so at the time—you remember, Amelia? I said I had never seen such eyes in a human head."

"I'm glad *I* never had any children," said Cousin Sarah. "If they don't break your heart in one way they do it in another."

"Isn't it better to have your heart broken than to have it wither up?" queried Valancy. "Before it could be broken it must have felt something splendid. *That* would be worth the pain."

"Dipp—clean dippy," muttered Uncle Benjamin, with a vague, unsatisfactory feeling that somebody had said something like that before.

"Valancy," said Mrs. Frederick solemnly, "do you ever pray to be forgiven for disobeying your mother?"

"I *should* pray to be forgiven for obeying you so long," said Valancy stubbornly. "But I don't pray about that at all. I just thank God every day for my happiness."

"I would rather," said Mrs. Frederick, beginning to cry rather belatedly, "see you dead before me than listen to what you have told me today."

Valancy looked at her mother and aunts, and wondered if they could ever have known anything of the real meaning of love. She felt sorrier for them than ever. They were so very pitiable. And they never suspected it.

"Barney Snaith is a scoundrel to have deluded you into marrying him," said Uncle James violently.

"Oh, *I* did the deluding. I asked *him* to marry me," said Valancy, with a wicked smile.

"Have you *no* pride?" demanded Aunt Wellington.

"Lots of it. I am proud that I have achieved a husband by my own unaided efforts. Cousin Georgiana here wanted to help me to Edward Beck."

"Edward Beck is worth twenty thousand dollars and has the finest house between here and Port Lawrence," said Uncle Benjamin.

"That sounds very fine," said Valancy scornfully, "but it isn't worth *that*"—she snapped her fingers—"compared to feeling Barney's arms around me and his cheek against mine."

"*Oh*, Doss!" said Cousin Stickles. Cousin Sarah said, "Oh, *Doss!*" Aunt Wellington said, "Valancy, you need not be indecent."

"Why, it surely isn't indecent to like to have your husband put his arm around you? I should think it would be indecent if you didn't."

"Why expect decency from her?" inquired Uncle James sarcastically. "She has cut herself off from decency forevermore. She has made her bed. Let her lie on it."

"Thanks," said Valancy very gratefully. "How you would have enjoyed being Torquemada! Now, I must really be getting back. Mother, may I have those three woollen cushions I worked last winter?"

"Take them—take everything!" said Mrs. Frederick.

"Oh, I don't want everything—or much. I don't want my Blue Castle cluttered. Just the cushions. I'll call for them some day when we motor in."

Valancy rose and went to the door. There she turned. She was sorrier than ever for them all. *They* had no Blue Castle in the purple solitudes of Mistawis.

"The trouble with you people is that you don't laugh enough," she said.

"Doss dear," said Cousin Georgiana mournfully, "some day you will discover that blood is thicker than water."

"Of course it is. But who wants water to be thick?" parried Valancy. "We want water to be thin—sparkling—crystal-clear."

Cousin Stickles groaned.

Valancy would not ask any of them to come and see her—she was afraid they *would* come out of curiosity. But she said:

"Do you mind if I drop in and see you once in a while, Mother?"

"My house will always be open to you," said Mrs. Frederick, with a mournful dignity.

"You should never recognise her again," said Uncle James sternly, as the door closed behind Valancy.

"I cannot quite forget that I am a mother," said Mrs. Frederick. "My poor, unfortunate girl!"

"I dare say the marriage isn't legal," said Uncle James comfortingly. "He has probably been married half a dozen times before. But *I* am through with her. I have done all I could, Amelia. I think you will admit that. Henceforth"—Uncle James was terribly solemn about it—"Valancy is to me as one dead."

"Mrs. Barney Snaith," said Cousin Georgiana, as if trying it out to see how it would sound.

"He has a score of aliases, no doubt," said Uncle Benjamin. "For my part, I believe the man is half Indian. I haven't a doubt they're living in a wigwam."

"If he has married her under the name of Snaith and it isn't his real name wouldn't that make the marriage null and void?" asked Cousin Stickles hopefully.

Uncle James shook his head.

"No, it is the man who marries, not the name."

"You know," said Cousin Gladys, who had recovered and returned but was still shaky, "I had a distinct premonition of this at Herbert's silver dinner. I remarked it at the time. When she was defending Snaith. You remember, of course. It came over me like a revelation. I spoke to David when I went home about it."

"What—*what*," demanded Aunt Wellington of the universe, "has come over Valancy? *Valancy*!"

The universe did not answer but Uncle James did.

"Isn't there something coming up of late about secondary personalities cropping out? I don't hold with many of those new-fangled notions, but there may be something in this one. It would account for her incomprehensible conduct."

"Valancy is so fond of mushrooms," sighed Cousin Georgiana. "I'm afraid she'll get poisoned eating toadstools by mistake living up back in the woods."

"There are worse things than death," said Uncle James, believing that it was the first time in the world that such statement had been made.

"Nothing can ever be the same again!" sobbed Cousin Stickles.

Valancy, hurrying along the dusty road, back to cool Mistawis and her purple island, had forgotten all about them—just as she had forgotten that she might drop dead at any moment if she hurried.

CHAPTER XXVIII

Summer passed by. The Stirling clan—with the insignificant exception of Cousin Georgiana—had tacitly agreed to follow Uncle James' example and look upon Valancy as one dead. To be sure, Valancy had an unquiet, ghostly habit of recurring resurrections when she and Barney clattered through Deerwood and out to the Port in that unspeakable car. Valancy bareheaded, with stars in her eyes. Barney, bareheaded, smoking his pipe. But shaved. Always shaved now, if any of them had noticed it. They even had the audacity to go in to Uncle Benjamin's store to buy groceries. Twice Uncle Benjamin ignored them. Was not Valancy one of the dead? While Snaith had never existed. But the third time he told Barney he was a scroundrel who should be hung for luring an unfortunate, weak-minded girl away from her home and friends.

Barney's one straight eyebrow went up.

"I have made her happy," he said coolly, "and she was miserable with her friends. So that's that."

Uncle Benjamin stared. It had never occurred to him that women had to be, or ought to be, "made happy."

"You—you pup!" he said.

"Why be so unoriginal?" queried Barney amiably. "Anybody could call me a pup. Why not think of something worthy of the Stirlings? Besides, I'm not a pup. I'm really quite a middle-aged dog. Thirty-five, if you're interested in knowing."

Uncle Benjamin remembered just in time that Valancy was dead. He turned his back on Barney.

Valancy *was* happy—gloriously and entirely so. She seemed to be living in a wonderful house of life and every day opened a new, mysterious room. It was in a world which had nothing in

157

common with the one she had left behind—a world where time was not—which was young with immortal youth—where there was neither past nor future but only the present. She surrendered herself utterly to the charm of it.

The absolute freedom of it all was unbelievable. They could do exactly as they liked. No Mrs. Grundy. No traditions. No relatives. Or in-laws. "Peace, perfect peace, with loved ones far away," as Barney quoted shamelessly.

Valancy had gone home once and got her cushions. And Cousin Georgiana had given her one of her famous candlewick spreads of most elaborate design. "For your spare-room bed, dear," she said.

"But I haven't got any spare-room," said Valancy.

Cousin Georgiana looked horrified. A house without a spare-room was monstrous to her.

"But it's a lovely spread," said Valanacy, with a kiss, "and I'm so glad to have it. I'll put it on my own bed. Barney's old patch-work quilt is getting ragged."

"I don't see how you can be contented to live up back," sighed Cousin Georgiana. "It's so out of the world."

"Contented!" Valancy laughed. What was the use of trying to explain to Cousin Georgiana. "It is," she agreed, "most gloriously and entirely out of the world."

"And you are really happy, dear?" asked Cousin Georgiana wistfully.

"I really am," said Valancy gravely, her eyes dancing.

"Marriage is such a serious thing," sighed Cousin Georgiana.

"When it's going to last long," agreed Valancy.

Cousin Georgiana did not understand this at all. But it worried her and she lay awake at nights wondering what Valancy meant by it.

Valancy loved her Blue Castle and was completely satisfied with it. The big living-room had three windows, all commanding exquisite views of exquisite Mistawis. The one in the end of the room was an oriel window—which Tom MacMurray, Barney explained, had got out of some little, old "up back" church that had been sold. It faced the west and when the sunsets flooded it Valancy's whole being knelt in prayer as if in some great cathedral. The new moons always looked down through it, the lower pine boughs swayed about the top of it, and all through the nights the soft, dim silver of the lake dreamed through it.

There was a stone fireplace on the other side. No desecrating gas imitation but a real fireplace where you could burn real logs. With a big grizzly bearskin on the floor before it, and beside it a hideous, red-plush sofa of Tom MacMurray's régime. But its ugliness was hidden by silver-grey timber wolf skins, and Valancy's cushions made it gay and comfortable. In a corner a nice, tall, lazy old clock ticked—the right kind of a clock. One that did not hurry the hours away but ticked them off deliberately. It was the jolliest looking old clock. A fat, corpulent clock with a great, round, man's face painted on it, the hands stretching out of its nose and the hours encircling it like a halo.

There was a big glass case of stuffed owls and several deer heads—likewise of Tom MacMurray's vintage. Some comfortable old chairs that asked to be sat upon. A squat little chair with a cushion was prescriptively Banjo's. If anybody else dared sit on it Banjo glared him out of it with his topaz-hued, black-ringed eyes. Banjo had an adorable habit of hanging over the back of it, trying to catch his own tail. Losing his temper because he couldn't catch it. Giving it a fierce bite for spite when he *did* catch it. Yowling malignantly with pain. Barney and Valancy laughed at him until they ached. But it was Good Luck they loved. They were both agreed that Good Luck was so lovable that he practically amounted to an obsession.

One side of the wall was lined with rough, homemade bookshelves filled with books, and between the two side windows hung an old mirror in a faded gilt-frame, with fat cupids gamboling in the panel over the glass. A mirror, Valancy thought, that must be like the fabled mirror into which Venus had once looked and which thereafter reflected as beautiful every woman who looked into it. Valancy thought she was almost pretty in that mirror. But that may have been because she had shingled her hair.

This was before the day of bobs and was regarded as a wild, unheard-of proceeding—unless you had typhoid. When Mrs. Frederick heard of it she almost decided to erase Valancy's name from the family Bible. Barney cut the hair, square off at the back of Valancy's neck, bringing it down in a short black fringe over her forehead. It gave a meaning and a purpose to her little, three-cornered face that it never had possessed before. Even her nose ceased to irritate her. Her eyes were bright, and her sallow skin had cleared to the hue of creamy ivory. The old family joke had come true—she was really fat at last—anyway, no longer skinny. Valancy might never be beautiful, but she was of the type that looks its best in the woods—elfin—mocking—alluring. Her heart bothered her very little. When an attack threatened she was generally able to head it off with Dr. Trent's prescription. The only bad one she had was one night when she was temporarily out of medicine. And it *was* a bad one. For the time being, Valancy realised keenly that death was actually waiting to pounce on her any moment. But the rest of the time she would not—did not—let herself remember it at all.

CHAPTER XXIX

Valancy toiled not, neither did she spin. There was really very little work to do. She cooked their meals on a coal-oil stove, performing all her little domestic rites carefully and exultingly, and they ate out on the verandah that almost overhung the lake. Before them lay Mistawis, like a scene out of some fairy tale of old time. And Barney smiling his twisted, enigmatical smile at her across the table.

"What a view old Tom picked out when he built this shack!" Barney would say exultantly.

Supper was the meal Valancy liked best. The faint laughter of winds was always about them and the colours of Mistawis, imperial and spiritual, under the changing clouds were something that cannot be expressed in mere words. Shadows, too. Clustering in the pines until a wind shook them out and pursued them over Mistawis. They lay all day along the shores, threaded by ferns and wild blossoms. They stole around the headlands in the glow of the sunset, until twilight wove them all into one great web of dusk.

The cats, with their wise, innocent little faces, would sit on the verandah railing and eat the tidbits Barney flung them. And how good everything tasted! Valancy, amid all the romance of Mistawis, never forgot that men had stomachs. Barney paid her no end of compliments on her cooking.

"After all," he admitted, "there's something to be said for square meals. I've mostly got along by boiling two or three dozen eggs hard at once and eating a few when I got hungry, with a slice of bacon once in a while and a jorum or tea."

Valancy poured tea out of Barney's little battered old pewter teapot of incredible age. She had not even a set of dishes—only

Barney's mismatched chipped bits—and a dear, big, pobby old jug of robin's-egg blue.

After the meal was over they would sit there and talk for hours—or sit and say nothing, in all the languages of the world, Barney pulling away at his pipe, Valancy dreaming idly and deliciously, gazing at the far-off hills beyond Mistawis where the spires of firs came out against the sunset. The moonlight would begin to silver the Mistawis. Bats would begin to swoop darkly against the pale, western gold. The little waterfall that came down on the high bank not far away would, by some whim of the wildwood gods, begin to look like a wonderful white woman beckoning through the spicy, fragrant evergreens. And Leander would begin to chuckle diabolically on the mainland shore. How sweet it was to sit there and do nothing in the beautiful silence, with Barney at the other side of the table, smoking!

There were plenty of other islands in sight, though none were near enough to be troublesome as neighbours. There was one little group of islets far off to the west which they called the Fortunate Isles. At sunrise they looked like a cluster of emeralds, at sunset like a cluster of amethysts. They were too small for houses; but the lights on the larger islands would bloom out all over the lake, and bonfires would be lighted on their shores, streaming up into the wood shadows and throwing great, blood-red ribbons over the waters. Music would drift to them alluringly from boats here and there, or from the verandahs on the big house of the millionaire on the biggest island.

"Would you like a house like that, Moonlight?" Barney asked once, waving his hand at it. He had taken to calling her Moonlight, and Valancy loved it.

"No," said Valancy, who had once dreamed of a mountain castle ten times the size of the rich man's "cottage" and now pitied the poor inhabitants of palaces. "No. It's too elegant. I would have to carry it with me everywhere I went. On my back like a snail. It would own me—possess me, body and soul. I like a house I can love and cuddle and boss. Just like ours here. I don't envy Hamilton Gossard 'the finest summer residence in Canada.' It is magnificent, but it isn't my Blue Castle."

Away down at the far end of the lake they got every night a glimpse of a big, continental train rushing through a clearing. Valancy liked to watch its lighted windows flash by and wonder who was on it and what hopes and fears it carried. She also amused herself by picturing Barney and herself going to the dances and dinners in the houses on the islands, but she did not want to go in reality. Once they did go to a masquerade dance in the pavilion at one of the hotels up the lake, and had a glorious evening, but slipped away in their canoe, before unmasking time, back to the Blue Castle.

"It was lovely—but I don't want to go again," said Valancy.

So many hours a day Barney shut himself up in Bluebeard's Chamber. Valancy never saw the inside of it. From the smells that filtered through at times she concluded he must be conducting chemical experiments—or counterfeiting money. Valancy supposed there must be smelly processes in making counterfeit money. But she did not trouble herself about it. She had no desire to peer into the locked chambers of Barney's house of life. His past and his future concerned her not. Only this rapturous present. Nothing else mattered.

Once he went away and stayed away two days and nights. He had asked Valancy if she would be afraid to stay alone and she had said she would not. He never told her where he had been. She was not afraid to be alone, but she was horribly lonely. The sweetest sound she had ever heard was Lady Jane's clatter through the woods when Barney returned. And then his signal whistle from the shore. She ran down to the landing rock to greet him—to nestle herself into his eager arms—they *did* seem eager.

"Have you missed me, Moonlight?" Barney was whispering.

"It seems a hundred years since you went away," said Valancy.

"I won't leave you again."

"You must," protested Valancy, "if you want to. I'd be miserable if I thought you wanted to go and didn't, because of me. I want you to feel perfectly free."

Barney laughed—a little cynically.

"There is no such thing as freedom on earth," he said. "Only different kinds of bondages. And comparative bondages. *You* think you are free now because you've escaped from a peculiarly unbearable kind of bondage. But are you? You love me—*that's* a bondage."

"Who said or wrote that 'the prison unto which we doom ourselves no prison is'?" asked Valancy dreamily, clinging to his arm as they climbed up the rock steps.

"Ah, now you have it," said Barney. "That's all the freedom we can hope for—the freedom to choose our prison. But, Moonlight,"—he stopped at the door of the Blue Castle and looked about him—at the glorious lake, the great, shadowy woods, the bonfires, the twinkling lights—"Moonlight, I'm glad to be home again. When I came down through the woods and saw my home lights—mine—gleaming out under the old pines— something I'd never seen before—oh, girl, I was glad—glad!"

But in spite of Barney's doctrine of bondage, Valancy thought they were splendidly free. It was amazing to be able to sit up half the night and look at the moon if you wanted to. To be late for meals if you wanted to—she who had always been rebuked so sharply by her mother and so reproachfully by Cousin Stickles if she were one minute late. Dawdle over meals as long as you wanted to. Leave your crusts if you wanted to. Not come home at all for meals if you wanted to. Sit on a sun-warm rock and paddle your bare feet in the hot sand if you wanted to. Just sit and do nothing in the beautiful silence if you wanted to. In short, do any fool thing you wanted to whenever the notion took you. If *that* wasn't freedom, what was?

CHAPTER XXX

They didn't spend all their days on the island. They spent more than half of them wandering at will through the enchanted Muskoka country. Barney knew the woods as a book and he taught their lore and craft to Valancy. He could always find trail and haunt of the shy wood people. Valancy learned the different fairy-likenesses of the mosses—the charm and exquisiteness of woodland blossoms. She learned to know every bird at sight and mimic its call—though never so perfectly as Barney. She made friends with every kind of tree. She learned to paddle a canoe as well as Barney himself. She liked to be out in the rain and she never caught cold.

Sometimes they took a lunch with them and went berrying— strawberries and blueberries. How pretty blueberries were—the dainty green of the unripe berries, the glossy pinks and scarlets of the half ripes, the misty blue of the fully matured! And Valancy learned the real flavour of the strawberry in its highest perfection. There was a certain sunlit dell on the banks of Mistawis along which white birches grew on one side and on the other still, changeless ranks of young spruces. There were long grasses at the roots of the birches, combed down by the winds and wet with morning dew late into the afternoons. Here they found berries that might have graced the banquets of Lucullus, great ambrosial sweetnesses hanging like rubies to long, rosy stalks. They lifted them by the stalk and ate them from it, uncrushed and virgin, tasting each berry by itself with all its wild fragrance ensphered therein. When Valancy carried any of these berries home that elusive essence escaped and they became nothing more than the common berries of the market-place—very kitchenly good indeed, but not as they would have been, eaten in their birch dell until her fingers were stained as pink as Aurora's eyelids.

Or they went after water-lilies. Barney knew where to find them in the creeks and bays of Mistawis. Then the Blue Castle was glorious with them, every receptacle that Valancy could contrive filled with the exquisite things. If not water lilies then cardinal flowers, fresh and vivid from the swamps of Mistawis, where they burned like ribbons of flame.

Sometimes they went trouting on little nameless rivers or hidden brooks on whose banks Naiads might have sunned their white, wet limbs. Then all they took with them were some raw potatoes and salt. They roasted the potatoes over a fire and Barney showed Valancy how to cook the trout by wrapping them in leaves, coating them with mud and baking them in a bed of hot coals. Never were such delicious meals. Valancy had such an appetite it was no wonder she put flesh on her bones.

Or they just prowled and explored through woods that always seemed to be expecting something wonderful to happen. At least, that was the way Valancy felt about them. Down the next hollow—over the next hill—you would find it.

"We don't know where we're going, but isn't it fun to go?" Barney used to say.

Once or twice night overtook them, too far from their Blue Castle to get back. But Barney made a fragrant bed of bracken and fir boughs and they slept on it dreamlessly, under a ceiling of old spruces with moss hanging from them, while beyond them moonlight and the murmur of pines blended together so that one could hardly tell which was light and which was sound.

There were rainy days, of course, when Muskoka was a wet green land. Days when showers drifted across Mistawis like pale ghosts of rain and they never thought of staying in because of it. Days when it rained in right good earnest and they had to stay in. Then Barney shut himself up in Bluebeard's Chamber and Valancy read, or dreamed on the wolfskins with Good Luck purring beside her and Banjo watching them suspiciously from his own peculiar chair. On Sunday evenings they paddled across to a point of land and walked from there through the woods to the little Free Methodist church. One felt really too happy for Sunday. Valancy had never really liked Sundays before.

And always, Sundays and weekdays, she was with Barney. Nothing else really mattered. And what a companion he was! How understanding! How jolly! How—how Barney-like! That summed it all up.

Valancy had taken some of her two hundred dollars out of the bank and spent it in pretty clothes. She had a little smoke-blue chiffon which she always put on when they spent the evenings at home—smoke-blue with touches of silver about it. It was after she began wearing it that Barney began calling her Moonlight.

"Moonlight and blue twilight—that is what you look like in that dress. I like it. It belongs to you. You aren't exactly pretty, but you have some adorable beauty-spots. Your eyes. And that little kissable dent just between your collar bones. You have the wrist and ankle of an aristocrat. That little head of yours is beautifully shaped. And when you look backward over your shoulder you're maddening—especially in twilight or moonlight. An elf maiden. A wood sprite. You belong to the woods, Moonlight—you should never be out of them. In spite of your ancestry, there is something wild and remote and untamed about you. And you have such a nice, sweet, throaty, summery voice. Such a nice voice for love-making."

"Shure an' ye've kissed the Blarney Stone," scoffed Valancy. But she tasted these compliments for weeks.

She got a pale green bathing-suit, too—a garment which would have given her clan their deaths if they had ever seen her in it. Barney taught her how to swim. Sometimes she put her bathing-dress on when she got up and didn't take it off until she went to bed—running down to the water for a plunge whenever she felt like it and sprawling on the sun-warm rocks to dry.

She had forgotten all the old humiliating things that used to come up against her in the night—the injustices and the disappointments. It was as if they had all happened to some other person—not to her, Valancy Snaith, who had always been happy.

"I understand now what it means to be born again," she told Barney.

Holmes speaks of grief "staining backward" through the pages of life; but Valancy found her happiness had stained backward likewise and flooded with rose-colour her whole previous drab existence. She found it hard to believe that she had ever been lonely and unhappy and afraid.

"When death comes, I shall have lived," thought Valancy. "I shall have had my hour."

And her dust-pile!

One day Valancy had heaped up the sand in the little island cove in a tremendous cone and stuck a gay little Union Jack on top of it.

"What are you celebrating?" Barney wanted to know.

"I'm just exorcising an old demon," Valancy told him.

CHAPTER XXXI

Autumn came. Late September with cool nights. They had to forsake the verandah; but they kindled a fire in the big fireplace and sat before it with jest and laughter. They left the doors open, and Banjo and Good Luck came and went at pleasure. Sometimes they sat gravely on the bearskin rug between Barney and Valancy; sometimes they slunk off into the mystery of the chill night outside. The stars smouldered in the horizon mists through the old oriel. The haunting, persistent croon of the pine-trees filled the air. The little waves began to make soft, sobbing splashes on the rocks below them in the rising winds. They needed no light but the firelight that sometimes leaped up and revealed them—sometimes shrouded them in shadow. When the night wind rose higher Barney would shut the door and light a lamp and read to her—poetry and essays and gorgeous, dim chronicles of ancient wars. Barney never would read novels: he vowed they bored him. But sometimes she read them herself, curled up on the wolf skins, laughing aloud in peace. For Barney was not one of those aggravating people who can never hear you smiling audibly over something you've read without inquiring placidly, "What is the joke?"

October—with a gorgeous pageant of colour around Mistawis, into which Valancy plunged her soul. Never had she imagined anything so splendid. A great, tinted peace. Blue, wind-winnowed skies. Sunlight sleeping in the glades of that fairyland. Long dreamy purple days paddling idly in their canoe along shores and up the rivers of crimson and gold. A sleepy, red hunter's moon. Enchanted tempests that stripped the leaves from the trees and heaped them along the shores. Flying shadows of clouds. What had all the smug, opulent lands out front to

169

compare with this?

November—with uncanny witchery in its changed trees. With murky red sunsets flaming in smoky crimson behind the westering hills. With dear days when the austere woods were beautiful and gracious in a dignified serenity of folded hands and closed eyes—days full of a fine, pale sunshine that sifted through the late, leafless gold of the juniper-trees and glimmered among the grey beeches, lighting up evergreen banks of moss and washing the colonnades of the pines. Days with a high-sprung sky of flawless turquoise. Days when an exquisite melancholy seemed to hang over the landscape and dream about the lake. But days, too, of the wild blackness of great autumn storms, followed by dank, wet, streaming nights when there was witch-laughter in the pines and fitful moans among the mainland trees. What cared they? Old Tom had built his roof well, and his chimney drew.

"Warm fire—books—comfort—safety from storm—our cats on the rug. Moonlight," said Barney, "would you be any happier now if you had a million dollars?"

"No—nor half so happy. I'd be bored by conventions and obligations then."

December. Early snows and Orion. The pale fires of the Milky Way. It was really winter now—wonderful, cold, starry winter. How Valancy had always hated winter! Dull, brief, uneventful days. Long, cold, companionless nights. Cousin Stickles with her back that had to be rubbed continually. Cousin Stickles making weird noises gargling her throat in the mornings. Cousin Stickles whining over the price of coal. Her mother, probing, questioning, ignoring. Endless colds and bronchitis—or the dread of it. Redfern's Liniment and Purple Pills.

But now she loved winter. Winter was beautiful "up back"— almost intolerably beautiful. Days of clear brilliance. Evenings that were like cups of glamour—the purest vintage of winter's wine. Nights with their fire of stars. Cold, exquisite winter sunrises. Lovely ferns of ice all over the windows of the Blue

Castle. Moonlight on birches in a silver thaw. Ragged shadows on windy evenings—torn, twisted, fantastic shadows. Great silences, austere and searching. Jewelled, barbaric hills. The sun suddenly breaking through grey clouds over long, white Mistawis. Icy-grey twilights, broken by snow-squalls, when their cosy living-room, with its goblins of firelight and inscrutable cats seemed cosier than ever. Every hour brought a new revelation and wonder.

Barney ran Lady Jane into Roaring Abel's barn and taught Valancy how to snowshoe—Valancy, who ought to be laid up with bronchitis. But Valancy had not even a cold. Later on in the winter Barney had a terrible one and Valancy nursed him through it with a dread of pneumonia in her heart. But Valancy's colds seemed to have gone where old moons go. Which was luck—for she hadn't even Redfern's Liniment. She had thoughtfully bought a bottle at the Port and Barney had hurled it into frozen Mistawis with a scowl.

"Bring no more of that devilish stuff here," he had ordered briefly. It was the first and last time he had spoken harshly to her.

They went for long tramps through the exquisite reticence of winter woods and the silver jungles of frosted trees, and found loveliness everywhere.

At times they seemed to be walking through a spellbound world of crystal and pearl, so white and radiant were clearings and lakes and sky. The air was so crisp and clear that it was half intoxicating.

Once they stood in a hesitation of ecstasy at the entrance of a narrow path between ranks of birches. Every twig and spray was outlined in snow. The undergrowth along its sides was a little fairy forest cut out of marble. The shadows cast by the pale sunshine were fine and spiritual.

"Come away," said Barney, turning. "We must not commit the desecration of tramping through there."

One evening they came upon a snowdrift far back in an old clearing which was in the exact likeness of a beautiful woman's profile. Seen too close by, the resemblance was lost, as in the fairy-tale of the Castle of St. John. Seen from behind, it was a shapeless oddity. But at just the right distance and angle the outline was so perfect that when they came suddenly upon it, gleaming out against the dark background of spruce in the glow of winter sunset they both exclaimed in amazement. There was a low, noble brow, a straight, classic nose, lips and chin and cheek-curve modelled as if some goddess of old time had sat to the sculptor, and a breast of such cold, swelling purity as the very spirit of the winter woods might display.

"'All the beauty that old Greece and Rome, sung, painted, taught'," quoted Barney.

"And to think no human eyes save ours have seen or will see it," breathed Valancy, who felt at times as if she were living in a book by John Foster. As she looked around her she recalled some passages she had marked in the new Foster book Barney had brought her from the Port—with an adjuration not to expect *him* to read or listen to it.

"'All the tintings of winter woods are extremely delicate and elusive'," recalled Valancy. "'When the brief afternoon wanes and the sun just touches the tops of the hills, there seems to be all over the woods an abundance, not of colour, but of the spirit of colour. There is really nothing but pure white after all, but one has the impression of fairy-like blendings of rose and violet, opal and heliotrope on the slopes—in the dingles and along the curves of the forest-land. You feel sure the tint is there, but when you look at it directly it is gone. From the corner of your eye you are aware that it is lurking over yonder in a spot where there was nothing but pale purity a moment ago. Only just when the sun is setting is there a fleeting moment of real colour. Then the redness streams out over the snow and incarnadines the hills and rivers and smites the crest of the pines with flame. Just a few minutes of transfiguration and revelation—and it is gone.'

"I wonder if John Foster ever spent a winter in Mistawis," said Valancy.

"Not likely," scoffed Barney. "People who write tosh like that generally write it in a warm house on some smug city street."

"You are too hard on John Foster," said Valancy severely. "No one could have written that little paragraph I read you last night without having seen it first—you know he couldn't."

"I didn't listen to it," said Barney morosely. "You know I told you I wouldn't."

"Then you've got to listen to it now," persisted Valancy. She made him stand still on his snowshoes while she repeated it.

"'She is a rare artist, this old Mother Nature, who works "for the joy of working" and not in any spirit of vain show. Today the fir woods are a symphony of greens and greys, so subtle that you cannot tell where one shade begins to be the other. Grey trunk, green bough, grey-green moss above the white, grey-shadowed floor. Yet the old gypsy doesn't like unrelieved monotones. She must have a dash of colour. See it. A broken dead fir bough, of a beautiful red-brown, swinging among the beards of moss'."

"Good Lord, do you learn all that fellow's books by heart?" was Barney's disgusted reaction as he strode off.

"John Foster's books were all that saved my soul alive the past five years," averred Valancy. "Oh, Barney, look at that exquisite filigree of snow in the furrows of that old elm-tree trunk."

When they came out to the lake they changed from snowshoes to skates and skated home. For a wonder Valancy had learned, when she was a little schoolgirl, to skate on the pond behind the Deerwood school. She never had any skates of her own, but some of the other girls had lent her theirs and she seemed to have a natural knack of it. Uncle Benjamin had once promised her a pair of skates for Christmas, but when Christmas came he had given her rubbers instead. She had never skated since she grew up, but the old trick came back quickly, and glorious were the hours she and Barney spent skimming over the white lakes and past the dark islands where the summer cottages were closed and silent. Tonight they flew down Mistawis before the wind, in an exhilaration that crimsoned Valancy's cheeks under her white tam. And at the end was her dear little house, on the island of pines, with a coating of snow on its roof, sparkling in the moonlight. Its windows glinted impishly at her in the stray gleams.

"Looks exactly like a picture-book, doesn't it?" said Barney.

They had a lovely Christmas. No rush. No scramble. No niggling attempts to make ends meet. No wild effort to remember whether she hadn't given the same kind of present to the same person two Christmases before—no mob of last-minute shoppers—no dreary family "reunions" where she sat mute and unimportant—no attacks of "nerves." They decorated the Blue Castle with pine boughs, and Valancy made delightful little tinsel stars and hung them up amid the greenery. She cooked a dinner to which Barney did full justice, while Good Luck and Banjo picked the bones.

"A land that can produce a goose like that is an admirable land," vowed Barney. "Canada forever!" And they drank to the Union Jack a bottle of dandelion wine that Cousin Georgiana had given Valancy along with the bedspread.

"One never knows," Cousin Georgiana had said solemnly, "when one may need a little stimulant."

Barney had asked Valancy what she wanted for a Christmas present.

"Something frivolous and unnecessary," said Valancy, who had got a pair of goloshes last Christmas and two long-sleeved, woolen undervests the year before. And so on back.

To her delight, Barney gave her a necklace of pearl beads. Valancy had wanted a string of milky pearl beads—like congealed moonshine—all her life. And these were so pretty. All that worried her was that they were really too good. They must have cost a great deal—fifteen dollars, at least. Could Barney afford that? She didn't know a thing about his finances. She had refused to let him buy any of her clothes—she had enough for that, she told him, as long as she would need clothes. In a round, black jar on the chimney-piece Barney put money for their household expenses—always enough. The jar was never empty, though Valancy never caught him replenishing it. He couldn't have much, of course, and that necklace—but Valancy tossed care aside. She would wear it and enjoy it. It was the first pretty thing she had ever had.

CHAPTER XXXII

New year. The old, shabby, inglorious outlived calendar came down. The new one went up. January was a month of storms. It snowed for three weeks on end. The thermometer went miles below zero and stayed there. But, as Barney and Valancy pointed out to each other, there were no mosquitoes. And the roar and crackle of their big fire drowned the howls of the north wind. Good Luck and Banjo waxed fat and developed resplendent coats of thick, silky fur. Nip and Tuck had gone.

"But they'll come back in spring," promised Barney.

There was no monotony. Sometimes they had dramatic little private spats that never even thought of becoming quarrels. Sometimes Roaring Abel dropped in—for an evening or a whole day—with his old tartan cap and his long red beard coated with snow. He generally brought his fiddle and played for them, to the delight of all except Banjo, who would go temporarily insane and retreat under Valancy's bed. Sometimes Abel and Barney talked while Valancy made candy for them; sometimes they sat and smoked in silence *à la* Tennyson and Carlyle, until the Blue Castle reeked and Valancy fled to the open. Sometimes they played checkers fiercely and silently the whole night through. Sometimes they all ate the russet apples Abel had brought, while the jolly old clock ticked the delightful minutes away.

"A plate of apples, an open fire, and 'a jolly goode booke' are a fair substitute for heaven," vowed Barney. "Any one can have the streets of gold. Let's have another whack at Carman."

It was easier now for the Stirlings to believe Valancy of the dead. Not even dim rumours of her having been over at the Port came to trouble them, though she and Barney used to skate there occasionally to see a movie and eat hot dogs shamelessly at the corner stand afterwards. Presumably none of the Stirlings ever thought about her—except Cousin Georgiana, who used to lie awake worrying about poor Doss. Did she have enough to eat? Was that dreadful creature good to her? Was she warm enough at nights?

Valancy was quite warm at nights. She used to wake up and revel silently in the cosiness of those winter nights on that little island in the frozen lake. The nights of other winters had been so cold and long. Valancy hated to wake up in them and think about the bleakness and emptiness of the day that had passed and the bleakness and emptiness of the day that would come. Now she almost counted that night lost on which she didn't wake up and lie awake for half an hour just being happy, while Barney's regular breathing went on beside her, and through the open door the smouldering brands in the fireplace winked at her in the gloom. It was very nice to feel a little Lucky cat jump up on your bed in the darkness and snuggle down at your feet, purring; but Banjo would be sitting dourly by himself out in front of the fire like a brooding demon. At such moments Banjo was anything but canny, but Valancy loved his uncanniness.

The side of the bed had to be right against the window. There was no other place for it in the tiny room. Valancy, lying there, could look out of the window, through the big pine boughs that actually touched it, away up Mistawis, white and lustrous as a pavement of pearl, or dark and terrible in the storm. Sometimes the pine boughs tapped against the panes with friendly signals. Sometimes she heard the little hissing whisper of snow against them right at her side. Some nights the whole outer world seemed given over to the empery of silence; then came nights when there would be a majestic sweep of wind in the pines; nights of dear starlight when it whistled freakishly and joyously around the Blue Castle; brooding nights before storm when it crept along the floor of the lake with a low, wailing cry of brooding and mystery. Valancy wasted many perfectly good sleeping hours in these delightful communings. But she could sleep as long in the morning as she wanted to. Nobody cared. Barney cooked his own breakfast of bacon and eggs and then shut himself up in Bluebeard's Chamber till supper time. Then they had an evening of reading and talk. They talked about everything in this world and a good many things in other worlds. They laughed over their own jokes until the Blue Castle re-echoed.

"You *do* laugh beautifully," Barney told her once. "It makes me want to laugh just to hear you laugh. There's a trick about your laugh—as if there were so much more fun back of it that you wouldn't let out. Did you laugh like that before you came to Mistawis, Moonlight?"

"I never laughed at all—really. I used to giggle foolishly when I felt I was expected to. But now—the laugh just comes."

It struck Valancy more than once that Barney himself laughed a great deal oftener than he used to and that his laugh had changed. It had become wholesome. She rarely heard the little cynical note in it now. Could a man laugh like that who had crimes on his conscience? Yet Barney *must* have done something. Valancy had indifferently made up her mind as to what he had done. She concluded he was a defaulting bank cashier. She had found in one of Barney's books an old clipping cut from a Montreal paper in which a vanished, defaulting cashier was described. The description applied to Barney—as well as to half a dozen other men Valancy knew—and from some casual remarks he had dropped from time to time she concluded he knew Montreal rather well. Valancy had it all figured out in the back of her mind. Barney had been in a bank. He was tempted to take some money to speculate—meaning, of course, to put it back. He had got in deeper and deeper, until he found there was nothing for it but flight. It had happened so to scores of men. He had, Valancy was absolutely certain, never meant to do wrong. Of course, the name of the man in the clipping was Bernard Craig. But Valancy had always thought Snaith was an alias. Not that it mattered.

Valancy had only one unhappy night that winter. It came in late March when most of the snow had gone and Nip and Tuck had returned. Barney had gone off in the afternoon for a long, woodland tramp, saying he would be back by dark if all went well. Soon after he had gone it had begun to snow. The wind rose and presently Mistawis was in the grip of one of the worst storms of the winter. It tore up the lake and struck at the little house. The dark angry woods on the mainland scowled at Valancy, menace in the toss of their boughs, threats in their windy gloom, terror in the roar of their hearts. The trees on the island crouched in fear. Valancy spent the night huddled on the rug before the fire, her face buried in her hands, when she was not vainly peering from the oriel in a futile effort to see through the furious smoke of wind and snow that had once been blue-dimpled Mistawis. Where was Barney? Lost on the merciless lakes? Sinking exhausted in the drifts of the pathless woods? Valancy died a hundred deaths that night and paid in full for all the happiness of her Blue Castle. When morning came the storm broke and cleared; the sun shone gloriously over Mistawis; and at noon Barney came home. Valancy saw him from the oriel as he came around a wooded point, slender and black against the glistening white world. She did not run to meet him. Something happened to her knees and she dropped down on Banjo's chair. Luckily Banjo got out from under in time, his whiskers bristling with indignation. Barney found her there, her head buried in her hands.

"Barney, I thought you were dead," she whispered.

Barney hooted.

"After two years of the Klondike did you think a baby storm like this could get me? I spent the night in that old lumber shanty over by Muskoka. At bit cold but snug enough. Little goose! Your eyes look like burnt holes in a blanket. Did you sit up here all night worrying over an old woodsman like me?"

"Yes," said Valancy. "I—couldn't help it. The storm seemed so wild. Anybody might have been lost in it. When—I saw you—come round the point—there—something happened to me. I don't know what. It was as if I had died and come back to life. I can't describe it any other way."

CHAPTER XXXIII

Spring. Mistawis black and sullen for a week or two, then flaming in sapphire and turquoise, lilac and rose again, laughing through the oriel, caressing its amethyst islands, rippling under winds soft as silk. Frogs, little green wizards of swamp and pool, singing everywhere in the long twilights and long into the nights; islands fairy-like in a green haze; the evanescent beauty of wild young trees in early leaf; frost-like loveliness of the new foliage of juniper-trees; the woods putting on a fashion of spring flowers, dainty, spiritual things akin to the soul of the wilderness; red mist on the maples; willows decked out with glossy silver pussies; all the forgotten violets of Mistawis blooming again; lure of April moons.

"Think how many thousands of springs have been here on Mistawis—and all of them beautiful," said Valancy. "Oh, Barney, look at that wild plum! I will—I must quote from John Foster. There's a passage in one of his books—I've re-read it a hundred times. He must have written it before a tree just like that:

"'Behold the young wild plum-tree which has adorned herself after immemorial fashion in a wedding-veil of fine lace. The fingers of wood pixies must have woven it, for nothing like it ever came from an earthly loom. I vow the tree is conscious of its loveliness. It is bridling before our very eyes—as if its beauty were not the most ephemeral thing in the woods, as it is the rarest and most exceeding, for today it is and tomorrow it is not. Every south wind purring through the boughs will winnow away a shower of slender petals. But what matter? Today it is queen of the wild places and it is always today in the woods.'"

"I'm sure you feel much better since you've got that out of your system," said Barney heartlessly.

"Here's a patch of dandelions," said Valancy, unsubdued. "Dandelions shouldn't grow in the woods, though. They haven't any sense of the fitness of things at all. They are too cheerful and self-satisfied. They haven't any of the mystery and reserve of the real wood-flowers."

"In short, they've no secrets," said Barney. "But wait a bit. The woods will have their own way even with those obvious dandelions. In a little while all that obtrusive yellowness and complacency will be gone and we'll find here misty, phantom-like globes hovering over those long grasses in full harmony with the traditions of the forest."

"That sounds John Fosterish," teased Valancy.

"What have I done that deserved a slam like that?" complained Barney.

One of the earliest signs of spring was the renaissance of Lady Jane. Barney put her on roads that no other car would look at, and they went through Deerwood in mud to the axles. They passed several Stirlings, who groaned and reflected that now spring was come they would encounter that shameless pair everywhere. Valancy, prowling about Deerwood shops, met Uncle Benjamin on the street; but he did not realise until he had gone two blocks further on that the girl in the scarlet-collared blanket coat, with cheeks reddened in the sharp April air and the fringe of black hair over laughing, slanted eyes, was Valancy. When he did realise it, Uncle Benjamin was indignant. What business had Valancy to look like—like—like a young girl? The way of the transgressor was hard. Had to be. Scriptural and proper. Yet Valancy's path couldn't be hard. She wouldn't look like that if it were. There was something wrong. It was almost enough to make a man turn modernist.

Barney and Valancy clanged on to the Port, so that it was dark when they went through Deerwood again. At her old home Valancy, seized with a sudden impulse, got out, opened the little gate and tiptoed around to the sitting-room window. There sat her mother and Cousin Stickles drearily, grimly knitting.

181

Baffling and inhuman as ever. If they had looked the least bit lonesome Valancy would have gone in. But they did not. Valancy would not disturb them for worlds.

CHAPTER XXXIV

Valancy had two wonderful moments that spring.

One day, coming home through the woods, with her arms full of trailing arbutus and creeping spruce, she met a man who she knew must be Allan Tierney. Allan Tierney, the celebrated painter of beautiful women. He lived in New York in winter, but he owned an island cottage at the northern end of Mistawis to which he always came the minute the ice was out of the lake. He was reputed to be a lonely, eccentric man. He never flattered his sitters. There was no need to, for he would not paint any one who required flattery. To be painted by Allan Tierney was all the *cachet* of beauty a woman could desire. Valancy had heard so much about him that she couldn't help turning her head back over her shoulder for another shy, curious look at him. A shaft of pale spring sunlight fell through a great pine athwart her bare black head and her slanted eyes. She wore a pale green sweater and had bound a fillet of linnaea vine about her hair. The feathery fountain of trailing spruce overflower her arms and fell around her. Allan Tierney's eyes lighted up.

"I've had a caller," said Barney the next afternoon, when Valancy had returned from another flower quest.

"Who?" Valancy was surprised but indifferent. She began filling a basket with arbutus.

"Allan Tierney. He wants to paint you, Moonlight."

"Me!" Valancy dropped her basket and her arbutus. "You're laughing at me, Barney."

"I'm not. That's what Tierney came for. To ask my permission to paint my wife—as the Spirit of Muskoka, or something like that."

"But—but—" stammered Valancy, "Allan Tierney never paints

183

any but—any but—"

"Beautiful women," finished Barney. "Conceded. Q. E. D., Mistress Barney Snaith is a beautiful woman."

"Nonsense," said Valancy, stooping to retrieve her arbutus. "You *know* that's nonsense, Barney. I know I'm a heap better-looking than I was a year ago, but I'm not beautiful."

"Allan Tierney never makes a mistake," said Barney. "You forget, Moonlight, that there are different kinds of beauty. Your imagination is obsessed by the very obvious type of your cousin Olive. Oh, I've seen her—she's a stunner—but you'd never catch Allan Tierney wanting to paint her. In the horrible but expressive slang phrase, she keeps all her goods in the shop-window. But in your subconscious mind you have a conviction that nobody can be beautiful who doesn't look like Olive. Also, you remember your face as it was in the days when your soul was not allowed to shine through it. Tierney said something about the curve of your cheek as you looked back over your shoulder. You know I've often told you it was distracting. And he's quite batty about your eyes. If I wasn't absolutely sure it was solely professional—he's really a crabbed old bachelor, you know—I'd be jealous."

"Well, I don't want to be painted," said Valancy. "I hope you told him that."

"I couldn't tell him that. I didn't know what *you* wanted. But I told him *I* didn't want my wife painted—hung up in a salon for the mob to stare at. Belonging to another man. For of course I couldn't buy the picture. So even if you had wanted to be painted, Moonlight, your tyrannous husband would not have permitted it. Tierney was a bit squiffy. He isn't used to being turned down like that. His requests are almost like royalty's."

"But we are outlaws," laughed Valancy. "We bow to no decrees—we acknowledge no sovereignty."

In her heart she thought unashamedly:

"I wish Olive could know that Allan Tierney wanted to paint me. *Me!* Little-old-maid-Valancy-Stirling-that-was."

Her second wonder-moment came one evening in May. She

realised that Barney actually liked her. She had always hoped he did, but sometimes she had a little, disagreeable, haunting dread that he was just kind and nice and chummy out of pity; knowing that she hadn't long to live and determined she should have a good time as long as she did live; but away back in his mind rather looking forward to freedom again, with no intrusive woman creature in his island fastness and no chattering thing beside him in his woodland prowls. She knew he could never love her. She did not even want him to. If he loved her he would be unhappy when she died—Valancy never flinched from the plain word. No "passing away" for her. And she did not want him to be the least unhappy. But neither did she want him to be glad—or relieved. She wanted him to like her and miss her as a good chum. But she had never been sure until this night that he did.

They had walked over the hills in the sunset. They had the delight of discovering a virgin spring in a ferny hollow and had drunk together from it out of a birch-bark cup; they had come to an old tumble-down rail fence and sat on it for a long time. They didn't talk much, but Valancy had a curious sense of *oneness*. She knew that she couldn't have felt that if he hadn't liked her.

"You nice little thing," said Barney suddenly. "Oh, you nice little thing! Sometimes I feel you're too nice to be real—that I'm just dreaming you."

"Why can't I die now—this very minute—when I am so happy!" thought Valancy.

Well, it couldn't be so very long now. Somehow, Valancy had always felt she would live out the year Dr. Trent had allotted. She had not been careful—she had never tried to be. But, somehow, she had always counted on living out her year. She had not let herself think about it at all. But now, sitting here beside Barney, with her hand in his, a sudden realisation came to her. She had not had a heart attack for a long while—two months at least. The last one she had had was two or three nights before Barney was out in the storm. Since then she had not remembered she had a heart. Well, no doubt, it betokened the nearness of the end. Nature had given up the struggle. There would be no more pain.

"I'm afraid heaven will be very dull after this past year," thought Valancy. "But perhaps one will not remember. Would that be—nice? No, no. I don't want to forget Barney. I'd rather be miserable in heaven remembering him than happy forgetting him. And I'll always remember through all eternity—that he really, *really* liked me."

CHAPTER XXXV

Thirty seconds can be very long sometimes. Long enough to work a miracle or a revolution. In thirty seconds life changed wholly for Barney and Valancy Snaith.

They had gone around the lake one June evening in their disappearing propeller, fished for an hour in a little creek, left their boat there, and walked up through the woods to Port Lawrence two miles away. Valancy prowled a bit in the shops and got herself a new pair of sensible shoes. Her old pair had suddenly and completely given out, and this evening she had been compelled to put on the little fancy pair of patent-leather with rather high, slender heels, which she had bought in a fit of folly one day in the winter because of their beauty and because she wanted to make one foolish, extravagant purchase in her life. She sometimes put them on of an evening in the Blue Castle, but this was the first time she had worn them outside. She had not found it any too easy walking up through the woods in them, and Barney guyed her unmercifully about them. But in spite of the inconvenience, Valancy secretly rather liked the look of her trim ankles and high instep above those pretty, foolish shoes and did not change them in the shop as she might have done.

The sun was hanging low above the pines when they left Port Lawrence. To the north of it the woods closed around the town quite suddenly. Valancy always had a sense of stepping from one world to another—from reality to fairyland—when she went out of Port Lawrence and in a twinkling found it shut off behind her by the armies of the pines.

A mile and a half from Port Lawrence there was a small railroad station with a little station-house which at this hour of the day was deserted, since no local train was due. Not a soul was in sight when Barney and Valancy emerged from the woods. Off to the left a sudden curve in the track hid it from view, but over the tree-tops beyond, the long plume of smoke betokened the approach of a through train. The rails were vibrating to its thunder as Barney stepped across the switch. Valancy was a few steps behind him, loitering to gather June-bells along the little, winding path. But there was plenty of time to get across before the train came. She stepped unconcernedly over the first rail.

She could never tell how it happened. The ensuing thirty seconds always seemed in her recollection like a chaotic nightmare in which she endured the agony of a thousand lifetimes.

The heel of her pretty, foolish shoe caught in a crevice of the switch. She could not pull it loose. "Barney—Barney!" she called in alarm. Barney turned—saw her predicament—saw her ashen face—dashed back. He tried to pull her clear—he tried to wrench her foot from the prisoning hold. In vain. In a moment the train would sweep around the curve—would be on them.

"Go—go—quick—you'll be killed, Barney!" shrieked Valancy, trying to push him away.

Barney dropped on his knees, ghost-white, frantically tearing at her shoe-lace. The knot defied his trembling fingers. He snatched a knife from his pocket and slashed at it. Valancy still strove blindly to push him away. Her mind was full of the hideous thought that Barney was going to be killed. She had no thought for her own danger.

"Barney—go—go—for God's sake—go!"

"Never!" muttered Barney between his set teeth. He gave one mad wrench at the lace. As the train thundered around the curve he sprang up and caught Valancy—dragging her clear, leaving the shoe behind her. The wind from the train as it swept by turned to icy cold the streaming perspiration on his face.

"Thank God!" he breathed.

For a moment they stood stupidly staring at each other, two white, shaken, wild-eyed creatures. Then they stumbled over to the little seat at the end of the station-house and dropped on it.

Barney buried his face in his hands and said not a word. Valancy sat, staring straight ahead of her with unseeing eyes at the great pine woods, the stumps of the clearing, the long, gleaming rails. There was only one thought in her dazed mind—a thought that seemed to burn it as a shaving of fire might burn her body.

Dr. Trent had told her over a year ago that she had a serious form of heart-disease—that any excitement might to fatal.

If that were so, why was she not dead now? This very minute? She had just experienced as much and as terrible excitement as most people experience in a lifetime, crowded into that endless thirty seconds. Yet she had not died of it. She was not an iota the worse for it. A little wobbly at the knees, as any one would have been; a quicker heart-beat, as any one would have; nothing more.

Why!

Was it possible Dr. Trent had made a mistake?

Valancy shivered as if a cold wind had suddenly chilled her to the soul. She looked at Barney, hunched up beside her. His silence was very eloquent: Had the same thought occurred to him? Did he suddenly find himself confronted by the appalling suspicion that he was married, not for a few months or a year, but for good and all to a woman he did not love and who had foisted herself upon him by some trick or lie? Valancy turned sick before the horror of it. It could not be. It would be too cruel—too devilish. Dr. Trent *couldn't* have made a mistake. Impossible. He was one of the best heart specialists in Ontario. She was foolish—unnerved by the recent horror. She remembered some of the hideous spasms of pain she had had. There must be something serious the matter with her heart to account for them.

But she had not had any for nearly three months.

Why!

Presently Barney bestirred himself. He stood up, without looking at Valancy, and said casually:

"I suppose we'd better be hiking back. Sun's getting low. Are your good for the rest of the road?"

"I think so," said Valancy miserably.

Barney went across the clearing and picked up the parcel he had dropped—the parcel containing her new shoes. He brought it to her and let her take out the shoes and put them on without any assistance, while he stood with his back to her and looked out over the pines.

They walked in silence down the shadowy trail to the lake. In silence Barney steered his boat into the sunset miracle that was Mistawis. In silence they went around feathery headlands and across coral bays and silver rivers where canoes were slipping up and down in the afterglow. In silence they went past cottages echoing with music and laughter. In silence drew up at the landing-place below the Blue Castle.

Valancy went up the rock steps and into the house. She dropped miserably on the first chair she came to and sat there staring through the oriel, oblivious of Good Luck's frantic purrs of joy and Banjo's savage glares of protest at her occupancy of his chair.

Barney came in a few minutes later. He did not come near her, but he stood behind her and asked gently if she felt any the worse for her experience. Valancy would have given her year of happiness to have been able honesty to answer "Yes."

"No," she said flatly.

Barney went into Bluebeard's Chamber and shut the door. She heard him pacing up and down—up and down. He had never paced like that before.

And an hour ago—only an hour ago—she had been so happy!

CHAPTER XXXVI

Finally Valancy went to bed. Before she went she re-read Dr. Trent's letter. It comforted her a little. So positive. So assured. The writing so black and steady. Not the writing of a man who didn't know what he was writing about. But she could not sleep. She pretended to be asleep when Barney came in. Barney pretended to go to sleep. But Valancy knew perfectly well he wasn't sleeping any more than she was. She knew he was lying there, staring through the darkness. Thinking of what? Trying to face—what?

Valancy, who had spent so many happy wakeful hours of night lying by that window, now paid the price of them all in this one night of misery. A horrible, portentous fact was slowly looming out before her from the nebula of surmise and fear. She could not shut her eyes to it—push it away—ignore it.

There could be nothing seriously wrong with her heart, no matter what Dr. Trent had said. If there had been, those thirty seconds would have killed her. It was no use to recall Dr. Trent's letter and reputation. The greatest specialists made mistakes sometimes. Dr. Trent had made one.

Towards morning Valancy fell into a fitful dose with ridiculous dreams. One of them was of Barney taunting her with having tricked him. In her dream she lost her temper and struck him violently on the head with her rolling-pin. He proved to be made of glass and shivered into splinters all over the floor. She woke with a cry of horror—a gasp of relief—a short laugh over the absurdity of her dream—a miserable sickening recollection of what had happened.

Barney was gone. Valancy knew, as people sometimes know things—inescapably, without being told—that he was not in the house or in Bluebeard's Chamber either. There was a curious

191

silence in the living-room. A silence with something uncanny about it. The old clock had stopped. Barney must have forgotten to wind it up, something he had never done before. The room without it was dead, though the sunshine streamed in through the oriel and dimples of light from the dancing waves beyond quivered over the walls.

The canoe was gone but Lady Jane was under the mainland trees. So Barney had betaken himself to the wilds. He would not return till night—perhaps not even then. He must be angry with her. That furious silence of his must mean anger—cold, deep, justifiable resentment. Well, Valancy knew what she must do first. She was not suffering very keenly now. Yet the curious numbness that pervaded her being was in a way worse than pain. It was as if something in her had died. She forced herself to cook and eat a little breakfast. Mechanically she put the Blue Castle in perfect order. Then she put on her hat and coat, locked the door and hid the key in the hollow of the old pine and crossed to the mainland in the motor boat. She was going into Deerwood to see Dr. Trent. She must *know*.

CHAPTER XXXVII

Dr. Trent looked at her blankly and fumbled among his recollections.

"Er—Miss—Miss—"

"Mrs. Snaith," said Valancy quietly. "I was Miss Valancy Stirling when I came to you last May—over a year ago. I wanted to consult you about my heart."

Dr. Trent's face cleared.

"Oh, of course. I remember now. I'm really not to blame for not knowing you. You've changed—splendidly. And married. Well, well, it has agreed with you. You don't look much like an invalid now, hey? I remember that day. I was badly upset. Hearing about poor Ned bowled me over. But Ned's as good as new and you, too, evidently. I told you so, you know—told you there was nothing to worry over."

Valancy looked at him.

"You told me, in your letter," she said slowly, with a curious feeling that some one else was talking through her lips, "that I had angina pectoris—in the last stages—complicated with an aneurism. That I might die any minute—that I couldn't live longer than a year."

Dr. Trent stared at her.

"Impossible!" he said blankly. "I couldn't have told you that!"

Valancy took his letter from her bag and handed it to him.

"Miss Valancy Stirling," he read. "Yes—yes. Of course I wrote you—on the train—that night. But I *told* you there was nothing serious—"

"Read your letter," insisted Valancy.

Dr. Trent took it out—unfolded it—glanced over it. A dismayed look came into his face. He jumped to his feet and strode agitatedly about the room.

"Good heavens! This is the letter I meant for old Miss Jane Sterling. From Port Lawrence. She was here that day, too. I sent you the wrong letter. What unpardonable carelessness! But I was beside myself that night. My God, and you believed that—you believed—but you didn't—you went to another doctor—"

Valancy stood up, turned round, looked foolishly about her and sat down again.

"I believed it," she said faintly. "I didn't go to any other doctor. I—I—it would take too long to explain. But I believed I was going to die soon."

Dr. Trent halted before her.

"I can never forgive myself. What a year you must have had! But you don't look—I can't understand!"

"Never mind," said Valancy dully. "And so there's nothing the matter with my heart?"

"Well, nothing serious. You had what is called pseudo-angina. It's never fatal—passes away completely with proper treatment. Or sometimes with a shock of joy. Have you been troubled much with it?"

"Not at all since March," answered Valancy. She remembered the marvellous feeling of re-creation she had had when she saw Barney coming home safe after the storm. Had that "shock of joy" cured her?

"Then likely you're all right. I told you what to do in the letter you should have got. *And* of course I supposed you'd go to another doctor. Child, why didn't you?"

"I didn't want anybody to know."

"Idiot," said Dr. Trent bluntly. "I can't understand such folly. And poor old Miss Sterling. She must have got your letter—telling her there was nothing serious the matter. Well, well, it couldn't have made any difference. Her case was hopeless. Nothing that she could have done or left undone could have made any difference. I was surprised she lived as long as she did—two months. She was here that day—not long before you. I hated to tell her the truth.

You think I'm a blunt old curmudgeon—and my letters *are* blunt enough. I can't soften things. But I'm a snivelling coward when it comes to telling a woman face to face that she's got to die soon. I told her I'd look up some features of the case I wasn't quite sure of and let her know next day. But you got her letter—look here, "Dear Miss S-t-*e*-r-l-i-n-g."'

"Yes. I noticed that. But I thought it a mistake. I didn't know there were any Sterlings in Port Lawrence."

"She was the only one. A lonely old soul. Lived by herself with only a little home girl. She died two months after she was here—died in her sleep. My mistake couldn't have made any difference to her. But you! I can't forgive myself for inflicting a year's misery on you. It's time I retired, all right, when I do things like that—even if my son was supposed to be fatally injured. Can you ever forgive me?"

A year of misery! Valancy smiled a tortured smile as she thought of all the happiness Dr. Trent's mistake had bought her. But she was paying for it now—oh, she was paying. If to feel was to live she was living with a vengeance.

She let Dr. Trent examine her and answered all his questions. When he told her she was fit as a fiddle and would probably live to be a hundred, she got up and went away silently. She knew that there were a great many horrible things outside waiting to be thought over. Dr. Trent thought she was odd. Anybody would have thought, from her hopeless eyes and woebegone face, that he had given her a sentence of death instead of life. Snaith? Snaith? Who the devil had she married? He had never heard of Snaiths in Deerwood. And she had been such a sallow, faded, little old maid. Gad, but marriage *had* made a difference in her, anyhow, whoever Snaith was. Snaith? Dr. Trent remembered. That rapscallion "up back!" Had Valancy Stirling married *him?* And her clan had let her! Well, probably that solved the mystery. She had married in haste and repented at leisure, and that was why she wasn't overjoyed at learning she was a good insurance prospect, after all. Married! To God knew whom! Or what!

Jailbird? Defaulter? Fugitive from justice? It must be pretty bad if she had looked to death as a release, poor girl. But why were women such fools? Dr. Trent dismissed Valancy from his mind, though to the day of his death he was ashamed of putting those letters into the wrong envelopes.

CHAPTER XXXVIII

Valancy walked quickly through the back streets and through Lover's Lane. She did not want to meet any one she knew. She didn't want to meet even people she didn't know. She hated to be seen. Her mind was so confused, so torn, so messy. She felt that her appearance must be the same. She drew a sobbing breath of relief as she left the village behind and found herself on the "up back" road. There was little fear of meeting any one she knew here. The cars that fled by her with raucous shrieks were filled with strangers. One of them was packed with young people who whirled past her singing uproariously:

"My wife has the fever, O then,
My wife has the fever, O then,
My wife has the fever,
Oh, I hope it won't leave her,
For I want to be single again."

Valancy flinched as if one of them had leaned from the car and cut her across the face with a whip.

She had made a covenant with death and death had cheated her. Now life stood mocking her. She had trapped Barney. Trapped him into marrying her. And divorce was so hard to get in Ontario. So expensive. And Barney was poor.

With life, fear had come back into her heart. Sickening fear. Fear of what Barney would think. Would say. Fear of the future that must be lived without him. Fear of her insulted, repudiated clan.

She had had one draught from a divine cup and now it was dashed from her lips. With no kind, friendly death to rescue her.

She must go on living and longing for it. Everything was spoiled, smirched, defaced. Even that year in the Blue Castle. Even her unashamed love for Barney. It had been beautiful because death waited. Now it was only sordid because death was gone. How could any one bear an unbearable thing?

She must go back and tell him. Make him believe she had not meant to trick him—she *must* make him believe that. She must say good-bye to her Blue Castle and return to the brick house on Elm Street. Back to everything she had thought left behind forever. The old bondage—the old fears. But that did not matter. All that mattered now was that Barney must somehow be made to believe she had not consciously tricked him.

When Valancy reached the pines by the lake she was brought out of her daze of pain by a startling sight. There, parked by the side of old, battered ragged Lady Jane, was another car. A wonderful car. A purple car. Not a dark, royal purple but a blatant, screaming purple. It shone like a mirror and its interior plainly indicated the car caste of Vere de Vere. In the driver's seat sat a haughty chauffeur in livery. And in the tonneau sat a man who opened the door and bounced out nimbly as Valancy came down the path to the landing-place. He stood under the pines waiting for her and Valancy took in every detail of him.

A stout, short, pudgy man, with a broad, rubicund, good-humoured face—a clean-shaven face, though an unparalysed little imp at the back of Valancy's paralysed mind suggested the thought, "Such a face should have a fringe of white whisker around it." Old-fashioned, steel-rimmed spectacles on prominent blue eyes. A pursey mouth; a little round, knobby nose. Where—where—where, groped Valancy, had she seen that face before? It seemed as familiar to her as her own.

The stranger wore a green hat and a light fawn overcoat over a suit of a loud check pattern. His tie was a brilliant green of lighter shade; on the plump hand he outstretched to intercept Valancy an enormous diamond winked at her. But he had a pleasant, fatherly smile, and in his hearty, unmodulated voice was a ring of something that attracted her.

"Can you tell me, Miss, if that house yonder belongs to a Mr. Redfern? And if so, how can I get to it?"

Redfern! A vision of bottles seemed to dance before Valancy's eyes—long bottles of bitters—round bottles of hair tonic—square bottles of liniment—short, corpulent little bottles of purple pills—and all of them bearing that very prosperous, beaming moon-face and steel-rimmed spectacles on the label. Dr. Redfern!

"No," said Valancy faintly. "No—that house belongs to Mr. Snaith."

Dr. Redfern nodded.

"Yes, I understand Bernie's been calling himself Snaith. Well, it's his middle name—was his poor mother's. Bernard Snaith Redfern—that's him. And now, Miss, you can tell me how to get over to that island? Nobody seems to be home there. I've done some waving and yelling. Henry, there, wouldn't yell. He's a one-job man. But old Doc Redfern can yell with the best of them yet, and ain't above doing it. Raised nothing but a couple of crows. Guess Bernie's out for the day."

"He was away when I left this morning," said Valancy. "I suppose he hasn't come home yet."

She spoke flatly and tonelessly. This last shock had temporarily bereft her of whatever little power of reasoning had been left her by Dr. Trent's revelation. In the back of her mind the aforesaid little imp was jeeringly repeating a silly old proverb, "It never rains but it pours." But she was not trying to think. What was the use?

Dr. Redfern was gazing at her in perplexity.

"When you left this morning? Do you live—over there?"

He waved his diamond at the Blue Castle.

"Of course," said Valancy stupidly. "I'm his wife."

Dr. Redfern took out a yellow silk handkerchief, removed his hat and mopped his brow. He was very bald, and Valancy's imp whispered, "Why be bald? Why lose your manly beauty? Try

Redfern's Hair Vigor. It keeps you young."

"Excuse me," said Dr. Redfern. "This is a bit of a shock."

"Shocks seem to be in the air this morning." The imp said this out loud before Valancy could prevent it.

"I didn't know Bernie was—married. I didn't think he *would* have got married without telling his old dad."

Were Dr. Redfern's eyes misty? Amid her own dull ache of misery and fear and dread, Valancy felt a pang of pity for him.

"Don't blame him," she said hurriedly. "It—it wasn't his fault. It—was all my doing."

"You didn't ask him to marry you, I suppose," twinkled Dr. Redfern. "He might have let me know. I'd have got acquainted with my daughter-in-law before this if he had. But I'm glad to meet you now, my dear—very glad. You look like a sensible young woman. I used to sorter fear Barney'd pick out some pretty bit of fluff just because she was good-looking. They were all after him, of course. Wanted his money? Eh? Didn't like the pills and the bitters but liked the dollars. Eh? Wanted to dip their pretty little fingers in old Doc's millions. Eh?"

"Millions!" said Valancy faintly. She wished she could sit down somewhere—she wished she could have a chance to think—she wished she and the Blue Castle could sink to the bottom of Mistawis and vanish from human sight forevermore.

"Millions," said Dr. Redfern complacently. "And Bernie chucks them for—that." Again he shook the diamond contemptuously at the Blue Castle, "Wouldn't you think he'd have more sense? And all on account of a white bit of a girl. He must have got over *that* feeling, anyhow, since he's married. You must persuade him to come back to civilisation. All nonsense wasting his life like this. Ain't you going to take me over to your house, my dear? I suppose you've some way of getting there."

"Of course," said Valancy stupidly. She led the way down to the little cove where the disappearing propeller boat was snuggled.

"Does your—your man want to come, too?"

"Who? Henry. Not he. Look at him sitting there disapproving.

Disapproves of the whole expedition. The trail up from the road nearly gave him a conniption. Well, it *was* a devilish road to put a car on. Whose old bus is that up there?"

"Barney's."

"Good Lord! Does Bernie Redfern ride in a thing like that? It looks like the great-great-grandmother of all the Fords."

"It isn't a Ford. It's a Grey Slosson," said Valancy spiritedly. For some occult reason, Dr. Redfern's good-humoured ridicule of dear old Lady Jane stung her to life. A life that was all pain but still *life*. Better than the horrible half-dead-and-half-aliveness of the past few minutes—or years. She waved Dr. Redfern curtly into the boat and took him over to the Blue Castle. The key was still in the old pine—the house still silent and deserted. Valancy took the doctor through the living-room to the western verandah. She must at least be out where there was air. It was still sunny, but in the southwest a great thundercloud, with white crests and gorges of purple shadow, was slowly rising over Mistawis. The doctor dropped with a gasp on a rustic chair and mopped his brow again.

"Warm, eh? Lord, what a view! Wonder if it would soften Henry if he could see it."

"Have you had dinner?" asked Valancy.

"Yes, my dear—had it before we left Port Lawrence. Didn't know what sort of wild hermit's hollow we were coming to, you see. Hadn't any idea I was going to find a nice little daughter-in-law here all ready to toss me up a meal. Cats, eh? Puss, puss! See that. Cats love me. Bernie was always fond of cats! It's about the only thing he took from me. He's his poor mother's boy."

Valancy had been thinking idly that Barney must resemble his mother. She had remained standing by the steps, but Dr. Redfern waved her to the swing seat.

"Sit down, dear. Never stand when you can sit. I want to get a good look at Barney's wife. Well, well, I like your face. No beauty—you don't mind my saying that—you've sense enough to know it, I reckon. Sit down."

Valancy sat down. To be obliged to sit still when mental agony urges us to stride up and down is the refinement of torture. Every nerve in her being was crying out to be alone—to be hidden. But she had to sit and listen to Dr. Redfern, who didn't mind talking at all.

"When do you think Bernie will be back?"

"I don't know—not before night probably."

"Where did he go?"

"I don't know that either. Likely to the woods—up back."

"So he doesn't tell you his comings and goings, either? Bernie was always a secretive young devil. Never understood him. Just like his poor mother. But I thought a lot of him. It hurts me when he disappeared as he did. Eleven years ago. I haven't seen my boy for eleven years."

"Eleven years." Valancy was surprised. "It's only six since he came here."

"Oh, he was in the Klondike before that—and all over the world. He used to drop me a line now and then—never give any clue to where he was but just a line to say he was all right. I s'pose he's told you all about it."

"No. I know nothing of his past life," said Valancy with sudden eagerness. She wanted to know—she must know now. It hadn't mattered before. Now she must know all. And she could never hear it from Barney. She might never even see him again. If she did, it would not be to talk of his past.

"What happened? Why did he leave his home? Tell me. Tell me."

"Well, it ain't much of a story. Just a young fool gone mad because of a quarrel with his girl. Only Bernie was a stubborn fool. Always stubborn. You never could make that boy do anything he didn't want to do. From the day he was born. Yet he was always a quiet, gentle little chap, too. Good as gold. His poor mother died when he was only two years old. I'd just begun to make money with my Hair Vigor. I'd dreamed the formula for it, you see. Some dream that. The cash rolled in. Bernie had everything he wanted. I sent him to the best schools—private schools. I meant to make a gentleman of him. Never had any chance myself. Meant he should have every chance. He went through McGill. Got honours and all that. I wanted him to go in for law. He hankered after journalism and stuff like that. Wanted me to buy a paper for him—or back him in publishing what he called a 'real, worthwhile, honest-to-goodness Canadian Magazine.' I s'pose I'd have done it—I always did what he wanted me to do. Wasn't he all I had to live for? I wanted him to be happy. And he never was happy. Can you believe it? Not that he said so. But I'd always a feeling that he wasn't happy. Everything he wanted—all the money he could spend—his own bank account—travel—seeing the world—but he wasn't happy. Not till he fell in love with Ethel Traverse. Then he was happy for a little while."

The cloud had reached the sun and a great, chill, purple shadow came swiftly over Mistawis. It touched the Blue Castle—rolled over it. Valancy shivered.

"Yes," she said, with painful eagerness, though every word was cutting her to the heart. "What—was—she—like?"

"Prettiest girl in Montreal," said Dr. Redfern. "Oh, she was a looker, all right. Eh? Gold hair—shiny as silk—great, big, soft, black eyes—skin like milk and roses. Don't wonder Bernie fell for her. And brains as well. *She* wasn't a bit of fluff. B.A. from McGill. A thoroughbred, too. One of the best families. But a bit lean in the purse. Eh! Bernie was mad about her. Happiest young fool you ever saw. Then—the bust-up."

"What happened?" Valancy had taken off her hat and was absently thrusting a pin in and out of it. Good Luck was purring beside her. Banjo was regarding Dr. Redfern with suspicion. Nip and Tuck were lazily cawing in the pines. Mistawis was beckoning. Everything was the same. Nothing was the same. It was a hundred years since yesterday. Yesterday, at this time, she and Barney had been eating a belated dinner here with laughter. Laughter? Valancy felt that she had done with laughter forever. And with tears, for that matter. She had no further use for either of them.

"Blest if I know, my dear. Some fool quarrel, I suppose. Bernie just lit out—disappeared. He wrote me from the Yukon. Said his engagement was broken and he wasn't coming back. And not to try to hunt him up because he was never coming back. I didn't. What was the use? I knew Bernie. I went on piling up money because there wasn't anything else to do. But I was mighty lonely. All I lived for was them little notes now and then from Bernie—Klondike—England—South   Africa—China—everywhere.   I thought maybe he'd come back some day to his lonesome old dad. Then six years ago even the letters stopped. I didn't hear a word of or from him till last Christmas."

"Did he write?"

"No. But he drew a check for fifteen thousand dollars on his bank account. The bank manager is a friend of mine—one of my biggest shareholders. He'd always promised me he'd let me know if Bernie drew any checks. Bernie had fifty thousand there. And he'd never touched a cent of it till last Christmas. The check was made out to Aynsley's, Toronto—"

"Anysley's?" Valancy heard herself saying Aynsley's! She had a box on her dressing-table with the Aynsley trademark.

"Yes. The big jewellery house there. After I'd thought it over a while, I got brisk. I wanted to locate Bernie. Had a special reason for it. It was time he gave up his fool hoboing and come to his senses. Drawing that fifteen told me there was something in the wind. The manager communicated with the Aynsleys—his wife was an Aynsley—and found out that Bernard Redfern had bought a pearl necklace there. His address was given as Box 444, Port Lawrence, Muskoka, Ont. First I thought I'd write. Then I thought I'd wait till the open season for cars and come down myself. Ain't no hand at writing. I've motored from Montreal. Got to Port Lawrence yesterday. Enquired at the post-office. Told me they knew nothing of any Bernard Snaith Redfern, but there was a Barney Snaith had a P. O. box there. Lived on an island out here, they said. So here I am. And where's Barney?"

Valancy was fingering her necklace. She was wearing fifteen thousand dollars around her neck. And she had worried lest Barney had paid fifteen dollars for it and couldn't afford it. Suddenly she laughed in Dr. Redfern's face.

"Excuse me. It's so—amusing," said poor Valancy.

"Isn't it?" said Dr. Redfern, seeing a joke—but not exactly hers. "Now, you seem like a sensible young woman, and I dare say you've lots of influence over Bernie. Can't you get him to come back to civilisation and live like other people? I've a house up there. Big as a castle. Furnished like a palace. I want company in it—Bernie's wife—Bernie's children."

"Did Ethel Traverse ever marry?" queried Valancy irrelevantly.

"Bless you, yes. Two years after Bernie levanted. But she's a widow now. Pretty as ever. To be frank, that was my special reason for wanting to find Bernie. I thought they'd make it up, maybe. But, of course, that's all off now. Doesn't matter. Bernie's choice of a wife is good enough for me. It's my boy I want. Think he'll soon be back?"

"I don't know. But I don't think he'll come before night. Quite late, perhaps. And perhaps not till tomorrow. But I can put you up comfortably. He'll certainly be back tomorrow."

Dr. Redfern shook his head.

"Too damp. I'll take no chances with rheumatism."

"Why suffer that ceaseless anguish? Why not try Redfern's Liniment?" quoted the imp in the back of Valancy's mind.

"I must get back to Port Lawrence before rain starts. Henry goes quite mad when he gets mud on the car. But I'll come back tomorrow. Meanwhile you talk Bernie into reason."

He shook her hand and patted her kindly on the shoulder. He looked as if he would have kissed her, with a little encouragement, but Valancy did not give it. Not that she would have minded. He was rather dreadful and loud—and—and—dreadful. But there was something about him she liked. She thought dully that she might have liked being his daughter-in-law if he had not been a millionaire. A score of times over. And Barney was his son—and heir.

She took him over in the motor boat and watched the lordly purple car roll away through the woods with Henry at the wheel looking things not lawful to be uttered. Then she went back to the Blue Castle. What she had to do must be done quickly. Barney *might* return at any moment. And it was certainly going to rain. She was thankful she no longer felt very bad. When you are bludgeoned on the head repeatedly, you naturally and mercifully become more or less insensible and stupid.

She stood briefly like a faded flower bitten by frost, by the hearth, looking down on the white ashes of the last fire that had blazed in the Blue Castle.

"At any rate," she thought wearily, "Barney isn't poor. He will be able to afford a divorce. Quite nicely."

CHAPTER XXXIX

She must write a note. The imp in the back of her mind laughed. In every story she had ever read when a runaway wife decamped from home she left a note, generally on the pin-cushion. It was not a very original idea. But one had to leave something intelligible. What was there to do but write a note? She looked vaguely about her for something to write with. Ink? There was none. Valancy had never written anything since she had come to the Blue Castle, save memoranda of household necessaries for Barney. A pencil sufficed for them, but now the pencil was not to be found. Valancy absently crossed to the door of Bluebeard's Chamber and tried it. She vaguely expected to find it locked, but it opened unresistingly. She had never tried it before, and did not know whether Barney habitually kept it locked or not. If he did, he must have been badly upset to leave it unlocked. She did not realise that she was doing something he had told her not to do. She was only looking for something to write with. All her faculties were concentrated on deciding just what she would say and how she would say it. There was not the slightest curiosity in her as she went into the lean-to.

There were no beautiful women hanging by their hair on the walls. It seemed a very harmless apartment, with a commonplace little sheet-iron stove in the middle of it, its pipe sticking out through the roof. At one end was a table or counter crowded with odd-looking utensils. Used no doubt by Barney in his smelly operations. Chemical experiments, probably, she reflected dully. At the other end was a big writing desk and swivel-chair. The side walls were lined with books.

Valancy went blindly to the desk. There she stood motionless for a few minutes, looking down at something that lay on it.

A bundle of galleyproofs. The page on top bore the title *Wild Honey,* and under the title were the words "by John Foster."

The opening sentence—"Pines are the trees of myth and legend. They strike their roots deep into the traditions of an older world, but wind and star love their lofty tops. What music when old Æolus draws his bow across the branches of the pines—" She had heard Barney say that one day when they walked under them.

So Barney was John Foster!

Valancy was not excited. She had absorbed all the shocks and sensations that she could compass for one day. This affected her neither one way nor the other. She only thought:

"So this explains it."

"It" was a small matter that had, somehow, stuck in her mind more persistently than its importance seemed to justify. Soon after Barney had brought her John Foster's latest book she had been in a Port Lawrence bookshop and heard a customer ask the proprietor for John Foster's new book. The proprietor had said curtly, "Not out yet. Won't be out till next week."

Valancy had opened her lips to say, "Oh, yes, it *is* out," but closed them again. After all, it was none of her business. She supposed the proprietor wanted to cover up his negligence in not getting the book in promptly. Now she knew. The book Barney had given her had been one of the author's complimentary copies, sent in advance.

Well! Valancy pushed the proofs indifferently aside and sat down in the swivel-chair. She took up Barney's pen—and a vile one it was—pulled a sheet of paper to her and began to write. She could not think of anything to say except bald facts.

"Dear Barney:—

I went to Dr. Trent this morning and found out he had sent me the wrong letter by mistake. There never was anything serious the matter with my heart and I am quite well now.

I did not mean to trick you. Please believe that. I could not bear it if you did not believe that. I am very sorry for the mistake.

But surely you can get a divorce if I leave you. Is desertion a ground for divorce in Canada? Of course if there is anything I can do to help or hasten it I will do it gladly, if your lawyer will let me know.

I thank you for all your kindness to me. I shall never forget it. Think as kindly of me as you can, because I did not mean to trap you. Good-bye.

Yours gratefully,
Valancy."

It was very cold and stiff, she knew. But to try to say anything else would be dangerous—like tearing away a dam. She didn't know what torrent of wild incoherences and passionate anguish might pour out. In a postscript she added:

"Your father was here today. He is coming back tomorrow. He told me everything. I think you should go back to him. He is very lonely for you."

She put the letter in an envelope, wrote "Barney" across it, and left it on the desk. On it she laid the string of pearls. If they had been the beads she believed them she would have kept them in memory of that wonderful year. But she could not keep the fifteen thousand dollar gift of a man who had married her of pity and whom she was now leaving. It hurt her to give *up* her pretty bauble. That was an odd thing, she reflected. The fact that she was leaving Barney did not hurt her—yet. It lay at her heart like a cold, insensible thing. If it came to life—Valancy shuddered and went out—

She put on her hat and mechanically fed Good Luck and Banjo. She locked the door and carefully hid the key in the old pine. Then she crossed to the mainland in the disappearing propeller. She stood for a moment on the bank, looking at her Blue Castle. The rain had not yet come, but the sky was dark, and Mistawis grey and sullen. The little house under the pines looked very pathetic—a casket rifled of its jewels—a lamp with its flame blown out.

"I shall never again hear the wind crying over Mistawis

209

at night," thought Valancy. This hurt her, too. She could have laughed to think that such a trifle could hurt her at such a time.

CHAPTER XL

Valancy paused a moment on the porch of the brick house in Elm Street. She felt that she ought to knock like a stranger. Her rosebush, she idly noticed, was loaded with buds. The rubber-plant stood beside the prim door. A momentary horror overcame her—a horror of the existence to which she was returning. Then she opened the door and walked in.

"I wonder if the Prodigal Son ever felt really at home again," she thought.

Mrs. Frederick and Cousin Stickles were in the sitting-room. Uncle Benjamin was there, too. They looked blankly at Valancy, realising at once that something was wrong. This was not the saucy, impudent thing who had laughed at them in this very room last summer. This was a grey-faced woman with the eyes of a creature who had been stricken by a mortal blow.

Valancy looked indifferently around the room. She had changed so much—and it had changed so little. The same pictures hung on the walls. The little orphan who knelt at her never-finished prayer by the bed whereon reposed the black kitten that never grew up into cat. The grey "steel engraving" of Quatre Bras, where the British regiment forever stood at bay. The crayon enlargement of the boyish father she had never known. There they all hung in the same places. The green cascade of "Wandering Jew" still tumbled out of the old granite saucepan on the windowstand. The same elaborate, never-used pitcher stood at the same angle on the sideboard shelf. The blue and gilt vases that had been among her mother's wedding-presents still primly adorned the mantelpiece, flanking the china clock of berosed and besprayed ware that never went. The chairs in exactly the same places. Her mother and Cousin Stickles, likewise unchanged,

211

regarding her with stony unwelcome.

Valancy had to speak first.

"I've come home, Mother," she said tiredly.

"So I see." Mrs. Frederick's voice was very icy. She had resigned herself to Valancy's desertion. She had almost succeeded in forgetting there was a Valancy. She had rearranged and organised her systematic life without any reference to an ungrateful, rebellious child. She had taken her place again in a society which ignored the fact that she had ever had a daughter and pitied her, if it pitied her at all, only in discreet whispers and asides. The plain truth was that, by this time, Mrs. Frederick did not want Valancy to come back—did not want ever to see or hear of her again.

And now, of course, Valancy was here. With tragedy and disgrace and scandal trailing after her visibly.

"So I see," said Mrs. Frederick. "May I ask why?"

"Because—I'm—not—going to die," said Valancy huskily.

"God bless my soul!" said Uncle Benjamin. "Who said you were going to die?"

"I suppose," said Cousin Stickles shrewishly—Cousin Stickles did not want Valancy back either—"I suppose you've found out he has another wife—as we've been sure all along."

"No. I only wish he had," said Valancy. She was not suffering particularly, but she was very tired. If only the explanations were all over and she were upstairs in her old, ugly room—alone. Just alone! The rattle of the beads on her mother's sleeves, as they swung on the arms of the reed chair, almost drove her crazy. Nothing else was worrying her; but all at once it seemed that she simply could not endure that thin, insistent rattle.

"My home, as I told you, is always open to you," said Mrs. Frederick stonily, "but I can never forgive you."

Valancy gave a mirthless laugh.

"I'd care very little for that if I could only forgive myself," she said.

"Come, come," said Uncle Benjamin testily. But rather

enjoying himself. He felt he had Valancy under his thumb again. "We've had enough of mystery. What has happened? Why have you left that fellow? No doubt there's reason enough—but what particular reason is it?"

Valancy began to speak mechanically. She told her tale bluntly and barely.

"A year ago Dr. Trent told me I had angina pectoris and could not live long. I wanted to have some—life—before I died. That's why I went away. Why I married Barney. And now I've found it is all a mistake. There is nothing wrong with my heart. I've got to live—and Barney only married me out of pity. So I have to leave him—free."

"God bless me!" said Uncle Benjamin. Cousin Stickles began to cry.

"Valancy, if you'd only had confidence in your own mother—"

"Yes, yes, I know," said Valancy impatiently, "What's the use of going into that now? I can't undo this year. God knows I wish I could. I've tricked Barney into marrying me—and he's really Bernard Redfern. Dr. Redfern's son, of Montreal. And his father wants him to go back to him."

Uncle Benjamin made a queer sound. Cousin Stickles took her black-bordered handkerchief away from her eyes and stared at Valancy. A queer gleam suddenly shot into Mrs. Frederick's stone-grey orbs.

"Dr. Redfern—not the Purple Pill man?" she said.

Valancy nodded. "He's John Foster, too—the writer of those nature books."

"But—but—" Mrs. Frederick was visibly agitated, though not over the thought that she was the mother-in-law of John Foster— "*Dr. Redfern is a millionaire!*"

Uncle Benjamin shut his mouth with a snap.

"Ten times over," he said.

Valancy nodded.

"Yes. Barney left home years ago—because of—of some trouble—some—disappointment. Now he will likely go back. So you see—I had to come home. He doesn't love me. I can't hold him to a bond he was tricked into."

Uncle Benjamin looked incredibly sly.

"Did he say so? Does he want to get rid of you?"

"No. I haven't seen him since I found out. But I tell you—he only married me out of pity—because I asked him to—because he thought it would only be for a little while."

Mrs. Frederick and Cousin Stickles both tried to speak, but Uncle Benjamin waved a hand at them and frowned portentously.

"Let *me* handle this," wave and wave and frown seemed to say. To Valancy:

"Well, well, dear, we'll talk it over later. You see, we don't quite understand everything yet. As Cousin Stickles says, you should have confided in us before. Later on—I dare say we can find a way out of this."

"You think Barney can easily get a divorce, don't you?" said Valancy eagerly.

Uncle Benjamin silenced with another wave the exclamation of horror he knew was trembling on Mrs. Frederick's lips.

"Trust to me, Valancy. Everything will arrange itself. Tell me this, Dossie. Have you been happy up back? Was Sn—Mr. Redfern good to you?"

"I have been very happy and Barney was very good to me," said Valancy, as if reciting a lesson. She remembered when she studied grammar at school she had disliked the past and perfect tenses. They had always seemed so pathetic. "I have been"—it was all over and done with.

"Then don't worry, little girl." How amazingly paternal Uncle Benjamin was! "Your family will stand behind you. We'll see what can be done."

"Thank you," said Valancy dully. Really, it was quite decent of Uncle Benjamin. "Can I go and lie down a little while? I'm—I'm—tired."

"Of course you're tired." Uncle Benjamin patted her hand gently—very gently. "All worn out and nervous. Go and lie down, by all means. You'll see things in quite a different light after you've had a good sleep."

He held the door open. As she went through he whispered, "What is the best way to keep a man's love?"

Valancy smiled wanly. But she had come back to the old life—the old shackles. "What?" she asked as meekly as of yore.

"Not to return it," said Uncle Benjamin with a chuckle. He shut the door and rubbed his hands. Nodded and smiled mysteriously round the room.

"Poor little Doss!" he said pathetically.

"Do you really suppose that—Snaith—can actually be Dr. Redfern's son?" gasped Mrs. Frederick.

"I see no reason for doubting it. She says Dr. Redfern has been there. Why, the man is rich as wedding-cake. Amelia, I've always believed there was more in Doss than most people thought. You kept her down too much—repressed her. She never had a chance to show what was in her. And now she's landed a millionaire for a husband."

"But—" hesitated Mrs. Frederick, "he—he—they told terrible tales about him."

"All gossip and invention—all gossip and invention. It's always been a mystery to me why people should be so ready to invent and circulate slanders about other people they know absolutely nothing about. I can't understand why you paid so much attention to gossip and surmise. Just because he didn't choose to mix up with everybody, people resented it. I was surprised to find what a decent fellow he seemed to be that time he came into my store with Valancy. I discounted all the yarns then and there."

"But he was seen dead drunk in Port Lawrence once," said Cousin Stickles. Doubtfully, yet as one very willing to be convinced to the contrary.

"Who saw him?" demanded Uncle Benjamin truculently. "Who saw him? Old Jemmy Strang *said* he saw him. I wouldn't take old Jemmy Strang's word on oath. He's too drunk himself half the time to see straight. He said he saw him lying drunk on

215

a bench in the Park. Pshaw! Redfern's been asleep there. Don't worry over *that.*"

"But his clothes—and that awful old car—" said Mrs. Frederick uncertainly.

"Eccentricities of genius," declared Uncle Benjamin. "You heard Doss say he was John Foster. I'm not up in literature myself, but I heard a lecturer from Toronto say that John Foster's books had put Canada on the literary map of the world."

"I—suppose—we must forgive her," yielded Mrs. Frederick.

"Forgive her!" Uncle Benjamin snorted. Really, Amelia was an incredibly stupid woman. No wonder poor Doss had gone sick and tired of living with her. "Well, yes, I think you'd better forgive her! The question is—will Snaith forgive *us!*"

"What if she persists in leaving him? You've no idea how stubborn she can be," said Mrs. Frederick.

"Leave it all to me, Amelia. Leave it all to me. You women have muddled it enough. This whole affair has been bungled from start to finish. If you had put yourself to a little trouble years ago, Amelia, she would not have bolted over the traces as she did. Just let her alone—don't worry her with advice or questions till she's ready to talk. She's evidently run away in a panic because she's afraid he'd be angry with her for fooling him. Most extraordinary thing of Trent to tell her such a yarn! That's what comes of going to strange doctors. Well, well, we mustn't blame her too harshly, poor child. Redfern will come after her. If he doesn't, I'll hunt him up and talk to him as man to man. He may be a millionaire, but Valancy is a Stirling. He can't repudiate her just because she was mistaken about her heart disease. Not likely he'll want to. Doss is a little overstrung. Bless me, I must get in the habit of calling her Valancy. She isn't a baby any longer. Now, remember, Amelia. Be very kind and sympathetic."

It was something of a large order to expect Mrs. Frederick to be kind and sympathetic. But she did her best. When supper was ready she went up and asked Valancy if she wouldn't like a cup of tea. Valancy, lying on her bed, declined. She just wanted to be left alone for a while. Mrs. Frederick left her alone. She did not even remind Valancy that her plight was the outcome of her own lack of daughterly respect and obedience. One could not—exactly—say things like that to the daughter-in-law of a millionaire.

CHAPTER XLI

Valancy looked dully about her old room. It, too, was so exactly the same that it seemed almost impossible to believe in the changes that had come to her since she had last slept in it. It seemed—somehow—indecent that it should be so much the same. There was Queen Louise everlastingly coming down the stairway, and nobody had let the forlorn puppy in out of the rain. Here was the purple paper blind and the greenish mirror. Outside, the old carriage-shop with its blatant advertisements. Beyond it, the station with the same derelicts and flirtatious flappers.

Here the old life waited for her, like some grim ogre that bided his time and licked his chops. A monstrous horror of it suddenly possessed her. When night fell and she had undressed and got into bed, the merciful numbness passed away and she lay in anguish and thought of her island under the stars. The camp-fires—all their little household jokes and phrases and catch words—their furry beautiful cats—the lights agleam on the fairy islands—canoes skimming over Mistawis in the magic of morning—white birches shining among the dark spruces like beautiful women's bodies—winter snows and rose-red sunset fires—lakes drunken with moonshine—all the delights of her lost paradise. She would not let herself think of Barney. Only of these lesser things. She could not endure to think of Barney.

Then she thought of him inescapably. She ached for him. She wanted his arms around her—his face against hers—his whispers in her ear. She recalled all his friendly looks and quips and jests—his little compliments—his caresses. She counted them all over as a woman might count her jewels—not one did she miss from the first day they had met. These memories were all she could have now. She shut her eyes and prayed.

"Let me remember every one, God! Let me never forget one of them!"

Yet it would be better to forget. This agony of longing and loneliness would not be so terrible if one could forget. And Ethel Traverse. That shimmering witch woman with her white skin and black eyes and shining hair. The woman Barney had loved. The woman whom he still loved. Hadn't he told her he never changed his mind? Who was waiting for him in Montreal. Who was the right wife for a rich and famous man. Barney would marry her, of course, when he got his divorce. How Valancy hated her! And envied her! Barney had said, "I love you," to *her*. Valancy had wondered what tone Barney would say "I love you" in—how his dark-blue eyes would look when he said it. Ethel Traverse knew. Valancy hated her for the knowledge—hated and envied her.

"She can never have those hours in the Blue Castle. They are *mine*," thought Valancy savagely. Ethel would never make strawberry jam or dance to old Abel's fiddle or fry bacon for Barney over a camp-fire. She would never come to the little Mistawis shack at all.

What was Barney doing—thinking—feeling now? Had he come home and found her letter? Was he still angry with her? Or a little pitiful. Was he lying on their bed looking out on stormy Mistawis and listening to the rain streaming down on the roof? Or was he still wandering in the wilderness, raging at the predicament in which he found himself? Hating her? Pain took her and wrung her like some great pitiless giant. She got up and walked the floor. Would morning never come to end this hideous night? And yet what could morning bring her? The old life without the old stagnation that was at least bearable. The old life with the new memories, the new longings, the new anguish.

"Oh, why can't I die?" moaned Valancy.

CHAPTER XLII

It was not until early afternoon the next day that a dreadful old car clanked up Elm Street and stopped in front of the brick house. A hatless man sprang from it and rushed up the steps. The bell was rung as it had never been rung before—vehemently, intensely. The ringer was demanding entrance, not asking it. Uncle Benjamin chuckled as he hurried to the door. Uncle Benjamin had "just dropped in" to enquire how dear Doss—Valancy was. Dear Doss—Valancy, he had been informed, was the same. She had come down for breakfast—which she didn't eat—gone back to her room, come down for dinner—which she didn't eat—gone back to her room. That was all. She had not talked. And she had been let, kindly, considerately, alone.

"Very good. Redfern will be here today," said Uncle Benjamin. And now Uncle Benjamin's reputation as a prophet was made. Redfern was here—unmistakably so.

"Is my wife here?" he demanded of Uncle Benjamin without preface.

Uncle Benjamin smiled expressively.

"Mr. Redfern, I believe? Very glad to meet you, sir. Yes, that naughty little girl of yours is here. We have been—"

"I must see her," Barney cut Uncle Benjamin ruthlessly short.

"Certainly, Mr. Redfern. Just step in here. Valancy will be down in a minute."

He ushered Barney into the parlour and betook himself to the sitting-room and Mrs. Frederick.

"Go up and tell Valancy to come down. Her husband is here."

But so dubious was Uncle Benjamin as to whether Valancy could really come down in a minute—or at all—that he followed Mrs. Frederick on tiptoe up the stairs and listened in the hall.

"Valancy dear," said Mrs. Frederick tenderly, "your husband is in the parlour, asking for you."

"Oh Mother." Valancy got up from the window and wrung her hands. "I cannot see him—I cannot! Tell him to go away—*ask* him to go away. I can't see him!"

"Tell her," hissed Uncle Benjamin through the keyhole, "that Redfern says he won't go away until he *has* seen her."

Redfern had not said anything of the kind, but Uncle Benjamin thought he was that sort of a fellow. Valancy knew he was. She understood that she might as well go down first as last.

She did not even look at Uncle Benjamin as she passed him on the landing. Uncle Benjamin did not mind. Rubbing his hands and chuckling, he retreated to the kitchen, where he genially demanded of Cousin Stickles:

"Why are good husbands like bread?"

Cousin Stickles asked why.

"Because women need them," beamed Uncle Benjamin.

Valancy was looking anything but beautiful when she entered the parlour. Her white night had played fearful havoc with her face. She wore an ugly old brown-and-blue gingham, having left all her pretty dresses in the Blue Castle. But Barney dashed across the room and caught her in his arms.

"Valancy, darling—oh, you darling little idiot! Whatever possessed you to run away like that? When I came home last night and found your letter I went quite mad. It was twelve o'clock—I knew it was too late to come here then. I walked the floor all night. Then this morning Dad came—I couldn't get away till now. Valancy, whatever got into you? Divorce, forsooth! Don't you know—"

"I know you only married me out of pity," said Valancy, brushing him away feebly. "I know you don't love me—I know—"

"You've been lying awake at three o'clock too long," said Barney, shaking her. "That's all that's the matter with you. Love you! Oh, don't I love you! My girl, when I saw that train coming down on you I knew whether I loved you or not!"

221

"Oh, I was afraid you would try to make me think you cared," cried Valancy passionately. "Don't—don't! I know all about Ethel Traverse—your father told me everything. Oh, Barney, don't torture me! I can never go back to you!"

Barney released her and looked at her for a moment. Something in her pallid, resolute face spoke more convincingly than words of her determination.

"Valancy," he said quietly, "Father couldn't have told you everything because he didn't know it. Will you let *me* tell you— everything?"

"Yes," said Valancy wearily. Oh, how dear he was! How she longed to throw herself into his arms! As he put her gently down in a chair, she could have kissed the slender, brown hands that touched her arms. She could not look up as he stood before her. She dared not meet his eyes. For his sake, she must be brave. She knew him—kind, unselfish. Of course he would pretend he did not want his freedom—she might have known he would pretend that, once the first shock of realisation was over. He was so sorry for her—he understood her terrible position. When had he ever failed to understand? But she would never accept his sacrifice. Never!

"You've seen Dad and you know I'm Bernard Redfern. And I suppose you've guessed that I'm John Foster—since you went into Bluebeard's Chamber."

"Yes. But I didn't go in out of curiosity. I forgot you had told me not to go in—I forgot—"

"Never mind. I'm not going to kill you and hang you up on the wall, so there's no need to call for Sister Anne. I'm only going to tell you my story from the beginning. I came back last night intending to do it. Yes, I'm 'old Doc. Redfern's son'—of Purple Pills and Bitters fame. Oh, don't I know it? Wasn't it rubbed into me for years?"

Barney laughed bitterly and strode up and down the room a few times. Uncle Benjamin, tiptoeing through the hall, heard the laugh and frowned. Surely Doss wasn't going to be a stubborn little fool. Barney threw himself into a chair before Valancy.

"Yes. As long as I can remember I've been a millionaire's son. But when I was born Dad wasn't a millionaire. He wasn't even a doctor—isn't yet. He was a veterinary and a failure at it. He and Mother lived in a little village up in Quebec and were abominably poor. I don't remember Mother. Haven't even a picture of her. She died when I was two years old. She was fifteen years younger than Father—a little school teacher. When she died Dad moved into Montreal and formed a company to sell his hair tonic. He'd dreamed the prescription one night, it seems. Well, it caught on. Money began to flow in. Dad invented—or dreamed—the other things, too—Pills, Bitters, Liniment and so on. He was a millionaire by the time I was ten, with a house so big a small chap like myself always felt lost in it. I had every toy a boy could wish for—and I was the loneliest little devil in the world. I remember only one happy day in my childhood, Valancy. Only one. Even you were better off than that. Dad had gone out to see an old friend in the country and took me along. I was turned loose in the barnyard and I spent the whole day hammering nails in a . block of wood. I had a glorious day. When I had to go back to my roomful of playthings in the big house in Montreal I cried. But I didn't tell Dad why. I never told him anything. It's always been a hard thing for me to tell things, Valancy—anything that went deep. And most things went deep with me. I was a sensitive child and I was even more sensitive as a boy. No one ever knew what I suffered. Dad never dreamed of it.

"When he sent me to a private school—I was only eleven— the boys ducked me in the swimming-tank until I stood on a table and read aloud all the advertisements of Father's patent abominations. I did it—then"—Barney clinched his fists—"I was frightened and half drowned and all my world was against me. But when I went to college and the sophs tried the same stunt I didn't do it." Barney smiled grimly. "They couldn't make me do it. But they could—and did—make my life miserable. I never heard the last of the Pills and the Bitters and the Hair Tonic.

'After using' was my nickname—you see I'd always such a thick thatch. My four college years were a nightmare. You know—or you don't know—what merciless beasts boys can be when they get a victim like me. I had few friends—there was always some barrier between me and the kind of people I cared for. And the other kind—who would have been very willing to be intimate with rich old Doc. Redfern's son—I didn't care for. But I had one friend—or thought I had. A clever, bookish chap—a bit of a writer. That was a bond between us—I had some secret aspirations along that line. He was older than I was—I looked up to him and worshipped him. For a year I was happier than I'd ever been. Then—a burlesque sketch came out in the college magazine—a mordant thing, ridiculing Dad's remedies. The names were changed, of course, but everybody knew what and who was meant. Oh, it was clever—damnably so—and witty. McGill rocked with laughter over it. I found out *he* had written it."

"Oh, were you sure?" Valancy's dull eyes flamed with indignation.

"Yes. He admitted it when I asked him. Said a good idea was worth more to him than a friend, any time. And he added a gratuitous thrust. 'You know, Redfern, there are some things money won't buy. For instance—it won't buy you a grandfather.' Well, it was a nasty slam. I was young enough to feel cut up. And it destroyed a lot of my ideals and illusions, which was the worst thing about it. I was a young misanthrope after that. Didn't want to be friends with any one. And then—the year after I left college—I met Ethel Traverse."

Valancy shivered. Barney, his hands stuck in his pockets, was regarding the floor moodily and didn't notice it.

"Dad told you about her, I suppose. She was very beautiful. And I loved her. Oh, yes, I loved her. I won't deny it or belittle it now. It was a lonely, romantic boy's first passionate love, and it was very real. And I thought she loved me. I was fool enough to think that. I was wildly happy when she promised to marry me. For a few months. Then—I found out she didn't. I was an involuntary eavesdropper on a certain occasion for a moment. That moment was enough. The proverbial fate of the eavesdropper overtook me. A girl friend of hers was asking her how she could stomach Doc. Redfern's son and the patent-medicine background.

"'His money will gild the Pills and sweeten the Bitters,' said Ethel, with a laugh. 'Mother told me to catch him if I could. We're on the rocks. But pah! I smell turpentine whenever he comes near me.'"

"Oh, Barney!" cried Valancy, wrung with pity for him. She had forgotten all about herself and was filled with compassion for Barney and rage against Ethel Traverse. How dared she?

"Well,"—Barney got up and began pacing round the room—"that finished me. Completely. I left civilisation and those accursed dopes behind me and went to the Yukon. For five years I knocked about the world—in all sorts of outlandish places. I earned enough to live on—I wouldn't touch a cent of Dad's money. Then one day I woke up to the fact that I no longer cared a hang about Ethel, one way or another. She was somebody I'd known in another world—that was all. But I had no hankering to go back to the old life. None of that for me. I was free and I meant to keep so. I came to Mistawis—saw Tom MacMurray's island. My first book had been published the year before, and made a hit—I had a bit of money from my royalties. I bought my island. But I kept away from people. I had no faith in anybody. I didn't believe there was such a thing as real friendship or true love in the world—not for me, anyhow—the son of Purple Pills. I used to revel in all the wild yarns they told of me. In fact, I'm afraid I suggested a few of them myself. By mysterious remarks which people interpreted in the light of their own prepossessions.

"Then—you came. I *had* to believe you loved me—really loved *me*—not my father's millions. There was no other reason why you should want to marry a penniless devil with my supposed record. And I was sorry for you. Oh, yes, I don't deny I married you because I was sorry for you. And then—I found you the best and jolliest and dearest little pal and chum a fellow ever had. Witty—loyal—sweet. You made me believe again in the reality of friendship and love. The world seemed good again just because you were in it, honey. I'd have been willing to go on forever just as we were. I knew that, the night I came home and saw my homelight shining out from the island for the first time. And knew you were there waiting for me. After being homeless all my life it was beautiful to have a home. To come home hungry at night and know there was a good supper and a cheery fire—and *you*.

"But I didn't realise what you actually meant to me till that moment at the switch. Then it came like a lightning flash. I knew I couldn't live without you—that if I couldn't pull you loose in time I'd have to die with you. I admit it bowled me over—knocked me silly. I couldn't get my bearings for a while. That's why I acted like a mule. But the thought that drove me to the tall timber was the awful one that you were going to die. I'd always hated the thought of it—but I supposed there wasn't any chance for you, so I put it out of my mind. Now I had to face it—you were under sentence of death and I couldn't live without you. When I came home last night I had made up my mind that I'd take you to all the specialists in the world—that something surely could be done for you. I felt sure you couldn't be as bad as Dr. Trent thought, when those moments on the track hadn't even hurt you. And I found your note—and went mad with happiness—and a little terror for fear you didn't care much for me, after all, and had gone away to get rid of me. But now, it's all right, isn't it, darling?"

Was she, Valancy being called "darling"?

"I can't believe you care for me," she said helplessly. "I *know* you can't. What's the use, Barney? Of course, you're sorry for me—of course you want to do the best you can to straighten out the mess. But it can't be straightened out that way. You couldn't love me—me." She stood up and pointed tragically to the mirror over the mantel. Certainly, not even Allan Tierney could have seen beauty in the woeful, haggard little face reflected there.

Barney didn't look at the mirror. He looked at Valancy as if he would like to snatch her—or beat her.

"Love you! Girl, you're in the very core of my heart. I hold you there like a jewel. Didn't I promise you I'd never tell you a lie? Love you! I love you with all there is of me to love. Heart, soul, brain. Every fibre of body and spirit thrilling to the sweetness of you. There's nobody in the world for me but you, Valancy."

"You're—a good actor, Barney," said Valancy, with a wan little smile.

Barney looked at her.

"So you don't believe me—yet?"

"I—can't."

"Oh—damn!" said Barney violently.

Valancy looked up startled. She had never seen *this* Barney. Scowling! Eyes black with anger. Sneering lips. Dead-white face.

"You don't want to believe it," said Barney in the silk-smooth voice of ultimate rage. "You're tired of me. You want to get out of it—free from me. You're ashamed of the Pills and the Liniment, just as she was. Your Stirling pride can't stomach them. It was all right as long as you thought you hadn't long to live. A good lark—you could put up with me. But a lifetime with old Doc Redfern's son is a different thing. Oh, I understand—perfectly. I've been very dense—but I understand, at last."

Valancy stood up. She stared into his furious face. Then—she suddenly laughed.

"You darling!" she said. "You do mean it! You do really love me! You wouldn't be so enraged if you didn't."

Barney stared at her for a moment. Then he caught her in his arms with the little low laugh of the triumphant lover.

Uncle Benjamin, who had been frozen with horror at the keyhole, suddenly thawed out and tiptoed back to Mrs. Frederick and Cousin Stickles.

"Everything is all right," he announced jubilantly.

Dear little Doss! He would send for his lawyer right away and alter his will again. Doss should be his sole heiress. To her that had should certainly be given.

Mrs. Frederick, returning to her comfortable belief in an overruling Providence, got out the family Bible and made an entry under "Marriages."

CHAPTER XLIII

"But, barney," protested Valancy after a few minutes, "your father—somehow—gave me to understand that you *still* loved *her*."

"He would. Dad holds the championship for making blunders. If there's a thing that's better left unsaid you can trust him to say it. But he isn't a bad old soul, Valancy. You'll like him."

"I do, now."

"And his money isn't tainted money. He made it honestly. His medicines are quite harmless. Even his Purple Pills do people whole heaps of good when they believe in them."

"But—I'm not fit for your life," sighed Valancy. "I'm not—clever—or well-educated—or—"

"My life is in Mistawis—and all the wild places of the world. I'm not going to ask you to live the life of a society woman. Of course, we must spend a bit of the time with Dad—he's lonely and old—"

"But not in that big house of his," pleaded Valancy. "I can't live in a palace."

"Can't come down to that after your Blue Castle," grinned Barney. "Don't worry, sweet. I couldn't live in that house myself. It has a white marble stairway with gilt bannisters and looks like a furniture shop with the labels off. Likewise it's the pride of Dad's heart. We'll get a little house somewhere outside of Montreal—in the real country—near enough to see Dad often. I think we'll build one for ourselves. A house you build for yourself is so much nicer than a hand-me-down. But we'll spend our summers in Mistawis. And our autumns travelling. I want you to see the Alhambra—it's the nearest thing to the Blue Castle of your dreams I can think of. And there's an old-world garden in Italy where I want to show you the moon rising over Rome through the dark cypress-trees."

"Will that be any lovelier than the moon rising over Mistawis?"

"Not lovelier. But a different kind of loveliness. There are so many kinds of loveliness. Valancy, before this year you've spent all your life in ugliness. You know nothing of the beauty of the world. We'll climb mountains—hunt for treasures in the bazaars of Samarcand—search out the magic of east and west—run hand in hand to the rim of the world. I want to show you it all—see it again through your eyes. Girl, there are a million things I want to show you—do with you—say to you. It will take a lifetime. And we must see about that picture by Tierney, after all."

"Will you promise me one thing?" asked Valancy solemnly.

"Anything," said Barney recklessly.

"Only one thing. You are never, under any circumstances or under any provocation, to cast it up to me that I asked you to marry me."

CHAPTER XLIV

Extract from letter written by Miss Olive Stirling to Mr. Cecil Bruce:

"It's really disgusting that Doss' crazy adventures should have turned out like this. It makes one feel that there is no use in behaving properly.

"I'm *sure* her mind was unbalanced when she left home. What she said about a dust-pile showed that. Of course I don't think there was ever a thing the matter with her heart. Or perhaps Snaith or Redfern or whatever his name really is fed Purple Pills to her, back in that Mistawis hut and cured her. It would make quite a testimonial for the family ads, wouldn't it?

"He's such an insignificant-looking creature. I mentioned this to Doss but all she said was, 'I don't like collar ad men.'

"Well, he's certainly no collar ad man. Though I must say there is something rather distinguished about him, now that he has cut his hair and put on decent clothes. I really think, Cecil, you should exercise more. It doesn't do to get too fleshy.

"He also claims, I believe, to be John Foster. We can believe *that* or not, as we like, I suppose.

"Old Doc Redfern has given them two millions for a wedding-present. Evidently the Purple Pills bring in the bacon. They're going to spend the fall in Italy and the winter in Egypt and motor through Normandy in apple-blossom time. Not in that dreadful old Lizzie, though. Redfern has got a wonderful new car.

"Well, I think I'll run away, too, and disgrace myself. It seems to pay.

"Uncle Ben is a scream. Likewise Uncle James. The fuss they all make over Doss now is absolutely sickening. To hear Aunt Amelia talking of 'my son-in-law, Bernard Redfern' and 'my

231

daughter, Mrs. Bernard Redfern.' Mother and Father are as bad as the rest. And they can't see that Valancy is just laughing at them all in her sleeve."

CHAPTER XLV

Valancy and Barney turned under the mainland pines in the cool dusk of the September night for a farewell look at the Blue Castle. Mistawis was drowned in sunset lilac light, incredibly delicate and elusive. Nip and Tuck were cawing lazily in the old pines. Good Luck and Banjo were mewed and mewing in separate baskets in Barney's new, dark-green car *en route* to Cousin Georgiana's. Cousin Georgiana was going to take care of them until Barney and Valancy came back. Aunt Wellington and Cousin Sarah and Aunt Alberta had also entreated the privilege of looking after them, but to Cousin Georgiana was it given. Valancy was in tears.

"Don't cry, Moonlight. We'll be back next summer. And now we're off for a real honeymoon."

Valancy smiled through her tears. She was so happy that her happiness terrified her. But, despite the delights before her—'the glory that was Greece and the grandeur that was Rome'—lure of the ageless Nile—glamour of the Riviera—mosque and palace and minaret—she knew perfectly well that no spot or place or home in the world could ever possess the sorcery of her Blue Castle.

THE END

A TANGLED WEB

First published in 1931

AUNT BECKY'S LEVEE

A dozen stories have been told about the old Dark jug. This is the true one.

Several things happened in the Dark and Penhallow clan because of it. Several other things did *not* happen. As Uncle Pippin said, this may have been Providence or it may have been the devil that certainly possessed the jug. At any rate, had it not been for the jug, Peter Penhallow might to-day have been photographing lions alone in African jungles, and Big Sam Dark would, in all probability, never have learned to appreciate the beauty of the unclothed female form. As for Dandy Dark and Penny Dark, they have never ceased to congratulate themselves that they got out of the affair with whole hides.

Legally, the jug was the property of Aunt Becky Dark, *née* Rebecca Penhallow. For that matter, most of the Darks had been *née* Penhallow, and most of the Penhallows had been *née* Dark, save a goodly minority who had been Darks *née* Dark or Penhallows *née* Penhallow. In three generations sixty Darks had been married to sixty Penhallows. The resultant genealogical tangle baffled everybody except Uncle Pippin. There was really nobody for a Dark to marry except a Penhallow and nobody for a Penhallow to marry except a Dark. Once, it had been said, they wouldn't take anybody else. Now, nobody else would take them. At least, so Uncle Pippin said. But it was necessary to take Uncle Pippin's speeches with a large pinch of salt. Neither the Darks nor the Penhallows were gone to seed as far as that. They were still a proud, vigorous, and virile clan who hacked and hewed among themselves but presented an unbroken front to any alien or hostile force.

In a sense, Aunt Becky was the head of the clan. In point of seniority Crosby Penhallow, who was eighty-seven when she was eighty-five, might have contested her supremacy had he cared to do so. But at eighty-seven Crosby Penhallow cared only about one thing. As long as he could foregather every evening with his old crony, Erasmus Dark, to play duets on their flutes and violins, Aunt Becky might hold the sceptre of the clan if she wanted to.

It must be admitted frankly that Aunt Becky was not particularly beloved by her clan. She was too fond of telling them what she called the plain truth. And, as Uncle Pippin said, while the truth was all right, *in its place,* there was no sense in pouring out great gobs of it around where it wasn't wanted. To Aunt Becky, however, tact and diplomacy and discretion, never to mention any consideration for any one's feelings, were things unknown. When she wanted to say a thing she said it. Consequently Aunt Becky's company was never dull whatever else it might be. One endured the digs and slams one got oneself for the fun of seeing other people writhing under *their* digs and slams. As Aunt Becky knew from A to Z all the sad or fantastic or terrible little histories of the clan, no one had armour which her shafts could not penetrate. Little Uncle Pippin said that he wouldn't miss one of Aunt Becky's "levees" for a dog-fight. "She's a personality," Dr Harry Penhallow had once remarked condescendingly, on one of his visits home to attend some clan funeral.

"She's a crank," growled Drowned John Penhallow, who, being a notorious crank himself, tolerated no rivals.

"It's the same thing," chuckled Uncle Pippin. "You're all afraid of her because she knows too much about you. I tell you, boys, it's only Aunt Becky and the likes of her that keeps us all from dry-rotting."

Aunt Becky had been "Aunt Becky" to everybody for twenty years. Once when a letter came to the Indian Spring post-office addressed to "Mrs Theodore Dark" the new postmaster returned it marked "Person unknown." Legally, it was Aunt Becky's name. Once she had had a husband and two children. They were all dead long ago—so long ago that even Aunt Becky herself had practically forgotten them. For years she had lived in her two rented rooms in The Pinery—otherwise the house of her old friend, Camilla Jackson, at Indian Spring. Many Dark and Penhallow homes would have been open to her, for the clan were never unmindful of their obligations, but Aunt Becky would have none of them. She had a tiny income of her own and Camilla, being neither a Dark nor a Penhallow, was easily bossed.

"I'm going to have a levee," Aunt Becky told Uncle Pippin one afternoon when he had dropped in to see her. He had heard she was not very well. But he found her sitting up in bed, supported by pillows, her broad, griddled old face looking as keen and venomous as usual. He reflected that it was not likely there was much the matter with her. Aunt Becky had taken to her bed before now when she fancied herself neglected by her clan.

Aunt Becky had held occasional gatherings that she called "levees" ever since she had gone to live at The Pinery. It was her habit to announce in the local papers that Mrs Rebecca Dark would entertain her friends on such and such an afternoon. Everybody went who couldn't trump up a watertight excuse for not going. They spent two hours of clan gossip, punctuated by Aunt Becky's gibes and the malice of her smile, and had a cup of tea, sandwiches, and several slices of cake. Then they went home and licked their wounds.

"That's good," said Uncle Pippin. "Things are pretty dull in the clan. Nothing exciting has happened for a long time."

"This will be exciting enough," said Aunt Becky. "I'm going to tell them something—not everything—about who's to get the old Dark jug when I'm gone."

"Whew!" Uncle Pippin was intrigued at once. Still he did not forget his manners. "But why bother about that for a while? You're going to see the century out."

"No, I'm not," said Aunt Becky. "Roger told Camilla this morning that I wouldn't live this year out. He didn't tell *me*, the person most interested, but I wormed it out of Camilla."

It was a shock to Uncle Pippin and he was silent for a few

moments. He had had a death-bell ringing in his ear for three days, but he had not connected it with Aunt Becky. Really, no one had ever thought of Aunt Becky dying. Death, like life, seemed to have forgotten her. He didn't know what to say.

"Doctors often make mistakes," he stammered feebly.

"Roger doesn't," said Aunt Becky grimly. "I've got to die, I suppose. Anyhow, I might as well die. Nobody cares anything about me now."

"Why do you say that, Becky?" said Camilla, betraying symptoms of tears. "I'm sure I do."

"No, you don't really. You're too old. We're both too old to care really for anybody or anything. You know perfectly well that in the back of your mind you're thinking, 'After she dies I'll be able to have my tea strong.' There's no use blinking the truth or trying to cover it up with sentiment. I've survived all my real friends."

"Come, come, what about me?" protested Uncle Pippin.

Aunt Becky turned her cronelike old grey head towards him.

"You!" she was almost contemptuous. "Why, you're only sixty-four. I was married before you were born. You're nothing but an acquaintance if it comes to that. Hardly even a relative. You were only an adopted Penhallow, remember. Your mother always vowed you were Ned Penhallow's son, but I can tell you some of us had our doubts. Funny things come in with the tide, Pippin."

This, reflected Uncle Pippin, was barely civil. He decided that it was not necessary to protest any more friendship for Aunt Becky.

"Camilla," snapped Aunt Becky, "I beg of you to stop trying to cry. It's painful to watch you. I had to send Ambrosine out because I couldn't put up with her mewing. Ambrosine cries over everything alike—a death or a spoiled pudding. But one excuses her. It's about the only fun she's ever got out of life. I am ready to die. I've felt almost everything in life there is to feel—ay, I've drained my cup. But I mean to die decently and in order. I'm going to have one last grand rally. The date will be announced in the paper. But if you want anything to eat you'll have to bring it with you. I'm not going to bother with that sort of thing on my death-bed."

Uncle Pippin was genuinely disappointed. Living alone as he did, subsisting on widower's fare, the occasional meals and lunches he got in friends' houses meant much to him. And now Aunt Becky was going to ask people to come and see her and wasn't going to give them a bite. It was inhospitable, that's what it was. Everybody would be resentful, but everybody would be there. Uncle Pippin knew his Darks and his Penhallows. Every last one of them would be keen to know who was to get the old Dark jug. Everybody would think he or she ought to have it. The Darks had always resented the fact of Aunt Becky owning it, anyhow. She was only a Penhallow. The jug should be the property of a born Dark. But old Theodore Dark had expressly left it to his dearly beloved wife in his will, and there you were. The jug was hers to do as she liked with. And nobody in eighty-five years had ever been able to predict what Aunt Becky would do about anything.

Uncle Pippin climbed into what he called his "gig" and drove away behind his meek white horse down the narrow, leisurely red side-road that ran from Indian Spring to Bay Silver. There was a grin of enjoyment on his little, wrinkled face with its curious resemblance to a shrivelled apple, and his astonishingly young, vivid blue eyes twinkled. It would be fun to watch the antics of the clan over the jug. The thorough-going, impartial fun of one who was not vitally concerned. Uncle Pippin knew he had no chance of getting the jug. He was only a fourth cousin at best, even granting the dubious paternity about which Aunt Becky had twitted him.

"I've a hunch that the old lady is going to start something," said Uncle Pippin to his white nag.

II

In spite of the fact that no refreshments were to be served, every Dark and every Penhallow, by birth, marriage or adoption, who could possibly get to Aunt Becky's "levee" was there. Even old rheumatic Christian Dark, who hadn't been anywhere for years, made her son-in-law draw her through the woods behind The Pinery on a milk-cart. The folding doors between Aunt Becky's two rooms were thrown open, the parlour was filled with chairs, and Aunt Becky, her eyes as bright as a cat's, was ready to receive her guests, sitting up in her big old walnut bed under its tent canopy hung with yellowed net. Aunt Becky had slept in that bed ever since she was married and intended to die in it. Several women of the tribe had their eye on it, and each had hoped she would get it, but just now nobody thought of anything but the jug.

Aunt Becky had refused to dress up for her guests. She wasn't going to be bothered, she told Camilla—they weren't really worth it. So she received them regally with a faded old red sweater pinned tightly around her shrunken throat and her grey hair twisted into a hard knot on the crown of her head. But she wore her diamond ring and she had made the scandalized Ambrosine put a little rouge on her cheeks. "It's no more than decent at your age," protested Ambrosine.

"Decency's a dull dog," retorted Aunt Becky. "I parted company with it long ago. You do as you're bid, Ambrosine Winkworth, and you'll get your reward. I'm not going to have Uncle Pippin saying, 'The old girl *used to have* good colour.' Dab it on good and thick, Ambrosine. None of them will imagine they can bully me as they probably would if they found me looking lean and washed-out. My golly, Ambrosine, but I'm looking forward to this afternoon. It's the last bit of fun I'll have this side of eternity and I'm going to lap it up, Ambrosine. Harpies all of 'em, coming here just to see what pickings they're going to get. Ay, I'm going to make them squirm."

The Darks and Penhallows knew this perfectly well, and every new arrival approached the walnut bed with a secret harrowing conviction that Aunt Becky would certainly ask any especially atrocious question that occurred to her. Uncle Pippin had come early, provided with several wads of his favourite chewing-gum, and selected a seat near the folding doors—a point of vantage from which he could see everybody and hear everything Aunt Becky said. He had his reward.

"Ay, so you're the man who burned his wife," remarked Aunt Becky to Stanton Grundy, a long, lean man with a satiric smile who was an outsider, long ago married to Robina Dark, whom he had cremated. Her clan had never forgiven him for it, but Stanton Grundy was insensitive and only smiled hollowly at what he regarded as an attempted witticism.

"All this fuss over a jug worth no more than a few dollars at most," he said scornfully, sitting down beside Uncle Pippin.

Uncle Pippin shifted his wad of gum to the other side of his mouth and manufactured a cheerful lie instantly for the credit of the clan.

"A collector offered Aunt Becky a hundred dollars for it four years ago," he said impressively. Stanton Grundy *was* impressed, and to hide it remarked that *he* wouldn't give ten dollars for it.

"Then, why are you here?" demanded Uncle Pippin.

"To see the fun," returned Mr Grundy coolly. "This jug business is going to set everybody by the ears."

Uncle Pippin nearly swallowed his gum in his indignation. What right had this outsider, who was strongly suspected of being a Swedenborgian, whatever that was, to amuse himself over Dark whimsies and Penhallow peculiarities? It was quite in order for him, Pippin Penhallow, baptized Alexander, to do it. He was one of the tribe, however crookedly. But that a Grundy from God knew where should come for such a purpose made Uncle Pippin furious. Before he could administer catisgation, however, another arrival temporarily diverted his attention from the outrageous Grundy.

"Been having any more babies on the King's Highway?" Aunt Becky was saying to poor Mrs Paul Dark, who had brought her son into a censorious world in a Ford coupé on the way to the hospital. Uncle Pippin had voiced the general clan feeling on that occasion when he said gloomily,

"Sad mismanagement somewhere."

A little snicker drifted over the room, and Mrs Paul made her way to a chair with a burning face. But interest had already shifted from her to Murray Dark, a handsome middle-aged man who was shaking Aunt Becky's hand.

"Well, well, come to get a peep at Thora, hey? She's here—over there beyond Pippin and that Grundy man."

Murray Dark stalked to a chair, reflecting that when you belonged to a clan like this you really lived a dog's life. Of course he had come to see Thora. Everybody knew that, including Thora herself. Murray cared not a hoot about the Dark jug, but he did care tremendously about a chance to look at Thora. He did not have too many of them. He had been in love with Thora ever since the Sunday he had first seen her sitting in the church, the bride of Christopher Dark—drunken ne'er-do-well Chris Dark, with his insidious charm that no girl had ever been able to resist. All the clan knew it, too, but there had never been any scandal. Murray was simply waiting for Chris to pass out. Then he would marry Thora. He was a clever, well-to-do farmer and he had any amount of patience. In time he would attain his heart's desire— though sometimes he wondered a little uneasily how long that devil of a Chris *would* hang on. That family of Darks had such damn' good constitutions. They could live after a fashion that would kill any ordinary man in five years, and flourish for twenty. Chris had been dying by inches for ten years, and there was no knowing how many inches were left of him yet.

"Do get some hair tonic," Aunt Becky was advising William Y. Penhallow, who even as a baby had looked deadly serious and who had never been called Bill in his life. He had hated Aunt Becky ever since she had been the first person to tell him he was beginning to get bald.

"My dear"—to Mrs Percy Dark—"it's such a pity you haven't taken more care of your complexion. You had a fairly nice skin when you came to Indian Spring. Why, *you* here?"—this to Mrs Jim Trent, who had been Helen Dark.

"Of course I'm here," retorted Mrs Jim. "Am I so transparent that there's any doubt?"

"It's a long time since you remembered my existence," snapped Aunt Becky. "But the jug is bringing more things in than the cat."

"Oh, *I* don't want your jug, I'm sure," lied Mrs Jim. Everybody knew she was lying. Only a very foolish person would lie to Aunt Becky, to whom nobody had ever as yet told a lie successfully. But then Mrs Jim Trent lived at Three Hills, and nobody who lived at Three Hills was supposed to have much sense.

"Got your history finished yet, Miller?" asked Aunt Becky.

Old Miller Dark looked foolish. He had been talking for years of writing a history of the clan, but had never got started. It didn't do to hurry these things. The longer he waited the more history there would be. These women were always in such a confounded hurry. He thankfully made way for Palmer Dark, who was known as the man who was proud of his wife.

"Looks as young as ever, doesn't she?" he demanded beamingly of Aunt Becky.

"Yes—if it's any good to look young when you're not—" conceded Aunt Becky, adding by way of a grace note, "Got the beginnings of a dowager's cushion, I see. It's a long time since I saw you, Palmer. But you're just the same, only more so. Well, well, and here's Mrs Denzil Penhallow. Looking fine and dandy, too. I've always heard a fruit diet was healthy. I'm told you ate all the fruit folks sent in for Denzil when he was sick last winter."

"Well, what of it? *He* couldn't eat it. Was it to be wasted?" retorted Mrs Denzil. Jug or no jug, *she* wasn't going to be insulted by Aunt Becky.

Two widows came in together—Mrs Toynbee Dark, who had had her mourning all ready when her third and last husband had died, and Virginia Powell, whose husband had been dead eight years and who was young and tolerably beautiful, but who still wore her black and had vowed, it was well known, never to marry again. Not, as Uncle Pippin remarked, that any one was known to have asked her.

Aunt Becky let Mrs Toynbee off with a coldly civil greeting. Mrs Toynbee had been known to go into hysterics when snubbed or crossed, and Aunt Becky did not intend to let any one else usurp the limelight at her last levee. But she gave poor Virginia a jab.

"Is your heart dug up yet?"

Virginia had once said sentimentally, "My heart is buried in Rose River churchyard," and Aunt Becky never let her forget it.

"Any of that jam left yet?" asked Aunt Becky slyly of Mrs Titus Dark, who had once gathered blueberries that grew in the graveyard and preserved them. Lawyer Tom Penhallow, who had been found guilty of appropriating his clients' money, was counted less of a clan disgrace. Mrs Titus always considered herself an ill-used woman. Fruit had been scarce that year—she had five men to cater for who didn't like butter—and all those big luscious blueberries going to waste in the lower corner of the Bay Silver graveyard. There were *very* few graves there; it was not the fashionable part of the graveyard.

"And how's your namesake?" Aunt Becky was asking Mrs Emily Frost. Kennedy Penhallow, who had been jilted by his cousin Emily, sixty-five years before, had called his old spavined mare after her to insult her. Kennedy, happily married for many years to Julia Dark, had forgotten all about it, but Emily Frost, *née* Penhallow, had never forgotten or forgiven.

"Hello, Margaret; going to write a poem about this? 'Weary and worn and sad the train rattled on.'" Aunt Becky went off into a cackle of laughter and Margaret Penhallow, her thin, sensitive face flushing pitifully and her peculiarly large, soft, grey-blue eyes filling with tears, went blindly to the first vacant chair. Once she had written rather awful little poems for a Summerside paper, but never after a conscienceless printer had deleted her punctuation marks, producing that terrible line which haunted the clan forever afterwards like an unquiet ghost which refused to be laid. Margaret could never feel safe from hearing it quoted somewhere with a snicker or a bellow. Even here at Aunt Becky's death-bed levee it must be dragged up. Perhaps Margaret still wrote poems. A little shell-covered box in her trunk might know something about that. But the public press knew them no more, much to the clan's thankfulness.

"What's the matter with you, Penny? You're not as good-looking as you generally believe you are."

"Stung on the eye by a bee," said Pennycuik Dark sulkily. He was a fat, tubby little fellow, with a curly grey beard and none-too-plentiful curly hair. As usual, he was as well-groomed as a cat. He still considered himself a gay young wag, and felt that nothing but the jug could have lured him into a public appearance under the circumstances. Just like this devilish old woman to call the attention of the world to his eye. But he was her oldest nephew and he had a right to the jug which he would maintain, eye or no eye. He always felt that his branch of the family had been unjustly done out of it two generations back. In his annoyance and excitement he sat down on the first vacant chair he spied, and then to his dismay discovered that he was sitting beside Mrs William Y., of whom he had the liveliest terror ever since she had asked him what to do for a child who had worms. As if he, Pennycuik Dark, confirmed bachelor, knew anything about either children or worms.

"Go and sit in that far corner by the door so that I can't smell that damn' perfume. Even a poor old nonentity like myself has a right to pure air," Aunt Becky was telling poor Mrs Artemas Dark, whose taste in perfumes had always annoyed Aunt Becky. Mrs Artemas *did* use them somewhat too lavishly, but even so, the clan reflected as a unit, Aunt Becky was employing rather strong language for a woman—especially on her death-bed. The Darks and the Penhallows prided themselves on keeping up with the times, but they were not so far advanced as to condone profanity in a woman. *That* was still taboo. The joke of it was that Aunt Becky herself had always been down on swearing and was supposed to hold in special disfavour the two clansmen who habitually swore—Titus Dark because he could not help it and Drowned John Penhallow, who could help it but didn't want to.

The arrival of Mrs Alpheus Penhallow and her daughter created a sensation. Mrs Alpheus lived in St. John and happened to be visiting her old home in Rose River when Aunt Becky's levee was announced. She was an enormously fat woman, with a rather deplorable penchant for wearing bright colours and over-rich materials, who had been very slim and beautiful in a youth during which she had been no great favourite with Aunt Becky. Mrs Alpheus expected some unpleasant greeting from Aunt Becky and meant to take it with a smile, for she wanted badly to get the jug, and the walnut bed into the bargain, if the fates were propitious. But Aunt Becky, though she said to herself that Annabel Penhallow's dress was worth more than her carcass, let her off very leniently with,

"Humph! Smooth as a cat's ear, just as always," and looked past her at Nan Penhallow, about whom clan gossip had been very busy ever since her arrival in Rose River. It was whispered breathlessly that she wore pyjamas and smoked cigarettes. It was well known that she had plucked eyebrows and wore breeches when she rode or "hiked," but even Rose River was resigned to that. Aunt Becky saw a snaky hipless thing with a shingle bob and long barbaric ear-rings. A silky, sophisticated creature in a smart black satin dress who instantly made every other girl in the room seem outmoded and Victorian. But Aunt Becky took her measure on the spot.

"So this is Hannah," she remarked, hitting instinctively on Nan's sore spot. Nan would rather have been slapped than called Hannah. "Well—well—well!" Aunt Becky's "wells" were a crescendo of contempt mingled with pity. "I understand you consider yourself a modern. Well, there were girls that chased the boys in my time, too. It's only names that change. Your mouth looks as if you'd been making a meal of blood my dear. But see what time does to us. When you're forty you'll be exactly like this"—with a gesture towards Mrs Alpheus' avoirdupois.

Nan was determined she wouldn't let this frumpy old harridan put her out. Besides, she had her own hankerings after the jug.

"Oh, no, Aunt Becky darling. I take after father's people. They stay thin, you know."

Aunt Becky did not like being "darlinged."

"Go upstairs and wash that stuff off your lips and cheeks," she said. "I won't have any painted snips around here."

"You—why, you've got rouge on yourself," cried Nan, despite her mother's piteous nudge.

"And who are you to say I should not?" demanded Aunt Becky. "Now, never mind standing there switching your tail at me. Go and do as you're told or else go home."

Nan was minded to do the latter. But Mrs Alpheus was whispering agitatedly at her neck,

"Go, darling, go—do exactly as she tells you—or—or—"

"Or you'll stand no chance of getting the jug," chuckled Aunt Becky, who at eighty-five had ears that could hear the grass grow.

Nan went, sulky and contemptuous, determined that she would get even with somebody for her manhandling by this cantankerous old despot. Perhaps it was at this moment, when Gay Penhallow was entering the room in a yellow dress that seemed woven out of sunshine, that Nan made up her mind to capture Noel Gibson. It was intolerable that Gay of all people should be a witness of her discomfiture.

"Green-eyed girls for trouble," said Uncle Pippin.

"She's a man-eater I reckon," agreed Stanton Grundy.

Gay Penhallow, a slight, blossom-like girl whom only the Family Bible knew as Gabrielle Alexandrina, was shaking Aunt Becky's hand but would not bend down to kiss her as Aunt Becky expected.

"Hey, hey, what's the matter?" demanded Aunt Becky. "Some

249

boy been kissing you? And you don't want to spoil the flavour, hey?"

Gay fled to a corner and sat down. It was true. But *how* did Aunt Becky know it? Noel *had* kissed her the evening before—Gay's first kiss in all her eighteen years—Nan would have hooted over *that!* An exquisite fleeting kiss under a golden June moon. Gay felt that she could *not* kiss any one, especially dreadful old Aunt Becky, after *that.* It would be sacrilege. Never mind if Aunt Becky wouldn't give her the jug. What difference did it make about her old jug, anyway? What difference did anything make in the whole wide beautiful world except that Noel loved her and she loved him?

But something seemed to have come into the now crowded room with the arrival of Gay—something like a sudden quick-passing breeze on a sultry day—something as indescribably sweet and elusive as the fragrance of a forest flower—something of youth and love and hope. Everybody felt inexplicably happier—more charitable—more courageous. Stanton Grundy's lantern-jaws looked less grim and Uncle Pippin momentarily felt that, after all, Grundy had undoubtedly married a Dark and so had a right to be where he was. Miller Dark thought he really would get started on his history next week—Margaret had an inspiration for a new poem—Penny Dark reflected that he was only fifty-two, after all—William Y. forgot that he had a bald spot—Curtis Dark, who had the reputation of being an incurably disagreeable husband, thought his wife's new hat became her and that he would tell her so on the way home. Even Aunt Becky grew less inhuman and, although she had several more shots in her locker and hated to miss the fun of firing them, allowed the remainder of her guests to pass to their seats without insult or innuendo, except that she asked old Cousin Skilly Penhallow how his brother Angus was. All the assembly laughed and Cousin Skilly smiled amiably. Aunt Becky couldn't put *him* out. He knew the whole clan quoted his Spoonerisms and that the one about his brother Angus, now dead for thirty years, never failed to evoke hilarity. The minister had come along that windy morning long ago, after Angus Penhallow's mill-dam had been swept away in the March flood, and had been greeted excitedly by Skilly.

"We're all upset here to-day, Mr MacPherson—ye'll kindly excuse us—my dam brother Angus burst in the night."

"Well, I think everybody is here at last," said Aunt Becky— "everybody I expected, at least, and some I didn't. I don't see Peter Penhallow or the Moon Man, but I suppose one couldn't expect either of them to behave like rational beings."

"Peter *is* here," said his sister Nancy Dark eagerly. "He's out on the veranda. You know Peter hates to be cooped up in a room. He's so accustomed to—to—"

"The great open spaces of God's outdoors," murmured Aunt Becky ironically.

"Yes, that's it—that's what I mean—that's what I meant to say. Peter is just as interested in you as any of us, dear Aunt."

"I daresay—if *that* means much. Or in the jug."

"No, Peter doesn't care a particle about the jug," said Nancy Dark, thankful to find solid ground under her feet in this at least.

"The Moon Man's here, too," said William Y. "I can see him sitting on the steps of the veranda. He's been away for weeks— just turned up to-day. Queer how he always seems to get wind of things."

"He was back yesterday evening. I heard him yelping to the moon all last night down at his shanty," boomed Drowned John. "He ought to be locked up. It's a family disgrace the way he carries on, wandering over the whole Island bareheaded and in rags, as if he hadn't a friend in the world to care for him. I don't care if he isn't mad enough for the asylum. He should be under *some* restraint."

Pounce went Aunt Becky.

"So should most of you. Leave Oswald Dark alone. He's perfectly happy on nights when there's a moon, anyhow, and who among us can say that. If we're perfectly happy for an hour or two at a time, it's as much as the gods will do for us. Oswald's in luck. Ambrosine, here's the key of my brass-bound trunk. Go up to the attic and bring down Harriet Dark's jug."

III

While Ambrosine Winkworth has gone for the jug and a hush of excitement and suspense has fallen over the assembled clan, let us look at them a little more closely, partly through Aunt Becky's eyes and partly through our own, and get better acquainted with them, especially with those whose lives were to be more or less affected and altered by the jug. There were all kinds of people there with their family secrets and their personal secrets, their outer lives of which everything—nearly—was known, and their inner lives of which nothing was known—not even to lean, lank Mercy Penhallow, whose lankness and leanness were attributed to the chronic curiosity about every one which gave her no rest day or night. Most of them looked like the dull, sedate folks they were, but some of them had had shocking adventures. Some of them were very beautiful; some were very funny; some were clever; some were mean; some were happy; some were not; some were liked by everybody and some were liked by nobody; some had reached the stodgy plane where nothing more was to be expected from life; and some were still adventurous and expectant, cherishing secret, unsatisfied dreams.

Margaret Penhallow, for instance—dreamy, poetical Margaret Penhallow, who was the clan dressmaker and lived with her brother, Denzil Penhallow, in Bay Silver. Always overworked and snubbed and patronized. She spent her life making pretty clothes for other people and never had any for herself. Yet she took an artist's pride in her work and something in her starved soul sprang into sudden transforming bloom when a pretty girl floated into church in a gown of her making. *She* had a part in creating that beauty. That slim vision of loveliness owed something of its loveliness to *her,* "old Margaret Penhallow."

Margaret loved beauty; and there was so little of it in her life. She had no beauty herself, save in her overlarge, strangely lustrous eyes, and her slender hands—the beautiful hands of an old portrait. Yet there was a certain attractiveness about her that had not been dependent on youth and had not left her with the years. Stanton Grundy, looking at her, was thinking that she was more ladylike than any other woman of her age in the room and that, if he were looking for a second wife—which, thank God, he wasn't—Margaret would be the one he'd pick.

Margaret would have been a little fluttered had she known he was thinking even this much. The truth was, though Margaret would have died any horrible death you could devise before she admitted it, she longed to be married. If you were married you were somebody. If not, you were nobody. In the Dark and Penhallow clan, anyhow.

She wanted a dear little homey place to call her own; and she wanted to adopt a baby. She knew the very kind of baby she wanted—a baby with golden hair and great blue eyes, dimples and creases and adorable chubby knees. And sweet sleepy little kisses. Margaret's bones seemed to melt in her body as water when she thought of it. Margaret had never cared for the pack of young demons Denzil called his family. They were saucy and unattractive youngsters who made fun of her. All her love was centred in her imaginary baby and her imaginary little house—which was not quite as imaginary as the baby, if truth were known. Yet she had no real hope of ever owning the house, while, if she could get married, she might be able to adopt a baby.

Margaret also wanted very much to get the Dark jug. She wanted it for the sake of that far-off unknown Harriet Dark, concerning whom she had always had a strange feeling, half pity, half envy. Harriet Dark had been loved; the jug was the visible and tangible proof of that, outlasting the love by a hundred years. And what if her lover had been drowned! At least, she had *had* a lover.

Besides, the jug would give her a certain importance. She

had never been of any importance to any one. She was only "old Margaret Penhallow," with fifty drab, snubbed years behind her and nothing ahead of her but drab, snubbed old age. And why should she not have the jug? She was a real niece. A Penhallow, to be sure, but her mother had been a Dark. Of course Aunt Becky didn't like her, but then whom did Aunt Becky like? Margaret felt that she ought to have the jug—must have the jug. Momentarily, she hated every other claimant in the room. She knew if she had the jug she could make Mrs Denzil give her a room to herself in return for the concession of allowing the jug to be put on the parlour mantelpiece. A room to herself! It sounded heavenly. She knew she could never have her little dream-house or her blue-eyed, golden baby, but surely she might have a room to herself—a room where Gladys Penhallow and her shrieking chums could never come—girls who thought there was no fun in having a beau unless you could tell the world all about him and what he did and what he said—girls who always made her feel old and silly and dowdy. Margaret sighed and looked at the great sheaf of mauve and yellow iris Mrs William Y. had brought up for Aunt Becky, who had never cared for flowers. If their delicate, exotic beauty was wasted on Aunt Becky, it was not lost on Margaret. While she gazed at them she was happy. There was a neglected clump of mauve iris in the garden of "her" house.

IV

Gay Penhallow was sitting next to Margaret and was not thinking of the jug at all. She did not want the jug, though her mother was wild about it. Spring was singing in her blood and she was lost in glamorous recollections of Noel's kiss—and equally glamorous anticipations of Noel's letter, which she had got at the post-office on her way up. As she heard it crackle in its hiding-place she felt the little thrill of joy which had tingled over her when old Mrs Conroy had passed it out to her—his wonderful letter held profanely between a mailorder catalogue and a millinery advertisement. She had not dreamed of getting a letter, for she had seen him—and been kissed—only the night before. Now she had it, tucked away under her dress, next to her white satin skin, and all she wished was that this silly old levee was over and she was away somewhere by herself, reading Noel's letter. What time was it? Gay looked at Aunt Becky's solemn old grandfather clock that had ticked off the days and hours of four forgotten generations and was still ticking them relentlessly off for the fifth. Three! At half-past three she must think of Noel. They had made a compact to think of each other every afternoon at exactly half-past three. Such a dear, delightful, foolish compact—because was she not thinking of Noel all the time? And now she had his kiss to think about—that kiss which it seemed every one must see on her lips. She had thought about it all night—the first night of her life she had never slept for joy. Oh, she was so happy! So happy that she felt friendly to everybody—even to the people she had never liked before. Pompous old William Y. with his enormous opinion of himself—lean, curious, gossipy Mercy Penhallow— overtragic Virginia Powell with her tiresome poses—Drowned John, who had shouted two wives to death—Stanton Grundy, who had cremated poor Cousin Robina and who always looked at everybody as if he were secretly amused. One didn't like a person who was amused at everybody. Dapper Penny Dark, who thought he was witty when he called eggs cackleberries—Uncle Pippin with his old jaws always chewing something—most of all, poor piteous Aunt Becky herself. Aunt Becky was going to die soon and no one was sorry. Gay was so sorry because she wasn't sorry that the tears came into her eyes. Yet Aunt Becky had been loved once—courted once—kissed once—ridiculous and unbelievable as it seemed now. Gay looked curiously at this solitary old crone who had once been young and beautiful and the mother of little children. *Could* that old wrinkled face ever have been flower-like? Would she, Gay, ever look like that? No, of course not. Nobody whom Noel loved would ever grow old and unlovely.

She could see herself in the oval mirror that hung on the wall over Stanton Grundy's head, and she was not dissatisfied with the reflection. She had the colouring of a tea-rose, with golden-brown hair, and eyes to match it—eyes that looked like brown marigolds flecked with glints of gold. Long black lashes and eyebrows that might have been drawn in soot, so finely dark were they against her face. And there was a delicious spot here and there on her skin, like a little drop of gold—sole survivor of the freckles that had plagued her in childhood. She knew quite well that she was counted the beauty of the whole clan—"the prettiest girl that walked the aisles of the Rose River Church," Uncle Pippin averred gallantly. And she always looked the least little bit timid and frightened, so men always wanted to assure her there was nothing to be frightened of and she had more beaus than you could shake a stick at. But there had never been any one who really mattered but Noel. Every lane in Gay's thoughts to-day turned back to Noel. Fifteen minutes past three. Just fifteen more minutes and she would be *sure* that Noel was thinking of her.

There was a tiny dark fleck or two on Gay's happiness. For one, she knew all the Penhallows rather disapproved of Noel Gibson. The Darks were more tolerant—after all, Noel's mother had been a Dark, although a rather off-colour one. The Gibsons were considered a cut or two beneath the Penhallows. Gay knew very well that her clan wanted her to marry Dr Roger Penhallow. She looked across the room at him in kindly amusement. Dear old Roger, with his untidy mop of red hair, his softly luminous eyes under straight heavy brows and his long, twisted mouth with a funny quirk in the left corner—who was thirty if he were a day. She was awfully fond of Roger. Somehow, there was a good tang to him. She could never forget what he had done for her at her first dance. She had been so shy and awkward and plain—or was sure she was. Nobody asked her to dance till Roger came and swept her out triumphantly and paid her such darling compliments that she bloomed out into beauty and confidence—and the boys woke up—and handsome Noel Gibson from town singled her out for attention. Oh, she was very very fond of Roger—and very proud of him. A fourth cousin who had been a noted ace in the war Gay so dimly remembered and had brought down fifty enemy planes. But as a husband Gay really had to laugh. Besides, why should any one suppose he wanted to marry her? *He* had never said so. It was just one of those queer ideas that floated about the clan at times—and had a trick of turning out abominably correct. Gay hoped this one wouldn't. She would hate to hurt Roger. She was so happy she couldn't bear to think of hurting any one.

The second little fleck was Nan Penhallow. Gay had never been too fond of Nan Penhallow, though they had been chums of a sort, ever since childhood, when Nan would come to the Island with her father and mother for summer vacations. Gay never forgot the first day she and Nan had met. They were both ten years old; and Nan, who was even then counted a beauty, had dragged Gay to a mirror, and mercilessly pointed out all the contrasts. Gay had never thought of her looks before, but now she saw fatally that she was ugly. Thin and sunburned and pale—freckles galore—hair bleached too light a shade by Rose River sunshine—funny, black unfaded eyebrows that looked as if they had just lighted on her face—how Nan made fun of those eyebrows! Gay was unhappy for years because she believed in her plainness. It had taken many a compliment to convince her that she had grown into beauty. As years went by she did not like Nan much better. Nan, with her subtle, mysterious face, her ashgold hair, her strange liquid emerald eyes, her thin red lips, who was not now really half as pretty as Gay but had odd exotic charms unknown to Rose River. How she patronized Gay—"You quaint child,"—"So Victorian." Gay did not want to be quaint and Victorian. She wanted to be smart and up-to-date and sophisticated like Nan. Though not exactly like Nan. She didn't want to smoke. It always made her think of that dreadful old Mrs Fidele Blacquiere down at the harbour and old moustached Highland Janet at Three Hills, who were always smoking big black pipes like the men. And then—Noel didn't like girls who smoked. He didn't approve of them at all. Nevertheless, Gay, deep down in her heart, was glad the visit of the Alpheus Penhallows to Rose River was to be a brief one this summer. Mrs Alpheus was going to a more fashionable place.

V

Hugh Dark and Joscelyn Dark *(née* Penhallow) were sitting on opposite sides of the room, never looking at each other, and seeing and thinking of nothing but each other. And everybody looked at Joscelyn and wondered as they had wondered for ten years, what terrible secret lay behind her locked lips.

The affair of Hugh and Joscelyn was the mystery and tragedy of the clan—a mystery that no one had ever been able to solve, though not for lack of trying. Ten years before, Hugh Dark and Joscelyn Penhallow had been married after an eminently respectable and somewhat prolonged courtship. Joscelyn had not been too easily won. It was a match which pleased everybody, except Pauline Dark, who was mad about Hugh, and Mrs Conrad Dark, his mother, who had never liked Joscelyn's branch of the Penhallows.

It had been a gay, old-fashioned evening wedding, according to the best Penhallow traditions. Everybody was there to the fourth degree of relationship, and every one agreed that they had never seen a prettier bride or a more indisputable happy and enraptured bridegroom. After the supper and the festivities were over, Hugh had taken his bride home to "Treewoofe,'" the farm he had bought at Three Hills. As to what had happened between the time when Joscelyn, still wearing her veil and satin in the soft coolness and brilliance of the September moonlight—a whim of Hugh's, that, who had some romantic idea of leading a veiled and shimmering bride over the threshold of his new home—had driven away from her widowed mother's house at Bay Silver and the time when, three hours later, she returned to it on foot, still in her dishevelled bridal attire, no one ever knew or could obtain the least inkling in spite of all their prying and surmising. All Joscelyn would ever say, even to her distracted relatives, was that she could never live with Hugh Dark. As for Hugh, he said absolutely nothing and very few people ever dared say anything to him.

Failing to discover the truth, surmise and gossip ran riot. All sorts of explanations were hinted or manufactured—most of them ridiculous enough. One was that Hugh, as soon as he got his bride home, told her that he would be master. He told her certain rules she must keep. He would have no woman bossing *him*. The story grew till it ran that Hugh, by way of starting in properly, had made or tried to make Joscelyn walk around the room on all fours just to teach her he was head of the house. No girl of any spirit, especially Clifford Penhallow's daughter, would endure such a thing. Joscelyn had thrown her wedding-ring at him and flown out of the house.

Others had it that Joscelyn had left Hugh because he wouldn't promise to give up a cat she had hated. "And now," as Uncle Pippin said mournfully, "the cat is dead." Some averred they had quarrelled because Joscelyn had criticized his grammar. Some that she had found out he was an infidel. "You know, his grandfather reads those horrid Ingersoll books. And Hugh had them all on a shelf in his bedroom." Some that she had contradicted him. "His father was like that, you know. Couldn't tolerate the least contradiction. If he only said, 'It's going to rain to-morrow,' it put him in a fury if you said you thought it would be fair."

Then Hugh had told Joscelyn she was too proud—he wasn't going to put up with it any longer. He had danced to her piping for three years but, by heck, the tune was going to be changed. Well, of course Joscelyn *was* proud. The clan admitted that. No woman could have carried such a wonderful crown of red-gold on her head without some pride to hold it up. But was that any excuse for a bridegroom setting wide open the door of his house and politely telling his bride to take her damned superior airs back to where they belonged?

The Darks would none of these crazy yarns. It was not Hugh's fault at all. Joscelyn had confessed she was a kleptomaniac. It ran in her family. A fourth cousin of her mother's was terrible that way. Hugh had the welfare of generations unborn to think of. What else could he do?

Darker hints obtained.

After all, though these little yarns were circulated and giggled over, few really believed there was a grain of truth in them. Most of the clan felt sure that Joscelyn's soft rose-red lips were fast shut on some far more terrible secret than a silly quarrel over cats or grammar. She had discovered something undoubtedly. But what was it?

She had found a love letter some other woman had written him and gone mad with jealousy. After all, Joscelyn's great-grandmother had been a Spanish girl from the West Indies. Spanish blood, you know. All the vagaries of Joscelyn's branch of the Penhallows were attributed to the fact of that Spanish great-grandmother. Captain Alec Penhallow had married her. She died leaving only one son—luckily. But that son had a family of eight. And they were all kittle cattle to handle. So intense in everything. Whatever they were, they were ten times more so than any one else would be.

No, it was worse than a letter. Joscelyn had discovered that Hugh had another wife. Those years out west. Hugh had never talked much about them. But at the last he broke down and confessed.

Nothing of the sort. That child down at the harbour, though. It was certain *some* Dark was its father. Perhaps Hugh—

Naturally, it made a dreadful scandal and sensation. The clan nearly died of it. It had been an old clan saying that nothing ever happened in Bay Silver. Rose River had a fire. Three Hills had an elopement. Even Indian Spring years ago had an actual murder.

But nothing ever happened in Bay Silver. And now something had happened with a vengeance.

That Joscelyn should behave like this! If it had been her rattle-brained sister Milly! They were always expecting Milly to do crazy things, so they were prepared to forgive her. But they had never thought of Joscelyn doing a crazy thing so they could not forgive her for amazing them. Not that it seemed to matter much to Joscelyn whether they forgave her or not. No entreaty availed to budge her an inch. "Her father was like that, you know," Mrs Clifford Penhallow wept. "He was noted for never changing his mind."

"Joscelyn evidently changed hers after she went up to Treewoofe that night," somebody replied. "*What* happened, Cynthia? Surely you, her mother, ought to know."

"How can I know when she won't tell me?" wailed Mrs Clifford. "None of you have ever had any idea how stubborn Joscelyn really is. She simply says she will never go back to Hugh and not another word will she say. She won't even wear her wedding-ring." Mrs Clifford thought this was really the worst thing in it all. "I *never* saw any one so unnaturally obstinate."

"And what in the world are we to *call* her?" wailed the clan. "She *is* Mrs Dark. Nothing can alter that."

Nothing *could* alter it in Prince Edward Island, where there had been only one divorce in sixty years. Nobody ever thought of Hugh and Joscelyn being divorced. One and all, Darks and Penhallows, would have expired of the disgrace of it.

In ten years the matter had naturally simmered down, though a few people kept wondering if the wife from the west would ever turn up. The state of affairs was accepted as something permanent and immutable. People even forgot to think about it, except when, as rarely happened, they saw Hugh and Joscelyn in the same room. Then they wondered fruitlessly again.

Hugh was a very fine-looking man—far handsomer now at thirty-five than he had been at twenty-five, when he was rather lank and weedy. He gave you a feeling that he was able to do anything—a feeling of great, calm power. He had gone on living at Treewoofe with an old aunt keeping house for him, and in agricultural circles he was regarded as a coming man. It was whispered that that Conservative party meant to bring him out as a candidate at the next election of the Provincial House. Yet his eyes with their savage bitterness were the eyes of a man who had failed, and nobody had ever heard him laugh since that mysterious wedding-night.

He had had one keen greedy look at Joscelyn when he had paused a moment in the doorway. He had not seen her for a long time. The tragic years had passed over her without dimming her beauty. Her hair massed round her head in shining defiant protest against the day of bobs, was as wonderful as ever. She had left her roses behind her—her cheeks were pale. But the throat he had once kissed so tenderly and passionately was as exquisite and ivory-like as ever, and her great eyes, that were blue or green or grey as the mood took her, were as lustrous and appealing, as defiant and ecstatic as they had been when she had looked down at him in the hall up at Treewoofe, that night ten years before. Hugh clenched his hands and set his lips. That lean fox of a Stanton Grundy was watching him—everybody was always watching him. The bridegroom jilted on his wedding night. From whom his bride had run in supposed horror or rebellion over three miles of dark solitary road. Well, let them watch and let them guess. Only he and Joscelyn knew the truth—the tragic absurd truth that had separated them.

Joscelyn had seen Hugh when he came into the room. He looked older; that unmanageable lock of dark hair was sticking up on the crown of his head as usual. Joscelyn knew she wanted to go over and coax it down. Kate Muir was sitting beside him ogling him; she had always detested and despised Kate Muir, née Kate Dark, who had been an ugly swarthy little girl and was now an ugly swarthy little widow with more money than she knew what to do with. Having married for money, Joscelyn reflected contemptuously, she had a right to it. But was that any excuse for her sitting in Hugh's pocket and gazing up at him as if she thought him wonderful. She knew that Kate had once said, "I always told Hugh she wouldn't make him a suitable wife." Joscelyn shivered slightly and locked her slender hands, on which was no wedding-ring, a little more tightly on her knee. She was not—never had been—sorry for what she had done ten years ago. She *couldn't* have done anything else, not *she,* Joscelyn Penhallow, with that touch of Spanish blood in her. But she had always felt a little outside of things and the feeling had deepened with the years. She seemed to have no part or lot in the life that went on around her. She learned to smile like a queen, with lips not eyes.

She saw her face reflected in the glass beside Gay Penhallow and suddenly thought that she looked old. Gay, wearing her youth like a golden rose, was so happy, so radiant, as if lighted by some inner flame. Joscelyn felt a queer pang of envy. She had never envied any one in all these ten years, borne up by the rapture of a certain strange, spiritual, sacrificial passion and renunciation. All at once, she felt an odd flatness, as if her wings had let her down. A chill of consternation and fright swept over her. She wished she had not come to this silly levee. She cared nothing about the old Dark jug, though her mother and Aunt Rachel both wanted it. She would not have come if she had thought Hugh would be there. Who would have expected him? Surely *he* didn't want the jug. She would have despised him if she thought he did. No doubt he had had to bring his mother and his sister, Mrs Jim Trent. They were both glowering at her. Her sisters-in-law, Mrs Penny Dark and Mrs Palmer Dark, were pretending not to see her. She knew they all hated her. Well, it didn't matter. After all, could you blame them, considering the insult she had offered to the House of Dark? No, it didn't matter—Joscelyn wondered a little dreamily if anything mattered. She looked at Lawson Dark, with the V.C. he had won at Amiens pinned on his breast, in his wheel-chair behind Stanton Grundy, for ten years a paralytic from shell-shock. At Naomi Dark beside him, with her patient, haggard face and her dark, hollow eyes in which still burned the fires of the hope that kept her alive. Joscelyn was amazed to find suddenly stirring in her heart a queer envy of Naomi Dark. Why should she envy Naomi Dark, whose husband didn't recognize her—never, had recognized her since his return from the war? His mind was normal in every other respect, but he had forgotten all about the bride he had met and married only a few weeks before his departure for the front. She knew Naomi lived by the belief that Lawson would remember her some day. Meanwhile she took care of him and worshipped him. Lawson had grown quite fond of her as a nurse, but no recollection ever came to him of his sudden love and his brief honeymoon. Yet Joscelyn envied her. She *had* had something. Life had not been an empty cup for her, whatever bitter brew was mingled in it. Even Mrs Foster Dark had something to live for. Happy Dark had run away from home years ago, leaving a note—"I'll come back some time, Mother." Mrs Foster would never lock her door at night lest Happy come, and it was well-known that she always left a supper on the table for him. Nobody else believed Happy would ever come back—the young devil was undoubtedly dead years ago and good riddance! But the hope kept Mrs Foster going, and Joscelyn envied her!

She saw Murray Dark devouring Thora Dark with his eyes, satisfied if she gave him only one look in return. He would, Joscelyn knew, rather have one of those long, deep, remote looks of Thora's than a kiss from any other woman. Well, it was no wonder he loved Thora. She was one of those women men can't help loving—except Chris Dark, who had given up loving her six weeks after he had married her. Yet other women did not dislike Thora. Whenever she came into a room people felt happier. She lighted life like a friendly beaming candle. She had a face that was charming without being in the least beautiful. A fascinating square face with a wide space between her blue almond-shaped eyes and a sweet, crooked mouth. She was very nicely dressed. Her peculiarly dark auburn hair was parted on her forehead and coronetted on her crown. There were milky pearl drops in her ears. What a wife she would make for Murray if that detestable Chris would only be so obliging as to die. The winter before, he had had double pneumonia and everybody was sure he would die. But he hadn't—owed his life, no doubt, to Thora's faithful nursing. And Matthew Penhallow at Three Hills, whom everybody loved and who had a family that needed him, died of *his* pneumonia. Another proof of the contrariness of life.

Pauline Dark wasn't here. Was she still in love with Hugh? She had never married. What a tangled, criss-crossed thing life was, anyhow. And here they were all sitting in rows, waiting for Ambrosine Winkworth to bring down the jug about which they were all ready to tear each other in pieces. Truly a mad world. Joscelyn was unblessed with the sense of humour which was making the affair a treat to Tempest Dark, sitting behind her. Tempest had made up his mind on considered opinion to shoot himself that night. He had nearly done it the night before, but he had reflected that he might as well wait till after the levee. He wanted, as a mere matter of curiosity, to see who got the old Dark jug. Winnifred had liked that jug. He knew he had no chance of it himself. Aunt Becky had no use for a bankrupt. He was bankrupt and the wife he had adored had died a few weeks previously. He couldn't see any sense in living on. But just at this moment he was enjoying himself.

VI

Donna Dark and Virginia Powell sat together as usual. They were first cousins, who were born the same day and married the same day,—Donna to her own second cousin, Barry Dark, and Virginia to Edmond Powell—two weeks before they had left for Valcartier. Edmond Powell had died of pneumonia in the training camp, but Barry Dark had his crowded hour of glorious life somewhere in France. Virginia and Donna were "war widows" and had made a solemn compact to remain widows for ever. It was Virginia's idea, but Donna was very ready to fall in with it. She knew she could never care for any man again. She had never said her heart was buried in any especial place—though rumour sometimes attributed Virginia's famous utterance to her—but she felt that way about it. For ten years they had continued to wear weeds, though Virginia was always much weedier than Donna.

Most of the clan thought Virginia, with her spiritual beauty of pale gold hair and over-large forget-me-not eyes, was the prettier of the two devoted. Donna was as dark as her name—a slight, ivory-coloured thing with very black hair which she always wore brushed straight back from her forehead, as hair should be worn only by a really pretty woman or by a woman who doesn't care whether she looks pretty or not. Donna didn't care—or thought she didn't—but it was her good luck to have been born with a widow's peak and that saved her. Her best features were her eyes, like star-sapphires, and her mouth with its corners tucked up into dimples. She had bobbed her hair at last, though her father kicked up a fearful domestic hullabaloo over it, and Virginia was horrified.

"Do you think Barry would have liked it, dear?"

"Why not?" said Donna rebelliously. "Barry wouldn't have liked a dowdy wife. He was always up-to-date."

Virginia sighed and shook her head. *She* would never cut off her hair—never. The hair Edmond had caressed and admired.

"He used to bury his face in it and say it was like perfumed sunshine," she moaned gently.

Donna had continued to live with her father, Drowned John Penhallow—so called to distinguish him from another John Penhallow who had not been drowned—and her older half-sister, Thekla, ever since Barry's death. She had wanted to go away and train for nursing, but Drowned John had put his not inconsiderable foot down on that. Donna had yielded—it saved trouble to yield to Drowned John at the outset. He simply yelled people down. His rages were notorious in the clan. When reproached with them he said,

"If I didn't go into a rage now and then, life here would be so dull my females would hang themselves."

Drowned John was twice a widower. With his first wife, Jennie Penhallow, he had quarrelled from the time they were married. When they knew their first baby was coming, they quarrelled over what college they would send him to. As the baby turned out to be Thekla, there was no question—in Drowned John's mind, at least—of college. But the rows went on and became such a scandal that the clan hinted at a separation—not divorce of course. That never entered their heads. But Drowned John did not see the sense of it. He would have to have a housekeeper.

"Might as well be quarrelling with Jennie as with any other woman," he said.

When Jennie died—"from sheer exhaustion," the clan said— Drowned John married Emmy Dark, destined to be Donna's mother. The clan thought Emmy was more than a little mad to take him, and pointed out to her what an existence she would have. But Drowned John never quarrelled with Emmy. Emmy simply would not quarrel—and Drowned John had secretly thought life with her was very flat. Yet, although he always had two sets of manners and used his second best at home, Thekla and Donna were rather fond of him. When he got his own way he was quite agreeable. Hate what Drowned John hated—love what Drowned John loved—give him a bit of blarney now and again—and you couldn't find a nicer man.

All sorts of weird yarns were told of Drowned John's young days, culminating in his quarrel with his father, during which Drowned John, who had a tremendous voice, shouted so loud that they heard him over at Three Hills, two miles away. After which he had run away to sea on a ship that was bound for New Zealand. He had fallen overboard on the voyage and was reported drowned. The clan held a funeral service and his father had his name chiselled on the big family monument in the graveyard. After two years young John came home, unchanged save for a huge snake tattooed around his right arm, having acquired a lavish vocabulary of profanity and an abiding distaste for sea-faring. Some thought the ship which had picked him up unnecessarily meddlesome. But John settled down on the farm, told Jennie Penhallow he was going to marry her, and refused to have his name erased from the monument. It was too good a joke. Every Sunday Drowned John went into the graveyard and guffawed over it.

He was sitting now behind William Y. and wondering if William Y. really was presumptuous enough to imagine *he* should have the jug. Why, there was no manner of doubt in the world that he, John Penhallow, should have it. It would be a damned outrage if Aunt Becky gave it to any one else and he'd tell her so, by asterisk and by asterisk. His very long face crimsoned with fury at the mere thought—a crimson that covered his ugly bald forehead, running back to his crown. His bushy white moustache bristled. His pop-eyes glared. By—more asterisks and very lurid ones—if any one else got that jug they'd have to reckon with *him*.

"I wonder what Drowned John is swearing so viciously inside himself about," thought Uncle Pippin.

Donna wanted the jug, too. She was really quite crazy about it. She felt she ought to have it. Long, long ago, when Barry was just a little boy, Aunt Becky had told him she was going to leave it to him when she died. So she, Barry's widow, should have it now. It was such a lovely old thing, with its romantic history. Donna had always hankered after it. She did not swear internally as her father did, but she thought crossly she had never seen such a bunch of old harpies.

VII

Outside on the railing of the veranda Peter Penhallow was sitting, swinging one of his long legs idly in the air. A rather contemptuous scowl was on his lean, bronzed, weary face.

Peter's face always looked bored and weary—at least in scenes of civilization. He wasn't going in. You would not catch Peter mewed up in a room full of heirloom hunters. Indeed, to Peter any room, even a vacant one, was simply a place to get out of as soon as possible. He always averred he could not breathe with four walls around him. He had come to this confounded levee—a curse on Aunt Becky's whims!—sorely against his will, but at least he would stay outside where there was a distant view of the jewelled harbour and a glorious wind that had never known fetters, blowing right up from the gulf—Peter loved wind—and a big tree of apple blossom that was fairer to look upon than any woman's face had ever seemed to Peter. The clan wrote Peter down as a woman-hater, but he was nothing of the sort. The only woman he hated was Donna Dark; he was simply not interested in women and had never tried to be because he felt sure no woman would ever be willing to share the only life he could live. And as for giving up that life and adopting a settled existence, the idea simply could never have occurred to Peter. Women regretted this, for they found him very attractive. Not handsome but "so distinguished, you know." He had grey eagle eyes, that turned black in excitement or deep feeling. Women did not like his eyes—they made them uncomfortable—but they thought his mouth very beautiful, and even liked it for its strength and tenderness and humour. As Uncle Pippin said, the clan would likely have been very fond of Peter Penhallow if they had ever had any chance to get acquainted with him. As it was, he remained only a tantalizing hop-out-of-kin, out of whose goings-on they got several vicarious thrills and of whom they were proud because his explorations and discoveries had won him fame—"notoriety," Drowned John called it—but whom they never pretended to understand and of whose satiric winks they were all a little afraid. Peter hated sham of any kind; and a clan like the Penhallows and the Darks were full of it. Had to be, or they couldn't have carried on as a clan at all. But Peter never made any allowances for that.

"Look at Donna Dark," he was wont to sneer. "Pretending to be devoted to Barry's memory when all the time she'd jump at a second husband if there was any chance of one."

Not that Peter ever did look at Donna. He had never seen her since she was a child of eight, sitting across from him in church on the last Sunday he had been there before he ran away on the cattle-ship. But people reported what he said to Donna and Donna had it in for him. She never expected any such good luck as a chance to get square. But one of her day-dreams was that in some mysterious and unthinkable way Peter Penhallow should fall in love with her and sue for her hand, only to be spurned with contumely. Oh, how she would spurn him! How she would show him that she was "a widow indeed." Meanwhile she had to content herself with hating him as bitterly as Drowned John himself could hate.

Peter, who was by trade a civil engineer and by taste an explorer, had been born in a blizzard and had nearly been the death of three people in the process—his mother, to begin with, and his father and the doctor, who were blocked and all but frozen to death on that night of storm. When they were eventually dug out and thawed out Peter was there. And never, so old Aunty But averred, had such an infant been born. When she had carried him out to the kitchen to dress him, he had lifted his head of his own power and stared all around the room with bright eager eyes. Aunty But had never seen anything like it. It seemed uncanny and gave her such a turn that she let Peter drop. Luckily, he landed unhurt on a cushion of the lounge, but it was the first of his many narrow shaves. Aunty But always told with awe that Peter had not cried when he came into the world, as all properly behaved babies do.

"He seemed to like the change," said Aunty But. "He's a fine, healthy child but"—and Aunt But shook her head forebodingly. The Jeff Penhallows did not bother over her "buts." She had got her nickname from them. *But* they lived to think that her foreboding on this occasion was justified.

Peter continued to like change. He had been born with the soul of Balboa or Columbus. He felt to the full the lure of treading where no human foot had ever trod. He had a thirst for life that was never quenched—"Life," he used to say, "that grand glorious adventure we share with the gods." When he was fourteen he had earned his way around the world, starting out with ten cents and working his passage to Australia on a cattle-ship. Then he had come home—with the skin of a man-eating tiger he had killed himself for his mother's decorous parlour floor and a collection of magnificent blue African butterflies which became a clan boast—gone back to school, toiled slavishly, and eventually graduated in civil engineering. His profession took him all over the world. When he had made enough money out of a job to keep him for awhile, he stopped working and simply explored. He was always daring the unknown—the uncharted—the undiscovered. His family had resigned themselves to it. As Uncle Pippin said, Peter was "not domestic," and they knew now he would never become so. He had had many wild adventures of which his clan knew and a thousand more of which they never heard. They were always expecting him to be killed.

"He'll be clapped into a cooking-pot some day," said Drowned John, but he did not say it to Peter, for the simple reason that he never spoke to him. There was an old feud between those two Penhallow families, dating back to the day when Jeff Penhallow had killed Drowned John's dog and hung it at his gate, because Drowned John's dog had worried his sheep and Drowned John had refused to believe it or to get rid of his dog. From that day none of Drowned John's family had had any dealings, verbal or otherwise, with any of Jeff Penhallow's. Drowned John knocked down and otherwise maltreated in the square at Charlottetown a man who said that Jeff Penhallow's word was as good as his bond because neither was any good. And Peter Penhallow, meeting a fellow Islander somewhere along the Congo, slapped his face because the said Islander laughed over Thekla Dark having once flavoured some gingerbread with mustard. But this was clan loyalty and had nothing whatever to do with personal feeling, which continued to harden and embitter through the years. When Barry Dark, Peter's cousin and well-beloved chum, told Peter he was going to marry Donna Dark, Peter was neither to hold nor bind. He refused to countenance the affair at all and kicked up such a rumpus that even the Jeff Penhallows thought he was going entirely too far. When the wedding came off, Peter was hunting wapiti in New Zealand, full of bitterness of soul, partly because Barry had married one of the accursed race and partly because he, Peter, being notoriously and incurably left-handed, had not been accepted for overseas service. Barry had been rather annoyed over Peter's behaviour and a slight coolness had arisen between them, which was never quite removed because Barry never came back from the front. This left a sore spot in Peter's soul which envenomed still further his hatred of Donna Dark. Peter had had no intention of coming to Aunt Becky's levee. He had fully meant to leave that afternoon en route for an exploring expedition in the upper reaches of the Amazon. He had packed and strapped and locked his trunk, whistling with sheer boyish delight in being off once more. He had had a month at home—a month too much. Thank God, no more of it. In a few weeks he would be thousands of miles away from the petty gossips and petty loves and petty hates of the Darks and Penhallows—away from a world where women bobbed their hair and you couldn't tell who were grandmothers and who were flappers—from behind—and in a place where nobody would ever make moan, "Oh, what will people think of you, Peter, if you do—or don't do—that?"

"And I swear by the nine gods of Clusium that this place will not see me again for the next ten years," said Peter Penhallow, running downstairs to his brother's car, waiting to take him to the station.

Just then Destiny, with an impish chuckle, tapped him on the shoulder. His half-sister Nancy was coming into the yard almost in tears. She couldn't get to the levee if he wouldn't take her. Her husband's car had broken down. And she *must* get to the levee. She would have no chance at all of getting that darling old jug if she did not go.

"Young Jeff here can take you. I'll wait for the evening train," said Peter obligingly.

Young Jeff demurred. He had to hoe his turnips. He could spare half an hour to take Peter to the station, but spend a whole afternoon down at Indian Spring he would not.

"Take her yourself," he said. "If the evening train suits you as well, you've nothing else to do this afternoon."

Peter yielded unwillingly. It was almost the first time in his life he had done anything he really didn't want to do. But Nancy had always been a sweet little dear—his favourite in his own family. She "Oh—Petered" him far less than any of the others. If she had set her heart on that confounded jug, he wasn't going to spoil her chance.

If Peter could have foreseen the trick Fate had it in mind to play him, would he really have gone to the levee, Nancy to the contrary withstanding. Well, would he now? Ask him yourself.

So Peter came to the levee, but he felt a bit grim and into the house he would not go. He did not give his real reason—for all his hatred of sham. Perhaps he did not acknowledge it even to himself. Peter, who was not afraid of any other living creature from snakes and tigers up, was at the very bottom of his heart afraid of Aunt Becky. The devil himself, Peter reflected, would be afraid of that blistering old tongue. It would not have been so bad if she had dealt him the direct thwacks she handed out to most people. But Aunt Becky had a different technique for Peter. She made little smiling speeches to him, as mean and subtle and nasty as a cut made with paper, and Peter had no defence against them. So he thankfully draped himself over the railing of the veranda. The Moon Man was standing at the other end, and Big Sam Dark and Little Sam Dark were in the two rocking-chairs. Peter didn't mind them, but he had a bad moment when Mrs Toynbee Dark dropped into the only remaining chair with her usual whines about her health, ending up with pseudo-thankfulness that she was as well as she was.

"The girls of to-day are *so* healthy," sighed Mrs Toynbee. "Almost vulgarly so, don't you think, Peter? When I was a girl I was extremely delicate. Once I fainted six times in one day. I don't really think I *ought* to go into that close room."

Peter, who hadn't been so scared since the time he had mistaken an alligator for a log, decided that he had every excuse for being beastly.

"If you stay out here with four unwedded men, my dear Alicia, Aunt Becky will think you have new matrimonial designs and you'll stand no chance of the jug at all."

Mrs Toynbee turned a horrible shade of pea-green with suppressed fury, gave him a look containing things not lawful to be uttered and went in with Virginia Powell. Peter took the precaution of dropping the surplus chair over the railing into the spirea bushes.

"Excuse me if I weep," said Little Sam, winking at Peter while he wiped away large imaginary tears from his eyes.

"Vindictive. Very vindictive," said Big Sam, jerking his head at the retreating Mrs Toynbee. "And sly as Satan. You shouldn't have put her back up, Peter. She'll do you a bad turn if she can."

Peter laughed. What did Mrs Toynbee's vindictiveness matter to him, bound for the luring mysteries of untrod Amazon jungles? He drifted off into a reverie over them, while the two Sams smoked their pipes and reflected, each according to his bent.

VIII

"Little" Sam Dark—who was six-feet-two—and "Big" Sam Dark—who was five-feet-one—were first cousins. "Big" Sam was six years the elder, and the adjective that had been appropriate in childhood stuck to him, as things stick in Rose River and

Little Friday Cove, all his life. The two Sams were old sailors and longshore fishermen, and they had lived together for thirty years in Little Sam's little house that clung like a limpet to the red "cape" at Little Friday Cove. Big Sam had been born a bachelor. Little Sam was a widower. His marriage was so far in the dim past that Big Sam had almost forgiven him for it, though he occasionally cast it up to him in the frequent quarrels by which they enlivened what might otherwise have been the rather monotonous life of retired sea-folk.

They were not, and never had been, beautiful, though that fact worried them little. Big Sam had a face that was actually broader than it was long and a flaming red beard—a rare thing among the Darks, who generally lived up to their name. He had never been able to learn how to cook, but he was a good washer and mender. He could also knit socks and write poetry. Big Sam quite fancied himself as a poet. He had written an epic which he was fond of declaiming in a surprisingly great voice for his thin body. Drowned John himself could hardly bellow louder. When he was low in his mind he felt that he had missed his calling and that nobody understood him. Also that nearly everybody in the world was going to be damned.

"I should have been a poet," he would say mournfully to his orange-hued cat—whose name was Mustard. The cat always agreed with him, but Little Sam sometimes snorted contemptuously. If he had a vanity it was in the elaborate anchors tattooed on the back of his hands. He considered them far more tasty and much more in keeping with the sea than Drowned John's snake. He had always been a Liberal in politics and had Sir Wilfrid Laurier's picture hanging over his bed. Sir Wilfrid was dead and gone, but in Big Sam's opinion no modern leader could fill his shoes. Premiers and would-be premiers, like everything else, were degenerating. He thought Little Friday Cove the most desirable spot on earth and resented any insinuation to the contrary.

"I like to have the sea, 'the blue lone sea,' at my very doorstep like this," he boomed to the "writing man" who was living in a rented summer cottage at the cove and had asked if they never found Little Friday lonesome.

"Jest part of his poetical nature," Little Sam had explained aside, so that the writing man should not think that Big Sam had rats in his garret. Little Sam lived in secret fear—and Big Sam in secret hope—that the writing man would "put them in a book."

By the side of the wizened Big Sam Little Sam looked enormous. His freckled face was literally half forehead and a network of large, purplish-red veins over nose and cheeks looked like some monstrous spider. He wore a great drooping moustache like a horse-shoe that did not seem to belong to his face at all. But he was a genial soul and enjoyed his own good cooking, especially his famous pea soups and clam chowders. His political idol was Sir John Macdonald, whose picture hung over the clock shelf, and he had been heard to say—not in Big Sam's hearing—that he admired weemen in the abstract. He had a harmless hobby of collecting skulls from the old Indian graveyard down at Big Friday Cove and ornamenting the fence of his potato plot with them. He and Big Sam quarrelled about it every time he brought a new skull home. Big Sam declared it was indecent and unnatural and unchristian. But the skulls remained on the poles.

Little Sam was not, however, always inconsiderate of Big Sam's feelings. He had once worn large, round, gold earrings in his ears, but he had given up wearing them because Big Sam was a fundamentalist and didn't think they were Presbyterian ornaments.

Both Big and Little Sam had only an academic interest in the old Dark jug. Their cousinship was too far off to give them any claim on it. But they never missed attending any clan gathering. Big Sam might get material for a poem out of it and Little Sam might see a pretty girl or two. He was reflecting now that Gay Penhallow had got to be a regular little beauty and that Thora Dark was by way of being a fine armful. And there was *something* about Donna Dark—something confoundly seductive. William

Y.'s Sara was undeniably handsome, but she was a trained nurse and Little Sam always felt that she knew too much about her own and other people's insides to be really charming. As for Mrs Alpheus Penhallow's Nan, about whom there had been so much talk, Little Sam gravely decided that she was "too jazzy."

But Joscelyn Dark, now. She had always been a looker. What the divvle could have come between her and Hugh? Little Sam thought "divvle" was far less profane than "devil"—softer like. For an old sea-dog Little Sam was fussy about his language.

Oswald Dark had been standing at the far end of the veranda, his large, agate-grey, expressionless eyes fixed on the sky and the golden edge of the world that was the valley of Bay Silver. He wore, as usual, a long black linen coat reaching to his feet and, as usual, he was bareheaded. His long brown hair, in which there was not a white thread, parted in the middle, was as wavy as a woman's. His cheeks were hollow but his face was strangely unlined. The Darks and Penhallows were as ashamed of him as they had once been proud. In his youth Oswald Dark had been a brilliant student, with the ministry in view. Nobody knew why he "went off." Some hinted at an unhappy love affair; some maintained it was simply overwork. A few shook their heads over the fact that Oswald's grandmother had been an outsider—a Moorland from down east. Who knew what sinister strain she might have brought into the pure Dark and Penhallow blood?

Whatever the reason, Oswald Dark was now considered a harmless lunatic. He wandered at will over the pleasant red roads of the Island, and on moonlight nights sang happily as he strode along, with an occasional genuflection to the moon. On moonless nights he was bitterly unhappy and wept to himself in woods and remote corners. When he grew hungry he would call in at the first house, knock thunderingly on the door as if it had no right to be shut, and demand food regally. As everybody knew him he always got it, and no house was shut to him in the cold of a winter night. Sometimes he would disappear from human ken for weeks at a time. But, as William Y. said, he had an uncanny instinct for clan pow-wows of any sort and invariably turned up at them, though he could seldom be persuaded to enter the house where they were being held. As a rule he took no notice of people he met in his wanderings—except to scowl darkly at them when they demanded jocularly, "How's the moon?"—but he never passed Joscelyn Dark without smiling at her—a strange eerie smile—and once he had spoken to her.

"You are seeking the moon, too. I know it. And you're unhappy because you can't get it. But it's better to want the moon, even if you can't get it—the beautiful silvery remote Lady Moon—as unattainable as things of perfect beauty ever are—than to want and get anything else. Nobody knows that but you and me. It's a wonderful secret, isn't it? Nothing else matters."

IX

The folks in the parlour were getting a bit restless. What—the devil or the mischief—according to sex—was keeping Ambrosine Winkworth so long getting the jug? Aunt Becky lay impassive, gazing immovably at a plaster decoration on the ceiling which, Stanton Grundy reflected, looked exactly like a sore. Drowned John nearly blew the roof off with one of his famous sneezes and half the women jumped nervously. Uncle Pippin absent-mindedly began to hum *Nearer My God to Thee,* but was squelched by a glare from William Y. Oswald Dark suddenly came to the open window and looked in at these foolish and distracted people.

"Satan has just passed the door," he said in his intense dramatic fashion.

"What a blessing he didn't come in," said Uncle Pippin imperturbably. But Rachel Penhallow was disturbed. It had seemed so *real* when the Moon Man said it. She wished Uncle Pippin would not be so flippant and jocose. Every one again wondered why Ambrosine didn't come in with the jug. Had she taken a weak spell? Couldn't she find it? Had she dropped and broken it on the garret floor?

Then Ambrosine entered, like a priestess bearing a chalice. She placed the jug on the little round table between the two rooms. A sigh of relieved tension went over the assemblage, succeeded by an almost painful stillness. Ambrosine went back and sat down at Aunt Becky's right hand. Miss Jackson was sitting on the left.

"Good gosh," whispered Stanton Grundy to Uncle Pippin, "did you ever see three such ugly women living together in your life?"

That night at three o'clock Uncle Pippin woke up and thought of a marvellous retort he might have made to Stanton Grundy. But at the time he could think of absolutely nothing to say. So he turned his back on Stanton and gazed at the jug, as every one else was doing—some covetously, a few indifferently, all with the interest natural to this exhibition of an old family heirloom they had been hearing about all their lives and had had few and far between opportunities of seeing.

Nobody thought the jug very beautiful in itself. Taste must have changed notably in a hundred years if anybody had ever thought it beautiful. Yet it was undoubtedly a delectable thing, with its history and its legend, and even Tempest Dark leaned forward to get a better view of it. A thing like that, he reflected, deserved a certain reverence because it was the symbol of a love it had outlasted on earth and so had a sacredness of its own.

It was an enormous, pot-bellied thing of a type that had been popular in pre-Victorian days. George the Fourth had been king when the old Dark jug came into being. Half its nose was gone and a violent crack extended around its middle. The decorations consisted of pink-gilt scrolls, green and brown leaves and red and blue roses. On one side was a picture of two convivial tars, backed with the British Ensign and the Union Jack, who had evidently been imbibing deeply of the cup which cheers *and* inebriates, and who were expressing the feelings of their inmost hearts in singing the verse printed above them:

Thus smiling at peril at sea or on shore
We'll box the old compass right cheerly,
Pass the grog, boys, about, with a song or two more,
Then we'll drink to the girls we love dearly.

On the opposite side the designer of the jug, whose strong point had not been spelling, had filled in the vacant place with a pathetic verse from Byron:

The man is doomed to sail
With the blast of the gale
Through billows attalantic to steer.
As he bends o'er the wave
Which may soon be his grave
He remembers his home with a tear.

Rachel Penhallow felt a tear start to her eyes and roll down her long face as she read it. It had been, she thought mournfully, so sadly prophetic.

In the middle of the jug, below its broken nose, was a name and date. Harriet Dark, Aldboro, 1826, surrounded by a wreath of pink and green tied with a true-lover's knot. The jug was full of old pot-pourri and the room was instantly filled with its faint fragrance—a delicate spicy smell, old-maidishly sweet, virginally elusive, yet with such penetrating, fleeting suggestions of warm passion and torrid emotions. Everybody in the room suddenly felt its influence. For one infinitesimal moment Joscelyn and Hugh looked at each other—Margaret Penhallow was young again—Virginia put her hand over Donna's in a convulsive grasp—Thora Dark moved restlessly—and a strange expression flickered over Lawson Dark's face. Uncle Pippin caught it as it vanished and felt his scalp crinkle. For just a second, he thought Lawson was remembering.

Even Drowned John found himself recalling how pretty and flower-like Jennie had been when he married her. What a hell of

280

a pity one couldn't stay always young.

Every one present knew the romantic story of the old Dark jug. Harriet Dark, who had been sleeping for one hundred years in a quaint English churchyard, had been a slim fair creature with faint rose cheeks and big grey eyes, in 1826, with a gallant sea-captain for a lover. And this lover, on what proved to be his last voyage, had sailed to Amsterdam and there had caused to be made the jug of scroll and verse and true-lover's knot for a birthday gift to his Harriet, it being the fashion of the time to give the lady of your heart such a robust and capacious jug. Alas for true loves and true lovers! On the voyage home the Captain was drowned. The jug was sent to the broken-hearted Harriet. Hearts *did* break a hundred years ago, it is said. A year later Harriet, her spring of love so suddenly turned to autumn, was buried in the Aldboro churchyard and the jug passed into the keeping of her sister, Sarah Dark, who had married her cousin, Robert Penhallow. Sarah, being perhaps of a practical and unromantic turn of mind, used the jug to hold the black currant jam for the concoction of which she was noted. Six years later, when Robert Penhallow decided to emigrate to Canada, his wife carried the jug with her, full of black currant jam. The voyage was long and stormy; the currant jam was all eaten; and the jug was broken by some mischance into three large pieces. But Sarah Penhallow was a resourceful woman. When she was finally settled in her new home, she took the jug and mended it carefully with white lead. It was done thoroughly and lastingly but not exactly artistically. Sarah smeared the white lead rather lavishly over the cracks, pressing it down with her capable thumb. And in a good light to this very day the lines of Sarah Penhallow's thumb could be clearly seen in the hardened spats of white lead.

Thereafter for years Sarah Penhallow kept the jug in her dairy, filled with cream skimmed from her broad, golden-brown, earthenware milk-pans. On her death-bed she had given it to her daughter Rachel, who had married Thomas Dark. Rachel Dark left it to her son Theodore. By this time it had been advanced to the dignity of an heirloom and was no longer degraded to menial uses. Aunt Becky kept it in her china cabinet, and it was passed around and its story told at all clan gatherings. It was said a collector had offered Aunt Becky a fabulous sum for it. But no Dark or Penhallow would ever have dreamed of selling such a household god. Absolutely it must remain in the family. To whom would Aunt Becky give it? This was the question every one in the room was silently asking; Aunt Becky alone knew the answer and she did not mean to be in any hurry to give it. This was her last levee; she had much to do and still more to say before she came to the question of the jug at all. She was going to take her time about it and enjoy it. She knew perfectly well that what she was going to do would set everybody by the ears, but all she regretted was that she would not be alive to see the sport. Look at all those female animals with their eyes popping out at the jug! Aunt Becky began to laugh and laughed until her bed shook.

"I think," she said, finally, wiping the tears of mirth from her eyes, "that a solemn assembly like this should be opened with prayer."

This was by way of being a bombshell. Who but Aunt Becky would have thought of such a thing? Everybody looked at each other and then at David Dark, who was the only man in the clan who was known to have a gift of prayer. David Dark was usually very ready to lead in prayer, but he was not prepared for this.

"David," said Aunt Becky inexorably. "I'm sorry to say this clan haven't the reputation of wearing their knees out praying. I shall have to ask you to do the proper thing."

His wife looked at him appealingly. She was very proud because her husband could make such fine prayers. She forgave him all else for it, even the fact that he made all his family go to bed early to save kerosene and had a dreadful habit of licking his fingers after eating tarts. David's prayers were her only claim to distinction, and she was afraid he was going to refuse now.

David, poor wretch, had no intention of refusing, much as he disliked the prospect. To do so would offend Aunt Becky and lose him all chance of the jug. He cleared his throat and rose to his feet. Everybody bowed. Outside the two Sams, realizing what was going on as David's sonorous voice floated out to them, took their pipes out of their mouths. David's prayer was not up to his best, as his wife admitted to herself, but it was an eloquent and appropriate petition and David felt himself badly used when after his "Amen" Aunt Becky said:

"Giving God information isn't praying, David. It's just as well to leave something to His imagination, you know. But I suppose you did your best. Thank you. By the way, do you remember the time, forty years ago, when you put Aaron Dark's old ram in the church basement?"

David looked silly and Mrs David was indignant. Aunt Becky certainly had a vile habit of referring in company to whatever incident in your life you were most anxious to forget. But she was like that. And you couldn't resent it if you wanted the jug. The David Darks managed a feeble smile.

"Noel," thought Gay, "is leaving the bank now."

"I wonder," said Aunt Becky reflectively, "who was the first man who ever prayed. And what he prayed for. And how many prayers have been uttered since then."

"And how many have been answered," said Naomi Dark, speaking bitterly and suddenly for the first time.

"Perhaps William Y. could throw some light on that," chuckled Uncle Pippin maliciously. "I understand he keeps a systematic record of all his prayers, which are answered and which ain't. How about it, William Y.?"

"It averages up about fifty-fifty," said William Y. solemnly, not understanding at all why some were giggling. "I am bound to say, though," he added, "that some of the answers were—peculiar."

As for Ambrosine Winkworth, David had made an enemy for life of her because he had referred to her as "Thine aged handmaiden." Ambrosine shot a venomous glance at David.

"Aged—aged," she muttered rebelliously. "Why, I'm only seventy-two—not so old as all that—not so old."

283

"Hush, Ambrosine," said Aunt Becky authoritatively. "It's a long time since you were young. Put another cushion under my head. Thanks. I'm going to have the fun of reading my own will. And I've had the fun of writing my own obituary. It's going to be printed just as I've written it, too. Camilla has sworn to see to that. Good Lord, the obituaries I've read! Listen to mine."

Aunt Becky produced a folded paper from under her pillow.

"'No gloom was cast over the communities of Indian Spring, Three Hills, Rose River or Bay Silver when it became known that Mrs Theodore Dark—Aunt Becky as she was generally called, less from affection than habit—had died on'—whatever the date will be—*'at the age of eighty-five.'*

"You notice," said Aunt Becky, interrupting herself, "that I say *died*. I shall not pass away or pass out or pay my debt to nature or depart this life or join the great majority or be summoned to my long home. I intend simply and solely to die.

"'Everybody concerned felt that it was high time the old lady did die. She had lived a long life, respectably if not brilliantly, had experienced almost everything a decent female could experience, had outlived husband and children and anybody who had ever really cared anything for her. There was therefore neither sense, reason nor profit in pretending gloom or grief. The funeral took place on'—whatever date it does take place on—*'from the home of Miss Camilla Jackson at Indian Spring. It was a cheerful funeral, in accordance with Aunt Becky's strongly expressed wish, the arrangements being made by Mr Henry Trent, undertaker, Rose River.'*

"Henry will never forgive me for not calling him a mortician," said Aunt Becky. "Mortician—Humph! But Henry has a genius for arranging funerals and I've picked on him to plan mine.

"'Flowers were omitted by request'—no horrors of funeral wreaths for me, mind. No bought harps and pillows and crosses. But if anybody cares to bring a bouquet from their own garden, they may—*'and the services were conducted by the Rev. Mr Trackley of Rose River. The pall-bearers were Hugh Dark, Robert*

Dark'—mind you don't stumble, Dandy, as you did at Selina Dark's funeral. What a jolt you must have given the poor old girl—*'Palmer Dark, Homer Penhallow'*—put them on opposite sides of the casket so they can't fight—*'Murray Dark, Roger Penhallow, David Dark, and John Penhallow'*—Drowned John, mind you, not that simpering nincompoop at Bay Silver—*'who contrived to get through the performance without swearing as he did at his father's funeral.'*"

"I didn't," shouted Drowned John furiously, springing to his feet. "And don't you dare publish such a thing about me in your damned obituary. You—you—"

"Sit down, John, sit down. That really isn't in the obituary. I just stuck it in this minute to get a rise out of you. Sit down."

"I didn't swear at my father's funeral," muttered Drowned John sullenly as he obeyed.

"Well, maybe it was your mother's. Don't interrupt me again please. Courtesy costs nothing as the Scotchman said. *'Aunt Becky was born a Presbyterian, lived a Presbyterian, and died a Presbyterian. She had a hard man to please in Theodore Dark, but she made him quite as good a wife as he deserved. She was a good neighbour as neighbours go and did not quarrel more than anybody else in the clan. She had a knack of taking the wind out of people's sails that did not make for popularity. She seldom suffered in silence. Her temper was about the average, neither worse nor better and did not sweeten as she grew older. She always behaved herself decently, although many a time it would have been a relief to be indecent. She told the truth almost always, thereby doing a great deal of good and some harm, but she could tell a lie without straining her conscience when people asked questions they had no business to ask. She occasionally used a naughty word under great stress and she could listen to a risky story without turning white around the gills, but obscenity never took the place of wit with her. She paid her debts, went to church regularly, thought gossip was very interesting, liked to be the first to hear a piece of news, and was always especially interested in things that were none of her business. She could see a baby without wanting to eat it, but she was always a very good mother to her own. She longed for freedom, as all women do, but had sense enough to understand that real freedom is impossible in this kind of a world, the lucky people being those who can choose their masters, so she never made the mistake of kicking uselessly over the traces. Sometimes she was mean, treacherous and greedy. Sometimes she was generous, faithful and unselfish. In short, she was an average person who had lived as long as anybody should live.'*

"There," said Aunt Becky, tucking her obituary under the pillow, quite happy in the assurance that she had made a sensation. "You will observe that I have not called myself 'the late Mrs Dark' or 'the deceased lady' or 'relict.' And that's that."

"God bless me, did you ever hear the equal of that?" muttered Uncle Pippin blankly.

Every one else was silent in a chill of outraged horror. Surely—surely—that appalling document would never be published. It must *not* be published, if anything short of the assassination of Camilla Jackson could prevent it. Why, strangers would suppose it had been written by some surviving member of the clan.

But Aunt Becky was bringing out another document, and all the Darks and Penhallows bottled up their indignation for the time being and uncorked their ears. Who was to get the jug? Until that was settled the matter of the obituary would be left in abeyance.

Aunt Becky unfolded her will, and settled her owlish shell-ringed glasses on her beaky nose.

"I've left my little bit of money to Camilla for her life," she said. "After her death it's to go to the hospital in Charlottetown."

Aunt Becky looked sharply over the throng. But she did not see any particular disappointment. To do the Darks and Penhallows justice, they were not money-grabbers. No one grudged Camilla Jackson her legacy. Money was a thing one could and should earn for oneself; but old family heirlooms, crusted with the sentiment of dead and gone hopes and fears for generations, were different matters. Suppose Aunt Becky left the jug to some rank outsider? Or a museum? She was quite capable of it. If she did, William Y. Penhallow mentally registered a vow that he would see his lawyer about it.

"Any debts are to be paid," continued Aunt Becky, "and my grave is to be heaped up—not left flat. I insist on that. Make a note of it, Artemas."

Artemas Dark nodded uncomfortably. He was caretaker of the Rose River graveyard, and he knew he would have trouble with the cemetery committee about that. Besides, it made it so confoundedly difficult to mow. Aunt Becky probably read his thoughts, for she said:

"I won't have a lawn-mower running over me. You can clip my grave nicely with the shears. I've left directions for my tombstone, too. I want one as big as anybody else's. And I want my lace shawl draped around me in my coffin. It's the only thing I mean to take with me. Theodore gave it to me when Ronald was born. There were times when Theodore could do as graceful a thing as anybody. It's as good as new. I've always kept it wrapped in silver paper at the bottom of my third bureau drawer. Remember, Camilla."

Camilla nodded. The first sign of disappointment appeared on Mrs Clifford Penhallow's face. She had set her heart on getting the lace shawl, for she feared she had very little chance of getting the jug. The shawl was said to have cost Theodore Dark two hundred dollars. To think of burying two hundred dollars!

Mrs Toynbee Dark, who had been waiting all the afternoon for an opportunity to cry, thought she saw it at the mention of Aunt Becky's baby son who had been dead for sixty years, and got out her handkerchief. But Aunt Becky headed her off.

"Don't start crying yet, Alicia. By the way, while I think of it, will you tell me something? I've always wanted to know and I'll never have another chance. Which of your three husbands did you like best—Morton Dark, Edgar Penhallow, or Toynbee Dark? Come now, make a clean breast of it."

Mrs Toynbee put her handkerchief back in her bag and shut the latter with a vicious snap.

"I had a deep affection for all my partners," she said.

Aunt Becky wagged her head.

"Why didn't you say 'deceased' partners? You were thinking it, you know. You have that type of mind. Alicia, tell me honestly, don't you think you ought to have been more economical with husbands? Three! And poor Mercy and Margaret there haven't been able even to get one."

Mercy reflected bitterly that if *she* had employed the methods Alicia Dark had, she might have had husbands and to spare, too. Margaret coloured softly and looked piteous. Why, oh, why, must cruel old Aunt Becky hold her up to public ridicule like this?

"I've divided all my belongings among you," said Aunt Becky. "I hate the thought of dying and leaving all my nice things. But since it must be, I'm not going to have any quarrelling over them before I'm cold in my grave. Everything's down here in black and white. I've just left the things according to my own whims. I'll read the list. And let me say that the fact that any one of you gets something doesn't mean that you've no chance for the jug as well. I'm coming to that later."

Aunt Becky took off her spectacles, polished them, put them on again, and took a drink of water. Drowned John nearly groaned with impatience. Heaven only knew how long it would be before she would get to the jug. He had no interest in her other paltry knick-knacks.

"Mrs Denzil Penhallow is to have my pink china candlesticks," announced Aunt Becky. "I know you'll be delighted at this, Martha dear. You've given me so many hints about candlesticks."

Mrs Denzil had wanted Aunt Becky's beautiful silver Georgian candlesticks. And now she was saddled with a pair of unspeakable china horrors, in colour a deep magenta-pink with what looked like black worms wriggling all over them. But she tried to look pleased, because if she didn't, it might spoil her chances for the jug. Denzil scowled, jug or no jug, and Aunt

Becky saw it. Pompous old Denzil! She would get even with him.

"I remember when Denzil was about five years old he came down to my place with his mother, one day, and our old turkey gobbler took after him. I suppose the poor bird thought no one else had a right to be strutting around there. 'Member, Denzil? Lord, how you ran and blubbered! You certainly thought Old Nick was after you. Do you know, Denzil, I've never seen you parading up the church aisle since but I've thought of that."

Well, it had to be endured. Denzil cleared his throat and endured it.

"I haven't much jewellery," Aunt Becky was saying. "Two rings. One is an opal. I'm giving that to Virginia Powell. They say it brings bad luck, but you're too modern to believe that old superstition, Virginia. Though *I* never had any luck after I got it."

Virginia tried to look happy, though she had wanted the Chinese screen. As for luck or no luck, how could that matter? Life was over for her. Nobody grudged her the opal, but when Aunt Becky mentioned rings many ears were pricked up. Who would get her diamond ring? It was a fine one and worth several hundreds of dollars.

"Ambrosine Winkworth is to have my diamond ring," said Aunt Becky.

Half those present could not repress a gasp of disapproval and the collective effect was quite pronounced. This, thought the gaspers, was absurd. Ambrosine Winkworth had no right whatever to that ring. And what good would it do her—an old broken-down servant? Really, Aunt Becky's brain must be softening.

"Here it is, Ambrosine," said Aunt Becky, taking it from her bony finger and handing it to the trembling Ambrosine. "I'll give it to you now, so there'll be no mistake. Put it on."

Ambrosine obeyed. Her old wrinkled face was aglow with the joy of a long-cherished dream suddenly and unexpectedly realized. Ambrosine Winkworth, through a drab life spent in other people's kitchens, had hankered all through that life for a diamond ring. She had never hoped to have it; and now here it was on her hand, a great starry wonderful thing, glittering in the June sunshine that fell through the window. Everything came true for Ambrosine in that moment. She asked no more of fate.

Perhaps Aunt Becky had divined that wistful dream of the old woman. Or perhaps she had just given Ambrosine the ring to annoy the clan. If the latter, she had certainly succeeded. Nan Penhallow was especially furious. *She* should have the diamond ring. Thekla Penhallow felt the same way. Joscelyn, who once had had a diamond ring, Donna, who still had one, and Gay, who expected she soon would have one, looked amused and indifferent. Chuckling to herself Aunt Becky picked up her will and gave Mrs Clifford Penhallow her Chinese screen.

"As if I wanted her old Chinese screen," thought Mrs Clifford, almost on the point of tears.

Margaret Penhallow was the only one whom nobody envied. She got Aunt Becky's *Pilgrim's Progress*, a very old, battered book. The covers had been sewed on; the leaves were yellow with age. One was afraid to touch it lest it might fall to pieces. It was a most disreputable old volume which Theodore Dark, for some unknown reason, had prized when alive. Since his death, Aunt Becky had kept it in an old box in the garret where it had got musty and dusty. But Margaret was not disappointed. She had expected nothing.

"My green pickle leaf is to go to Rachel Penhallow," said Aunt Becky.

Rachel's long face grew longer. She had wanted the Apostle spoons. But Gay Penhallow got the Apostle spoons—to her surprise and delight. They were quaint and lovely, and would accord charmingly with a certain little house of dreams that was faintly taking shape in her imagination. Aunt Becky looked at Gay's sparkling face with less grimness than she usually showed and proceeded to give her dinner-set to Mrs Howard Penhallow, who wanted the Chippendale sideboard.

"It was my wedding-set," said Aunt Becky. "There's only one

piece broken. Theodore brought his fist down on the cover of one of the tureens one day when he got excited in an argument at dinner. I won out in the argument, though—at least I got my own way, tureen or no tureen. Emily, you're to have the bed."

Mrs Emily Frost, *née* Dark, a gentle, faded little person, who also had yearned for the Apostle spoons, tried to look grateful for a bed which was too big for any of her tiny rooms. And Mrs Alpheus Penhallow, who wanted the bed, had to put up with the Chippendale sideboard. Donna Dark got an old egg-dish in the guise of a gaily coloured china hen sitting on a yellow china nest, and was glad because she had liked the old thing when she was a child. Joscelyn Dark got the claw-footed mahogany table Mrs Palmer Dark had hoped for, and Roger Dark got the Georgian candlesticks and Mrs Denzil's eternal hatred. The beautiful old Queen Anne bookcase went to Murray Dark, who never read books, and Hugh Dark got the old hour-glass—early eighteenth century—and wondered bitterly what use it would be to a man for whom time had stopped ten years ago. He knew, none better, how long an hour can be and what devastating things can happen in it.

"Crosby, you're to have my old cut-glass whisky decanter," Aunt Becky was saying. "There hasn't been any whisky in it for many a year, more's the pity. It'll hold the water you're always drinking in the night. I heard you admire it once."

Old Crosby Penhallow, who had been nodding, wakened up and looked pleased. He really hadn't expected anything. It was kind of Becky to remember him. They had been young together.

Aunt Becky looked at him—at his smooth, shining bald head, his sunken blue eyes, his toothless mouth. Old Crosby would never have false teeth. Yet in spite of the bald head and faded eyes and shrunken mouth, Crosby Dark was not an ill-looking old man—quite the reverse.

"I have a mind to tell you something, Crosby," said Aunt Becky. "*You* never knew it—nobody ever knew it—but you were the only man I ever loved."

291

The announcement made a sensation. Everybody—so ridiculous is outworn passion—wanted to laugh but dared not. Crosby blushed painfully all over his wrinkled face. Hang it all, was old Becky making fun of him? And whether or no, how dared she make a show of him like this before everybody?

"I was quite mad about you," said Aunt Becky musingly. "Why? I don't know. You were handsomer sixty years ago than any man has a right to be, but you had no brains. Yet you were the man for me. And you never looked at me. You married Annette Dark— and I married Theodore. Nobody knows how much I hated him when I married him. But I got quite fond of him after awhile. That's life, you know—though those three romantic young geese here, Gay and Donna and Virginia, think I'm talking rank heresy. I got over caring for you in time, even though for years after I did, my heart used to beat like mad every time I saw you walk up the church aisle with your meek little Annette trotting behind you. I got a lot of thrills out of loving you, Crosby—many more I don't doubt than if I'd married you. And Theodore was really a much better husband for me than you'd have been—he had a sense of humour. And it doesn't matter now whether he was or wasn't. I don't even wish now that you had loved me, though I wished it for so many years. Lord, the nights I couldn't sleep for thinking of you—and Theodore snoring beside me. But there it is. Somehow, I've always wanted you to know it and at last I've had the courage to tell you."

Old Crosby wiped his brow with his handkerchief. Erasmus would never let him hear the last of this—never. And suppose it got into the papers! If he had dreamed anything like this was going to happen, he would never have come to the levee. He glowered at the jug. It was to blame, durn it.

"I wonder how many of us will get out of this alive," whispered Stanton Grundy to Uncle Pippin.

But Aunt Becky had switched over to Penny Dark and was giving him her bottle of Jordan water.

"What the deuce do I care for Jordan water," thought Penny.

Perhaps his face was too expressive, for Aunt Becky suddenly grinned dangerously.

"Mind the time, Penny, you moved a vote of thanks to Rob Dufferin on the death of his wife?"

There was a chorus of laughs of varying timbre, among which Drowned John's boomed like an earthquake. Penny's thoughts were as profane as the others' had been. That a little mistake between thanks and condolence, made in the nervousness of public speaking, should be everlastingly coming up against a man like this. From old Aunt Becky, too, who had just confessed that most of her life she had loved a man who wasn't her husband, the scandalous old body.

Mercy Penhallow sighed. *She* would have liked the Jordan water. Rachel Penhallow had one and Mercy had always envied her for it. There must be a blessing in any household that had a bottle of Jordan water. Aunt Becky heard the sigh and looked at Mercy.

"Mercy," she said apropos of nothing, "do you remember that forgotten pie you brought out after everybody had finished eating at the Stanley Penhallow's silver-wedding dinner?"

But Mercy was not afraid of Aunt Becky. She had a spirit of her own.

"Yes, I do. And do *you* remember, Aunt Becky, that the first time *you* killed and roasted a chicken after you were married, you brought it to the table with the insides still in it?"

Nobody dared to laugh, but everybody was glad Mercy had the spunk. Aunt Becky nodded undisturbed.

"Yes, and I remember how it smelled! We had company, too. I don't think Theodore ever fully forgave me. I thought that had been forgotten years ago. *Is* anything ever forgotten? Can people *ever* live anything down? The honours are to you, Mercy, but I must get square with somebody. Junius Penhallow, do *you* remember—since Mercy has started digging up the past—how drunk you were at your wedding?"

Junius Penhallow turned a violent crimson but couldn't deny

it. Of what use was it, with Mrs Junius at his elbow, to plead that he had been in such a blue funk on his wedding-morning that he'd never have had the courage to go through with it if he hadn't got drunk? He had never been drunk since, and it was hard to have it raked up now, when he was an elder in the church and noted for his avowed temperance principles.

"I'm not the only one who ever got drunk in this clan," he dared to mutter, despite the jug.

"No, to be sure. There's Artemas over there. Do you remember, Artemas, the evening you walked up the church aisle in your nightshirt?"

Artemas, a tall, raw-boned, red-haired fellow, had been too drunk on that occasion to remember it, but he always roared when reminded of it. He thought it the best joke ever.

"You should have all been thankful I had that much on myself," he said with a chuckle.

Mrs Artemas wished she were dead. What was a joke to Artemas was a tragedy to her. She had never forgotten—never could forget—the humiliation of that unspeakable evening. She had forgiven Artemas certain violations of his marriage vow of which every one was aware. But she had never forgiven—never would forgive—the episode of the nightshirt. If it had been pyjamas, it would not have been quite so terrible. But in those days pyjamas were unknown.

Aunt Becky was at Mrs Conrad Dark.

"I'm giving you my silver saltcellars. Alec Dark's mother gave them to me for a wedding-present. Do you remember the time you and Mrs Clifford there quarrelled over Alec Dark and she slapped your face? And neither of you got Alec after all. There, there, don't crack the spectrum. It's all dead and vanished, just like my affair with Crosby."

("As if there was ever any affair," thought Crosby piteously.)

"Pippin's to have my grandfather clock. Mrs Digby Dark thinks she should have that because her father gave it to me. But no. Do you remember, Fanny, that you once put a tract in a book you lent me? Do you know what I did with it? I used it for curl papers. I've never forgiven you for the insult. Tracts, indeed. Did I need tracts?"

"You—weren't a member of the church," said Mrs Digby, on the point of tears.

"No—nor am yet. Theodore and I could never agree which church to join. I wanted Rose River and he wanted Bay Silver. And after he died it seemed sort of disrespectful to his memory to join Rose River. Besides, I was so old then it would have seemed funny. Marrying and church-joining should be done in youth. But I was as good a Christian as any one. Naomi Dark."

Naomi, who had been fanning Lawson, looked up with a start as Aunt Becky hurled her name at her.

"You're to get my Wedgwood teapot. It's a pretty thing. Cauliflower pattern, as it's called, picked out with gold lustre. It's the only thing it really hurts me to give up. Letty gave it to me—she bought it at a sale in town with some of her first quarter's salary. Have you all forgotten Letty? It's forty years since she died. She would have been sixty if she were living now—as old as you, Fanny. Oh, I know you don't own to more than fifty, but you and Letty were born within three weeks of each other. It seems funny to think of Letty being sixty—she was always so young—she was the youngest thing I ever knew. I used to wonder how Theodore and I ever produced her. She *couldn't* have been sixty ever—that's why she had to die. After all, it was better. It hurt me to have her die—but I think it would have hurt me more to see her sixty—wrinkled—faded—grey-haired—my pretty Letty, like a rose tossing in a breeze. Have you all forgotten that gold hair of hers—such *living* hair? Be good to her teapot, Naomi. Well, that's the end of my valuable belongings—except the jug. I'm a bit tired—I want a rest before I tackle *that* business. I'm going to ask you all to sit in absolute silence for ten minutes and think about a question I'm going to ask you at the end of that time—all of you who are over forty. How many of you would like to live your lives over again if you could?"

X

Another whim of Aunt Becky's! They resigned themselves to it with what grace they could. A silence of ten minutes seems like a century—under certain conditions. Aunt Becky lay as if tranquilly asleep. Ambrosine was gazing raptly at her diamond ring. Hugh thought about the night of his wedding. Margaret tried to compose a verse of her new poem. Drowned John became conscious that his new boots were exceedingly tight and uncomfortable and uneasily remembered his new litter of pigs. He ought to be home attending to them. Uncle Pippin wondered irritably what that fellow Grundy was looking so amused about. Uncle Pippin would have been still more scandalized had he known that Grundy was imagining himself God, rearranging all these twisted lives properly, and enjoying himself hugely. Murray Dark devoured Thora with his eyes and Thora went on placidly shining with her own light. Gay began to pick out her flower-girls. Little Jill Penhallow and little Chrissie Dark. They were such darlings. They must wear pink and yellow crêpe and carry baskets of pink and yellow flowers—roses or 'mums, according to the time of year. Palmer Dark enjoyed in imagination the pleasure of kicking Homer Penhallow. Old Crosby was asleep and old Miller was nodding. Mercy Penhallow sat stiffly still and criticized the universe. Many of them were already sore and disappointed; nerves were strained and tenuous; when Junius Penhallow cleared his throat the sound was like a blasphemy.

"Two minutes more of this and I shall throw back my head and howl," thought Donna Dark. She suddenly felt sick and tired of the whole thing—of the whole clan—of her whole tame existence. What was she living for, anyhow? She felt as out of place as the blank, unfaded space left on the wall where a picture had hung. Life had no meaning—this silly little round of gossip and venom and malicious laughter. Here was a roomful of people ready to fly at each other's throats because of an old broken-nosed jug and a few paltry knick-knacks. She forgot that she had been as keen as anybody about the jug when she came. She wondered impatiently if anything pleasant or interesting or thrilling were ever going to happen to her again. Drowned John's early wanderlust suddenly emerged in her. She wanted to have wings—wide sweeping wings to fly into the sunset—skim over the waves—battle with the winds—soar to the stars—in short, do everything that was never done by her smug, prosperous, sensible home-keeping clan. She was in rebellion against all the facts of her life. Probably the whole secret of Donna's unrest at that moment was simply a lack of oxygen in the air. But it came pat to the psychological moment.

The sudden and lasting cessation of all the undertones and rustlings and stirrings in the room behind them at first arrested the attention and finally aroused the wonder of the outsiders on the veranda. Peter, who never knew why he should not gratify his curiosity about anything the moment he felt it, got off the railing, walked to the open window, and looked in. The first thing he saw was the discontented face of Donna Dark, who was sitting by the opposite window in the shadow of a great pine outside. Its emerald gloom threw still darker shadows on her glossy hair and deepened the lustre of her long blue eyes. She turned towards Peter's window as he laid his arms on the sill and bent inward. It was one of those moments all the rest of life can't undo. Their eyes met, Donna's richly quilled about with dark lashes, somewhat turbulent and mutinous under eyebrows flying up like little wings, Peter's grey and amazed, under a puzzled frown.

Then it happened.

Neither Donna nor Peter knew at first just what *had* happened. They only knew *something* had. Peter continued to stare at Donna as if mesmerized. Who was this creature of strange dark loveliness? She must be one of the clan or she wouldn't be here, but he couldn't place her at all. Wait—wait—what old memory flickered tantalizingly before him—now approaching—now receding? He *must* grasp it—the old church at Rose River—himself, a boy of twelve sitting in his father's pew—across

297

the aisle a little girl of eight—blue-eyed, black-haired, wing-browed—a little girl, *sitting in Drowned John's pew!* He knew he must hate her because she sat in Drowned John's pew. So he made an impudent face at her. And the little girl had laughed—*laughed*. She was amused at him. Peter, who had hated her before impersonally, hated her now personally. He had kept on hating her although he had never seen her again—never again till now. Now he was looking at her across Aunt Becky's parlour. At that moment Peter understood what had happened to him. He was no longer a free man—forevermore he must be in the power of this pale girl. He had fallen in love fathoms deep with Drowned John's daughter and Barry Dark's detested widow. Since he never did anything by halves he did not fall in love by halves either.

Peter felt a bit dizzy. It is a staggering thing to look in at a casual window and see the woman you now realize you have been subconsciously waiting for all your life. It is a still more staggering thing to have your hate suddenly dissolve into love, as though your very bones had melted to water. It rather lets you down. Peter was actually afraid to try to walk back to the veranda railing for fear his legs would give way. He knew, without stopping to argue with himself about it, that he would take no train from Three Hills that night and the lure of Amazon jungles had ceased—temporarily at least—to exist. Mystery and magic enfolded Peter as a garment. What he wanted to do was to vault over the window-sill, hurl aside those absurd men and women sitting between them, snatch up Donna Dark, strip off those ridiculous weeds she was wearing for another man, and carry her off bodily. It was quite on the cards that he would have done it—Peter had such a habit of doing everything he wanted to do—but at that moment the ten-minute silence was over and Aunt Becky opened her eyes. Everybody sighed with relief, and Peter, finding that all eyes were directed towards him, dragged himself back to the railing and sat on it, trying to collect his scattered wits and able only to see that subtle, deep-eyed face with its skin as delicate as a white night moth, under its cap of flat dark hair.

Well, he had fallen in love with Donna Dark. He realized that he had been sent there by the powers that govern to fall in love with her. It was predestined in the councils of eternity that he should look through that particular window at that particular moment. Good heavens, the years he had wasted insensately hating her! Hopeless idiot! Blind bat! Now the only thing to do was to marry her as quickly as possible. Everything else could wait, but that could not. Even finding out what Donna thought about it could wait.

Donna could hardly be said to be thinking at all. She was not quite so quick as Peter was at finding out what had happened to her. She had recognized Peter the moment she had seen him—partly from that same old memory of an impudent boy across the aisle, partly from his photographs in the papers. Though they weren't good of him—not half as fascinating. Peter hated being photographed and always glared at the camera as if it were a foe. Still, Donna knew him for her enemy—and for something else.

She was trembling with the extraordinary excitement that tingled over her at the sight of him—she, who, a few seconds before, had been so bored—so tired—so disgusted that she wished she had the courage to poison herself.

She was sure Virginia noticed it. Oh, if he would only go away and not stand there at the window staring at her. She knew he was leaving for South America that night—she had heard Nancy Penhallow telling it to Mrs Homer. Donna put her hand up to her throat, as if she were choking. What was the matter with her? Who cared if Peter Penhallow went to the Amazon or the Congo? It was not she, not Donna Dark, Barry's inconsolable widow, who cared. Certainly not. It was this queer, wild, primitive creature who had, without any warning, somehow usurped her body and only wanted to spring to the window and feel Peter's arms around her. There is no saying but that this perfectly crazy impulse might have mastered Donna if Aunt Becky had not opened her eyes and Peter had not vanished from the window.

Donna gave a gasp, which, coming after the universal sigh,

escaped the notice of everybody but Virginia, who laid her hand over Donna's and squeezed it sympathetically.

"Darling, I saw it all. It must have been frightfully hard for you. You bore it splendidly."

"What—what did I bear?" stammered Donna idiotically.

"Why, seeing that dreadful Peter Penhallow staring at you like that—with his hate fairly sticking out of his eyes."

"Hate—hate—oh, do you think he hates me—really?" gasped Donna.

"Of course he does. He always has, ever since you married Barry. But you won't run the risk of meeting him again, darling. He's off to-night on some of his horrid explorations, so don't worry over it."

Donna was not worrying exactly. She only felt that she would die if Peter Penhallow did go away—like that—without a word or another glance. It was not to be borne. She would dare uncharted seas with him—she would face African cooking-pots—she would—oh, what mad things was she thinking? And *what* was Aunt Becky saying.

"Every one over forty who would be willing to live his or her life over again exactly as it has been lived, put up your hand."

Tempest Dark was the only one who put up his hand.

"Brave man! Or fortunate man—which?" inquired Aunt Becky satirically.

"Fortunate," said Tempest laconically. He *had* been fortunate. He had fifteen exquisite years with Winnifred Penhallow. He would face anything to have them again.

"Would *you* live your life over again, Donna?" whispered Virginia sentimentally.

"No—*no!!*" Donna felt that to live over again the years that Peter Penhallow had hated her would be unendurable. Virginia looked grieved and amazed. She had not expected such an answer. She felt that something had come between her and Donna— something that clouded the sweet, perfect understanding that had always existed between them. She had been wont to say that words were really unnecessary for them—they could read each other's thoughts. But Virginia could not read Donna's thoughts just now—which was perhaps quite as well. She wondered uneasily if the curse of Aunt Becky's opal was beginning to work already.

"Well, let's get down to business," Aunt Becky was saying.

"Thank the pigs," thought Drowned John fervently.

Aunt Becky looked over the room gloatingly. She had prolonged her sport as long as it was possible. She had got them just where she wanted them—all keyed up and furious—all except a few who were beyond the power of her venom and whom for that reason she did not despise. But look at the rest of them—squatting there on their ham-bones, pop-eyed, coveting the jug, ready to tear in pieces the one who got it. In a few minutes the lucky one would be known, they thought. Ah, would he? Aunt Becky chuckled. She still had a bomb to throw.

XI

"You're all dying to know who is to get the jug," she said, "but you're not going to know yet awhile. I did intend to tell you to-day who I meant to have it, but I've thought of a better plan. I've decided to leave the jug in keeping of a trustee until a year from the last day of next October. *Then,* and not till then, you'll find out who's to get it."

There was a stunned silence—broken by a laugh from Stanton Grundy.

"Sold!" he said laconically.

"Who's the trustee?" said William Y. hoarsely. He knew who *should* be trustee.

"Dandy Dark. I've selected him because he is the only man I ever knew who could keep a secret."

Everyone looked at Robert Dark, who squirmed uncomfortably, thus finding himself the centre of observation. Everybody disapproved. Dandy Dark was a nobody—his nickname told you that. It was a hangover from the days when he *had* been a dandy—something nobody would ever dream of calling the fat, shabby, old fellow now, with his double chin, his unkempt hair and his flabby, pendulous cheeks. Only his little, deep-set, beady black eyes seemed to justify Aunt Becky's opinion of his ability to keep a secret.

"Dandy is to be the sole executor of my will and the custodian of the jug until a year from the last day of next October," repeated Aunt Becky. "That's all the rest of you are to know about it. I'm not going to tell you how it will be decided then. It is possible that I may leave Dandy a sealed letter with the name of the legatee in it. In that case Dandy may know the name or he may not know it. Or it is equally possible that I may leave instructions in that same sealed letter that the ownership is to be settled by lot. And again, I may empower Dandy to choose for himself who is to have the jug, always bearing in his mind my opinions and prejudices regarding certain people and certain things. So in case I have chosen the last alternative, it behooves you all to watch your step from now on. The jug may not be given to any one older than a certain age or to any unmarried person who, in my judgment, should be married, or to any person who has been married too much. It may not be given to any one who has habits I don't like. It may not be given to any one who quarrels or wastes his time fiddling. It may not be given to any one addicted to swearing or drinking. It may not be given to any untruthful person or any dishonest person or any extravagant person. I've always hated to see any one wasting money, even if it isn't mine. It may not be given to any one who has *no* bad habits and never did anything disgraceful"—with a glance in the direction of the impeccable William Y. "It may not be given to any one who begins things and never finishes them, or any one who writes bad poetry. On the other hand, these things may not influence in the slightest my decision or Dandy's decision. And of course if the matter is to be decided by lot, it doesn't matter what you do or don't do.

And finally it may go to somebody who doesn't live on the island at all. Now, you know as much about it as you're going to know."

Aunt Becky sank back on her pillows and enjoyed their expressions. Nobody dared say anything, but how they thought! And looking at each other as if to say,

"Well, *you* won't have much chance. You heard what she said."

All the old bachelors and old maids reflected that they were practically out of it. Titus Dark and Drowned John were marked men because they swore. Chris Penhallow, a queer widower who lived by himself and played the violin when he should have been carpentering, wondered if he could live nearly a year and a half without touching it. Tom Dark, who had stolen a pot of jam from his aunt's pantry when he was a boy, wondered if Aunt Becky meant him when she spoke of dishonest people. Gosh, how hard it was to live some things down. Abel Dark, who had put a staging up to paint his house four years ago but had painted only a small patch and left the staging there, reflected that he really must get down to that job right away. Sim Dark wondered uneasily if Aunt Becky had or had not looked at him when she spoke of untruthful persons. She always seemed able to instil such venom into what she said. As for Penny Dark, the idea struck him then and there that it was time he got married.

Homer Penhallow and Palmer Dark wondered if they hadn't better forswear their ancient grudge. They had always been bad friends, ever since the day in school when a band of boys, headed and incited by Homer Penhallow, had taken the pants off little Palmer Dark and made him walk a mile home in his shirt-tail. Still, though this rankled for years, they had not been open enemies till the affair of the kittens. Homer Penhallow's cat went down to Palmer Dark's barn and had three kittens which were not discovered until they were old enough to run around. Palmer Dark, who was out of cats just then, claimed them as his. Born in his barn and nourished on his premises. Homer wanted the kittens but Palmer, secure in possession, snapped contemptuous fingers at him. Then Homer's cat did an ungrateful thing. She went home and took the kittens with her. Homer was openly triumphant. What a joke on Palmer! Palmer bided his time in an ominous calm. One Sunday when Homer and his family were all in church, Palmer sneaked up to Homer's barn, caught the kittens and carried them home in a bag. Homer's cat came down the next day and succeeded in retrieving one. The other two Palmer kept shut securely up until she had forgotten them. So Palmer thought he had come off best. He had the two handsome striped toms while Homer had only an ugly little spotted tabby, afflicted with a cough. Palmer told the story around the clan, and after that he and Homer were at open feud. This had lasted for years, although all the cats concerned had long since gone where good cats go.

"Now you've found out all you're going to find out, so you can go," said Aunt Becky. "Be sure to think nice thoughts. I leave you all my forgiveness. I've had an amusing afternoon. Heaven will be kind of tame after this, there's no manner of doubt. Speaking of heaven, would any of you like me to do any errands there for you?"

What a question! Nobody answered, although Drowned John would have liked to send word to Toynbee Dark that he had never repaid him the three dollars he had borrowed of him before his death. But as Aunt Becky had never spoken to Toynbee on earth, it was not likely she would do it in heaven, so it would be a waste of breath to ask her. Anyway, it was too late. Aunt Becky was saying,

"Ambrosine, shut the doors."

Ambrosine closed the sliding doors, shutting the table with the jug in with Aunt Becky. Tongues were loosed, though they still talked in undertones. They said all, or most, of the things they had been thinking. There was great dissatisfaction. The Darks felt that they had been slighted; the Penhallows thought the Darks had got everything. The idea of giving old Ambrosine Winkworth the diamond ring!

XII

Drowned John rose and stalked out. There was one thing he could do, and he did it thoroughly. He banged the door.

"Let's leave the females to fight it out," he said. But the men, as soon as they got outside, had plenty to say.

"Would you believe it?" demanded William Y., looking around him as if appealing to the world.

"Nobody got much change out of Aunt Becky, did they?" chuckled Murray Dark.

Dandy Dark was puffing himself out. He had never in all his life been of any importance, save what little accrued from the fact that he was the only man in the countryside who kept a bulldog. And now he had, in a wink, become the most important person in the clan.

"All the weemen will be wishing I was single," he chuckled. But his face was inscrutable—purposely so. No fear of his giving away the secret.

"Too mean to give anything away, even a secret," muttered Artemas Dark.

"The heathen are raging already," said Stanton Grundy to Uncle Pippin. "If that jug doesn't set everybody by the ears in a month's time, may I fight with Irishmen to the end of my life. Keep your eyes buttoned back for sights, Pippin."

"Oh, take in the slack of your jaw," said Uncle Pippin snappishly.

"Well, a nice lot of family skeletons have had a good airing," said Palmer Dark.

"I haven't had as much fun since the dog-fight in church," said Artemas Dark.

"Aunt Becky never liked any of us, you know," said Hugh. "She's bound to get all the rises she can out of us."

"She isn't like any other woman," growled Drowned John.

"Nobody is," said Grundy.

"You don't know much about women, John," said Sim Dark.

No man can endure being told he knows nothing about women—especially if he has coffined two wives. Drowned John went into an icy rage.

"Well, I know something about *you,* Sim Dark, and if you don't stop circulating lies about me as you've been doing for years, you'll have to reckon with me."

"But surely you don't want me to tell the *truth* about you," said Sim in bland amazement.

Drowned John did not reply in words—could not—since he dared not swear so near Aunt Becky. He simply spat.

"It's an outrageous way to leave the jug," growled William Y.

"You should be thankful she didn't make it a condition that everybody should turn a somersault in the church aisle," said Artemas. "She would if she'd thought of it."

"*You* would have liked that, I don't doubt," retorted William Y. "Grinning like a chessy cat over the very thought of it."

Oswald Dark turned around and surveyed the irritated William Y.

"Look at the moon," he said softly, waving his hand at a pale, silver bubble floating over the seaward valley. "Look at the moon," he repeated insistently, laying a long thin hand on the arm of William Y.

"Heavens, I've seen moons before—hundreds of them!" snorted William Y. peevishly.

"But can one see a thing of perfect beauty—like the moon—too often?" inquired Oswald, fixing his large agate eyes questioningly on William Y., who jerked his arm away and turned his back both on Oswald and his moon.

"That jug shouldn't be in a house where there is no responsible woman," said Denzil Penhallow sourly. Everybody knew that Mrs Dandy was as mad as a November partridge by spells.

"If any one has anything to say against my wife he'd better not let me hear him saying it," retorted Dandy ominously. "I'll smash his face for him."

"Any time and any place," said Denzil obligingly.

"Come, come, let us preserve decorum," implored Uncle Pippin nervously.

"Pippin, go home and soak your head in turpentine for three days," boomed Drowned John.

Uncle Pippin subsided. This, he reflected, was what came of Aunt Becky's not giving them anything to eat.

"Devil take the jug," he muttered.

"I doubt if the devil will be so obliging," said the irrepressible Grundy.

The women were coming out now and the men went off to get car or horse, according to purse or age. Tempest Dark, who was walking, sauntered out of the gate, reflecting that he wanted to see this comedy played out. He would live long enough to see who got the jug.

Titus Dark on the way home was importuned by a tearful wife to give up swearing.

"Damn it, I can't," groaned Titus. "And I ain't the only one in the tribe that swears. Take Drowned John."

"Drowned John knows when and when not to swear and you don't," sobbed Mrs Titus. "It's only for a year and a quarter, Titus. You *must*. Dandy'll never give us the jug if you don't."

"I don't believe Dandy'll have a thing to say about it. Aunt Becky wouldn't let any one else decide that," said Titus. "I'd just go for months in misery and not get a da—— not get a blessed thing out of it. Besides, Mary, how is any one going to live with me if I can't swear? When I swear for ten minutes on end a child could eat out of my hand. Isn't that better than bottling it up and thinking murder? Take this horse now. I've just gotter swear at him or he'd never travel. If I talked anything else to him he wouldn't understand what I was saying."

However, Titus had to promise to try. It would, he reflected, be damned hard. These women were so damned unreasonable. But he'd have a go at it, damned if he wouldn't. The race for the jug was on and the devil take the hindmost.

Gay slipped away alone. She knew a certain little ferny corner down the side road where she meant to stop and read Noel's letter. She looked so happy that the Moon Man shook his head at her.

"Take care," he whispered warningly. "It's dangerous to be too happy—those that sit in the high places don't like it. Look how they hide my Lady from me so much of the time."

But Gay only laughed at him and ran on down the side path and out by the side gate under the apple blossoms. Gay loved apple blossoms. It always hurt her that they lasted such a little while—such milky, wonderful things with hearts of love's own hue. To be sure, the roses came afterwards. But if one could only have the apple blossoms and the roses, too. Gay felt greedy of beauty. She wanted every kind all at once, now when life itself seemed just on the point of breaking into some marvellous blossom and all the coming days were in a hurry to be born. Youth is like that. It wants everything at once, not realizing that something must be saved for autumn days. Save? Nonsense! Pour it all out now, a libation to the approaching god. Gay did not think this—she only felt it, hurrying down the road, as sweet and virginal as the apple blossoms.

"A nice little cuddler that, if you ask me," chuckled Stanton Grundy admiringly, giving Uncle Pippin a dig in the ribs.

"I'm not asking you," said Uncle Pippin irritably. *He* had a sense of the fitness of things. Poke fun at old maids and fat married women if you like, but leave young things like Gay alone. Grundy's vulgar chuckle seemed to debase everything. Hadn't that man *any* reverence for anything? And why didn't he read a few halitosis advertisements? Heaven knew the magazines were full of them.

Gay read her letter in her ferny corner and kissed it and put it back in her bosom. There was only one terrible thing in it. Noel said he could not come out till Saturday. They were going to be extra busy in the bank. Had she to live three whole days without seeing him? Could she? A little cluster of silver daisies growing by a lichened old stone nodded at her. She picked one of them—

witch daisies that knew whether your sweetheart loved you or not. Too-wise daisies. Gay pulled away the tiny ivory petals one by one—he loves me—he loves me not—he loves me. Gay took out the letter again and kissed it and put the torn daisy petals into it. She was young and pretty and very much in love. And he loved her. The daisies said so. What a world! The poor old Moon Man! As if one could be too happy! As if God didn't like to see you happy! Why, people were made for happiness. And wasn't it the most miraculous thing that out of all the world she and Noel should have met and loved! When there were so many other girls he might have fancied. She seemed to be at the very heart of some exquisite magic that had changed everything in life for her.

XIII

Donna came out beside Virginia. She had begun to collect her wits, but she did not quite know yet exactly what had taken place. She knew Peter was sitting on the railing, and she meant to sweep past him haughtily in all her dark dignity of widowhood, with lids cast down. But as she passed him she had to look up. They had another momentary unforgettable exchange of eyes. Virginia saw it this time and was vaguely disturbed by it. It did not look like a glance of hatred. She clutched Donna's arm as they went down the steps.

"Donna, I believe that pig of a Peter is falling in love with you."

"Oh—do you think so—*do* you really think so?" said Donna. Virginia could not understand her tone at all. But it *must* be a horrified one.

"I'm afraid so. Wouldn't it be terrible for you? What a blessing he's leaving for South America to-night. Just *think* what it would be like to have him trying to make love to you."

Donna *did* think of it. A strange shiver of terror and delight went over her from head to foot. She felt thankful that Drowned John bellowed to her that instant to hurry up. She fled to his car, leaving a puzzled and somewhat alarmed Virginia on the steps. *What* had come over Donna?

Mrs Foster Dark went home and ate her supper under Happy's fiddle hanging on the wall. Murray Dark went home and thought about Thora. Artemas Dark reflected dismally that it wouldn't do for him to get drunk for over a year. Crosby Penhallow and Erasmus spent the evening with their flutes—on the whole happily, although Crosby had to put up with some sly digs from Erasmus about old Becky's being in love with him. Peter Penhallow went home and unpacked his trunk. He had searched the world over for the meaning of life's great secret and now he had found it in one look from Donna Dark's eyes. Was he a fool? Then welcome folly.

Big and Little Sam went home across windy sea-fields, and on the way home Little Sam bought a ticket from Little Mosey Gautier for the raffle Father Sullivan was getting up down at Chapel Point to raise funds for the Old Sailors' Home. Big Sam wouldn't buy a ticket. *He* wasn't going to have no truck with Catholics and their doings, and he thought Little Sam might have expended his quarter to far better advantage. They had the heathen to think of.

"No good's going to come of it," he remarked sourly.

Little Sam went home and, dismissing the old Dark jug from his mind, sat down to read his favourite volume, *Foxe's Book of Martyrs,* with the salt wind that even his battered and unromantic heart loved, blowing in at his window. Big Sam went down to the rocks and solaced himself by repeating the first canto of his epic to the gulf.

XIV

Denzil Penhallow told Margaret she must walk home—he and the wife were going down to have tea with the William Y's. Margaret was secretly well pleased. It was only a mile and the month was June. Besides, it would give her a chance to stop and see Whispering Winds.

Whispering Winds was the small secret which made poor Margaret's life endurable. It wound in and out of her drab life like a ribbon of rainbows. It was the little house on the Bay Silver side road where Aunt Louisa Dark had lived. At her death, two years ago, it had become the property of her son Richard, who lived in Halifax. It was for sale but nobody had ever wanted to buy it—nobody, that is, except Margaret, who had no money to buy anything, and would have been hooted at if it were so much as suspected that she wanted to buy a house. Hadn't she a perfectly good, ungrudged home with her brother? What in the world would *she* want of a house?

Margaret did want it—terribly. She had always loved that little house of Aunt Louisa's. It was she who gave it the dear secret name of Whispering Winds, and dreamed all kinds of foolish, sweet dreams about it. As soon as she got to the Bay Silver side road, she turned down it and very soon was at the lane of her house—an old, old lane, grassy and deep-rutted, with bleached old grey "longer" fences hemming it in. There were clumps of birches all along it for a little way—then young spruces growing up thickly on either side—then just between them, at the end, the little house, once white, now as grey as the longers. There it was, basking in the late sunlight—smiling at her with its twinkling windows. Back of it was a steep hill where tossing young maples were whitening in the wind, and off to the right was a glimpse of purple valley. There was an old well in one corner, with an apple tree spilling blossoms over it. A little field off to the right was cool and inviting in the shadow of a spruce wood. The scent of its clover drifted across to Whispering Winds. The air was like a thin golden wine and the quiet was a benediction.

Margaret caught her breath with the delight of it.

Whispering Winds was one of those houses you loved the minute you saw them, without being in the least able to tell why—perhaps because its roof-line was so lovely against the

311

green hill. She loved it so. She walked about the old garden, that was beginning to have such a look of neglect. She longed to prune it and weed it and dress it up. That delightful big bed of striped grass was encroaching on the path, those forget-me-nots were simply running wild. They and the house were just crying out for some one to take care of them. The house and the garden belonged together some way—you couldn't have separated them. The house seemed to grow out of the garden. The shrubs and vines reached up around it to hold it and caress it. If she could just have this house—with a baby in it—she would ask nothing more. Not even Aunt Becky's jug. Margaret realized pathetically that she must give up writing poetry for awhile, or she might have no chance of the jug. And she still hankered after it. Since she could never have Whispering Winds she wanted the jug. Dandy Dark had always been friendly to her. If it should rest with him to give the jug, she stood a better chance than from Aunt Becky. Cruel old Aunt Becky who had jeered at her and her poor little poems and her old-maidenhood before all the clan. Margaret knew that perhaps she *was* silly and faded and childish and unimportant and undesired, but it hurt to have it rubbed in so. She never harmed any one. Why couldn't they leave her alone? Denzil and Mrs Denzil were always giving her digs, too, about "single blessedness," and her nieces and nephews openly laughed at her. But here, in this remote shadowy little garden, she forgot all about it. Things ceased to sting. If she could only stay here forever, where the robins called to one another at evening in the maple wood. Listen to them.

But it was soon time to go home. Mrs Denzil would expect her to get the supper for the family and help milk the cows. She bade good-bye regretfully to Whispering Winds and went on to the square bare house in a treeless yard where the Denzil Penhallows lived. She went up to her hideous little room looking out on the hen-yard, which she had to share with Gladys Penhallow. Gladys was there with some of her friends, thinking at the tops of their voices as usual. It was always noisy. There were never any quiet moments. Margaret's head ached. She wished she had not gone to Aunt Becky's levee. It hadn't done any good. As for the old *Pilgrim's Progress,* it could lie on in The Pinery attic for all she cared.

How pretty Gay Penhallow had looked to-day! And so young. What was it like to be eighteen? Margaret had forgotten if she had ever really known. What had been the trouble between Hugh and Joscelyn? And how dared Thora Dark, who had a husband, be so attractive to other men? What would it be like to have a man look at you the way she had seen Murray looking at Thora— though of course he had no business to be looking at another man's wife like that. Poor Lawson! It was dreadful to see the hunger in Naomi's eyes. How tickled Ambrosine was over that ring! Margaret did not grudge her the ring. Perhaps Ambrosine felt about it the way *she* felt about Whispering Winds. Though of course poor old Ambrosine's hands *were* too thin and knotty to wear rings. Margaret looked with considerable satisfaction at her own slender, shapely fingers. Nobody could say she hadn't a pretty hand. Roger Dark was a nice fellow. Why didn't he get a nice girl for a wife? They said he was crazy about Gay Penhallow, who wouldn't look at him. There you were again. Love going to waste all around you and you starving for a little. The idea suddenly struck Margaret that God wasn't fair. She shuddered and dismissed it as a blasphemy. It sounded like something that dreadful Grundy man would say. Poor Cousin Robina! Peter Penhallow, they said, was off on another of his explorations. He always seemed to live life with such gusto. But Margaret did not envy him. She never wanted to go away from home. What she wanted was a place where she could put down roots and grow old quietly. Margaret thought she would not mind growing old if she could be left to do it in peace. It was hard to grow old gracefully when you were always being laughed at because you were not young. But there was only one career for women in her clan. Of course you could be a nurse or a teacher or dressmaker, or something like that, to fill in the time before marriage, but the

Darks and Penhallows did not take you seriously.

XV

"Tell Joscelyn Dark I want to see her before she goes home, Ambrosine," ordered Aunt Becky.

Joscelyn had walked the short distance up from Bay Silver and intended to walk back. Palmer Dark had taken her mother and her Aunt Rachel home in his car. She felt that she had had about enough of Aunt Becky for one day, but she went back to the bedroom readily enough. After all, the poor old soul was not long for this world.

Aunt Becky was lying back on her pillows. She was gazing earnestly on a little old tintype hanging on the wall near her bed. The picture was not decorative. At least so Joscelyn thought. But then she did not see it with Aunt Becky's eyes. Joscelyn saw only a tubby pompous old man, with a fringe of whisker around his face, and a thin, scrawny little woman in a preposterous dress. Aunt Becky saw a big, hearty, high-coloured man whose abounding vitality brought a gust of life into every existence and a vivid-eyed girl whose wit and sly mirth had been the spice of every company she was in and whose love affairs were stimulating and piquant. Aunt Becky sighed as she turned to Joscelyn. The fire had gone out of her eyes, the sting out of her voice. She looked exactly what she was—a very old, very ill, very tired woman.

"Sit down, Joscelyn. You know, I've been lying here thinking how many people will be glad when I'm dead? And not one to be sorry. And it seems to me that I wish I'd lived a bit differently, Joscelyn. I've always taken my fun out of them—I haven't spared them—they're all afraid of me. I'm just an ogress to them. It *was* fun to watch them squirming. But now—I don't know. I've a devilish sort of feeling that I wish I'd been a kind, gentle, stingless creature like—well, like Annette Dark, for instance. Everybody was sorry when she died—though she never said a clever thing in her life. But she was smart enough to die before she got too old. Women should, Joscelyn. I've sat up too late. Nobody will miss me."

Joscelyn looked levelly at Aunt Becky. She knew that what Aunt Becky said was true enough in a way. And she sensed the secret bitterness in the old woman's soul behind all her satire and bravado. She wanted to comfort her without telling a lie. Joscelyn could neither tell nor live a lie—which was what had made a clan existence hard for her.

"I think, Aunt Becky, that every one of us will miss you a great deal more than you suppose we will—a great deal more than we imagine ourselves. You're like—like mustard. Sometimes you bite—and a big dose of you *is* rather awful—"

"As to-day, for example," interjected Aunt Becky with a faint grin.

"But you *do* give a tang to things. They'd be flat without you. And you seem like—I don't know how to put it—the very essence of Dark and Penhallow. We won't be half so much a clan when you're gone. You've always made history for us somehow. If this had been an ordinary afternoon—if we'd come here and you'd been nice to us—"

"And fed you—"

"We'd have all gone away and forgotten the afternoon. There'd be nothing in it to remember. But this afternoon *will* be remembered—and talked about. When the girls are old women they'll tell their grandchildren about it—you'll live by it fifty years after you're in your grave, Aunt Becky."

"I *have* often thought it would be a frightfully dull world if everybody were perfectly good and sweet," conceded Aunt Becky. "I guess it's only because I'm tired that I'm wishing I'd been more like Annette. She was as sweet and good and unexciting as they make 'em. She never said a naughty word in her life. And I was far handsomer than she was, mind you. But Crosby loved *her*. Now, Joscelyn, here's a queer thing. You heard what I said to-day. There was a time I'd have given my soul if Crosby had loved me—

I'd have given and done anything—except be like Annette. Not even for Crosby would I have been willing to be like Annette—even though now I'm getting childish and wishing I had been. I'd rather sting people than bore them, after all. But—"

Aunt Becky paused and looked earnestly at Joscelyn. Joscelyn had held her own well. She was very good-looking. The evening light, falling through the window behind her, made a tremulous primrose nimbus around her shapely head. But her eyes—Aunt Becky wanted to solve the haunting mystery of Joscelyn's eyes.

"I didn't keep you here to talk about my own feelings. I'm going to die. And I'm not afraid of death. Isn't it strange? I was once so afraid of it. But before I die I want to ask you something. I've never asked you before—do me that justice. What went wrong between you and Hugh?"

Joscelyn started—flushed—paled—almost rose from her chair.

"No—sit down. I'm not going to try to make you tell if you don't want to. It isn't curiosity, Joscelyn. I'm done with that. I feel I'd just like to know the truth before I die. I remember your wedding. Hugh was the happiest-looking groom I ever saw. And you seemed very well pleased with yourself, too—when you came in first, at least. I remember thinking you were made for each other—the sort of people who should marry—and found a home—and have children. And I *would* like to know what wrecked it all."

Joscelyn sat silent a few minutes longer. Oddly enough, she was conscious of a strange desire to tell Aunt Becky everything. Aunt Becky would understand—she was sure Aunt Becky would understand. For ten years she had lived in an atmosphere of misunderstanding and disapproval and suspicion. She had not minded it, she thought—the inner flame which irradiated life had been her protection. But to-day she felt oddly that she *had*, after all, minded it more than she had supposed. There was a soreness in her spirit that seemed old, not new. She *would* tell Aunt Becky. No one else would ever know. It was a confidence to the grave itself. And it might help her—heal her. She bent forward and began to speak in a low, intense voice. Aunt Becky lay and listened movelessly until Joscelyn had finished.

"So that was it," she said, when the passionate voice had ceased. "Something none of us ever thought of. I never thought of it. I thought perhaps it was something quite small. So many of the tragedies of life come from little, silly, ridiculous things. Nobody ever knew why Roger Penhallow hanged himself forty years ago—nobody but me. He did it because he was eighteen years old and his father *spanked* him. Ah, the things I know of this clan! All the things I said to-day were things every one knows. But I didn't say a word about scores of things nobody dreams I know. But weren't you very cruel, Joscelyn?"

"What else could I have done?" said Joscelyn. "I *couldn't* have done anything else."

"Not with that Spanish blood in you, I suppose. At least we'll blame it on the Spanish blood. Everything that isn't right in your branch of the Penhallows is laid at the door of that Spanish blood. Peter Penhallow and his hurry to be born, for instance. It must be the Spanish blood that makes you all fall in love with such terrible suddenness. Most of Captain Martin's descendants have been lovers at sight or not at all. I thought you'd escaped *that* curse—Hugh took so long courting you. Have you ever felt sorry you did it, Joscelyn?"

"No—no—no," cried Joscelyn.

"Two 'no's' too many," said Aunt Becky.

"I want to tell you the exact truth," said Joscelyn slowly. "It is quite true—I've never been sorry I *did* do it. You can't be sorry you did a thing you *have* to do. But I have been sorry—not many times but all the time—that I *had* to do it. I didn't want to do it. I didn't want to hurt Hugh like that—and I *did* want to have Treewoofe. I want it yet—you don't know how much I want Treewoofe—and all the lovely life I had planned to have there. It was dreadful to have to give it up. But I couldn't do anything else, Aunt Becky—I *couldn't.*"

"Well, God bless you, child. The less we say about it the better. You'll probably hate me tonight because you've told me this. You'll feel I tricked you into it by being old and pitiful."

"No, you didn't trick me. I wanted to tell you. I don't know why—but I wanted to. And I'm glad you don't blame me too much, Aunt Becky."

"I don't blame you at all. I might even believe you were right if I were young enough to believe it. God save us all, what a world it is! The things that happen to people—things without rhyme or reason! Frank has never married, has he? Do you think it happened to him, too?"

Joscelyn's face crimsoned.

"I don't know. He went away the next morning, you know. Sometimes I think it might have—because—when I looked at him—oh, Aunt Becky, you remember that absurd thing Virginia Penhallow said about the first time she met Ned Powell. The whole clan has laughed over it. 'The moment I looked into his eyes I knew he was my predestined mate.' Of course it *was* ridiculous. But, Aunt Becky, that was just the way I felt, too."

"Of course." Aunt Becky nodded understandingly. "We all *feel* those things. They're not ridiculous when we feel them. It's only when we put them into words that they're ridiculous. They're not meant to be put in words. Well, when *I* couldn't get the man I wanted, I just decided to want the man I could get. That was Craig Penhallow's way of looking at it, too. Ever hear the story of Craig Penhallow and the trees in Treewoofe lane, Joscelyn?"

"No."

"Well, you've noticed—haven't you—something odd about the spruce trees up and down that lane? There's a gap in them every once in so long."

Joscelyn nodded. Aunt Becky could not tell her much she didn't know about the appearance of the trees in Treewoofe lane.

"Thirty years ago old Cornelius Treverne owned Treewoofe. Craig was courting his daughter Clara. And one night Clara turned him down. Hard. Craig was furious. He flung himself out of the house and stormed down the lane. Poor old Cornelius had spent that whole day setting out a hedge of little spruce trees all along both sides of that long lane. A hard day's work, mind you. And what do you think Craig did by way of relieving his feelings? As he stalked along he would tear up a handful of old Cornelius' trees on the right hand—a few steps more—up would come a bunch on the left. He kept that up all the way down the lane. You can imagine what it looked like when he got to the end of it. And you can imagine what old Cornelius felt when he saw it next morning. He never got time to replant the trees—Cornelius was a great hand to put things off. He was a good man—painfully good. It was a blessing he didn't have any sons, or they'd certainly have gone to the bad by way of keeping up the family average. But he was no hustler. So the trees that were left grew up as they were. As for Craig, by the time he had finished with the lane he felt a lot better. There were as good fish in the sea as ever came out of it—Maggie Penhallow was just as handsome as Clara Treverne. Or at least she managed her eyes and hands so well, she passed for handsome. You see, Craig was like me. He decided to be sensible. Perhaps your way is wiser, Joscelyn—and perhaps we're all fools together with the Moon Man's high-seated gods laughing at us. Joscelyn—and I don't know whether I should tell you this—but I think I should, for I don't think you know, and the things we don't know sometimes hurt us horribly, in spite of the old proverb. All Hugh's family are at him to go to the States and get a divorce. It's been done several times, you know. People brag that Prince Edward Island hasn't had but one divorce since Confederation. Stuff and nonsense! It's had a dozen."

"But—but—they're not really legal—here, are they?" stammered Joscelyn.

"Legal enough. They're winked at, anyhow. Mind, I don't say Hugh is going to do it. But they're at him—they're at him. Times have changed a bit these last ten years. No easy divorce for us—but in Hugh's case they'd condone it. Mrs Jim Trent is the moving spirit behind it, I understand. She lived so long in the States she got their viewpoint. And she and Pauline Dark are as friendly just now as two cats lapping from the same saucer. Pauline's as much in love with Hugh as she ever was, you know."

"It matters nothing to me," said Joscelyn stiffly, rising to go. She bade Aunt Becky good-bye rather shortly. Aunt Becky smiled cryptically after Joscelyn had gone out.

"I've made Joscelyn Dark tell one fib in her life, if she never tells another," she thought. "Poor little romantic, splendid fool. I don't know whether I feel envy or contempt. Yet I remember when I took myself almost as seriously as that. Lord, what *does* get into girls? Old Cy Dark's son!"

XVI

Joscelyn went home slowly through the glamour and perfume of the June evening. Slowly, because she was in no hurry to get home where her mother and her Aunt Rachel would be talking the afternoon over indignantly and expecting her to be as indignant as they were. Slowly, because some unwelcome shadow of imminent change seemed to go with her as she walked. Slowly, because she was living over again the story she had told Aunt Becky.

She had been very sure she loved Hugh when she had finally promised to marry him. She had been happy in their brief engagement. Everybody had been happy—everybody well enough pleased about it, except Hugh's mother, Mrs Conrad Dark, and his second cousin, Pauline Dark. Joscelyn did not care whether Pauline was pleased or not, but she was sorry Mrs Conrad wasn't. Mrs Conrad did not like her—never had liked her. Joscelyn had never been able to imagine why—until this very afternoon, when Aunt Becky had illuminated the mystery by her reference to Alec. Joscelyn had known Mrs Conrad detested her from their first meeting, when Mrs Conrad had told her that her petticoat was below her dress. Now, in the days of petticoats, there were three different ways you could tell a girl that her petticoat was below her dress. You could tell it as a kindly friend who felt it a duty to help get matters righted as soon as possible before any one else noticed it, but who felt a sympathy with her as the victim of an accident which might happen at any time to yourself. You could tell it as a disinterested onlooker who had no real concern with the affair but wanted to do as you would be done by. Or you could tell it with a certain suppressed venom and triumph, as if you rather delighted in catching her in such a scrape and wanted her to know you saw the fatal garment and had your own opinion of any girl who could be so careless.

The last way had been Mrs Conrad Dark's, and Joscelyn knew her for an enemy. But this did not disturb to any extent the happiness of her engagement. Joscelyn had a good deal of Peter Penhallow's power of detachment from the influence of any one else's opinion. As long as Hugh loved her it did not matter what Mrs Conrad thought; and Joscelyn knew how Hugh loved her.

Soon after their engagement Treewoofe Farm at Three Hills came into the market. Treewoofe had been so named from some old place in Cornwall whence the Trevernes had come. The house was built on a hill overlooking the valley of Bay Silver, and Hugh bought the farm because of its magnificent view. Most of the clan thought the idea of buying a farm because it was beautiful very amusing and suspected Joscelyn of putting him up to it. Luckily, they thought, the soil was good, though run down, and the house practically new. Hugh had not made such a bad purchase, if the winter winds didn't make him wish he'd picked a more sheltered home. As for the view, of course it was very fine. None of the Darks or Penhallows were so insensitive to beauty as not to admit that. There was no doubt old Cornelius had tacked another hundred on his price because of that view. But it was a lonely spot and rather out of the world, and most of them thought Hugh had made a mistake.

Hugh and Joscelyn had no qualms about it. They both loved Treewoofe. The splendour of many sunsets had flooded that hill

321

and the shadows of great clouds rolled over it. One evening after he had bought it, he and Joscelyn walked up to see it, going to it, not by the road but by a little crooked, ferny path through the Treewoofe beech woods, full of the surprises no straight path can ever give. They had run all over the house and orchard like children and then stood together at their front door and looked down—down—down—over the hill itself—over the farmsteads and groves in the valley below—over her own home, looking like a doll's house at that distance—over the mirror-like beauty of Bay Silver—over the harbour bar—out—out—out—to the great gulf—a grey sea, this evening, with streaks of silver—Joscelyn had drawn a breath of rapture. To live every day looking at that! And to know that glorious wind every day—sweeping up over the harbour, over the sheltered homesteads that hid from it— up—up—up—to their glorious free crest that welcomed it. And oh, what would dawn over those seaside meadows far below be like?

"We'll have three good neighbours up here," said Joscelyn. "The wind—and the rain—and the stars. They can come close to us here. All my life, Hugh, I've longed to live on a hill. I can't breathe in the valley."

Turning round she could see, past the other end of the hall that ran right through the house, the lovely old-fashioned garden behind—and behind it again the orchard in bloom. Their home, haunted by no ghosts of the past—only by wraiths of the future. Unborn eyes would look out of its windows—unborn voices sing in its rooms—unborn feet run lightly in the old orchard. Beautiful to-morrows—unknown lovely years were waiting there for them. Friends would come to them—hands of comrades would knock at their door—silken gowns would rustle through their chambers—there would be companionship and good smacking jests such as their clan loved. What a home they would make of Treewoofe! All the richness and ripeness of life would be theirs.

Joscelyn saw their faces reflected in the long mirror that was hanging over the fireplace in the corner. A mirror with an intriguing black cat a-top of it which had been brought out from Cornwall and sold with the house. Young, happy, merry faces against a background of blue sky and crystal air. Hugh put his arm about her neck and drew her cheek close to his.

"That's an old looking-glass, honey. It has reflected many a woman's face. But never, never one so beautiful as my queen's."

The wedding was in September. Milly, Joscelyn's harum-scarum younger sister, was bridesmaid. Frank Dark was best man. Joscelyn had never seen Frank Dark. He lived in Saskatchewan, where his father, Cyrus Dark, had gone when his family were small, and where Frank and Hugh had been cronies during the years Hugh had spent in the west. But he came east for the wedding, arriving there only on the afternoon of the day itself. Joscelyn saw him for the first time when her Uncle Jeff swept in with her and left her standing by the side of her waiting groom. Joscelyn raised her eyes to look at Hugh—and instead found herself looking past him straight into Frank Dark's eyes as he gazed with open curiosity at this bride of Hugh's.

Frank Dark was "dark by name and dark by nature" as the clan said. He had black, satiny hair, a thin olive-hued face and dark liquid eyes. A very handsome fellow, Frank Dark. Beside him, Hugh looked rather overgrown and raw-boned and unfinished. And at that moment Joscelyn Penhallow knew that she had never loved Hugh Dark, save with the affection of a good comrade. She loved Frank Dark, whom she had never seen until that minute.

The ceremony was well begun before Joscelyn realized what had happened. She always believed that if she had realized it a moment sooner she could have stopped the marriage somehow—anyhow—it did not matter how, so long as it was only stopped. But Hugh was saying, "I will" when she came to her senses—and Frank's shadow was on the floor before her as she said, "I will" herself, without knowing exactly what she was saying. Another moment and she was Hugh Dark's wife—Hugh Dark's wife in the throes of a wild passionate love for another man. And Hugh at that moment was making a vow in his heart that no pain, no sorrow, no heartache should ever touch her life if he could prevent it.

Joscelyn never knew how she got through the evening. It always seemed a nightmare of remembrance. Hugh kissed her on her lips—tenderly—possessively. The husband's kiss against which Joscelyn found herself suddenly in wild rebellion. Milly gave her a tear-wet peck next, and then Frank Dark, easy, debonair Frank Dark, bent forward with a smile and good-wishes for Hugh's wife on his lips and kissed her lightly on the cheek. It was the first and last time he ever touched her; but to-day, ten years after, that kiss burned on Joscelyn's cheek as she thought of it.

There was an orgy of kissing after that. At Dark and Penhallow weddings everybody kissed the bride and everybody else who could or would be kissed. Joscelyn, bewildered and terrified, had yet one clear thought in her mind—no one—*no one* must kiss the cheek where Frank's kiss had fallen. She gave them her lips or her left cheek blindly, but she kept the right to him. On and on they came with their good wishes and their tears or laughter— Joscelyn felt her mother's tears, she felt her bones almost crack in Drowned John's grip, she heard old Uncle Erasmus whisper one of the smutty little jokes he always got off at weddings, she saw Mrs Conrad's cold venomous face—no kiss from Mrs Conrad—she saw Pauline Dark's pale, quivering lips—Pauline's kiss was as cold as the grave—she heard jolly old Aunt Charlotte whispering, "Tell him he's wonderful at least once a week." It was all a dream—she must wake presently.

The ordeal of well-wishing over, the ordeal of supper came. Joscelyn was laughed at because she could not eat. Uncle Erasmus made another smutty jest and was punished by his wife's sharp elbow. After supper Hugh took his bride home. The rest of the young folks, Frank Dark among them, stayed at Bay Silver to dance the night away. Joscelyn went out with only a cloak over her bridal finery. Hugh had asked her to go home with him so.

The drive to Treewoofe had been very silent. Hugh sensed that somehow she did not want to talk. He was so happy he did not want to talk himself. Words might spoil it. At Treewoofe he lifted her from the buggy and led her by the hand—how cold the hand was. She was frightened, his little love—across the green before the house and over the threshold of his door. He turned to welcome her with the little verse of poetry he had composed for the occasion. Hugh had the knack of rhyme that flickered here and there in the clan, sometimes emerging in very unexpected brainpans. He had pictured himself doing this a hundred times—leading in a white-veiled, silk-clad bride—but not a bride with such white lips and such wide, horror-filled eyes. For the first time, Hugh realized that here was something most terribly wrong. This was not the pretty shrinking and confusion of the happy bride.

They stood in the entrance hall at Treewoofe and looked at each other. A fire was flickering in the fireplace—Hugh had lighted it with his own hands before he left and bade his hired boy to keep it alive—and the rosy flamelight bathed the hall and fell over his lovely golden bride—his no more.

"Joscelyn—my darling—what is wrong?"

She found her voice.

"I can't live with you, Hugh."

"Why not?"

She told him. She loved Frank Dark and loving him she could be wife to no other man. Now her eyes were no longer blue or green or grey, but a flame.

There was a terrible hour. In the end Hugh set open the door and looked at her, white anger falling over his face like a frost. One only word he said:

"Go."

Joscelyn had gone, wraithlike in her shimmer of satin and tulle, out into the cold September moonlight silvering over Treewoofe Hill. She had half walked, half run home to Bay Silver in a certain wild triumph. As she went past the graveyard, her own people buried there seemed to be reaching out after her to pluck her back. Not her father, though. He lay very quiet in his grave—quieter than he had ever lain in life. There had been Spanish blood in *him*. Mrs Clifford Penhallow could have told you that. Her clan thought—she thought herself—that she had had a hard life with Clifford's vagaries. Though when she became a widow she found there were a good many harder things he had fended from her.

Joscelyn cherished no delusion. She was Hugh's wife in law and she could marry no other man. The thought of divorce never entered her head. But she was free to be true to her love— this wonderful passion which had so suddenly filled her soul and given it wings, so that she seemed rather to fly than walk over the road. Its dark enchantment lifted her above fear and shame; nothing could touch her, not even what she knew was to be faced. And in this rapt mood she came back to her mother's door and the dismayed dancers scattered to their homes as if a ghost had walked in among them. Joscelyn, as she went upstairs with the frost of the autumn night wet on her limp wedding-veil, wondered if Frank saw her and what he would think. But Frank was not there. Ten minutes after Hugh had taken his bride away a telegram had come for Frank Dark. Cyrus Dark was dying in Saskatchewan. Frank left at once to pack his scarcely unpacked trunk and catch the early boat-train, thereby perhaps escaping the horsewhipping a madman at Treewoofe was silently threatening to give him and which, it must be admitted, he did not in the least deserve.

Frank Dark returned to the west without ever knowing that his friend's bride had fallen in love with him. He hadn't the slightest wish that she should fall in love with him—though he thought her a dashed pretty girl. A bit of money, too. Hugh had always been a lucky beggar.

XVII

Joscelyn paused at the gate of her home and looked at it with some distaste. The old Clifford Penhallow house was prim, old-fashioned and undecorated, but it was considered to be very quaint by the summer tourists who came to Bay Silver, and a post card had been made of it. The house was built on a little point running out into Bay Silver. On one side its roof sloped unbrokenly down to within a few feet of the ground. Its windows were high and narrow. A little green yard surrounded it, with nothing in it but green grass which Rachel Penhallow swept every day. To the right was a huddle of trees—a lombardy, a maple and three apple trees, girt by a tidy stone dyke. On the left a neat gate opened into a neat pasture—oh, everything was so neat and bare—where there were some windy willows and where Mrs Clifford kept her cow. Back of it was a straight blue line of harbour, a glimpse of pink sand-dunes and over them a hazy sunset.

For ten years this had been to Joscelyn merely a place to live her strange inner dream-life. She asked no more of it. But now she was suddenly conscious of this odd distaste for it. She had never cared very much for it. It lay too low—she wanted the wind and outlook of a hill. She did not want to go in. She could see her mother and Aunt Rachel at the living-room window. They seemed to be quarrelling as usual. Rather—bickering. They couldn't do anything as genuine and positive as quarrel. There was no Spanish blood in either of them. Joscelyn knew what was ahead of her if she went in—the whole afternoon would be threshed over and somehow they would make her feel that she was responsible for their not getting what they wanted. She could not endure that just now—so she walked around the pasture, as if she were going to the shore, and when she was out of their sight she slipped through the sweet-briar thicket, in at the kitchen door, and upstairs to her own room. With a sigh of relief and weariness she sank into a chair by the open window.

She suddenly felt tireder than she had ever felt in her life before. Was this to be her existence forever? She had not thought about the future for years—there was *no* future to think of— nothing but the strange present where her secret love burned like an altar flame she must tend forever, a devoted priestess. But now she thought of the future. A future lived with two old women who were always bickering—an aunt who was bitter and miserly, a mother who was always complaining of "slaving" and not being appreciated. Milly, gay, irresponsible Milly, was long since married and gone. Her going had been a relief to Joscelyn because Milly thought her a fool, but now she missed Milly's laughter. How still and quiet everything was. But up at Treewoofe there would be wind. There was always a wind there. She could see every dell and slope of Treewoofe Farm from where she sat, lying in the light of a queer red smoky sunset. Dear Treewoofe which seemed in some curious way to belong to her still, when she watched the moon sinking over its snowy hill on winter nights or the autumn stars burning over its misty harvest fields. Over it a cloud was drifting—a cloud like a woman with long, blowing, wet hair. She thought of Pauline Dark—Pauline, who still loved Hugh. Could it be true that Hugh's family really wanted him to get a U.S. divorce? Would Pauline ever be mistress of Treewoofe? Pauline with her thin malicious smile. Demure as a cat, too. At the thought Joscelyn felt a wave of home-sickness engulf her. Treewoofe was *hers*—hers, though she could never enter into her heritage. Hugh would never—could never—take another woman there in her place. It would be a sacrilege. Joscelyn shivered again. She had a bitter realization that her springtime suddenly seemed far away. She was no longer young—and all she had had out of life was a certain cool indifferent kiss dropped ten years ago on a cheek that no lips had ever touched since. Yet for that kiss she had given her soul.

Aunt Rachel came in without the useless formality of a knock. She had been crying and the knobby tip of her long nose was very red. But she was not without her consolation. Mercy

Penhallow hadn't got Aunt Becky's bottle of Jordan water, thank heaven. *She,* Rachel Penhallow, was now the only woman in the clan who had one. Penny Dark didn't count. Men had no real understanding about such sacred things.

"What did you think of the afternoon, Joscelyn?"

"Think—the afternoon—oh, it was funny," said Joscelyn.

Aunt Rachel stared. She thought the afternoon had been dreadful and scandalous but it would never have occurred to her to call it funny.

"*We* have no real chance for the jug, of course. I told your mother that before we went. And less than ever *now.* Dandy Dark and Mrs Conrad are first cousins. If you had not been so crazy—Joscelyn—" Joscelyn winced. She always winced when Aunt Rachel gave her jabs about her behaviour. She hated Aunt Rachel. Always had hated her. It was always a comfort to reflect that if she chose she could humiliate Aunt Rachel to the dust. Aunt Rachel with her poor pitiful pride in the possession of that bottle of Jordan water, one of several which an itinerant missionary had once sold for the benefit of his cause. She and Theodore Dark had been the only ones in the clan to buy one. The bottle stood in the middle of the parlour mantelpiece. Aunt Rachel dusted it every day with reverent hands.

One day when Joscelyn had been a little girl, she had found herself alone in the parlour, and she had boldly climbed up on a chair and taken the sacred bottle in her hand. It was a pretty bottle with a facetted glass stopper, and Aunt Rachel had tied a bow of blue satin ribbon lovingly around its throat. Somehow Joscelyn had dropped it. Luckily it fell on the soft, velvety, padded roses of one of Mrs Clifford's famous hooked rugs. So it did not break. But the stopper came out and before the horrified Joscelyn could leap down and rescue it, every drop of the priceless Jordan water had been spilled. At first Joscelyn was cold with horror. Even at ten she did not think there was anything special or sacred about that water. She had understood too well her father's satirical speeches about it. But she knew what Aunt Rachel would be like.

Then an impish idea entered her mind. Luckily she was alone in the house. She went out and deliberately filled up the bottle from the kitchen water-pail. It looked exactly the same. Aunt Rachel never knew the difference.

Joscelyn had never told a soul—less for her own sake than for Aunt Rachel's. That bottle of supposed Jordan water was all that gave any meaning to Aunt Rachel's life. It was the only thing she really loved—her god, in truth, though she would have been horrified if such a suggestion had ever been made to her.

As for Joscelyn, she could never have stood Aunt Rachel and her martyr airs at all had it not been for the knowledge of how securely she had her in her power.

"Where did you put that bottle of St. Jacob's oil when you housecleaned the pantry?" Aunt Rachel was asking. "I want to rub my joints. There's rain coming. I shouldn't have put off my flannels. A body should wear flannel next the skin till the end of June."

Joscelyn went silently and got the St. Jacob's oil.

XVIII

Hugh Dark leaned over the gate at Treewoofe for a time before going in, looking at the house dead black on its hill against the dull red sky—the house where he had once thought Joscelyn Penhallow would be mistress. He thought it looked lonely—as if it expected nothing more from life. Yet it had nothing of the desolate peace of a house whose life has been lived. It had an unlived look about it; it had a defrauded defiant air; it had been robbed of its birthright.

Before his marriage, Hugh had liked to stand so and look at his house when he came home, dreaming a young man's dreams. He imagined coming home to Joscelyn; he would stand awhile before going in, looking up at all its windows whence warm golden lights would be gleaming over winter snows or summer gardens or lovely, pale, clear autumn dusks. He would think of the significance of each window—the dining-room, where his supper would be laid, the kitchen, where Joscelyn was waiting for him, perhaps a dimly-lighted window upstairs in a room where small creatures slept. "*She* is the light of my house," he would think. Pretty? The word was too cheap and tawdry for Joscelyn. She was beautiful, with the beauty of a warm pearl or a star or a golden flower. And she was his. He would sit with her by rose-red fires on stormy winter nights and wild wet fall evenings, shut in with her for secret happy hours, while the winds howled about Treewoofe. He would walk with her in the twilit orchard on summer nights, and kiss her hair in that soft blue darkness of shadows.

For years he had not looked at his house when he came home. In a sense he hated it. But to-night he was restless and unhappy. Only after seeing Joscelyn did he realize to the full how empty his life was. Empty like his house. It was always difficult to believe that the incidents of his wedding-night had been real. We can never believe that terrible things really have happened. Years after they *have* happened we are still incredulous. So it was with Hugh. It simply could not be so. Joscelyn *must* be in that house, waiting for him to come to her. If he stood here patiently by the gate he would see her at the door looking for him and see the garland gold of her hair shining like a crown in the light behind her.

Would he get the divorce his mother and sisters were always hinting at? No, he would not. He struck his clenched fist furiously on the gate-post. Frank would come home then and marry Joscelyn. He should never have her.

There was no light in the house. His old housekeeper must be away. Hugh went in sullenly, not by the front door, though it was nearest. He knew that it was locked. He had locked it behind Joscelyn on their wedding-night and it had never been opened since. He went in by the kitchen door and lit a lamp. He was restless. He went all over the house—the dusty ill-kept house. It *was* lonely and unsatisfied. The chairs wanted to be sat upon. The mirrors wanted to reflect charming faces. The rooms wanted children to go singing through them. The walls wanted to re-echo to laughter. There had been no laughter in this house since that wedding-night—no real laughter. A house without remembered laughter is a pitiful thing. He came finally to the square front hall where the ashes of the bridal fire were still in the grate. His housekeeper had her orders never to meddle with anything in the front hall. The dust lay thick over everything. The mirror was turned to the wall. He hated it because it had once reflected her face and would reflect it no more forever. The clock on the mantelpiece was not going. It had stopped that night and had never been wound again. So time had stopped for Hugh Dark when he had looked at Joscelyn and realized that she was no longer his.

On the mantelpiece, just before the clock, a wedding-ring and a small diamond ring were lying. They had been there ever since Joscelyn had stripped them from her fingers.

The moonlight was looking in through the glass of the front door like a white hopeless face. Hugh recalled an old saying he had heard or read somewhere—"God had made a fool of him."

Ah, verily God had made a fool of *him*.

He would go out and roam about in the night as he often did to drive away haunting thoughts. In the house he could think of nothing but Joscelyn. Outside he could think of his plans for making money out of his farm and the possibilities that were looming up for him in local politics. But first he must feed his cat. The poor beast was hungry, crouched on the kitchen doorstep looking at him accusingly. It was not the cat he and Joscelyn were reputed to have quarrelled over.

"At least," thought Hugh bitterly, "a cat always knows its own mind."

XIX

So Aunt Becky's famous last "levee" was over with all its comedy and tragedy, its farce and humour, its jealousies and triumphs; and it may be concluded that very few people went home from it as happy as they went to it. The two Sams, perhaps, who were untroubled by love or ambition and had no suspicion of the dark clouds already lowering over their lives,—Gay Penhallow—and maybe Peter, who was tearing the bowels out of his trunk. He had said to Nancy on the way home:

"Nancy—Nancy, I've fallen in love—I have—I have—and it's glorious. Why did I never fall in love before?"

Nancy caught her breath as Peter whirled around a corner on two wheels.

"What *do* you mean? And who is it?"

"Donna Dark."

"Donna Dark!" Nancy gasped again as Peter shaved old Spencer Howey's team by the merest fraction of an inch. "Why, Peter, I thought you always hated her."

"So I did. But, dearest of Nancys, have you never heard the proverb, 'Hate is only love that has missed its way'?"

WHEELS WITHIN WHEELS

Most of the clan who were at The Pinery went home thinking it was all nonsense to talk of Aunt Becky's dying. Anybody as full of vim and devilment as she was would last for years. Roger must be mistaken.

But Roger had, as usual, made no mistake. Less than a week after the famous levee, Aunt Becky died—very quietly and unostentatiously. And tidily. Aunt Becky insisted on dying tidily. She made Ambrosine put on a smooth and spotless spread, tuck all the edges neatly in, and fold back the fresh sheet in unwrinkled purity.

"I've lived clean and I'll die clean," said Aunt Becky, folding her hands on the sheet. "And I'm glad I'm not dying in my sleep. Roger told me I might. I want to have all my wits about me when I die."

She was done with life. As she looked back in this last hour she saw how few things had really mattered. Her hates now seemed trivial and likewise many of her loves. Things she had once thought great, seemed small and a few trifles loomed vastly. Grief and joy had alike ceased to worry her. But she was glad she had told Crosby Dark that she had loved him. Yes, that was a satisfaction. She closed her sunken old eyes and did not open them again.

Of course there was a clan funeral and everybody with one exception came, even Mrs Allan Dark, who was dying of some chronic trouble but had determined—so it was reported—to live until she knew who got the Dark jug. The exception was Tom Dark, who was in bed with a dislocated shoulder. The night before, as he was sitting on his bed, studying if there were any way to wheedle the secret out of Dandy Dark, he had absently put both feet into one pyjama leg. Then when he stood up he fell on the floor in what his terrified wife at first thought was a fit. Very few of the clan sympathized with him as to his resulting shoulder. They thought it served him right for wearing new-fangled duds. If he had had a proper nightshirt on it couldn't have happened.

Thekla Penhallow, who always looked as if her nose were cold, appeared at the funeral in heavy mourning. Some of the other women wondered uneasily if they shouldn't have, too. To be sure, Aunt Becky had hated mourning; she called it "a relic of barbarism." But who knew what Dandy thought about it?

Everything proceeded decently and in order—until just at the last. Aunt Becky, who had never cared for flowers in her life, had her casket heaped with them. But her clan at least respected her wish as regards "made-up" flowers. There was nothing but clusters and bouquets gathered in old homestead gardens and breathing only of the things Aunt Becky had known—and perhaps loved—all her life.

Aunt Becky was sternly handsome in what some considered far too expensive a coffin, with her lace shawl draped about her and her cold white lips forever closed on all the clan secrets she knew—so handsome that her clan, who had thought of her for years only a gaunt unlovely old woman, with straggling hair and wrinkled face, were surprised. Crosby Dark, who had felt ashamed at the levee when she told him she had loved him, now felt flattered. The love of that stately old queen was a compliment. For the rest, they looked a her with interest, respect, and more grief than any of them had expected to feel. With considerable awe as well. She looked as if she might open her eyes with that terrible inquisitorial look of hers and shoot some ghastly question at them. It would be like her.

Very few tears were shed. Mrs Clifford cried; but then she shed gallons at everybody's funeral. And Grace Penhallow cried, which was so unusual that her husband whispered testily, "What are *you* crying for? You always hated her."

"That's why I'm crying," said Grace drearily. She could not explain how futile that old hate seemed to her now. And its futility made her feel sad and temporarily bereft of all things.

The Rev. Mr Trackley conducted the service very fittingly and gracefully, most people considered. Though Uncle Pippin thought, "Oh, you are drawing it rather strong" at some of the phrases used in Mr Trackley's eulogy of the departed. Aunt Becky had hardly been such a saint as *that*. And Drowned John thought shamelessly, when Mr Trackley said the Lord had taken her, "He's welcome to her." William Y. was by no means so sure of it as the minister seemed to be. Aunt Becky, he reflected, had never been a member of the church. But then she was a Penhallow. A Penhallow couldn't go anywhere but to the right place, William Y. felt comfortingly.

The funeral procession from The Pinery to the graveyard at Rose River was, so Camilla proudly remarked to Ambrosine that night, the longest that had ever been know in the clan. It was a day of heavy clouds with outbursts of sunshine between them; an occasional grey mist of rain drifted over the spruce barrens down by the harbour, much to the comfort of the superstitious. Aunt Becky was buried in the Theodore Dark plot, beside her husband and children, under a drift of blooming spirea. The old graveyard was full of the pathos of forgotten graves. Men and women of the clan lay there—men and women who had been victorious, and men and women who had been defeated. Their follies and adventures, their gallantries and mistakes, their fortunes and misfortunes, were buried and forgotten with them. And now Aunt Becky had come to take her place among them. People did not hurry away after the grave service had been concluded. A clan funeral was by way of being a bit of a social function as well as a funeral. They broke up into little groups and talked—with rather easier minds than they had brought to the funeral—for Camilla had told them that that dreadful obituary had simply been a hoax on Aunt Becky's part. She had wanted to give them one good final scare.

"Thank God," said William Y., who really hadn't slept anything to speak of since he had heard that obituary read.

Everybody looked at Dandy Dark with a new outward respect. People came up and spoke to him who did not ordinarily notice him unless they fell over him. He felt his importance, as the possessor of a dying trust, but did not presume on it too much. Folks felt sure he knew already who was going to get the jug. If Aunt Becky hadn't told him, no doubt he had steamed the letter open the night after the levee. Artemas Dark while the burial service was going on, was speculating as to whether there were any chance of getting Dandy "lit up" and worming the secret out of him that way. He sadly concluded there wasn't. Dandy had never tasted liquor in his life. Too mean—and unadventurous, thought Artemas. Titus Dark wondered if it would be any good to try the Sams' ouija-board. It was said to do wonderful things. But—would that be tampering with the powers of darkness? He knew Mr Trackley thought so.

Palmer Dark and Homer Penhallow nodded to each other shamefacedly. Young Jimmy Dark meowed very distinctly at this, but Palmer and Homer pretended not to have heard.

"Good thing they've made it up at last," said Uncle Pippin. "Never could see the sense of keeping up a mouldy old scrap like that."

"As for the sense of it, there's no sense in heaps of things we do," said Stanton Grundy. "Life would be tedious without a vendetta or two."

Everybody was on tiptoe. Abel Dark had already begun to finish painting his house and Miller Dark had actually commenced work on his clan history and had a genealogical table neatly made out. Chris Penhallow had never touched a violin. Drowned John and Titus Dark had not sworn for a week—at least nobody had heard them do it. Titus showed the strain but there was no shadow on Drowned John's brow as he strode across the graveyard, trampling on the graves, to look at Jennie's and Emmy's and read his own epitaph. Ambrosine Winkworth wore her diamond ring—most unfitting, it was thought. Mrs Toynbee Dark went faithfully to visit each husband's grave. People said Nan Penhallow might have left the lipstick off for a funeral.

"She's a flip piece," said Rachel Penhallow. "She tries to flirt with every man—why, she even tries to flirt with Pa," said Mrs William Y.

"Little Sam saw her digging clams down at the sea-run in her bathing-suit the other night," said Mercy Penhallow.

"Yes, and I warrant you she'd just as soon dig them with nothing at all on," said Mrs Clifford bitterly. "Such an example for our girls! What did Little Sam think of it?"

"Well, you know what men are," said Mercy. "He said of course it was hardly a decorous garb but she looked all right if she'd had a bit more meat on her legs."

"Dear me!" was all Mrs Clifford could say; but she said it adequately.

Mrs William Y. looked solemnly at Nan, who was wearing a dress Mrs William Y. thought was a sheer impertinence.

"I would like," she said bitterly, "to ask that girl how she would like to meet her God with those bare knees."

"Naked and ashamed," quoted Mrs Clifford vaguely.

"Oh, I think you exaggerate," said Stanton Grundy, passing by. "Naked and *not* ashamed."

"At any rate, she has *good* knees," said Mrs William Y. majestically. Stanton Grundy was not going to be allowed to sneer unrebuked at any Penhallow.

The little perverse lock stuck up on Hugh's head when he took off his hat for prayer, and Joscelyn had the same irrational impulse to go and smooth it down. Later on she saw Pauline talking to him and looking up at Treewoofe as she talked. Joscelyn resented the latter fact more than the former. Then Sim Penhallow came up and told her he had heard Hugh was going to sell Treewoofe— looking at her to see how she took it. Joscelyn did not let him see the sick dismay which invaded her soul. She took the news impassively, and Sim revenged himself nastily.

"You made a sad mess of things there, my girl."

Joscelyn turned her back on him without a word. Sim went off, vowing Hugh was well rid of *that,* and Joscelyn stood looking at Treewoofe, dim and austere and lovely on its distant hill. Oh, surely, surely Hugh would not sell it. But hadn't Pauline once said she wouldn't live on a bleak hill like that for anything?

Exaggerated reports of the value of the jug had already got around and mythical collectors had offered Aunt Becky fabulous sums for it. Another rumour was that it was to be left to the most truthful person in the clan. A group of men standing near the grave discussed it.

"Have we got to live for a year without telling any lies?" said Uncle Pippin sadly, but with a glint of mischief in his young blue eyes.

"There won't be many of us left in that case," said Stanton Grundy.

"*Us!*" grunted Uncle Pippin resentfully to himself.

Penny Dark went as always to look at what he thought the handsomest stone in the graveyard, which had been put up by Stephen Dark to the memory of a wife he hated. The gravestone was considered one of the sights of Rose River. A high pedestal of white marble surmounted by the life-size figure of an angel with outstretched wings. It had cost Stephen Dark—who never gave his wife a cent he could help giving—a thousand dollars. It was much admired by those who had never seen it on a wet day. *Then* the water ran down the angel's nose and poured off in a stream.

Penny minced past Margaret Penhallow without even noticing her. She thought his bandy legs bandier than ever and she detested his curly eyebrows.

Adam Penhallow was gloomy and would not be sociable. His wife had had twins the previous day. Not that Adam had anything against the poor twins, but—"that finishes us for the jug. Aunt Becky hated twins," he thought sadly. Murray Dark contrived to visit a few graves with Thora and went home satisfied.

The Moon Man was there, wandering about the graveyard,

talking to the dead people in a gruesome way.

"Do you remember Lisa, the first time I kissed you?" he said to the grave of a woman who had been dead for fifteen years. A group of young folks, overhearing him, giggled. To them the Moon Man had always been old and crazy. They could not conceive of him as young and sane, with eager eyes and seeking lips.

"What do you suppose they're thinking of down there?" he asked eerily of William Y., who had never supposed anything about it and shivered at the very idea. Oswald was entirely too friendly with dead people. They were standing by a gravestone on which was a notorious inscription. "She died of a broken heart." The girl whose broken heart was hidden in that neglected corner had been neither Dark nor Penhallow—for which mercy the clan were thankful. But the Moon Man looked at the old lichened stone gently. "If the truth were told, that line could be engraved on many another stone here," he said. "Your mother now—your mother, William Y.—wouldn't it be true on *her* stone, too?"

William Y. made off without a reply, and his place was filled by Gay Penhallow, who couldn't help looking pretty in a smart little hat of black velvet pulled down over her happy eyes, with tiny winglike things sticking up at the sides, as if black butterflies had alighted there. Entirely too smart a hat for a funeral, the matrons reflected. But the old Moon Man smiled at her.

"Don't stay too late at the dance to-night," he whispered. "They kept up a dance too late there once—and Satan entered."

His tone made Gay shiver a little. And how did he know she was going to the dance? She had kept it very secret, knowing many of the clan would disapprove of her going to a dance the night after a clan funeral. This queer old Moon Man knew everything.

The Moon Man turned to Amasa Tyler, who was standing near, and said:

"Have you thought out the pattern of your coffin yet? You'll be needing it soon."

Amasa, who was young and in the pink of health, smiled contemptuously. But when Amasa was killed in a motor-car accident a month later, people recalled what the Moon Man had said and shook their heads. How did he know? Say what you like, there was something in this second-sight business.

Nobody, as usual, took any notice of little Brian Dark. He had asked his uncle to take him to the funeral. Duncan Dark had at first refused. But Mr Conway interceded for him.

"Aw, take the kid," said Mr Conway—"he doesn't have much fun."

So Duncan Dark, being in one of his rare good-humoured moods, had taken him.

Brian knew nothing and cared nothing about Aunt Becky. But he wanted a chance to put a little bouquet of wild flowers on his mother's grave—he always did that when he could, because she had no headstone and nobody ever went near her grave. If she had had a stone the line about the broken heart might very well have been inscribed on it also, though Brian knew nothing about that. He only knew he had no father and that he was a disgrace and nobody loved him. Nobody spoke to him at the funeral—though this was not out of unkindness but simply because they did not think of him. If they had thought of it they would have spoken, for they had all forgotten poor Laura Dark's shame and in any case were not, with all their faults and prejudices, cruel enough to visit it on her child. Besides, Duncan Dark himself was very off colour, and the clan had little to do with him or his household. But Brian believed it was because he was a disgrace. He would have liked to join the group of boys, but he saw in it big Marshall Tracy, who had once taken his scanty lunch from him in school and trampled on it. So he drew back. Anyway, the boys wouldn't welcome him, he knew. He was a shy, delicate, dreamy little creature and the other boys at school tormented him for this. So he had no playmates and was almost always lonely. Sometimes he wished wistfully that he had just one chum. He felt tears coming into his eyes when he saw a sweet-looking woman come up to little Ted Penhallow and kiss him. Ted didn't like it, but Brian, who had never been kissed in his life that he could remember, envied him. He wished there was some one who cared enough to kiss him. There seemed to be so much love in the world and none of it for him.

"Everybody has some friends but me," he thought, his heart swelling under his shabby coat. On his way back from putting his little bouquet on his mother's grave, he passed Margaret Penhallow. Margaret would have spoken to him but Brian slipped by her before she could. He liked her looks—her eyes were kind and beautiful—but he was too shy and timid to linger. Margaret, who had once known and liked poor Laura Dark, thought it a pity her child was so sulky and unattractive. Sickly-looking, too. But likely Alethea Duncan starved him.

II

Peter Penhallow was at the first clan funeral he had ever attended and had already been held up by indignant Mrs Lawyer Dark of Summerside, who wanted to know why he hadn't come to her dinner Tuesday night.

"Your dinner—your dinner?" repeated Peter vaguely. "Why, I wasn't hungry." He had forgotten all about her confounded dinner. He had spent Tuesday evening wondering how he could get possession of Donna Dark. If he had been quite sure of her he would have simply gone to Drowned John and demanded her. But he must be quite sure before he could do that. So now he came boldly up to her at the funeral. She and Virginia were together of course. They had been together the evening before, too, because it had rained. Virginia and Donna had always made it a part of their ritual to spend every rainy evening together. They sat in what Virginia was pleased to call her "den," perfumed by burning incense—which Virginia defined as a "subtle suggestion of exotic romance." When Donna tried it once at home Drowned

John fired the burner out of the window and told her never to let him smell that damned stink in his house again.

Donna was still trying to be faithful to Barry's memory. Aided by Virginia's sentimentalities she succeeded for an hour in forgetting Peter and remembering Barry. It was like a wind blowing over an almost dead fire and for a brief space fanning one lingering ember into a fitful flame. After she went home she had got out Barry's letters and re-read them for the thousandth time. But they were suddenly lifeless—a casket rifled of its jewels—a vase with the perfume gone—a lamp with its flame blown out. The pulsing, vivid personality that was Peter Penhallow had banished the pale phantom that Barry had become.

Virginia was very suspicious. How dared Peter speak to Donna? He was actually holding out his hand.

And Donna was taking it.

"I thought you were on your way to South America," said Donna.

"I've postponed my trip there," said Peter, staring at her. "I think I'll take it as a honeymoon."

"Oh," said Donna, looking at him, too. Eyes can say a great deal in a second—especially when they are like twin deep pools with a star in them, as Peter was thinking Donna's were. And what a delicious mouth she had. He knew now that what he had been seeking for all his life was just the chance to kiss that dimpled mouth. To be sure, her nose was slightly irregular—rather too much like Drowned John's. When all was said and done he had seen hundreds of prettier women. But there was a charm about this Donna—a mighty and potent charm. And her voice was such a sweet, throaty, summery drawl. What a voice for love-making! Peter trembled before this slip—Peter who had never known fear. If he had been quite sure of her he would have put his arm around her and walked her out of the graveyard. But he was not sure, and before he knew what had happened Virginia had whisked Donna off to see the Richard Dark family plot, where Barry should have been buried, even if he wasn't, and where there was a monument to his memory. In the next plot to it Ned Powell was buried. Virginia had already knelt there in silent prayer for ten minutes, her long black veil sweeping picturesquely about her.

"I woke up last night thinking I heard him calling my name," she murmured with tears in her voice. Virginia could infuse tears into her voice at will.

Donna was conscious of a new feeling of disgust and impatience. Was Virginia really any better than old Cousin Matilda Dark, who was always whining about her dear departed husband? When did grief cease to be beautiful and become ridiculous? Donna knew. When it became a secondhand grief—a mere ghost of grief. Yet she had loved Barry very truly. When the word came of his death, her agony had been so great that she had thought it must tear her in pieces. It had seemed the most natural thing in the world to resolve on a dedication of her whole life to his memory. *What* was Virginia reciting as she gazed mournfully at Barry's monument?

Oh, that old verse of Mrs Browning's—

> Unless you can think when the song is done
> No other is soft in the rhythm,
> Unless you can feel when left by one
> That all other men go with him,
> Unless you can dream that his faith is fast
> In behoving or unbehoving,
> Unless you can die when the dream is past—
> Oh, never call it loving.

"That's so true of us, isn't it, Donna darling?" sobbed Virginia.

Donna felt still more impatient. Time was when she had thought that verse very beautiful and affecting. Well, it was so still. But not for her. Some mysterious hour of change had struck. All the melancholies and ecstasies of her young love belonged in a volume to which "finis" was at last written. With eyes suddenly made clear by what Donna, if she had ever heard the phrase, might have defined as "the expulsive power of a new affection," she saw Virginia and herself as they were. The dramatic lovers of grief—nothing else.

"After all, you know," she said coldly, "neither of us *did* die."

"No-o," admitted Virginia reluctantly. "But for weeks after Ned—died—I was tempted to drown myself. I never told you *that.*"

Donna reflected that it must be the only thing Virginia had *not* told her. It suddenly seemed to her that for ten years she had heard of nothing but Virginia's feelings when Ned died. It was an old story and a very boring one. Donna wondered if she were becoming heartless. But really poor Virginia was tiresome. Donna felt thankful she had never talked much about her feelings in Barry's case. She had no silly outpourings to blush over now and she was fortunately ignorant of how many of Virginia's absurdities were imputed to her. She walked away abruptly. After all, Barry's grave was not there. It was foolish to stand, a figure of woe, beside a plot where only his grandfather and grandmother were buried. She didn't believe for a moment that Virginia had ever had the faintest notion of drowning herself. She had been enjoying her weeds and her romantic position as a young war widow—Donna felt herself growing more hateful and cynical every moment—far too much for that. Aunty But came wandering along—an odd little figure in her rusty black and her queer old bonnet with its rampant spray of imitation osprey. Aunty But was seventy-five, but she was, as she claimed, spry as a cricket and still busy most of her time helping babies into the clan. She looked at the headstone of Barry's grandmother and sighed.

"She was his second wife—but she was a very nice woman," she said. "And hasn't it been a lovely funeral, dears? But—don't you think—a little bit *too* cheerful?"

"Aunt Becky wanted it cheerful," reminded Donna.

Aunty But shook her head. But what Aunty But would

have said was never known. For at that moment the scandal took place and everybody swarmed to the gate, where there was a great commotion among a crowd of men. *Outside* the graveyard—oh, most providentially outside of it—two men were fighting each other—Percy Dark and David Dark, two hitherto peaceful friends. Going at each other, hatless and coatless, red-faced and furious. Nobody ever knew just what had started the fight except that it was something one of them had said about the jug. From verbal warfare they resorted to fists. Percy was heard to exclaim, "I'll take some of the conceit out of you!" and assaulted first. William Y. tried to stop them and for reward got a whack on the nose that made it bleed profusely and robbed him of his pomposity for a week. Mrs David Dark fainted and Mrs Percy was never to go out anywhere the rest of the summer, so ashamed was she. Though at the time she behaved very well. She neither fainted nor had hysterics. Undismayed by William Y.'s fate she got between the two mad creatures and dared David to strike *her.* Before David could accept or refuse the challenge, both he and Percy were caught from behind and frog-marched to their respective cars. The fight was finished but the scandal was not. Before night it was all over the country that two of the Darks had fought at their aunt's funeral over her property and had to be dragged apart by their wives. It took years for them to live it down.

"Thank heaven, the minister was away before they started," sobbed Mrs Clifford.

Uncle Pippin pretended to be horrified, but in secret he thought the fight made the funeral more interesting and felt it a pity that Aunt Becky wasn't alive to see the prayerful David and the sanctimonious Percy pumelling each other like that. Tempest Dark laughed for the first time since his wife's death.

III

Donna and Virginia walked home together. Virginia contrived to tell Donna some weird tales about Peter—especially those yarns of his having "gone native" in the East Indies and having several dozens of dark-skinned wives. Donna didn't believe a word of them, but as yet she did not dare to defend Peter. She was not at all sure about him—especially about his attitude to her. Did she really exist for him at all? Until she was certain of that she was not going to commit herself. Let Virginia rave.

"I wonder if it's going to rain," said Virginia at Drowned John's gate.

"No—no, I'm sure it isn't—it's going to be a lovely evening. The moon will clear away the clouds," said Donna positively. She really couldn't stand any more of Virginia just then. Besides, she was dreadfully hungry and Virginia, who cared nothing for eating, always contrived to make the hearty Donna feel like a pig.

"I wish there was no moon to-night. I hate moonlight—it always reminds me of things I want to forget," said Virginia mournfully and inconsistently. For Virginia certainly did not want to forget things. But Virginia never allowed consistency to bother her when she got hold of what she thought a touching phrase. She floated off in her weeds uneasily. Certainly something had come over Donna. But it couldn't be Peter. It was absurd to suppose it could be Peter.

It *was* Peter. Donna knew that at last as she entered Drowned John's stodgy and comfortable home. She was in love with Peter Penhallow. And he, if eyes were to be believed, was in love with her. And what was to be done about it? Drowned John would raise the roof? Both he and Thekla were opposed to her marrying again—marrying anybody. But imagination faltered before the scenes they would make if she tried to marry Peter Penhallow. Well, Peter hadn't asked her to marry him. Perhaps he never would. Who in the world was laughing upstairs? Oh, that fool of a Thekla! Thekla was always trying some new health fad. Just now it was laughing for ten minutes every day. It got on Donna's nerves and she was raspy enough when she went to the supper-table. Drowned John was in a bad temper, too. He had come home from the funeral to find his favourite pig sick and couldn't swear about it. Thekla tried to placate him and ordinarily this would have appeased him. He liked to feel that his women-folk felt the need of placating him. But why wasn't Donna doing it? Donna was sitting in an absent silence as if his good or bad temper were nothing to her. Drowned John took his annoyance out in abusing everybody who had been at the funeral—especially Peter Penhallow. He expressed himself forcibly regarding Peter Penhallow.

"How would you like him for a son-in-law?" asked Donna.

Drowned John thought Donna was trying to be funny. He barked out a laugh.

"I'd sooner have the devil," he said, banging the table. "Thekla, is this knife *ever* sharpened? Two women to run this house and a man can't get a decent bread-knife!"

Donna escaped after supper. She could not spend the evening in the house. She was restless and unhappy and lonely. What had Peter meant about taking a honeymoon in South America. Who was to be the bride? Oh, she was tired of everything. The world was tired of everything. Even the very moon looked forlorn—a widow of the skies.

Donna walked along the winding drive by Rose River till she reached a little point running out into it. It was covered by an old orchard with an old ruined house in the middle of it. The Courting-House Uncle Pippin had named it, because spoony couples were in the habit of sitting on its steps; but there were none there when Donna reached it. She was just in time to meet Peter Penhallow, who had tied his boat to a bough and was coming up the old mossy path. They looked at each other, knowing it was Fate.

Peter had gone home from the funeral in a mood of black depression. What particular kind of an ass was he! Donna had deliberately turned her back on him and gone to weep at Barry's grave—or at least his gravestone. Her heart was still buried there. Peter had laughed when he had first heard Donna had said that. But he laughed no longer. It was now a tragedy.

In his despair he rushed to young Jeff's boat and began rowing down the river. He had some mad romantic notion of rowing down far enough to see Donna's light. Peter was so love-sick that there was no crazy juvenile thing he would not do. The day grew dimmer and dimmer. At first the river was of pale gold; then it was dim silver—then like a waiting woman in the darkness. Along its soft velvet shores home-lights twinkled out. He, Peter, had no home. No home except where Donna was. Where she was would always be home for him. And then he saw her coming up the winding drive.

When they came to their senses they were sitting side by side on the steps of the Courting-House between two white blooming spirea bushes. Peter had said, "Good evening," when what he had wanted to say was, "Hail, goddess." Donna could never recall what she said.

About them was night—and faint starlight—and scented winds. A dog was taking the countryside into his confidence two farms away.

Donna knew now that Peter loved her. She would share the flame and wonder that was his life—she would know the lure in the thought of treading where no white woman's foot had ever trod—they would gaze together on virgin mountain tops climbing upward into sunset skies—they would stand on peaks in Darien—they would spend nights together in the jungle—hot, scented, spicy nights—or under desert stars—didn't she hear the tinkling of camel-bells?

"I think I've been drunk ever since I saw you at Aunt Becky's levee—a week ago—a year ago—a lifetime ago," said Peter. "Drunk with the devilish magic of you, girl. And to think I've been hating you all my life! *You!*"

Donna sighed with rapture. She must keep this moment

forever. Adventure—mystery—love—the three most significant words in any language—were to be hers again. She was for the time being as perfectly, youngly, fearlessly happy as if she had never learned the bitter lesson that joy could die. She couldn't think of anything to say, but words did not seem necessary. She knew she was very beautiful—she had put on beauty like a garment. And the night was beautiful—and the sunken old rotten steps were beautiful—and the dog was beautiful. As for Peter—he was just Peter.

"Isn't that a jolly wind?" said Peter, as it blew around them from the river. "I hate an evening when there's no wind. It seems so dead. I always feel ten times more alive when there's a wind blowing."

"So do I," said Donna.

Then they spent some rapturous silent moments reflecting how wonderful it was that they should both love wind.

The moon came out from behind a cloud. Silver lights and ebon shadows played all about the old orchard. Peter had been silent so long that Donna had to ask him what he was thinking of. Just for the sake of hearing his dear voice again.

"Watch that dark cloud leaving the moon," said Peter, who had no notion of making love in the common way. "It's as good as an eclipse."

"How silvery it will be on the moon side," said Donna dreamily. "It must be wonderful."

"When I get my aeroplane we'll fly up in it when there's a cloud like that and see it from the moon side," said Peter, who had never thought of getting an aeroplane before but knew now he must have one and sweep in it with Donna through skies of dawn. "And I'll get you the Southern Cross for a brooch. Or would you prefer the belt of Orion for a girdle?"

"Oh," said Donna. She stood up and held out her arms to the moon. Perhaps she knew she had very beautiful arms, shining like warm marble through the sleeves of her filmy black dress. "I wish I could fly up there now."

"With me?" Peter had risen, too, and snatched at the dark blossom of her loveliness. He kissed her again and again. Donna returned his kisses—shamelessly, Virginia would have said. But there was no thought of Virginia or Barry or old feuds. They were alone in their exquisite night of moonlight and shadow and glamour.

"With me?" asked Peter again.

"With you," answered Donna between kisses.

Peter laughed down into her eyes triumphantly.

"I'm the only man in the world you could ever love," he said arrogantly and truthfully. "How soon can we be married?"

"Tee-hee—how very romantic" tittered Mrs Toynbee Dark, who had been standing for ten minutes at the corner of the old house watching them with sinister little black eyes.

"Ho, ho, my pet weasel, so you're there," said Peter. "Rejoice with me, widow of Toynbee, Donna has promised to marry me."

"So her heart has had a resurrection," said Mrs Toynbee. "It's an interesting idea. But what will Drowned John say about it?"

IV

Peter and Donna were not the only pair whose troth was plighted that night. The phrase was Gay's—she thought it sounded much more wonderful than just getting engaged. Nan, who was to go to the dance with Gay and Noel, went home with her from the funeral and on the way told Gay that her mother had decided to stay on the island until the matter of the jug was settled.

"She says she won't go back to St. John till it's known who is to get it. Poor mums! She'll certainly go loco if *she* doesn't. Dad is to be in China most of the year on business, so he won't miss us. We're taking the rooms at The Pinery Aunt Becky had. To think when life is so short I must be buried here for a year. It's poisonous."

Gay felt a little dashed. She didn't know why it chilled her to hear that Nan was going to stay around, but it did. She did not talk much and was rather relieved when they reached Maywood. Maywood had been one of the show-places of the clan when Howard Penhallow was alive, but it had gone to seed since— the shingles curled up a bit—the veranda roof was sagging—it needed paint badly. The grounds had run wild. But it had beauty of a sort yet, nestled under its steep hill of dark spruces with the near shore in its sapphire of sky and wave, and Gay loved it. It hurt and angered her when Nan called it a picturesque old ruin.

But she forgot all about Nan and her prickles as she dressed for the dance. It was delightful to make herself beautiful for Noel. She would wear her dress of primrose silk and her new, high-heeled fairy slippers. She always felt she was beautiful when she put on that dress. To slip such a lovely golden gown over her head—give her bobbed hair a shake like a daffodil tossing in the wind—and then look at the miracle.

All very fine till Nan slipped in and stood beside her— purposely perhaps. Nan in a wispy dress you could crumple in your hand—a shining, daring gown of red with a design of silver grapes all over it—hair with a filet of silver-green leaves, starred with one red bud, around her sleek, ash-gold head. Gay felt momentarily quenched.

"I look *home-made* beside her, that's the miserable truth," she thought. "Pretty, oh, yes, but home-made."

And her eyebrows looked so black and heavy beside the narrow line over Nan's subtle eyes. But Gay plucked up heart— the faint rose of her cheeks under the dark stain of her lashes was not make-up and say what you might about smartness, that curl of Nan's in front of her ear looked exactly like a side-whisker. Gay forgot Nan again as she ran down to the gate in the back of the garden whence she could see the curve in the Charlottetown road around which Noel's car must come.

She saw Mercy Penhallow and her mother in the glass porch as she ran. And she knew that quite likely they were clapperclawing Noel—Mercy, anyhow. When Gay had first begun to go about with Noel, her whole clan lifted their noses and keened. If people only wouldn't interfere so in one's life! The idea of them insinuating that Noel wasn't good enough for her—those inbred Darks and Penhallows! Don't dare marry outside of the Royal Family! Gay tossed her head in a fine scorn of them as she flitted through the garden on her slender and golden feet.

Mercy Penhallow had not yet begun on Noel. She and Mrs Howard had been discussing the funeral in all its details. Now Mercy's pale watery eyes were fixed on Nan, who was on the front veranda smoking a cigarette to the scandal of all Rose River folks who happened to go by.

"She must think her back beautiful—she shows so much of it," said Mercy. "But then it's old-fashioned to be modest."

Mrs Howard smiled tolerantly. Mrs Howard, her clan thought, was too tolerant. That was why matters had gone so far between Gay and Noel Gibson.

"She's going to the dance at the Charlottetown Country Club with Gay and Noel. I would have preferred Gay not to have gone, the night after the funeral—but the young people of to-day don't feel as we used to do about such things."

"The whole world is dancing mad," snapped Mercy. "The young fry of to-day have neither manners nor morals. As for Nan, she's out to catch a man, they say. Boys on the brain—running after them all the time, I'm told."

"The girls of our time let the boys do the running," smiled Mrs Howard. "It was more fun. I think—one could stop when one wanted to be caught."

Mercy, who had never been "caught," whether she wanted to be or not, sniffed.

"I suppose Gay is still crazy after Noel?" she said. "Why don't you put a stop to that, Lucilla?"

Mrs Howard looked distressed.

"How can I? Gay knows I don't like him. But the child is infatuated. Why, when I said something to her about his pedigree she said, 'Mother dear, Noel isn't a horse'."

"And Roger just mad about her!" moaned Mercy.

"A splendid fellow with gobs of money. He could give her *everything*—"

"Except happiness," said Mrs Howard sadly. But she said it only in thought and Mercy prattled on. "Noel hasn't a penny beyond his salary and I doubt if he'll ever have more. Besides, what are those Gibsons? Merely mushrooms. I wonder what her poor father would have thought of it."

Mrs Howard sighed. She was not as worldly as some of her clan. She did not want Gay to marry Roger, when she did not love him, simply because he had money. And it was not one of her counts against Noel that he had none. His Gibsonness mattered more. Mrs Howard knew her Gibsons as Gay could never know them. And she had, in spite of Gay's quip about the pedigree, an old-fashioned conviction about what was bred in the bone. The first time she had seen Noel she had thought, "A boy shouldn't know how to use his eyes like that. And he has the Gibson mouth."

But she couldn't bear to quarrel with Gay. Gay was all she had. Mercy didn't understand. It wasn't so simple "putting a stop" to things. Gay had a will of her own under all her youth and her sweetness, and Mrs Howard couldn't bear to make her child unhappy.

"Maybe he's only flirting with her," was Mercy's response to the sigh. "The Gibsons are very fickle."

Mrs Howard didn't like that either. It was unthinkable that a Gibson should be "only flirting" with a Penhallow. She resented the insinuation that Gay might be tossed aside.

"I'm afraid he's only too much in earnest and I think—I'm pretty sure—they're almost engaged already."

"Almost engaged. Lucilla dear, talk sense. Either people are engaged or they are *not*. And if Gay were *my* daughter—"

Mrs Howard hid a smile. She couldn't help thinking that if Gay had been Mercy's daughter neither Noel nor any other boy might have bothered her much. Poor Mercy! She was so very plain. With that terrible dewlap! And a face in which the features all seemed afraid of each other. Mrs Howard felt for her the complacent pity of a woman who had once been very pretty herself and was still agreeable to look upon.

Mrs Howard was by all odds the most popular woman in the clan. Wherever she was she always seemed to be in the right place without making any fuss about it. She generally got the best of any argument because she never argued—she only smiled. She did not know anything about a great many things, but she knew a great deal about loving and cooking and a woman can go far on that. She was no paw-and-claw friend, giving a dig now and a pat then, as so many were; and there was something about her that made people want to tell her their secrets—their beautiful secrets. Aunt Becky had always flattered herself that she knew all the clan secrets before anybody else, but Mrs Howard knew many things before Aunt Becky did.

Even Stanton Grundy, who seldom spoke well of a woman because he had a reputation for sardonic humour to keep up, had been heard to say of Mrs Howard that for once God knew what He was about when He made a woman.

Some of the clan thought Mrs Howard dressed too gay for a widow of her age, but Mrs Howard only laughed at this.

"I always liked bright colours and I'll wear them till I die," she told them. "You can bury me in black if you want to, but as long as breath's in me I'll wear blue."

"Talking of Roger," said Mercy, "he's looking miserable of late. Thin as a lath. Is he worrying over Gay? Or overworking?"

"A little of both, I'm afraid. Mrs Gateway died last week. No one on earth could have saved her, but Roger takes it terribly hard when he loses a patient."

"He's got more feeling than most doctors," said Mercy. "Gay's a blind little goose if she passes him over for Noel, that's all I've got to say."

It wasn't all Mercy had to say, but Mrs Howard deftly changed the unwelcome subject by switching to Aunt Becky's jug. Had Mercy heard? Two of Mrs Adam Penhallow's boarders at Indian Spring, Gerald Elmslie and Grosset Thompson, had quarrelled with each other over the jug and left. It was hard on Mrs Adam, who found it hard enough to make both ends meet.

"But what on earth made Gerald and Grosset quarrel over the jug?" asked Mercy. "*They've* nothing to do with it."

"Oh, Gerald is keeping company with Vera Dark and Grosset is engaged to Sally Penhallow," was the sufficient explanation. But that would not fill Mrs Adam's lean purse.

"It's my opinion that jug will drive somebody crazy yet," said Mercy.

Gay was watching for Noel at the gate, under an old spruce tree that was like a grim, black sorrowful priest. Evenings out of mind she had watched for him so. She could distinctly hear on the calm evening air Drowned John's Olympian laughter echoing along the shore down at Rose River and she resented it. When she came here to dream of Noel, only the loveliest of muted sounds should be heard—the faintest whisper of trees—the half-heard, half-felt moan of the surf—the airiest sigh of wind. It was the dearest half-hour of the whole day—this faint, gold, dusky one just before it got truly dark. She wanted to keep it wholly sacred to Noel—she was young and in love and it was spring, remember. So of course Drowned John had to be bellowing and Roger had to come stepping up behind her and stand beside her, looking down at her. Tall, grim, scarred Roger! At least Gay thought him grim, contrasting his thin face and mop of dark red hair with Noel's smoothness and sleekness. Yet she liked Roger very much and would have liked him more if her clan had not wanted her to marry him.

Roger looked at her—at the trim, shining, golden-brown head of her. Her fine black brows. Her fan-lashed, velvety eyes. That dimple just below the delightful red mouth of hers. That creamy throat above her golden dress. She was as shy and sweet and wilful as April, this little Gay. Who could help loving her? Her very look said, "Come and love me." What a soft, gentle little voice she had—one of the few women's voices he had ever heard with pleasure. He was very critical as regards women's voices, and very sensitive to them. Nothing hurt him quite so much as an unlovely voice—not even unloveliness of face.

She had something in her hand for him, if she would but open her hand and give it. He had ceased to hope she ever would. He knew the dream behind her lashes was not for him. He knew perfectly well that she was waiting there for another man, compared to whom he, Roger, was a mere shadow and puppet. Suddenly he realized that he had lived thirty-two years against Gay's eighteen.

Why on earth, he wondered, had he to love Gay when there were dozens of girls who would jump at him, as he knew perfectly well? But there it was. He did love her. And he wanted her to be happy. He was glad that in such a world any one could be as happy as Gay was. If that Gibson boy didn't *keep* her happy!

"This old gate is still here. I thought your mother was going to have it taken away."

"I wouldn't let her," said Gay. "This is *my* gate. I love it."

"I like any gate," said Roger whimsically. "A gate is a luring thing—a promise. There may be something wonderful beyond and you are not shut out. A gate is a mystery—a symbol. What would we find, you and I, Gay, if we opened that gate and went through?"

"A little green sunset hollow of white violets," laughed Gay. "But we're not going through, Roger—there's a dew on the grass and I'd spoil my new slippers."

She looked at him as she laughed—only for a moment, but that was the moment Noel's car flashed around the curve and she missed it. When she went back to the house, leaving Roger at the unopened gate, she found Noel sitting beside Nan on the steps. They had never met before but already they seemed to have known each other all their lives. And Nan was looking up at Noel with the eyes that instantly melted men but were not quite so effective with women. A strange, icy, little ripple ran all over Gay.

"I've just been asking Noel if he waves his hair with the curling-tongs," said Nan in her lazy, impudent voice.

Gay forgot her shivers and all other unpleasant things as she drifted through the dances. Noel said delicious things to her and looked things still more delicious; and when half way through it she sat out a dance with Noel in a shadowy corner of the balcony her cup brimmed full. For Noel whispered a question and Gay, smiling, blushing, yet with a queer little catch in her throat, and eyes strangely near to tears, whispered her answer. They were no longer "almost" engaged.

For the rest of the evening Gay floated—or seemed to float—in a rosy mist of something too rare and exquisite even to be called by so common a name as happiness. They left Nan at The Pinery on their way back and drove on to Maywood alone. They lingered over saying good-bye. It was such a sweet pleasure because they would meet so soon again. They stood under the big, late-blooming apple tree at the turn of the walk, among the soft, trembling shadows of the moonlit leaves. All around and beyond was a delicate, unreal moonlit world. The night was full of mystery and wonder; there never had—there never could have been—such a night before. Gay wondered as she gave her lips, red as the Rose of Love itself, to Noel, how many lovers all over the world were standing thus entranced—how many vows were being whispered thus in the starlight. The old tree suddenly waved its boughs over them as if in blessing. So many lovers had stood beneath it—it had screened so many kisses. Many of the lips that had kissed were ashes now. But the miracle of love renewed itself every springtime.

In her room Gay undressed by moonlight. She shredded the petals of the white June roses she had worn into the little blue rose-jar on her table. Her father had given her the jar when she was a child and had told her to drop a handful of rose leaves in it for every perfectly happy day she had. The jar was almost full now. There was only room really for one more handful. Gay smiled. She would put that handful in it on her wedding-day and then seal it up forever as a symbol of her girlhood.

Of course she didn't sleep. It would be a pity to waste a moment of such a night sleeping. It was nicer to lie awake thinking of Noel. Even planning a little bit about her wedding. It was to be in the fall. Her wedding-dress—satin as creamy as her own skin—"Your skin is like the petal of a white narcissus," Noel had told her—shimmering silk stockings—laces like sea-foam—one of those slender platinum wedding-rings—"the lovely Mrs Noel Gibson"—"one of the season's most charming brides"—a little house somewhere—perhaps one of those darling new bungalows—with yellow curtains like sunshine on its windows and yellow plates like circles of sunshine on its breakfast-table. With Noel opposite.

"Little love." She could hear him as he said it under the apple tree, looking down into the pools of darkness that were her eyes. How wonderful and unbelievable it was that out of a whole world of beautiful girls, his for the asking, he should have chosen *her.*

Just once she thought of the old Moon Man's warning—"Don't be too happy." That poor old crazy Moon Man. As if one could be too happy! As if God didn't like to see you happy! Why, people were made for happiness.

"I'll always love this night," thought Gay. "The eighth of June—it will always be the dearest date of the year. I'll always celebrate it in some dear secret little way of my own."

And they would always be together—always. On rough paths and smooth. Dawns and twilights would be more beautiful because they would be together.

"If I were dead," thought Gay, "and Noel came and looked at me I'd live again."

Next day Nan rang Gay up on the telephone.

"I think I like your Noel," Nan said, drawlingly. "I think I'll take him from you."

Gay laughed triumphantly.

"You can't," she said.

V

Gay was not the only one of the clan who kept vigil that night. Neither Donna nor Peter slept. Mrs David Dark and Mrs Palmer Dark lay awake in their shame beside snoring spouses, wondering dumbly why life should be so hard for decent women who had always tried to do what was right. Virginia was awake worrying. Mrs Toynbee Dark was awake nursing her venom. Pauline Dark was awake wondering if Hugh would really get that divorce. Thora Dark waited anxiously for a drunken, abusive husband to come home. The Sams slept, although both, did they but know it, had cause to be wakeful. Hugh Dark and Roger Penhallow slept soundly. Even William Y. slept, with a poultice on his nose. On the whole, the men seemed to have the best of it, unless Aunt Becky, sleeping so dreamlessly in her grave in the trim Rose River churchyard, evened things up for the women.

Joscelyn was not sleeping either. She went to bed and tossed restlessly for hours. Finally she rose softly, dressed, and slipped out of the house to the shore. The hollows among the dunes were filled with moonlight. The cool wind nestled in the grasses on the red "capes," bringing whiffs of the faint, cold, sweet perfumes of night. There was a wash of gleaming ripples all along the shore and a mist mirage over the harbour. Far out she heard the heart-breaking call of the sea that had called for thousands of years.

She felt old and cold and silly and empty. Suppose Hugh really loved Pauline and wanted to be free. Very well. Why not? Did not *she* love Frank Dark? Why could she not think philosophically, "Well, if Hugh gets a divorce *I* will be free, too, and perhaps Frank will come back"—no, she could not think that. Such a thought seemed to tarnish and cheapen the high flame of love she had nursed in her heart for years.

Dawn was breaking over the dunes and little shudders were running through the sand-hill grasses when she went back to the house. She had not dreamed of meeting any one at that early hour, but who should come trotting across Al Griscom's silent white pasture of morning dew but Aunty But, bent two-double, with her head wrapped in a grey shawl, out of which her bright little eyes peered curiously at Joscelyn. She seemed at once incredibly old and elfinly young.

"You're up early, Mrs Dark."

Joscelyn hated to be called Mrs Dark, just as she hated to take a letter out of the post-office addressed to "Mrs Hugh Dark." Once when she had had to sign some legal document "Joscelyn Dark," she had thrown down the pen and risen with lips as white as snow. Aunty But was the only one of the clan who ever addressed her as "Mrs Dark." And there was no use in snubbing Aunty But.

"And you, too, Aunty."

"Eh, but I've never been in bed at all. I've been up at Forest Myers' all night. A little girl there—a fine baby but got the Myers mouth, I'm afraid."

"And Alice?"

"Alice is fine but awful sorry for herself. Yet she didn't have a bad time at all. No caterwauling to speak of. It's a pleasure to help a woman like that to a baby. I might have done the same for you in that house up there"—Aunty But waved her hand at distant Treewoofe, taking shape in the pale grey light that was creeping over the hill—"if you hadn't behaved as you did. *I* brought babies into that house many a time—I was there when Clara Treewoofe was born. Such a time! Old Cornelius—but he was young Cornelius then—was crazy wild. You'd have thought nobody'd ever had a baby before. Finally I had to decoy him to the cellar and lock him up, or that child would never have got born. Poor Mrs Cornelius couldn't rightly give her mind to it for the racket Cornelius was making. Clara was the last baby at Treewoofe. It's high time there was some more. But there may be. I'm hearing Hugh is going to get a Yankee divorce. If that's so, Pauline won't let him slip through her fingers a second time. But she'll never have the babies you'd have had, Joscelyn. She hasn't the figger for it."

VI

Little Brian Dark had to walk home from the funeral because his Uncle Duncan took a notion to go on to town.

"Mind ye get the stones picked off the gore-field before milking," he told him.

Brian never had a day to play—never even half a day. He was very tired, for he had picked stones all the afternoon since early morning; and he was hungry. To be sure, he was always hungry; but the hunger in his heart was worse than any physical hunger. And there was no monument to his mother. Would he ever be able, when he grew up, to earn enough money to get one?

When he reached Duncan Dark's ugly yellow house among its lean trees, he took off his shabby "best suit," put on his ragged work-garb, and went out to the gore to pick stones. He picked stones until milking-time, his back aching as well as his heart. Then he helped Mr Conway milk the cows. Mr Conway was the only hired man Brian had ever heard of who was called "Mr." Mr Conway said he wouldn't work for any one who wouldn't call him "Mr." He was as good as any master, by gosh. Brian rather liked Mr Conway, who looked more like a poet gone to seed than a hired man. He had a shock of wavy, dark auburn hair, a drooping moustache and goatee, and round, brilliant, brown eyes. He was a stranger from Nova Scotia and called himself a Bluenose. Brian often wondered why, for Mr Conway's nose was far from blue. Red in fact.

When milking was over, Aunt Alethea, a tall, fair, slatternly woman, with a general air of shrewishness about her, told him to go down to Little Friday Cove and see if he could get a codfish from one of the Sams.

"Be smart about it, too," she admonished him. "None of your dawdling, or the Moon Man will cotch you."

What the Moon Man would do when he "cotched" him she never specified, perhaps reasoning that the unknown was always more terrible than the known. Brian's private opinion was that he would boil him in oil and pick his bones. He was more afraid of the Moon Man now than of the devil. He had once been dreadfully afraid of the devil. Somebody had told him that when a boy had no father, the devil was his father and would come along some night and carry him off. He had been sick with horror many a night after that. But Mr Conway had told him there was no devil and emphasized it with so many "By goshes" that Brian believed him. He wanted to believe him. But Mr Conway by-goshed heaven away, too, and that was not so good because it meant he would never see his mother again. Mr Conway didn't go so far as to say there was no God. He even admitted there probably was. Somebody had to run things, though he was making a poor job of it.

"Likely a young God who hain't learned his business yet, by gosh," said Mr Conway.

Brian was too young himself to be scandalized by this. He rather liked the idea of a young God. He had always thought of God as a stern, bearded Old Man.

If Brian had not been so tired he would have enjoyed the walk to Little Friday Cove. He loved to watch the harbour lights blossoming out in the blue of the twilight. He loved to watch the mysterious ships sailing out beyond the dunes to who knew what enchanted shores. He picked one that was just going over the bar and went with it in fancy. When he reached Little Friday Cove he found Big Sam alone and rather low in his mind. Trouble was coming; various signs and portents had pointed to it for days. No longer could he be blind to them. Salt, the dog, had howled dismally all Monday of the preceding week. On Tuesday Little Sam had smashed the looking-glass he had shaved by for forty years. On Wednesday Big Sam had failed to pick up a pin he had seen; on Thursday he had walked under Tom Appleby's ladder at the factory—and on Friday—Friday, mind you—Big and Little Sam between them had contrived to upset the salt at supper.

Big Sam was determined not to be superstitious. What did spilled salt and broken looking-glasses matter to good

Presbyterians? But he did believe in dreams—having Biblical warrant for the same. And he had had a horrible one the night after Aunt Becky died—of seeing the full moon, one moment burning black, the next livid red, coming nearer and nearer the earth. He woke, just as it seemed near enough to be touched, with a howl of agony that shattered the stillness of the spring night at Little Friday Cove for yards around. Big Sam, who had kept a careful and copious diary of his dreams for forty years, looked them all over and concluded that none of them had been as awe-inspiring as this one.

Then there was that peculiar sound the gulf had been making of late. When the Old Lady of the Gulf skirled like a witch, somebody was going to sup sorrow.

"Little Sam sneaked off somewhere's after supper," he told Brian. "I kinder thought I'd go up to the run myself and dig some clams. But I didn't—felt a bit tired. I'm beginning to feel my years. But I've got the key of the fish-house and I'll get a cod out for you. They're all most too big for you to carry, though. Stay and have a saucer of clam chowder. There's some left. That man can make chowder, I'll admit."

Brian would have liked the chowder well enough, for his supper had been of the sketchiest description, but it was getting dark. He must get home before it got very dark—he was afraid. He was ashamed of his cowardice, but there it was. Sometimes he thought if any one really loved him he would not be afraid of so many things. He looked so small and wistful that Big Sam gave the poor little shrimp a nickel to buy a chocolate bar at the Widow Terlizzick's little store on the way home. But Brian did not stop at the store. He did not like the Widow Terlizzick or the noisy crowd of loafers who were always in and around the store on summer nights. He hurried home with his heavy codfish and was told to clear off to bed—he would have to be up at four to help Mr Conway take some calves to market. Brian would have liked to sit out under the big apple tree for a little while and play his jew's-harp. He liked the old apple tree. It seemed like a friend to him—a great, kindly, fragrant, blooming creature stretching protecting arms over him. And he loved to play on his little jew's-harp. Once he had played on his jew's-harp in the evening at a house where he was planting potatoes, and two young people—one of them a girl in a white dress—had danced to his playing in the moonlit orchard. It was one of the few memories of beauty in his life. When he played his jew's-harp now he saw them again—dancing—dancing—dancing. With the grace of wind-blown leaves—white and mystic and lovely—to his elfin tune.

But Aunt Alethea was inexorable and Brian climbed the ladder to the kitchen loft, where he always slept alone and which he hated. He was afraid of the rats that infested it. There was only one thing he liked about it—from its window he could get a glimpse of the sea and a misty blue headland beyond which were wonderful sunsets. To-night there was a lovely rose and gold afterlight and the sea was blackly-blue under it. And he could see the pink-shaded lamp in the window of the Dollar house on the other side of the road. He loved to watch it, making a great glowing spot of colour in the darkness. When it suddenly went out he felt terribly lonely. Tears came to his eyes. He was such a little creature, alone in a great, dim, hostile world. Brian looked up at the sky. How dark the night was! How fearfully bright the stars!

"Dear God," he said softly, "dear *Young* God, please don't forget me."

He lay down on his hard little mattress. He was glad there was no moonlight yet. Moonlit nights in the loft frightened him. The things hanging from the rafters took on such queer shapes. And that hole in the wall of the loft that opened into the unfloored attic of the main house—it was dreadful on moonlit nights, when it looked so black and menacing. Who knew what might pop out of a hole like that? When it was dark he could not see it. It was a long while before he fell asleep. But at last he did—just about the time that Little Sam came home to Little Friday Cove.

VII

Little Sam had heard at the funeral that the raffle for which he had bought the ticket from Mosey Gautier, was to be held that night. So after supper he thought he might as well saunter around to Chapel Point and see if he had any luck.

He had.

Big Sam was sound asleep in his bunk, with Mustard rolled up in a golden ball on his stomach. Little Sam unwrapped something from the parcel he was carrying, looked at it rather dubiously, shook his head, and tried the effect of it on the clock shelf. Something in him liked it. Something else was uneasy.

"She's got a real fine figger," he reflected, with a speculative glance at the unconscious Big Sam. "But I dunno what he'll think of her—I really dunno. Nor the minister."

These considerations did not keep Little Sam awake. He fell asleep promptly and Aurora, goddess of the dawn, kept her vigil on the clock shelf through the hours of darkness, and was the first thing on which Big Sam's eyes rested when he opened them in the morning. There she stood, her lithe lovely form poised on tiptoe, smitten by a red-gold beam from the sun that was rising across the harbour.

"What the devil is that?" said Big Sam, thinking this was another dream. He flung himself out of his bunk, upsetting an indignant cat, and walked across the room.

"It ain't a dream," he said incredulously. "It's a statoo—a naked statoo."

Salt, who had been curled up at Little Sam's feet, bounded to the floor after Mustard. He liked Mustard well enough but he wasn't going to have her sitting there on the floor grinning at him. The resultant disturbance awoke Little Sam, who sat up drowsily and inquired what the row was about.

"Samuel Beelby Dark," said Big Sam ominously, "what's that up there?"

"Samuel Phemister Dark," returned Little Sam mockingly,

"that's an alabaster statooette—genuine alabaster. I drew it for fifth prize at the Chapel lottery last night. Pretty, ain't it?"

"Pretty?" Big Sam's voice boomed out. "Pretty! It's indecent and obscene, that's what *it* is. You take it right down and fire it out in the gulf as far as you can fire it."

If Big Sam had not thus flown off the handle it is probable that Little Sam would have done exactly that, being somewhat uneasy over the look of the thing generally and what Mr Trackley might say about it. But he was not going to be bullied into it by that little runt of a Big Sam and he'd let him see it.

"Oh, I guess not," he retorted coolly. "I guess it's going to stay right there. Stop yelping now and let your hair curl."

Big Sam's scanty love-locks showed no signs of curling, but his red beard fairly crackled with indignation. He began striding about the room in a fine rage, biting his right hand and then his left. Salt fled one way and Mustard another, leaving the Sams to fight it out.

"'Tain't right to have any kind of statoos, let alone naked ones. It's agin God's law. 'Thou shalt not make unto thee any graven immidge—'"

"Good gosh, I ain't made it, and I ain't worshipping it—"

"That'll come—that'll come. And a Catholic gee-gaw at that. S'pose likely it's the Virgin Mary."

Little Sam looked doubtful. He had been bred up in a good old Presbyterian hatred of Catholics and all their ways and works, but somehow he didn't think even they would go so far as to represent the Virgin Mary entirely unclothed.

"No, 'tain't. I think her name's there at the bottom—Aurorer. Just a gal, that's all."

"Do you think the Apostle Paul ever carried anything like that around with him?" demanded Big Sam. "Or"—as an afterthought that might carry more weight with Little Sam—"poor dear old Aunt Becky who isn't cold in her grave yet?"

"Not likely. St Paul was kind of a woman-hater like yourself. As for Aunt Becky, we ain't in the running for her jug, so why worry? Now stop chewing your fists and pretend you're grown up even if you ain't, Sammy. See if you can dress yourself like a man."

"Thank you. Thank you." Big Sam became ominously calm. "I'm entirely satisfied to be classed with the Apostle Paul. My conscience guides *my* conduct, you ribald old thing!"

"Been making a meal of the dictionary, it seems," retorted Little Sam, yanking his pants off their nail, "and it don't seem to have agreed with your stomach. Better take a dose of sody. Your conscience, as you call it, hasn't nothing to do with it—only your prejurdices. Look at that writing man. Hain't he got half a dozen of them statoos in his summer shanty up the river?"

"If he's a fool—and wuss—is that any reason why you should be? Think of that and your immortal soul, Sam Dark."

"This ain't my day for thinking," retorted the imperturbable Little Sam. "Now that you've blown off your steam, just set the porridge pot on. You'll feel better when you've had your breakfast. Can't 'preciate works of art properly on an empty stomach, Sammy."

Big Sam glared at him. Then he grabbed the porridge pot, yanked open the door, and hurled the pot through it. The pot bounded and clattered and leaped down the rocks to the sandy cove below. Salt and Mustard fled out after it.

"Some day you'll drive me too far," said Little Sam darkly. "You're just a narrow-minded, small-souled old maid, that's what you are. If you hadn't a dirty mind you wouldn't be throwing a fit 'cause you see a stone woman's legs. Your own don't look so artistic, prancing around in that shirt-tail, let me tell you. You really ought to wear pyjamas, Sammy."

"I fired your old pot out to show you I'm in earnest," roared Big Sam. "I tell you I won't have no naked hussy in this house, Sam Dark. I ain't over-squeamish but I draw the line at naked weemen."

"Yell louder, can't you? It's *my* house," said Little Sam.

"Oh, it is, is it? Very well. *Very* well. I'll tell you this right here and now. It ain't big enough for me and you and your Roarer."

"You ain't the first person that idee's occurred to," said Little Sam. "I've had too many tastes of your jaw of late."

Big Sam stopped prancing and tried to look as dignified as a man with nothing on but a shirt can look, as he laid down the ultimatum he never doubted would bring Little Sam to his senses.

"I've stood all I'm a-going to. I've stood them skulls of yours for years but I tell you right here and now, Sam Dark, I won't stand for that atrocity. If it's to remain—*I* leave."

"As for leaving or staying, suit yourself. Aurorer stays there on that clock shelf," retorted Little Sam, striding out and down the rocks to rescue his maltreated porridge pot.

Breakfast was a gloomy meal. Big Sam looked very determined, but Little Sam was not worried. They had had a worse row than this last week, when he had caught Big Sam stealing a piece of raisin pie he had put away for his own snack. But when the silent meal was over and Big Sam ostentatiously dragged an old, battered, bulging valise out from under his bunk and began packing his few chattels into it, Little Sam realized that the crisis was serious. Well, all right—all right. Big Sam needn't think he could bully *him* into giving up Aurorer. He had won her and he was going to keep her and Big Sam could go to Hades. Little Sam really thought Hades. He had picked up the word in his theological reading and thought it sounded more respectable than hell.

Little Sam watched Big Sam stealthily out of his pale woolly eyes as he washed up the dishes and fed Mustard, who came scratching at the window-pane. The morning's sunlit promise had been delusive and it was now, as Little Sam reflected testily, one of them still, dark, misty mornings calculated to dampen one's spirits. This was what came of ladders and looking-glasses.

Big Sam packed his picture of Laurier and the model of a ship, with crimson hull and white sails, that had long adorned the crater-cornered shelf above his bunk. These were indisputably his. But when it came to their small library there was difficulty.

"Which of these books am I to take?" he demanded frostily.

"Whichever you like," said Little Sam, getting out his baking-board. There were only two books in the lot he cared a hoot about, anyhow. *Foxe's Book of Martyrs* and *The Horrible Confession and Execution of John Murdoch (one of the Emigrants who lately left this country) who was hanged at Brockville (Upper Canada) on the 3rd day of September last for the inhuman Murder of His own brother.*

When Little Sam saw Big Sam pack the latter in his valise, he had much ado to repress a grisly groan.

"I'm leaving you the Martyrs and all the dime novels," said Big Sam defensively. "What about the dog and cat?"

"You'd better take the cat," said Little Sam, measuring out flour. "It'll match your whiskers."

This suited Big Sam. Mustard was his favourite.

"And the weegee-board?"

"Take it. I don't hold no dealings with the devil."

Big Sam shut and strapped his valise, put the reluctant Mustard into a bag, and with the bag over his shoulder and his Sunday hat on his head he strode out of the house and down the road without even a glance at Little Sam, who was ostentatiously making raisin pie.

Little Sam watched him out of sight still incredulously. Then he looked at the white, beautiful cause of all the mischief exulting on the clock itself.

"Well, he didn't get you out, my beauty, and I'm jiggered if he's ever going to. No, siree. I've said it and I'll stick to it. Anyhow, my ears won't have to ache any longer, listening to that old epic of his. And I can wear my earrings again."

Little Sam really thought Big Sam would come back when he had cooled down. But he underrated the strength of Big Sam's principles or his stubbornness. The first thing he heard was that Big Sam had rented Tom Wilkins' old shanty at Big Friday Cove and was living there. But not with Mustard. If Big Sam did not come back Mustard did. Mustard was scratching at the window three days after his ignominious departure in a bag. Little Sam let him in and fed him. It wasn't his fault if Big Sam couldn't keep his cat. He, Little Sam, wasn't going to see no dumb animal starve. Mustard stayed home until one Sunday when Big Sam, knowing Little Sam was safely in church, and remembering Homer Penhallow's tactics, came down to Little Friday Cove and got him. All to no purpose. Again Mustard came back—and yet again. After the third attempt Big Sam gave it up in bitterness of soul.

"Do I want his old yaller flannel cat?" he demanded of Stanton Grundy. "God knows I don't. What hurts my feelings is that he *knew* the critter would go back. That's why he offered him so free. The depth of that man! I hear he's going round circulating mean, false things about me and saying I'll soon be sick of living on salt codfish and glad to sneak back for a smell of good cooking. He'll see—he'll see. *I* ain't never made a god of my stomach as *he* does. You should have heard the riot he raised because I et a piece of mouldy old raisin pie he'd cached for himself the greedy pig. And saying it'll be too lonesome at Big Friday for one of my gabby propensities. Yessir, he said them words. Me, lonesome! This place just suits me down to the ground. See the scenery. I'm a lover of nature, sir, my favourite being the moon. And them contented cows up on the Point pasture—I could gaze at 'em by the hour. *They're* all the society I want, sir—present comp'ny always excepted. Not," added Big Sam feelingly, "but what Little Sam had his p'ints. The plum puddings that man could make! And them clam chowders of his stuck to the ribs better'n most things. But I had my soul to think of, hadn't I? And my morals?"

MIDSUMMER MADNESS

Gay did not find the first few weeks of her engagement to Noel all sunshine. One could not in a clan like hers. Among the Darks and Penhallows an engagement was tribal property, and every one claimed the right to comment and criticize, approve or disapprove, according to circumstances. In this instance disapproval was rampant, for none of the clan liked any Gibson and they did not spare Gay's feelings. It simply did not occur to them that a child of eighteen had any feelings to spare, so they dealt with her faithfully.

"Poor little fool, will she giggle as loud after she's been married to him for a couple of years?" said William Y., when he heard Gay's exquisite laugh as she and Noel whirled by in their car one night. To do him justice, William Y. would not have said it in Gay's hearing, but it was straightway carried to her. Gay only laughed again. And she laughed when Cousin Hannah from Summerside asked her if it could be true that she was going to marry "a certain young man." Cousin Hannah would not say "a Gibson." Her manner gave the impression that Gibsons did not really exist. They might imagine they did but they were mere emanations of the Evil One, to be resolutely disbelieved in by any one of good principles and proper breeding. One did not speak openly of the devil. Neither did one speak of the Gibsons. Her contempt stung Gay a bit, in spite of her laughter. But a letter from Noel, simply crammed with darlings, soon removed the sting.

"Do you *really* love him?" asked Mrs William Y. solemnly.

Gay wanted to say no because she detested Mrs William Y. But she also wanted to show her and every one just what Noel meant to her.

"He's the only man in the world for me, Aunty."

"H'm! That's a large order out of about five hundred million men," said Mrs William Y. sarcastically. "However, I remember I once felt that way, too."

This, although Mrs William Y. was unaware of it, was the most dreadful thing Gay had heard yet. Mrs William Y. couldn't have thought William Y. the only man in the world. Of course she had married him—but she *couldn't*. Gay, with the egotism of youth, couldn't believe that *any* woman had ever been in love with William Y., not realizing that when William Y. had been slender and hirsute, twenty-five years before, he had been quite a lady-killer.

"You could do better, you know," persisted Mrs William Y.

"Oh, I suppose you mean Roger," cried Gay petulantly. "You all think there's nobody like Roger."

"Neither there is," said Mrs William Y. with simple and sincere feeling. She loved Roger. Everybody loved him. If only Gay wasn't so silly and romantic. Just swept off her feet by Noel Gibson's eyes and hair.

"I suppose you think it's all fun being married," Mrs Clifford said.

Gay didn't think it was "fun" at all. That wasn't how she regarded marriage. But Aunt Rhoda Dark was just as bad.

"Do you realize what an important event marriage is in anybody's life, Gay?"

Gay was driven into a flippant answer that made Aunt Rhoda shake her head over modern youth.

Rachel Penhallow remarked in Gay's hearing that kidney trouble "ran" in the Gibsons. Mrs Clifford advised "not to let him feel too sure of you." Mrs Denzil raked Noel's father over the coals.

"The only way to get him to do anything was to coax him to do the opposite. I was there the day he threw a plate at his wife. She dodged it, but it made a dent on the mantel. You can see that dent there yet, Gay, if you don't believe me."

"What has all this got to do with me and Noel?" burst out Gay.

"These things are inherited. You can't get away from them."

But Aunt Kate Penhallow didn't think Noel was stubborn like his father. She thought Noel was the opposite—weak and easily swayed. She didn't like his chin; and Uncle Robert didn't like his eyes; and Cousin Amasa didn't like his ears—"They lie too close to his head. You never see such ears on a successful man," said Cousin Amasa, who had outstanding ears of his own but wasn't considered much of a success for all that.

"You would think they were the only people who ever got engaged in the world," said Mrs Toynbee, who, having come through three engagements, naturally didn't think it the wonder Gay and Noel did.

"All the Gibsons are very fickle," said Mrs Artemas Dark, who had been engaged to one herself before she married Artemas. He had treated her badly, but in her secret soul she sometimes thought she preferred him to Artemas still.

"You'd better wait until you're out of the cradle before you marry," growled Drowned John, who was having troubles of his own just then and was very touchy on the subject of engagements.

All this sort of thing only amused Gay. It didn't amount to anything. What did worry her was the subtle undercurrent of disapproval among those whose opinion she really valued. *Nobody* thought well of her engagement. Her mother cried bitterly over it and at first refused to give her consent at all.

"I can't stop you from marrying him, of course," she said, with what was great bitterness for the easy-going Mrs Howard. "But I'll never say I'm willing—never. I've never approved of him, Gay."

"Why—*Why?*" cried Gay piteously. She loved her mother and hated to go against her in anything. "*Why*, Mother? What can you say against him?"

"There's nothing in him," said Mrs Howard feebly. She thought it rather a poor reason, not realizing that she was actually uttering the most serious indictment in the world.

Altogether Gay had a hard time of it for a couple of weeks. Then Cousin Mahala swept down on the clan from her retreat up west—Cousin Mahala, who looked like a handsome old man with her short, crisp, virile grey hair and strong wise face. The eyes a little sunken. The mouth with a humorous quirk. The face of a woman who has *lived.*

"Let Gay marry him if she wants to," she told the harassed Mrs Howard, "and learn the ups and downs of life for herself, the same as the rest of us did. None of us have had perfect men."

"Oh, Cousin Mahala, you're the only person in this whole clan with a heart," cried Gay.

Cousin Mahala looked at her with a twinkle in her eye.

"Oh, no, I'm not, Gay. We've all got hearts, more or less. And the rest of us want to save you from the trouble and mistakes we've had. *I* don't. Mistakes and trouble are bound to come. Better come our own way than some one else's way. You'll be a lovely little bride, Gay. So young. I *do* like a young bride."

"Aunt Mavis asked me if I thought marriage 'all fun.' Of course I don't think it's all 'fun'—"

"You bet it isn't," said Cousin Mahala—

—"But I don't think it's all vexation either—"

"You're right there, too," said Cousin Mahala—

"—And whatever it is, I want to try it with Noel and nobody else."

Mrs Howard, thus attacked from the rear, surrendered. But only on one condition. Gay and Noel must wait a year before marriage. Eighteen was too young to marry. She couldn't give Gay up so soon. And Mrs Howard had another reason. Dandy Dark hated the Gibsons. If Dandy had the bestowal of the jug and if Gay were actually married to a Gibson, Mrs Howard felt she would have no chance of it at all. This secret thought stiffened her against all the pleading of Gay and the ardent Noel, to which she would probably have succumbed otherwise. Noel resigned himself sulkily to the condition. Gay, sweetly. After all, she was glad to purchase her mother's acquiescence by a little waiting.

She couldn't bear to do anything against her mother's will. And being engaged was very delightful. There was a big hope-chest to be filled. Of course she knew the clan hoped that in a year she would change her mind. As if anything could ever make her stop loving Noel. She kissed his ring in the dark that night before she went to sleep. Dear Cousin Mahala! If only she lived nearer. Gay wanted to have her about while she made ready to be married. She knew all the rest, although they had tacitly agreed to recognize the engagement and make the best of it, would rub all the bloom off her dear romance with their horrible practicalities and go on regretting all the time in their hearts that it wasn't Roger.

Roger had been lovely. He had wished her joy—in his dear caressing voice—Roger *had* such a nice voice—and told her he wanted every happiness to be hers.

"If I'd a black cat's wish-bone I'd give it to you, Gay," he said whimsically. "They tell me as long as you have a black cat's wish-bone you can get everything you want."

"But I've got everything I want, Roger," cried Gay. "Now that mother has come round so sweetly I haven't a thing left to wish for—except—except—that *you*—" Gay went crimson—"that *everybody* could be as happy as I am."

"I'm afraid it would take more than a black cat's wish-bone to bring *that* about," said Roger. But whether his "that" referred to the "you" or to the "everybody" Gay didn't know and dared not ask. She danced back to the house, flinging a smile over her shoulder to Roger as if she had thrown him a rose. Then she forgot all about him.

Roger overtook the Moon Man on the way home and asked him to take a lift. The Moon Man refused. He would never get in a car. But he looked piercingly at Roger.

"Why don't you set your love on my Lady Moon?" he said. "I would not be jealous. All men may love her but she loves no one. It doesn't hurt to love if you do not hope to be loved in return."

"I've never hoped to be loved in return—but it hurts damnably," said Roger.

II

The clan had its shock at Aunt Becky's levee and its sensation over the fight at the graveyard; but the affair of Peter and Donna burst upon it like a cyclone. It was, naturally, almost the death of Drowned John.

Peter and Donna would have liked to keep it a delightful secret until they had perfected their plans, but as soon as they saw Mrs Toynbee they knew there was no hope of that. Donna went home in a state of uplift that lasted until three o'clock at night. Then the terrors and doubts that stalk around at that hour swooped down on her. What—oh, what would Drowned John say? Of course, there was nothing he could *do*. She had only to walk out of the door and go with Peter. But Donna hated the thought of eloping. It was simply not done among Darks and Penhallows. And if she eloped she would have no chance of the jug. Not that the jug was to be compared to Peter. But if she could only have Peter and the jug, too! Donna thought she had a good chance of it if it rested with Dandy. She had always been a pet of Dandy's. But she had once heard Dandy's comments on an eloping couple.

Then there was Virginia. Virginia would never forgive her. Not that Virginia mattered beside Peter either. But she was fond of Virginia; she was the only chum she had ever had. And she was afraid of the reproachful things Virginia would say. In the morning she wouldn't feel like this. But at three o'clock one did have qualms.

It was all just as dreadful as Donna feared it would be. Mrs Toynbee saw Drowned John at the post-office next day, and Drowned John came home in a truly Drowned Johnian condition—aggravated by his determination not to swear. But in other respects he gave tongue.

Donna was plucky. She owned up fearlessly that she had kissed Peter at the Courting-House, just as Mrs Toynbee said. "You see, Daddy, I'm going to marry him."

"You're mad!" said Drowned John.

"I think I am," sighed Donna. "But oh, Daddy, it's such a nice madness."

Drowned John repented, as he had repented often before, that he had ever let Donna have that year at the Kingsport Ladies' College in her teens. It was there she learned to say those smart, flippant things which always knocked the wind out of him. He dared not swear but he banged the table and told Donna that she was never to speak to Peter Penhallow again. If she did—

"But I'll have to speak to him now and again, Daddy. One can't live on terms of absolute silence with one's husband, you know."

There it was again. But Donna, though flippant and seemingly fearless, was quaking inside. She knew her Drowned John. When Peter came down that afternoon Drowned John met him at the door and asked him his business.

"I've come to see Donna," Peter told him cheerfully. "I'm going to marry her, you know."

"My *dear* young man"—oh, the contempt Drowned John snorted into the phrase!—"you do yourself too much honour."

He went in and shut the door in Peter's face. Peter thought at first he would smash a window. But he knew Drowned John was quite capable of having him arrested for housebreaking. Where the devil was Donna! She might at least look out at him.

Donna, with a headache, was crying on her bed, quite ignorant of Peter's nearness. Thekla had been so nasty. Thekla had said that one husband, like one religion, should be enough for anybody. But then Thekla had always hated her for getting married at all. She had no friends—she was alone in a hostile, unfeeling clan world. But she *was* going to marry Peter.

It wasn't so easy. Peter, who would have made no bones of carrying off a bride from the Congo or Yucatan if he had happened to want one, found it a very different proposition to carry one off from the Darks and Penhallows. He couldn't even see Donna. Drowned John wouldn't let him in the house or let Donna out of it. Of course this couldn't have lasted. Drowned John couldn't keep Donna mewed up forever, and eventually

Peter and she would have found a way to each other. But the stars in their course, so poor Donna thought, fought against them. One night she sneezed; the next night her eyes were sore; the next night they had Roger, who told Donna she was down with measles.

It would, of course, have been more romantic if she had had consumption or brain fever or angina pectoris. But a veracious chronicler can tell only the truth. Donna Dark had measles and nearly died of them.

Once the rumour drifted to the distracted Peter that she *had* died. And he couldn't even see her. When he tore down to Rose River nobody answered his knock and the doors were locked and the lower windows shuttered. Peter thought of simply standing on the step and yelling until somebody had to come; but he was afraid any excitement might hurt Donna. Roger came along and tried to calm him down.

"Donna's not dead. She's a very sick girl yet and needs careful nursing, but I think she's out of danger. I was afraid of pneumonia. Don't be an ass, Peter. Go home and take things coolly till Donna recovers. Drowned John can't prevent your marrying her, though he'll make everything as unpleasant as he can, no doubt."

"Roger, were you ever in love with any one?" groaned Peter. "No, you couldn't have been. You wouldn't be such a cold-blooded fish if you were. Besides, you'd have fallen in love with Donna. I can't understand why every one isn't in love with Donna. Can you?"

"Easily," said Roger coolly.

"Oh, you like them buxom, I suppose," sneered Peter, "like Sally William Y.—or just out of the cradle like Gay Penhallow. Roger, you don't know what it's like to be in love. It's hellish— and heavenly—and terrible—and exquisite. Oh, Roger, why don't you fall in love?"

Roger had never been in any danger of falling in love with Donna Dark. As a matter of fact, he only half liked her and her poses, not realizing that the latter were only a pitiful device for filling an empty life. And he only half liked Peter. But he was sorry for him.

"I'll take a message to Donna for you—"

"A letter—"

"No. She couldn't read it. Her eyes are very bad—"

"Look here, Roger. I've got to see Donna—by the sacred baboon I've got to. Have a heart, Roger—smuggle me in. They'll have to open the door for you, and once I'm inside the devil himself shan't get me out till I've seen Donna—that Thekla is quite capable of murdering her—the whole pack are worrying her—that fiend of a Virginia is with her night and day, I hear, poisoning her mind against me."

"Stop gibbering, Peter. Think what effects a fracas in the house would have on Donna. It would set her back weeks if it didn't kill her. Thekla is a capital nurse whatever else she is—and Donna's mind is too full of you to be poisoned by anybody—through all her delirium she raved about you—you should have seen Drowned John's face."

"Was she delirious—my poor darling? Oh, Roger Penhallow, are you keeping anything back from me? I met the Moon Man coming down. He looked at me strangely. They say the old dud has second sight—he knows when people are going to die. Pneumonia has always been fatal to that family—Donna's mother died of it. For God's sake, tell me the truth—"

"Peter Penhallow, if you don't clear out of this at once I'll kick you twice—once for myself and once for Drowned John. Donna is going to be all right. You act as if you were the only man in the world who was ever in love before."

"I am," said Peter. "*You* don't know a thing about love, Roger. They tell me you were in love with Gay Penhallow. Well, I'd never be a cradle-snatcher, but if I were, Noel Gibson shouldn't have taken her from me—that tailor's mannequin. You're a white-livered hound, Roger, no blood in your veins."

"I've some sense in my noodle," said Roger drily.

"Which proves that you don't know anything about love," said Peter triumphantly. "Nobody's sensible if he's in love. It's a divine madness, Roger. Oh, Roger, I've never liked you over and above but I feel now as if I couldn't part from you. To think that you'll see Donna in a few minutes—oh, tell her—tell her—"

"Heaven grant me patience!" groaned Roger. "Peter, go out and get into my car and count up to five hundred slowly. I'll tell Donna anything you like and I'll bring back her message and then I'll take you home. It's not safe for you to be out alone—you damn' fool," concluded Roger under his breath.

"Roger—have you any idea how a man—"

"Tut—tut, Peter, you're not a man at all just now—you're only a state of mind."

Donna's convalescence was a tedious affair and not a very happy one. As soon as Drowned John suspected that Roger was fetching and carrying messages between Donna and Peter, he showed him to the door and sent for another doctor. Virginia haunted her pillow night and day and various relatives of her clique—a clan within a clan—came and went and "talked things over." Donna listened because she was too weak to argue. And all the talking-over in the world couldn't alter facts.

"You never loved Barry," sobbed Virginia, "It was only his uniform you loved."

"I did love Barry. But now I love Peter," said Donna.

"'The mind has a thousand eyes'," began Virginia—and finished the quotation. The trouble was she had quoted it so often before that it was rather stale to Donna.

"Love isn't done—for me. It's beginning all over again."

"I *don't* understand," said Virginia helplessly, "how you can be so fickle, Donna. It's a complete mystery to me. But *my* feelings have always been so very deep. I wonder you still keep poor Barry's picture over your dressing-table. Doesn't he look at you reproachfully?"

"No. Barry seems like a good old pal. He seems to say, 'I'm glad you've found some one to give you the happiness I can't now.' Virginia, we've been foolish and morbid—"

"I won't have you use such a word," sobbed Virginia. "I'm not morbid—I'm *true*. And you've broken our pact. Oh, Donna, how *can* you desert me? We've been through so many sad—and beau-tiful—and terrible things together. How *can* you break the bond?"

"Virginia, darling, I'm not breaking the bond. We can always be friends—dear friends—"

"Peter will take you away from me," sobbed Virginia. "He'll drag you all over the world—you'll never have any settled home, Donna—or any position in society."

"There'll be some adventure in marrying Peter," conceded Donna in a tone of satisfaction.

"And he'll never allow you to have any interest outside of him. He'll tell you what you are to think. He must possess exclusively."

"I don't want any interest outside of him," said Donna.

"You to say that—you who were Barry's wife—his *wife*. Why, to hear you talk—it might just as well have been some one else who was Barry's wife."

"Well, to be honest, Virginia, that's exactly the way I do feel about it. I'm *not* the girl who was married to Barry—I'm an entirely different creature. Perhaps I've drunk from some fairy pool of change, Virginia. I can't help it—and I don't want to help it. All I want just now is to have Peter come in and kiss me."

An aggravating sentence popped into Donna's head. She uttered it to annoy Virginia, who was annoying her.

"You've no idea how divinely Peter can kiss, Virginia."

"I've no doubt he has had plenty of practice," said Virginia bitterly. "As for me—*I* have my memories of Ned's kisses."

Donna permitted herself a pale smile. Ned Powell had had a little full red mouth with a little brown moustache above it. The very thought of being kissed by such a mouth had always made Donna shudder. She couldn't understand how Virginia could ever bear it.

"You can laugh," said Virginia coldly. "I suppose you can

laugh now at everything we have held sacred. But *I* happen to know that Peter Penhallow said that you were a nice little thing and he could have you for the asking."

"I don't believe he said it," retorted Donna, "but if he did— why not? It's quite true, you know."

Virginia went away crying. She told Drowned John that it was useless for her to come again; *she* had no longer any influence over Donna.

"I knew that opal would bring me bad luck."

Drowned John banged a table and glared at her. Drowned John went about those days banging tables. Drowned John was in an atrocious humour with everything and everybody, and determined to make them feel it. Had a father no rights at all? This was all it came to—all your years of sacrifice and care. They flouted you—just flouted you. They thought they could marry any fool fellow they pleased. Women were the very dickens. He had tamed his own two but the young ones were beyond him.

"She shall never marry him—never."

"She means to," said Virginia.

"She doesn't mean it—she only thinks she does," shouted Drowned John. Drowned John always thought that if he contradicted loud enough, people would come to believe him.

Bets were up in the clan about it. Some, like Stanton Grundy, thought it wouldn't last. "The hotter the fire the quicker it's over," said Stanton Grundy. Some thought Drowned John would never yield and some thought he'd likely crumple up at the last. And some thought it didn't matter a hoot whether he did or not. Peter Penhallow would take his own wherever he found it. To poor Donna, lying wearily in bed or reclining in an easy-chair, trying to endure the unfeeling way in which day followed day without Peter, they came with advice and innuendo and gossip. Peter had said, when Aunt But asked him how it was he was caught at last, "Oh, I just got tired of running." Peter, when a boy, had shot a pea at an elder in the church. Peter had flung a glass of water in his schoolmaster's face. Peter had taken a wasp's nest to prayer-meeting. Peter had set loose a trapped rat when the Sewing Circle met at his mother's house. They dragged up all the things they knew that Peter had done. And there were so many things he must have done that they knew nothing about.

"If you marry a rover like Peter what are you going to do with your family?" Mrs William Y. wanted to know.

"Oh, we're only going to have two children. A boy first and then a girl for good measure," said Donna. "We can manage to tote that many about with us."

Mrs William Y. was horrified. But Mrs Artemas, who had come with her, only remarked calmly,

"I couldn't ever get them to come in order that way."

"If I was a widow-woman I wouldn't be fool enough to want to marry again," said Mrs Sim Dark bitterly.

"That family of Penhallows are always doing such unexpected things and Peter is the worst of them," mourned Mrs Wilbur Dark.

"But if your husband does unexpected things at least he wouldn't bore you," said Donna. "I could endure anything but boredom."

Mrs Wilbur did not know what Donna meant by her husband's boring her. Of course men were tiresome at times. She told her especial friends that she thought the measles had gone to Donna's brain. They did that sometimes, she understood.

Dandy Dark came and asked her ominously how she thought Aunt Becky would have liked her taking a second helping after all her fine protestations.

"Aunt Becky liked consistency, that she did," said Dandy, who had a fondness for big words and used more of them than ever now that he was trustee of the jug.

This sounded like a threat. Donna pouted.

"Dandy," she coaxed, "you might tell me who's to get the jug—if you know. I wouldn't tell a soul."

Dandy chuckled.

"I've lost count how often that's been said to me the past

month. No use, Donna. Nobody's going to know more about that jug than Aunt Becky told them until the time comes. A dying trust"—Dandy was very important and solemn—"is a sacred thing. But think twice before you marry Peter, Donna—think twice."

"Oh, Aunty Con, some days I just hate life," Donna told a relative for whom she had some love. "And then again some days I just love it."

"That's the way with us all," said plump Aunty Con placidly.

Donna stared at her in amazement. Surely Aunty Con could never either love or hate life.

"Oh, Aunty Con, I'm really miserable. I seem to get better so slowly. And Peter and I can't get a word to each other. Father is so unreasonable—he seems to smell brimstone if any one mentions Peter's name. Thekla is barely civil to me—though she *was* an angel when I was really ill—and Virginia is sulking. I—I get so blue and discouraged—"

"You ain't real well yet," said Aunty Con soothingly. "Don't you worry, Donna. As soon as you're real strong Peter Penhallow will find a way. Rest you with that."

Donna looked out of her open window over her right shoulder into the July night. A little wet new moon was hanging over a curve of Rose River. There were sounds as if a car were dying in the yard. Nobody had told Donna that Peter came down to Drowned John's gate every night—where his father had hung the dog—and made all the weird noises possible with his claxon, but Donna suddenly felt he was very near her. She smiled. Yes, Peter would find a way.

III

Gay Penhallow could never quite remember when the first faint shadow fell across her happiness. It stole towards her so subtly. If you looked straight at it—it wasn't there. But turn away your eyes and out of the corners you could see it—a little nearer—still a little nearer—waiting to pounce.

Everything had been so wonderful at first. The weeks were not made up of days at all. Sunday was a flame, Monday a rainbow, Tuesday a perfume, Wednesday a bird-song, Thursday a wind-dance, Friday laughter, and Saturday—Noel always came Saturday night, whatever other night he missed—was something that was the soul of all the other six.

But now—the days were becoming just days again.

Nan and Noel were such friends. Well, why shouldn't they be? Weren't they going to be cousins! But still—there were moments when Gay felt like an outsider, as they talked to each other a patter she couldn't talk. Gay was not up-to-date in modern slang. They seemed to have so many mysterious catchwords and understandings—or perhaps Nan just made it appear so. Nan was an expert at that sort of thing—expert at catching and holding for herself the attention of any male creature, no matter what his affiliations might be. For Nan those affiliations didn't exist. She simply ignored them. Noel and Gay could not refuse to take her about with them—at least Gay couldn't and Noel didn't seem to want to. Nan continued to imply that she had no one to take her about—she was such a stranger. Gay felt it would be mean and catty to leave Nan out in the cold. But quite often—and oftener as the days went by—she felt as if it were she who was left out in the cold. And yet there was so little to take hold of—so little one could put into words or even into thoughts. She couldn't expect Noel to take no notice of any one but herself. But she thought wistfully of the old untroubled days when there had been no Nan at Indian Spring.

There was that dreadful afternoon when she had heard Nan and Noel exchanging airy persiflage over the phone. Gay hadn't meant to listen. She had taken down the receiver to see if the line were free and she had heard Noel's voice. Who was he talking to? Nan! Gay stood and listened—Gay who had been brought up to think listening on the phone the meanest form of eavesdropping. She didn't realize she was listening—all she realized was that Nan and Noel were carrying on a gay, semi-confidential conversation. Well, what of it? After all, what was really in it? They didn't say a word the whole world mightn't have heard. But it was the suggestion of intimacy in it—of something from which every one else was excluded. Why, Noel was talking to Nan as he should talk only to *her.*

When Gay hung up the receiver, after Nan had sent an impertinent kiss over the phone, she felt chilly and lost. For the first time she felt the sting of a bitter jealousy. And for the first time it occurred to her that she might not be happy all her life. But when Noel came that evening he was as dear and tender as ever and Gay went to bed laughing at herself. She was just a little fool to get worked up over nothing. It was only Nan's way. Even the kiss! Very likely Nan would have liked to make trouble between her and Noel. That was Nan's way, too. But she couldn't.

Gay was not so sure one evening two weeks later. Noel was to come that evening. Gay woke up in the morning expecting him. Her head lay in a warm pool of sunshine that spread itself over the pillow. She lay and stretched herself in it like a little lazy golden cat, sniffing delicately at the whiffs of heliotrope that blew in from the garden below. Noel would be out to-night. He had said so in his letter of the previous day. She had that to look forward to for a whole beautiful day. Perhaps they would go for a spin along the winding drive. Or perhaps they would go for a walk down to the shore? Or perhaps they would just linger at the side gate under the spruces and talk about themselves. There would be no Nan—Nan was away visiting friends in Summerside—she was sure of having Noel all to herself. She hadn't had him much to herself of late. Nan would be at Maywood or Noel would suggest that they go somewhere and pick her up—the poor kid was lonesome. Indian Spring was pretty quiet for a girl used to city life.

Gay lived the whole day in a mood of expectant happiness. A few weeks ago she had lived every day like that and she did not quite realize yet how different it had been lately. She dressed in the twilight especially for Noel. She had a new dress and she would wear it for him. Such a pretty dress. Powder-blue voile over a little slip of ivory silk. She wondered if Noel would like it and notice how the blue brought out the topaz tints of her hair and eyes and the creaminess of her slim throat. It was such a delight to make herself beautiful for Noel. It seemed like a sacrament. To brush her hair till it shone—to touch the shadowy hollow of her throat with a drop of perfume—to make her nails shine softly like pink pearls—to fasten about her neck the little string of tiny golden beads—Noel's last gift.

"Every bead on it is a kiss," he had whispered. "It's a rosary of our love, darling."

Then to look at herself and know he must find her fair and sweet. To know that she would see that little spark leap into his eyes as he looked at her.

Oh, Gay felt sorry for homely girls. How could they please their lovers? And she felt sorry for Donna Dark, who wasn't allowed to see *her* lover at all—though how could anybody care for that queer wild rover of a Peter Penhallow? And she felt sorry for Joscelyn, who had been so outrageously treated by her bridegroom—and she felt sorry for William Y.'s Sally, who was engaged to such an ugly, insignificant little man—and she felt sorry for Mercy Penhallow, who had never had a beau at all— and she felt sorry for poor Pauline Dark, who was hopelessly in love with Hugh—and for Naomi Dark, who was worse than widowed—even for poor silly Virginia Powell, who was so true and tiresome. In short, Gay felt sorry for almost every feminine creature she knew. Until late in the evening, when she was sorry only for herself.

Noel had not come. She had waited for him in the little green corner by the side gate, where Venus was shining over the dark trees, until ten o'clock and he had not come. Once she had got long-distance and called up his stepmother's house in town. But Noel was not there and his stepmother did not know where he was—or greatly care, her tone seemed to imply. Gay went back to her vigil by the gate. What had happened? Had his car acted up? But he could telephone. Suppose there had been an accident—a bad accident—suppose Noel had been hurt—killed? Or suppose he had just changed his mind? Had his good-bye kiss, three nights before, been just a little absent? And even his letter which had told her he was coming had begun with "dear" instead of "dearest" or "darling."

Once she thought she saw him coming through the garden. By the sudden uplift of her heart and spirit she knew how terrible had been her dread that he would not come. Then she saw that it was only Roger. Roger must not see her. She knew she was going to cry and he must not see her. Blindly she plunged into the green spruce copse beyond the gate—ran through it sobbing— the boughs caught and tore her dress—it didn't matter—nothing mattered except that Noel had not come. She gained her room and locked her door and huddled herself into bed. Oh, what a long night was before her to live through. She remembered a pet phrase of Roger's—he was always saying, "Don't worry—there's always to-morrow."

"I don't want to-morrow," sobbed Gay. "I'm afraid of it."

It was the first night in her life she had cried herself chokingly to sleep.

In the morning Noel telephoned his excuses. He had a-plenty. Nan had called him on the long-distance from Summerside early in the evening and wanted him to run up and bring her home. He had thought he had plenty of time for it. But when he got to Summerside Nan's friends were having an impromptu party and she wanted to wait for it. He had tried to get Gay on long-distance but couldn't. It was late when he had brought Nan home—too late to go on to Maywood. He was frightfully sorry and he'd be up the very first evening he was free. They were confoundedly busy in the bank just now. He had to work till midnight, etc.

Gay believed him because she had to. And when her mother said to her that folks were beginning to talk about Nan and Noel, Gay was scornful and indifferent.

"They have to talk about something, Mumsy. I suppose they've got tired gossiping about poor Donna and Peter and have to begin on Noel and me. Never mind them."

"*I* don't mind them. But the Gibsons—they've always had a name for being fickle—"

"I won't hear a word against Noel," flashed Gay. "Am I to keep him in my pocket? Is he never to speak to a girl but me? A nice life for him. *I* know Noel. But you always hated him—you're glad to believe anything against him—"

"Oh, Gay, child—no—no. I don't hate him—it's your happiness I'm thinking of—"

"Then don't worry me with malicious gossip," cried Gay so stormily that Mrs Howard dared not say another word on the subject. She switched to something safer.

"Have you written those chain letters yet, Gay?"

"No. And I'm not going to. Mumsy, you're really absurd."

"But, Gay—I don't know—no, I'm *not* superstitious—but you *know* it said if you broke the chain some misfortune would befall you—and it doesn't cost much—only six cents—"

"Mother, it *is* superstition. And I'm not going to be so foolish. Write the letters yourself, if you like—if it's worrying you."

"That wouldn't do any good. The letter was to you. It wouldn't take you long—"

"I'm not going to do it and that's all there is to it," said Gay, stubbornly. "You heard Roger on the subject, Mother."

"Oh, Roger—he's a good doctor but he doesn't know everything. There *are* things nobody understands—your father always laughed just as you do—but he was one of thirteen at a table just before he died. And say what you will, I knew a woman who wouldn't write the chain letters and she broke her knee-cap two weeks after she burned the one she got."

"Mrs Sim Dark broke her arm last week, but I haven't heard she burned any chain letters." Gay tried to laugh but she found it rather hard—she to whom laughter had always come so readily. There was such a strange, dreadful ache in her heart which she must hide from every one. And she would *not* be jealous and hateful and suspicious. Nan was trying to weave her cobweb spells around Noel of course. But she had faith in Noel—oh, she must have faith in him.

Noel did come up four evenings later. And Nan came, too. The three of them sat on the veranda steps and laughed and chattered. At least Noel and Nan did. Gay was a little bit silent. Nobody noticed it. At last she got up and strolled away to the twilight garden, through the gay ranks of the hollyhocks and the old orchard full of mysterious moonlit delights—the place of places for lovers—to the side gate. She expected Noel would follow her. He had always done so—yet. She listened for his following footsteps. When she reached the side gate she turned and peeped back through the spruce boughs. Noel was still sitting on the steps beside Nan. She could not see them but she could hear them. She knew quite well that Nan was looking up at Noel with those slanting green eyes of hers—eyes that did something to men that Gay's laughing, gold-flecked ones could never do. And no doubt—Gay's lip curled in contempt—she was implying that he was the most wonderful fellow in the world. Gay had heard her do that before. Well—he *was!* But Nan had no right to think him so—or make him think she thought so. Gay clenched her hands.

She waited there for what seemed a very long time. There was a pale green sunset sky, and idle, merry laughter came from far across the fields on the crystal clear air. Somewhere there was a faint fragrance on the air, as of something hidden—unseen— sweet.

Gay remembered a great many things that she had almost forgotten. Little things that Nan had done in their childhood vacations when she had come over to the Island every summer. There was that day Gay had been quite broken-hearted at the Sunday-school picnic because she hadn't a cent to pay for the peep-show Hicksy Dark was running. And then she had found a cent on the road—and was going to see the peep-show—and

Nan took the cent away from her and gave it to Hicksy and saw the show. Gay remembered how she had cried about that and how Nan had laughed.

The day when Nan had come in with a lovely big chocolate bar Uncle Pippin had given her. Chocolate bars were new things then.

"Oh, please give me a bite—just one bite," Gay had implored. She loved chocolate bars.

Nan had laughed and said,

"Maybe I'll give you the last one."

She sat down before Gay and ate the bar, slowly, deliberately, bite by bite. At last there was just one good bite left—a juicy, succulent bite, the lovely snowy filling oozing around a big Brazil-nut. And then Nan had laughed—and popped the bite into her own mouth—and laughed again at the tears that filled Gay's eyes.

"You cry so easy, Gay, that it's hardly any fun to make you cry," she said.

The day when Nan had snatched off Gay's new hair-bow, because it was bigger and crisper than her own, and slashed it to bits with the scissors. Mrs Alpheus *had* whipped Nan for it, but that didn't restore the hair-bow and Gay had to wear her old shabby one.

The time when Gay was to sing at the missionary concert in the church and Nan had broken up the song and reduced Gay to the verge of hysterics by suddenly pointing her finger at Gay's slippered feet and calling out, "Mouse!"

Oh, there were dozens of memories like that. Nan had always been the same—as sleek and self-indulgent and cruel as a little tiger. Taking whatever she had a whim for without caring who suffered. But Gay had never believed she could take Noel.

Gay was not Dark and Penhallow for nothing. She did not go back to the steps. She went into the house by the sun-porch door and up to her room, though it seemed as if at every step she trod on her own heart. In her room she looked at herself in the mirror. It was as if her young face had grown old in an hour. Her cheeks were a stormy red, but her eyes were strange to her. Surely such eyes had never looked out of her face before. She shuddered with cold—with anger—with sick longing—with incredulity. Then she blew out the lamp passionately and flung herself face downwards on her bed. The shadow had pounced at last. That other night she had cried herself to sleep—but she had slept. This was to be the first night of her life she could not sleep at all for pain.

IV

The quarrel and separation of the Sams had caused considerable sensation in the clan and for a time ousted Aunt Becky's jug, Gay Penhallow's engagement and Drowned John's tantrums over Peter and Donna as a topic of conversation in clan groups. Few thought it would last long. But the summer had passed without a reconciliation and folks gave up expecting it. That family of Darks had always been a stubborn gang. Neither of the Sams made any pretence of dignified reserve regarding their mutual wrongs. When they met, as they occasionally did, they glared at each other and passed on in silence. But each was forever waylaying neighbours and clansmen to tell his side of the story.

"I hear he's going about telling I kicked the dog in the abdomen," Little Sam would snort. "What's abdomen, anyhow?"

"Belly," said Stanton Grundy bluntly.

"Look at that now. I knew he was lying. I never kicked no dog in the belly. Touched his ribs with the toe of my boot once, that's all—for good and sufficient cause. Says I lured his cat back. What do I want of his old Persian Lamb cat? Always bringing dead rats in and leaving them lying around. And determined to sleep on *my* abdomen at nights. If he'd fed his cat properly she wouldn't have left him. But I ain't going to turn no broken-hearted, ill-

393

used beast out of *my* door. I hear he's raving round about moons and contented cows. The only use that man has for moons is to predict the weather, and as for contented cows or discontented cows, it's all one to him. But I'm glad he's happy. So am I. I can sing all I want to now without having some one sarcastically saying, 'A good voice for chawing turnips,' or, 'Hark from the tombs a doleful sound,' or maddening things like that. I had to endure that for years. But did I make a fuss about it? Or about his yelping that old epic of his half the night—cackling and chortling and guffawing and gurgling and yapping and yammering. You never heard such an ungodly caterwauling as that poor creature could make. 'Chanting,' *he* called it. Till I felt as if I'd been run through a meat-chopper. Did I mind his always conterdicting me? No; it kept life from being too tejus. Did I mind his being a fundamentalist? No; I respected his principles. Did I mind his getting up at unearthly hours Sunday mornings to pray? I did not. Some people might have said his method of praying was irrevent—talking to God same as he would to me or you. I didn't mind irreverence, but what I didn't like was his habit of swinging round right in the middle of a prayer and giving the devil a licking. Still, did I make a fuss over it? No; I overlooked all them things, and yet when I brings home a beautiful statooette like Aurorer there Big Sam up and throws three different kinds. Well, I'd rather have Aurorer than him any day and you can tell him so. She's easier to look at, for one thing, and she don't sneak into the pantry unbeknownst to me and eat up my private snacks for another. *I* ain't said much about the affair—I've let Big Sam do the talking—but some day when I git time I'm going to talk an awful lot, Grundy."

"I'm told that poor ass of a Little Sam spends most of his spare time imagining he's strewin' flowers on my grave," Big Sam told Mr Trackley. "And I hear he's been making fun of my prayers. Will you believe it, he had the impidence to tell me once I had to make my prayers shorter 'cause they interfered with his mornin' nap? Did I shorten 'em? Not by a jugful. Spun 'em out twice as long. What I put up with from that man! His dog nigh about chewed up my Victory bond, but did *I* complain? God knows I didn't. But when my cat had kittens on his sheet he tore up the turf. Talking of the cat, I hear she has kittens again. You'd think Little Sam might have sent me one. I hear there's three. And I haven't a thing except them two ducks I bought of Peter Gautier. They're company—but knowing you have to eat 'em up some day spoils things. Look a' here, Mr Trackley. Why did Jacob let out a howl and weep when he kissed Rachel?"

Mr Trackley didn't know, or if he did he kept it to himself. Some Rose Riverites thought Mr Trackley was too fond of drawing the Sams out.

"Because he found it wasn't what it was cracked up to be," chuckled Big Sam. He was happy all day because he had put one over on the minister.

But Big Sam was soon in no mood for joking about kisses, ancient or modern. He nearly had an apoplectic fit when he heard that some of the summer boarders up the river had gone to Little Sam under the mistaken impression that *he* was the poet, and asked him to recite his epic. The awful thing was that Little Sam *did*. Went through it from start to finish and never let on he wasn't the true author.

"From worshipping imidges to stealing poetry is only what you'd expect. You can see how that man's character's degen'rating," said Big Sam passionately.

V

Peter Penhallow was growing so lean and haggard that Nancy began to feel frightened about him. She tried to induce him to take some iron pills and got sworn at for her pains. A serious symptom, for Peter was not addicted to profanity. Nancy excused him, for she thought he was not getting a square deal, either from Drowned John or Providence. The very day Donna Dark was to be permitted to come downstairs she took tonsilitis. This meant three more weeks of seclusion. Peter sounded his horn at the enchanted portal every night or, in modern language, Drowned John's east lane gate—but that was all he could do. Drowned John, so it was reported, had sworn he would shoot Peter at sight and the clan waited daily in horrified expectancy, not knowing that Thekla had hidden Drowned John's gun under the spare-room bed. Drowned John, not being able to find it, ignored Peter and his caterwauling and took it out on poor sick Donna, who was by this time almost ready to die of misery. Sick in bed for weeks and weeks, staring at that horrible wallpaper Drowned John had selected and which she hated. Horrible greenish-blue paper with gilt stars on it, which Drowned John thought the last word in elegance.

She had lost all her good looks, she told herself. She cried and said she didn't want to get better. Peter couldn't love her any more—this pallid, washed-out skeleton she saw in her mirror when she got up after tonsilitis. The doctor said she must have her tonsils out as soon as she was strong enough for the ordeal. This was reported to Peter and drove him still further on what all his friends now believed was the road to madness. He didn't believe in operations. He wasn't going to have pieces of his darling Donna cut out. They were all trying to murder her, that was what they were doing—the whole darn tribe of them. He cursed Mrs Toynbee Dark a dozen times a day. Had it not been for her, Drowned John wouldn't have known of Donna's engagement, he wouldn't have kept such watch and ward—Peter would have been able to snatch her away, measles and tonsilitis to the contrary notwithstanding—and then a fig for your germs. But now—

"What am I to do?" groaned Peter to Nancy. "Nancy, tell a fellow what to do. I'm dying by inches—and they're going to carve Donna up."

Nancy could only reply soothingly that lots of people had had their tonsils out and there was nothing to do but to wait patiently.

Drowned John couldn't keep Donna shut up forever.

"You don't know him," said Peter darkly. "There's a plot. I believe Virginia Powell deliberately carried the tonsilitis germ to Donna. That woman would do anything to keep me and Donna apart. Next time it will be inflammatory rheumatism. They'll stick at nothing."

"Oh, Peter, don't be silly."

"Silly! Is it any wonder if I'm silly? The wonder is I'm not a blithering idiot."

"Some people think you are," said Nancy candidly.

"Nancy, it's eight weeks since I've seen Donna—eight hellish weeks."

"Well, you lived a good many years without seeing her at all."

"No—I merely existed."

"Cheer up—'It may be for years but it can't be forever'," quoted Nancy flippantly. "I did hear Donna was going to be out in Rose River Church next Sunday."

"Church! What can I do in church? Drowned John will be on one side of her and Thekla on the other. Virginia Powell will bring up the rear and Mrs Toynbee will watch everything. The only thing to do will be to sail in, hit Drowned John a wallop on the point of the jaw, snatch up Donna and rush out with her."

"Oh, Peter, don't make a scene in church—not in church," implored Nancy, wishing she hadn't told him.

She lived in misery until Sunday. Peter did make a bit of a scene, but not so bad as she feared. He was sitting in a pew under the gallery when the Drowned John's party came in—Drowned John first, Donna next, then Thekla—"I knew it would be like that," groaned Peter—then old Jonas Swan, the hired man—who had family privileges, being really a distant relative—then two visiting cousins. Peter ate Donna up with his eyes all through the service. They had nearly killed her, his poor darling. But she was more beautiful, more alluring than ever, with those great mauve shadows under her eyes and her thick creamy lids still heavy with the langour of illness. Peter thought the service would never end.

Did Trackley preach as long as this every Sunday and if so, why didn't they lynch him. Did that idiot who was yowling a solo in the choir imagine she could sing? People like that ought to be drowned young, like kittens. Would they never be done taking up the collection? There were *six* verses in the last hymn!

Peter shot up the aisle before the rest of the congregation had lifted their heads from the benediction. Drowned John had stepped out of his pew to speak to Elder MacPhee across the aisle. Thekla was talking unsuspiciously to Mrs Howard Penhallow in the pew ahead. Nobody was watching Donna just then, not dreaming that Peter would be in Rose River Church. None of his clique had ever darkened the door of Rose River Church since the sheep-fight. They went to Bay Silver.

Donna had turned and her large mournful eyes were roving listlessly over the rising assemblage. Then she saw Peter. He was in the pew behind her, having put his hands on either side of little Mrs Denby's plump waist and lifted her bodily out into the aisle to make way for him. Mrs Denby got the scare of her life. She talked about it breathlessly for years.

Peter and Donna had only a moment but it sufficed. He had planned exactly what to do and say. First he kissed Donna— kissed her before the whole churchful, under the minister's very eyes. Then he whispered:

"Be at your west lane gate at eleven o'clock tomorrow night. I'll come with a car. Can you?"

Donna hated the thought of eloping, but she knew there was nothing else to be done. If she shook her head Peter might simply vanish out of her life. Dear knows what he already thought of her for never sending him word or line. He couldn't know just how they watched her. It was now or never. So she nodded just as Drowned John turned to see what MacPhee was staring at. He saw Peter kiss Donna for a second time, vault airily over the central division of the pews and vanish through the side door by the pulpit. Drowned John started to say "damn" but caught himself in time. Dandy Dark's pew was next to his and Dandy had taken to attending church very regularly since the affair of the jug. People knew he went to keep tabs on them. Dandy had a pew in both Rose River and Bay Silver Churches and said shamelessly that he kept them because when he wasn't in one church he would get the credit of being in the other. The attendance at both churches had gone up with a rush since Aunt Becky's levee. Mr Trackley believed his sermons were making an impression at last and took heart of grace anew.

Dandy gave Donna a little facetious poke in the ribs as he went past her and whispered:

"Don't go and do anything silly, Donna."

By which Donna understood that it really would injure her chances for the jug if she ran away with Peter. Even Uncle Pippin shook his head disapprovingly at her. As he said, when he left the church, their love-making was entirely too public.

Donna heard something from her father when she got home. It was a wonder they *did* get home, for Drowned John drove so recklessly that he almost ran over a few foolish pedestrians and just missed two collisions. Thekla had her say, too. The visiting cousins giggled, but old Jonas went out stolidly to feed the pigs. Donna listened like a woman in a trance. Drowned John wasn't sure she even heard him. Then she went to her room to think things over.

She was committed to eloping the next night. It was not exactly a nice idea to a girl who had been brought up in the true Dark tradition—darker than the very Darkest. She thought of all the things the clan would say—of all the significant nods and winks. When Frank Penhallow and Lily Dark had eloped Aunt Becky had said to them on their return, "You were in a big hurry." Donna would hate to have any one say anything like that to her. But she and Peter would not be returning. That was the beauty of it. One thrust and the Gordian knot of their difficulties would be forever cut. Then freedom—and love—and escape from dull routine and stodginess—Thekla's jealousy and Drowned John's continual hectoring—and Virginia. Donna felt a pang of shame and self-reproach that there should be such relief in the thought of escaping from poor Virginia. But there it was. She couldn't *un*feel it. Thirty-six hours and she must meet Peter at the west lane gate and the old scandal-mongers could go hang, jug and all. Luckily Thekla had gone back to her own room. Drowned John slept below. It would be easy to slip out. Had Peter thought she had gone off very terribly? Virginia said the tonsilitis had made her look ten years older. It was dreadful to have Peter kiss her before the whole congregation like that—dreadful but splendid. Poor Virginia's face!

Somehow or other, Sunday passed—and Monday morning—and Monday afternoon—though Donna had never spent such interminable hours in her life. She was glad that she was in such disgrace with her father and Thekla that they wouldn't speak to her. But that had begun to wear off by supper-time. Thekla looked at her curiously. Donna couldn't help an air of excitement that hung about her like an aura, and under the mauve shadows her cheeks were faintly hued with rose. A bit of amusement flickered in her sapphire eyes. She was wondering just what Thekla and Drowned John would say if they knew she was going to run away with Peter Penhallow that very night. Of course she couldn't eat—who could, under the circumstances?

"Donna," said Thekla sharply, "you haven't been putting on rouge?"

Drowned John snorted. He always had a fit of indignation when he caught a glimpse of Donna's dressing-table. Entirely too many fal-als for trying to be beautiful! Decent women didn't try to be beautiful. But if he had ever found or suspected any rouge about it, he would probably have thrown table and all out of the window.

"Of course not," said Donna.

"Well, your cheeks are red," said Thekla. "If you aren't painted you're feverish. You've got a relapse. I knew you would, going out so soon. You'll stay in bed to-morrow."

Donna grasped at the opportunity. She had been wondering

if she and Peter could possibly get off the Island before Drowned John caught them. The Island was such a poor place to murder or elope. You were sure to be caught before you could get away from it. But by dinner-time next day they would be safely off, and then a fig for Drowned John.

"I—I think I will. For the forenoon, anyway. You can call me for dinner. I'm sure I haven't any relapse—but I'm tired."

Really, Providence at last seemed to be on her side.

Everybody in Drowned John's household went to bed early. At nine the lights were out and the door locked. This did not worry Donna. She knew quite well where Thekla hid the key, sly as she thought herself about it. She was ready at half-past ten, with a small suitcase packed. She opened her door and peered out. Everything was silent. Thekla's door was shut tight. Down the hall old Jonas was snoring. Fancy any one snoring on this wonderful night. Would the stairs creak? They did, of course, but nobody seemed to hear. What would happen if she sneezed? Drowned John slept in the little cubby-hole off the dining-room and the key was in the blue vase on the clock shelf. Drowned John was snoring too. Donna shuddered. She hoped Peter didn't snore. She unlocked the door, stepped out, and closed it behind her. Really, eloping was ridiculously easy.

Donna fled through the orchard to the west lane gate. She had nearly half an hour to wait. The tall black firs about the gate came out against the starlit sky. There were dancing northern lights over the dark harbour. The white birches down the west lane seemed to shine with a silvery light of their own. The night was full of wonder and delight and a subtle beauty that was not lost even on the excited Donna, who had inherited from her silent little mother a love and understanding for such things which sometimes amused and sometimes exasperated Drowned John, who would have thought it all of a piece with Virginia's maunderings if he could have realized the happiness Donna felt over a sunlight-patterned river—a silver shimmer on the harbour—starlight over fir trees—a blue dawn on dark hills—

daisies like a froth of silver on seaside meadows.

Donna waited, enjoying the night for a time. If Peter had only come when she was in that mood all would have gone well. Then she began to shiver in the cool shrewish wind of September darkness. The trees whispered eerily over her. There were strange rustlings and shadows in the orchard. William Y.'s dog was exchanging opinions with Adam Dark's dog across the river. A roar swooped out of nothing—passed into nothing—a car had gone by. Donna shrank back into the shadow of the firs. Had they seen her? Oh, why didn't Peter come? Would she ever get warm again. She would catch her death of cold. She should have put on a heavier coat. It had been summer when she became ill. She hadn't realized that summer was gone and autumn here. Her courage and excitement ebbed with her temperature. Surely it must be eleven now. He had said eleven. If he didn't care enough for her to be on time—to avoid keeping her here in the cold half the night! Waiting—waiting. Donna knew how long time always seemed to one who was waiting. But even allowing for that, she was sure it must be nearer twelve than eleven. If he didn't come soon she would go back to bed—and then let Peter Penhallow propose eloping to *her* again!

Then she saw his lights—and everything was changed. There was his car coming up the west lane, with her destiny in it. If Thekla woke up she would see the lights from her window. God send she didn't wake up!

Peter caught her in his arms, exultantly.

"I've had the most devilish luck. Two flat tires and something wrong with the carburettor. I was afraid you'd have gone back—afraid you wouldn't be able to get out at all. But it's all right now. We've heaps of time. I allowed for delays. Listen—my plan is this: We'll motor to Borden and catch the boat. And we'll stop at the Kirtland manse and get Charlie Blackford to marry us. I've had the licence for days. Charlie's a good sort—I know him well. He'll marry us like a shot and make no bones if it is a few minutes before six. Once we're on the mainland—heigh-ho for

New York in our own car—and we'll sail for South America from there. Girl of my heart, do you love me as much as ever. Lord, I could eat you. I feel famished. You're as lovely as dark moonlight. Donna—Donna—"

"Oh, Peter, don't smother me," gasped Donna. "Wait—wait—let us get away. I'm so afraid Father will come out. Oh, it seems I've been here for *years*."

"Don't worry. I'll settle him in a jiffy, now that I've got you out of the house. Donna, if you knew what I've been through—"

"Peter, stop! Let's get away."

Peter stopped, a bit sulkily. He thought Donna a trifle cool after such an agonizing separation. Surely she needn't grudge him a few kisses. He didn't realize how cold and frightened she really was or how endless had seemed her waiting.

"We can't get away for a minute or two. When I passed your Aunt Eudora's over there, young Eudora was in the yard saying good-bye to Mac Penhallow. We've got to wait till he's gone. Darling, you're shivering. Get into the car. It'll be warm there, out of this beastly wind."

"Put out your lights—if Thekla sees your lights—oh, Peter, it's rather awful running away like this. We've never done such things."

"If you are sorry it's not too late yet," said Peter in a changed, ominous voice.

"Don't be ridiculous, Peter." Donna was still cold and frightened and her nerves were bad after all she'd been through. She thought Peter might be a *little* more considerate. Instead, here he was being deliberately devilish. "Of course I'm not sorry. I'm only sorry it had to be like this. It's so—so *sneaky*."

"Well," said Peter, who had also been through something, especially with those fiendish tires, and had a good deal yet to learn about women, "what else do you propose?"

"Peter, you're horrid! Of course I know we must go through with it—"

"Go through with it. Is *that* how you look at it?"

Donna felt suddenly that Peter was a stranger.

"I don't know what you want me to say. I can't pick and choose words when I'm half frozen. And that isn't all—"

"I didn't think it would be," said Peter.

"You've been saying some funny things yourself—oh, I've heard—"

"Evidently. And listened, too."

"Well, I'm not deaf. You told Aunty But that—that—you let yourself be caught because you were tired of running."

"Good heavens, woman, I only said that to choke Aunty But off. Was I going to tell that old gossip I worshipped you?"

Donna had never really believed that he had said it at all. Now she felt as if she almost hated him for saying a thing like that in a clan like hers.

"As if I'd been *chasing* you—my friends have been telling me right along I was a fool."

If Donna had but known it, she was nearer having her ears boxed at that moment than ever in her life before. But Peter folded his arms and stared grimly ahead of him. What use was there in talking? Would that love-sick fool of a Mac ever get through making his farewells and clear out? Once they were on a clear road at fifty an hour Donna would be more reasonable.

"They'll think I was in such a hurry to run away like this—I know Dandy Dark will never give *me* the jug now—Aunt Becky always thought eloping was vulgar—"

The Spanish blood suddenly claimed right of way—or else the Penhallow temper.

"If you do get that filthy jug," said Peter between his teeth, "I'll smash it into forty thousand pieces."

That finished it. If it hadn't been for the jug this sudden tempest in a teapot might have blown off harmlessly, especially as Mac Penhallow's old Lizzie went clattering down the road at last. Donna opened the car door and sprang out, her eyes blazing in the pale starlight.

"Peter Penhallow—I deserve this—but—"

"You deserve a damn' good spanking," said Peter.

Donna had never sworn in her life before. But she was not Drowned John's daughter for nothing.

"Go to hell," she said.

Peter committed the only sin a woman cannot forgive. He took her at her word.

"All right," he said—and went.

Donna picked up the suitcase, which was lying where she had first set it down, and marched back through the orchard and into the house. She re-locked the door and put the key in the blue vase. Drowned John was still snoring—so was old Jonas. She got into her own room and into her own bed. She was no longer cold—she was burning hot with righteous anger. What an escape! To think she had been on the point of running away with a creature who could say such beastly things to her. But of course one couldn't expect the Bay Silver Penhallows to have any manners. It served her right for forgetting she had always hated him. Virginia had been right—poor dear ill-used Virginia. But from henceforth forever-more, she, Donna, would be a widow indeed. Oh, how she hated Peter! As she hated everybody and everything. Hate, Donna reflected for her comforting, was a good lasting passion. You got over loving but you never got over hating. She thought of a score of stinging things she could have said to Peter. And now she would never have the chance to say them. The pity of it!

Peter tore across the country all night and caught the boat. So she had Drowned John's temper as well as his nose! He was well out of *that*—by the sacred baboon he was! He had no use for women who swore—not knowing how lucky he had been that Donna hadn't gone into hysterics instead of swearing. Serve him right for taking up with that family at all. Well, madness was finished and hurrah for sanity! Thank heaven, he was his own man again—free to wander the world over, with no clog of a woman tied round his neck. No more love for him—he was through with love.

VI

Donna was not the only woman of the clan to be out that night. Gay Penhallow was lying among the ferns in the birch grove behind Maywood, weeping her heart out at midnight.

There was a dance at the Silver Slipper that evening—the closing dance of the summer season, before the last of the guests left the big hotel down by the harbour's mouth. Noel had promised to come for Gay. Of late a little hope had sprung up in Gay's heart that everything was coming right between her and Noel again. They had had a little quarrel after that night when Gay had left Noel and Nan on the steps. Gay found herself put in the wrong. Noel was very angry over the way she had acted. A nice position she had put him in, Gay, all her little bit of pride now worn down by suffering, had apologized humbly and been grudgingly forgiven. She even felt a little happy again.

But only a little. Her pretty, dewy visions were gone never to return. There was always a little cold fear lurking deep down in her heart now. Day by day Noel seemed to drift further away from her. He wrote oftener than he came—and his letters had got so thin. When she hungered for the touch of his hand and the sound of his voice, with a hunger and longing that devoured her soul, came only one of those thin letters of excuse—from Noel, who only a few weeks ago had vowed he could *not* go on living ten miles away from her.

But she could not believe he meant to jilt her—her, Gay Penhallow of the proud Penhallows. Gay knew girls had been jilted—even Penhallow girls. But not so soon—so suddenly. Not in a few weeks after your lover had asked you to marry him. Surely the process of cooling off should take longer.

After she dressed for the dance that night she did a certain thing in secret. She hunted that old chain letter out of her desk and wrote three neat, careful little copies of it. Enveloped and addressed and stamped them. And flung on her coat and slipped down to the post-office in the cool windy September twilight to

406

post them. Who knew? After all—there might be something in it.

When she got back long-distance was calling. Noel couldn't come after all. He had to work in the bank that night.

Gay went out and sat down on the steps, huddled in her grey coat. Her little face with its piteous eyes, rose whitely over her soft fur collar. Roger found her there when he dropped in on his return from a sick-call.

"I thought you'd be at the Silver Slipper to-night," said Roger—who knew and was furious and helpless over certain things—more things than Gay knew. He looked down at her—this lovely, sensitive little thing who must be suffering as only such a sensitive thing could—with clenched hands. But he avoided her eyes. He could not bear the thought of looking into her eyes and seeing no laughter in them.

"Noel couldn't come," said Gay lightly. Roger was not to know—to suspect. "He has to work tonight. It's rather a shame, isn't it? Here I am 'all dressed up and nowhere to go.' Roger,"—she bent forward suddenly—"will you run me down to the Silver Slipper? It's only a mile—it won't take you long—I can come home with Sally William Y."

Roger hesitated.

"Do you really want to go, Gay?"

"Of course." Gay pouted charmingly. "A dance is a dance, isn't it—even if your best beau can't be there? Don't you think it would be a shame to waste these lovely slippers, Roger?"

She poked out a slender little golden foot in a cobweb of a stocking. Gay knew she had the daintiest ankles in the clan. But she was thinking wildly—desperately—she must be *sure*—sure that Noel had not lied to her.

Roger yielded. He did not know what Gay might find at the Silver Slipper but whatever it was she had better know it, hard as it might be. After all, it might not be Noel's car he had passed where the road turned down to the dunes.

Gay thanked Roger prettily at the door of the dance-hall and would not let him wait—or come in. She ran along the veranda with laughing greetings to the folks she knew, her eyes darting hither and thither from one canoodling pair to another in shadowy corners. Across the hall to the dance-room, with its rustic seats and its red lanterns. It was full of whirling couples, and Gay felt her head go around. She steadied herself against the door-post and looked about the room. Her head grew steadier, her lips ceased to tremble. There was no sign of Noel—or Nan. Perhaps—after all—but there was a little room off the dance-room—she must see who was in there. She slipped down the hall and stepped in. There had been laughter in it before her entrance—laughter that ceased abruptly. Several groups of young folks were in the room, but Gay saw only Noel and Nan. They were perched on the edge of a table where the punch-bowl was, eating sandwiches. To speak the strict truth, *one* sandwich, taking bites from it turn about. Nan, laughing shrilly in a daring new frock of orchid and mauve tulle—a frock that was almost backless—was holding it up to Noel's mouth when the general hush that followed Gay's entrance made her look around. A malicious, triumphant sparkle flashed into her eyes.

"Just in time for the last bite, Gay darling." She tossed it insultingly at Gay—but Gay was gone, sick and cold with agony to the depths of her being. Through the hall—over the veranda—down the steps. Out into the night where she could be alone. If she could just get away where it was dark and cool and quiet—no lights—no laughter—oh, no laughter! She thought everybody was laughing at her—at her, Gay Penhallow, who had been jilted. Unconsciously she clutched at the little gold bead necklace around her neck as she ran—Noel's gift—and broke it. The gold beads rolled like tiny stars over the dusty road in the pale autumn moonlight, but she never thought of stopping to pick them up. She knew if she ceased for a moment to run she would shriek aloud with anguish and not be able to stop. Some late-coming cars drenched the distraught little figure with their radiance and one narrowly escaped running her down. Gay wished it had.

Would she never get away somewhere where no one could see her? The road seemed endless—endless—she must keep running like this forever—if she stopped her heart would break.

Eventually she did get to Maywood. There was a light in the living-room. Her mother was there still. Gay couldn't face her. She couldn't face any one then. She was breathless and sobbing. Her pretty honey-hued gown hung about her in shreds, limp with dew, torn by the wild shrubs along the dune road. But that didn't matter. Dresses would never matter again. Nothing would matter. Gay found her tear-blinded way to a little ferny corner in the birch grove and flung herself down in it in a dreadful little huddle of misery. All the bitterness of all betrayed women was distilled in her young heart. The world had ended for her. There was nothing beyond—nothing. Nobody ever had suffered like this before—nobody ever would suffer like this again. How could she go on living? Nobody could suffer like this and live.

And it was all the fault of that horrible jug. Aunt Becky seemed to be laughing derisively at her from her grave. As all the world would soon be laughing—with the William Y. brand of laughter.

VII

Pennycuik Dark had decided that he must get married. Not without long and painful cogitations on the subject. For years Penny had believed he would always remain a bachelor. In his youth he had rather prided himself on being a bit of a lady-killer. He had then every intention of being married sometime. But—somehow—while he was making up his mind the lady always got engaged to somebody else. Before he realized it he had drifted into the doldrums of matrimonial prospects. The young girls began to think him one of the old folks and all the desirable maids of his own generation were wedded wives. The clan began to count Penny among its confirmed old bachelors. At first Penny had resented this. But of late years he had been well content. Marriage, he said, had no charms for him. He had enough money to live on without working, a comfortable little house at Bay Silver and a fairly good housekeeper in old Aunty Ruth Penhallow, a smart little car to coast about in, and two magnificent cats forever at his heels. First Peter and Second Peter, who slept at the foot of his bed and ate at his table. What more could matrimony offer him? He compared his lot complacently with most of the married men he knew. He wouldn't, he vowed, take any of their wives as a gift. As for a family—well, there were enough Darks and Penhallows in the world without his contributing any more. "Better let the cursed breed die out," Penny had growled irritably when Uncle Pippin rallied him about not being married. He liked to sit in church and pity Charlie Penhallow in the pew ahead, who had to buy dresses for seven foolish daughters and looked it. Penny's pity had a special flavour for him by reason of the fact that Mrs Charlie had been the only girl he had ever seriously considered marrying. But before he could make up his mind positively that he wanted her she had married Charlie. Penny told himself he didn't care, but when now, in his mellow fifties, he sat and recalled his old flames, like a dog remembering how many bones he has buried, he did not linger on the recollection of Amy Dark. Which meant that the thought of her held a sting for him. Amy had been a pretty girl and was a pretty woman still, in spite of seven daughters and two sons, and sometimes when Penny looked at her in church he felt a vague regret that she hadn't waited until he had decided whether he wanted her or not.

But, on the whole, Penny's bachelor existence suited him very well. He was fond of saying he had "kept the boy's heart," and had no suspicion that the younger folks thought him a chronic valentine. He thought he was quite a dandy still, admired by all his clan. He could come and go as he liked; he had no responsibilities and few duties.

Nevertheless, now and then of late years, a doubt of his wisdom in remaining unmarried crept into his mind. Aunt Ruth was growing old and, with her heart, might drop off any time.

What in thunder would he do for a housekeeper then? He began to feel rheumatic twinges in his legs, and remembered that his grandfather, Roland Penhallow, had been a cripple for years. If he, Penny, went like that, who would wait on him? And if the rheumatism went to his heart, as it had gone to Uncle Alec's, and he had no housekeeper, he might die in the night and nobody know of it for weeks. The gruesome thought of himself lying there alone dead for weeks was more than Penny could endure. Perhaps, after all, he had better marry before it was too late. But these fleeting fears might not have stirred him to action had it not been for Aunt Becky and her jug. Penny wanted that jug. Not because he cared a hang for the dingus itself but as a question of right. His father was Theodore Dark's oldest brother and his family ought to have it. And he felt sure he would have no chance of it if he remained unwedded. Aunt Becky had as good as said so. This tipped the balance in favour of matrimony, and Penny, with a long sigh of regret for the carefree and light-hearted existence he was giving up, made up his mind that he would marry if it killed him.

VIII

It remained to decide on the lady. This was no easy matter. It should have been easier than it had been thirty years before. There was not such a wide range of choice, as Penny ruefully admitted to himself. He had no idea of marrying out of the clan. At twenty-five he had liked to toy with such a daring idea, but at fifty-three a sensible man does not take such a risk. But which of the old maids and widows should be Mrs Penny Dark? For old maid or widow it must be, Penny decided with another sigh. Penny was not quite a fool, in spite of his juvenile pretences, and he knew quite well no young girl would look at him. He had not, he said cynically, enough money for *that*. He balanced the abstract allurements of old maids and widows. Somehow, an old maid did not appeal to him. He hated the thought of marrying a woman no other man had ever wanted. But then—a widow! Too experienced in managing men. Better a grateful spinster who would always bear in mind what he had rescued her from.

Still, he would consider them all.

For several Sundays after he had made up his mind he went to both Rose River and Bay Silver Churches and looked all the possibilities over. It was an interesting experience. Much more fun than trying to count the beads on Mrs William Y.'s dress, which was how he had contrived for several Sundays to endure the tedium of the sermon. Penny felt quite youthful and exhilarated over it. He wondered slyly what Mr Trackley would think about it if he knew. And what excitement there would be among all the aforesaid possibilities if they dreamed what was hanging in the balance. Would Hester Penhallow in the choir look so sanctimonious and other-worldly if she knew that her chances of being Mrs Pennycuik Dark were being debated down in the pew? Not that Hester had much of a chance. Marry that terrible beak of a nose! Never! Not for forty jugs.

"I can't marry an ugly woman, you know," thought Penny plaintively. The rest of the old cats in the choir he dismissed without a second thought.

Edna Dark was ladylike but her face was too tame. Charlotte Penhallow was too dowdy and her mouth too wide. Violet Dark was handsome enough still—a high-coloured woman with small, light brown eyes and a nasal voice. Handsome but charmless. Penny felt that he could do without beauty and style but charm he must have. Besides, in the back of his mind was an unacknowledged doubt if she would take him.

Bertha Dark's face was presentable, but where did she get such thick legs? Penny did not think he could stand a pair of legs like that waddling up the church aisle after him every Sunday. Elva Penhallow had slim, dainty legs but Penny decided she was "too devout" for him. Religion was all very well—a certain amount became a woman—but Elva really had too much to make a comfortable wife. Wasn't there a story that she was so conscientious that she used to write down in her diary every night the time she had spent in idleness that day, and pray over it? Too strenuous—by far too strenuous.

Penny wondered how old Lorella Dark really was. Nobody ever seemed to know, beyond the idea that she was kind of thirtyish. She was a plump and juicy little person, and he would have picked her in a second if he had not been afraid that she was not yet old enough to have given up hope of any man except an old bachelor. Penny did not mean to run any risk of a refusal.

Jessie Dark might have done. But he had heard her say she liked cats "in their place." She would never believe their place was on the marriage-bed, of that Penny felt sure. First and Second Peter would forbid those banns.

Bessie Penhallow—no, quite out of the question. He couldn't endure the big mole with three long hairs on it she had on her chin. Besides, she was as religious in her way as Elva. She was—to quote Penny's phrase—a foreign-mission crank. The last time he had been talking with her she had told him that interest in Christian literature was increasing in China and had been peeved because he didn't get excited over it.

Mildred Dark, who was a stenographer in a law office in town and came home for the week-ends, was stylish and up-to-date. But what a terrible complexion of moth patches. It was very well to say all women were sisters under their skins—Penny wasn't quite sure whether that was in Shakespeare or in the Bible—but the skin made a difference, confound it.

As for her sister Harriet, who "went in" for spiritualism and declared she had a "spirit lover" on "the other side," let her continue to love spiritually. Penny had no intention of being her lover on *this* side. No spooky rivals for *him*.

Betty Moore would really have been his choice if she had been Dark or Penhallow. But one took too many chances in marrying a Moore. Emilia Trask had money but she had a temperish look. No, no, Dark or Penhallow it must be. Marriage was a risk at best, but better the devil you know than the devil you don't know.

There was Margaret Penhallow. She had been pretty and her eyes were still pretty. Mr Trackley said she had a beautiful soul. That was probably true—but her body was so confoundedly lean. Mrs Clarence Dark, now—ah, there was a fine armful of a woman for you! But she was a widow and there was a legend that she had once slapped her husband's face at prayer-meeting. And though Uncle Pippin had said that he would rather be slapped than kissed in public—as Andy Penhallow was—Penny could not see the necessity of either. After all, Margaret's figure was the more fashionable. All the young girls were skinny nowadays. None of the plump morsels he remembered in his youth. Where were the girls of yesteryear? Girls that *were* girls—ah! But Margaret was ladylike and gentle and would of course give up writing her silly poems when she had a husband. By the time Mr Trackley's sermon was finished Penny had decided that he would marry Margaret. He went out into the crisp sunshine of the October afternoon feeling himself already roped in and fettered. When all was said and done, he would have liked a little more—well—romance. Penny sighed. He wished he had got married years ago. He would have been used to it by now.

IX

Big Sam was not particularly happy. Summer had passed; autumn was coming in; winter loomed ominously near. The Wilkins shanty was draughty and Big Friday Cove was a dodgasted lonesome place. He was getting indigestion from eating his own cooking. Various clan housewives invited him frequently to meals, but he did not care to go because he felt that they were on Little Sam's side. Even the Darks and Penhallows were getting lax and modern, Big Sam reflected gloomily. They would tolerate anything.

But when Big Sam heard that Little Sam was going to see the

Widow Terlizzick on Sunday nights, he was struck dumb for a time; then he turned himself loose on the subject to all who would listen.

"Wants to work another wife to death, I s'pose. I really would have thought Little Sam had more sense. But you can't trust a man who's been married once—though you'd think he'd be the very one to know better. And him the ugliest man in the clan! Not that the fair Terlizzick is any beauty, what with all them moles and her sloppy ankles. I'd say she looked like a dog-fight. And fat! If he had to buy her by the pound he'd think it over. She's been married twice already. Some folks never know when to stop. I'm sorry for Little Sam but it's certainly coming to him. I hear he waddles home from church with her. Next thing he'll be serenading her. Did I ever tell you Little Sam imagines he can sing? Once I says to him, says I, 'D'ye call that ungodly caterwauling music?' But the Terlizzicks never had any ear. Well, she'll have her troubles. I could tell a few things, if I wanted to."

None of the clan approved of the hinted courtship. To be sure, they had all long ago tacitly agreed that the Sams were in a class by themselves and not to be judged by the regular clan standards. Still, the Terlizzicks were a little *too* rank. But none of them took Little Sam's supposed matrimonial designs to heart as much as Big Sam. When he was observed standing on a rock, waving his short arms wildly in the air, it was a safe bet that he was *not*, as heretofore, shouting his epic out to waves and stars, but abusing the Widow Terlizzick. She was, he told the world, a hooded cobra, a big fat slob, a rapacious female animal and a tigress. He professed profound pity for Little Sam. The poor fellow little dreamed what he was in for. He oughter have more sense! Taking two men's leavings! Huh! But them widows did bamboozle people so. And the Terlizzick had so much experience. Two husbands done-in.

All these compliments being duly reported to Little Sam and Mrs Terlizzick may or may not have pleased them. Little Sam kept his own counsel and brought up Mustard's three kittens ostentatiously. The white goddess of the morning still stood on the clock shelf but the dust had gathered on her shapely legs. When Father Sullivan started up another lottery at Chapel Point Little Sam said it oughter be stopped by law and what were the Protestants thinking of?

THE MOVING FINGER

The sudden arrival "home" of Frank Dark and his sister Edna fell on the clan like a mild bombshell. Frank announced that Edna thought she had as good a right to the jug as anybody and had given him no peace until he consented to come. Dandy was his uncle and who knew? They would be in at the killing, anyhow. And he was about sick of the west. Guessed he'd sell out there and buy on the Island. Settle down for the rest of his life among his own folks.

"And marry a nice little Island girl," said Uncle Pippin.

"Sure," laughed Frank. "They're hard to beat."

But after he had left the store amused smiles were exchanged.

"Doesn't look any too prosperous," was the comment.

"He's gone to seed. They say he's been going the pace," said William Y. "Drank up everything he made a little faster than he made it."

"Too handsome to be any good when he was young. That always spoils a man," growled Sim Dark, who had certainly never been spoiled for that reason.

Joscelyn heard he was home the next evening just as she was starting for church. Aunt Rachel mentioned it casually to Mrs Clifford—"They say Frank Dark's home again"—and Joscelyn's head reeled and her universe whirled about her. For a moment she thought she was going to faint, and clutched wildly at the table to steady herself. Frank home—Frank! For a moment ten years folded themselves back like a leaf that is turned in a book and she saw herself, mist-veiled, looking into Frank Dark's handsome eyes.

"Ain't you ready yet, Joscelyn?" said Aunt Rachel fretfully. "We're going to be late. And if we are we won't get a seat.

Everybody will be there to hear Joseph."

The Rev. Joseph Dark of Montreal was to preach in Bay Silver Church that night and naturally almost every Dark and every Penhallow would be there. They were very proud of Joe. He was the highest salaried minister in Canada—little Joe Dark who used to run around Bay Silver barefooted and work in the holidays for his wealthier relatives. They hadn't bothered their heads much about him then, but now his occasional visits home were events and when he preached in Bay Silver Church they had to put chairs in the aisles.

Joscelyn walked to the church with her aunt. It was on an October evening as warm as June. A frolicsome little wind was stripping all the gold from the maple trees. The western sky was like a great smoky chrysanthemum over hills that were soft violet and brown. A few early autumnal stars were burning over the misty, shorn harvest fields. A great orange moon was rising over Treewoofe Hill, bringing out a remote, austere quality in its beauty. There was a pleasant smell of damp mould from red ploughed fields. Everybody was ploughing now. Hugh had been ploughing on the big hill field up at Treewoofe all day. Joscelyn knew that he had always loved to plough that hill field. She had seen him from her window and wondered again if he were really going to sell Treewoofe. Every few weeks the rumour revived. Aunt Rachel had mentioned it again that day and it had frettered Joscelyn like a grumbling toothache. But everything was forgotten now in the shock of what she had just heard. She walked as one in a dream. She did not know whether she felt glad or sorry or exultant or—or—afraid. Ay, she *did* know. She was afraid. Suddenly and horribly afraid. Of seeing Frank.

She did not think there was any danger of seeing him that evening. He would be stopping with his brother Burton at Indian Spring and Burton never came to hear Joseph Dark preach. Joe Dark had married the girl Burt wanted and Burt always ascribed Joe's success in the ministry to the fact that he knew how to flatter the women. Besides, Burt always averred in his characteristic way

418

that that old church at Bay Silver was lousy with fleas. As Uncle Pippin had once said, Burt Dark was a realistic sort of cuss.

But Joscelyn knew she would meet Frank somewhere and soon. And she was mortally afraid, with a sick, cold, dreadful fear.

They were late; when they reached the church the Reverend Joseph was praying and they waited in the porch that was full of other late-comers. The inner doors were tightly shut and only a sonorous murmur penetrated outwards. Joseph Dark had a beautiful voice and there was something in the faint, unworded rhythm of his prayer that soothed Joscelyn. She rather liked standing there in the porch, listening to it. One could fit one's own words, one's own needs, one's own desires to it.

She did not see Hugh at first. He was standing just behind her, gazing at her with smouldering eyes. Palmer Dark and Homer Penhallow were in the porch also. They had nodded amicably and mentioned the weather. Then they stood hating each other while Joseph prayed. The truce of the jug still held but underneath it the old dear feud rankled. Ambrosine Winkworth sailed in past them and streamed up the aisle, her head held high, her diamond ring on her ungloved hand. Ambrosine had no intention of waiting in the draughty porch until little Joe Dark, whom she had spanked in years gone by, had finished praying. He always prayed too proudly, anyway, Ambrosine thought. Ambrosine never wore gloves now, and she was the happiest woman in the church that night. Envious people said that the airs Ambrosine put on over that ring were simply ridiculous,

"Ain't she the fine lady now?" whispered Uncle Pippin, sitting on the third step of the gallery stair, beside Big Sam, who had come to find out if there were any truth in the story that Little Sam came to Bay Silver Church every Sunday night to walk home with the Widow Terlizzick.

"What a long tail our cat has," whispered Big Sam in return.

Back in the shadowy corner Stanton Grundy loomed, lean and taciturn. He had never been able to hear Joe Dark preach before.

Something had always prevented. But now his chance had come to see the man his Robina had secretly loved all her life. Robina, who was now a handful of ashes in an urn in the churchyard outside—all ashes, even to the heart that had belonged to Joseph Dark instead of to its lawful owner, Stanton Grundy. Donna Dark and her father were there, although Drowned John was never over-anxious to hear Joe preach. Not that he had anything against Joe. But he thought it might give him a swelled head if too many of his own clan went to hear him. However, Donna was set on coming and Drowned John gave in. Drowned John was by way of getting into the habit of giving in now and then to Donna. It eased things up a bit. In the month that had passed, gossip about Peter and Donna had died down. There had been a good deal of it at first and much wonderment as to why everything had stopped so suddenly. Drowned John did not vex himself wondering why. It was very simple. He had ordered Donna to discard the fellow and she had of course obeyed. Some thought Peter's behaviour that notable Sunday had disgusted Donna. Virginia thought that dear Donna's higher nature had reasserted itself. Though Virginia did not get a great deal of comfort out of that. Dear Donna was frightfully changed, there was no doubt about it. So cynical. She laughed at Virginia's sentimental memories. She said that if Barry had lived they would probably have fought like cat and dog, half the time. At home Donna's behaviour was rather like that of a ladylike tigeress by times. Then Drowned John was driven to the reflection that life might have been more comfortable if he had let Peter have her. And there was no longer any fun in her. There had used to be a good bit when Virginia wasn't around. In short, she would, he confided to his pigs, neither gee nor haw.

Kate Muir was there, buxom and rosy and overdressed as usual, with the three little black curls every one made fun of lying sleekly and flatly on her forehead. Murray Dark was there, waiting impatiently for Joe to get through, that he might go in and look at Thora for an hour. Percy Dark and David Dark were there, but they glowered gloomily past each other. They had never "spoken" since their fight at the funeral and by heck, they never would speak, jug or no jug. Tempest Dark was there because he had been a crony of Joe's in boyhood and still liked the beggar in spite of his priestly ways.

All in all, it was an odd mélange of passions—hates and hopes and fears—that waited in the old church porch at Bay Silver for Joseph Dark to finish his seemingly interminable prayer.

Joscelyn had a love for Bay Silver Church—a tranquil old grey church among its sunken graves and mossy gravestones. She was glad the graveyard had never been ironed out and standardized like the one at Rose River.

Outside, the moon was shining calmly on the tombstones and the Moon Man was wandering about among them. Occasionally he stopped and told a dead crony something. Occasionally he bowed to the moon. Occasionally he would come to the porch door or a church window and peer in. Later on when the congregation sang he would sing, too. But he would never enter a church door.

"What's Joe so damn' long about?" thought Drowned John impatiently. He dared not swear in words but, thank God, thought was still free.

Frank Dark was in the porch, standing under the little hanging lamp, before Joscelyn saw him. He stood there, beaming rather fatuously around him. Joscelyn stared at him with eyes in which dawning horror struggled with amazement. *This* could not be Frank Dark—oh, *this* could never be the slim, gallant stripling to whom she had so suddenly lost her heart on her wedding night. *This* could not be the man she had loved in secret for ten years. *This!* Fat; half-bald; nose red; eyes puffy and bloodshot; sallow jowls; shabby. With failure written all over him. She saw him as he was; worse—as he had always been under all the charm of his vanished youth. Paltry—crude—cheap. She gazed at him in the stubborn incredulity with which we face the fact of a sudden death. It could not be! It could not be for *this* that she had torn Hugh's life in shreds and lost Treewoofe forever? Joscelyn wondered if it were she who was laughing—certainly some one was laughing. It was Hugh, behind her. A strange little laugh with nothing of mirth in it. So Hugh saw what she was seeing. Joscelyn wondered if there were any deeper depths of shame to which she could descend.

Hugh's laugh drew Frank's attention to them. He smiled broadly and came forward with outstretched hand, effusive and gushing.

"Hugh—and Joscelyn! How *do* you do! How *do* you do! My, it's good to see all you folks again. You don't look a day older, Joscelyn—handsomer than ever. It don't seem possible it's ten years since I danced at your wedding. How time does fly!"

Joscelyn felt sure she was in a nightmare. She must wake up. This ridiculous, hideous situation couldn't be real. She saw Hugh shaking hands with Frank—Frank whom he had vowed to thrash if he ever set eyes on him again. Now he would disdain to do it. Joscelyn saw the disdain in his eyes—in his bitter mouth. Thrash this poor creature for whom his bride had thrown him over. The idea was farcical.

"And how's the family?" said Frank with a sly wink.

Something in the electric silence that followed gave Frank time to think. There was a titter from some ill-bred young cub by the door. Frank had never heard the sequel to the wedding at which he had danced. But he felt he had put his foot in it somehow. Probably they had no family and were sensitive about it. His tongue was always getting him into trouble. But hang it, if they hadn't a family they ought to have. Hugh needn't glower like that. As for Joscelyn, she had always been a high and mighty piece of goods. But she needn't be looking at him as if he were some kind of a new and fancy worm. The airs some people gave themselves made him tired.

The Reverend Joseph had concluded his prayer and with a sigh of relief the waiting group passed into the church. Joscelyn, who only wanted to run—and run—and run, had to follow Aunt

Rachel in and sit quietly through a sermon of which she heard not one word. She felt as if she had been stripped naked to the gaze of a world that was laughing at her shame. It was of no avail to tell herself that no one but Hugh ever knew or suspected that she had loved Frank Dark—or something she had believed Frank Dark to be. The feeling of naked humiliation persisted. How Hugh must be mocking her! "You flouted me for this! What do you think of your bargain?"

Hugh was not thinking anything of the sort. He thought Frank Dark a pretty poor specimen of a man—not worth all the hatred he had lavished on him—but he did not know that Joscelyn saw what he did. After all, Frank was still handsome in a florid way and women's tastes were odd enough. Hugh was another who did not hear much of Joseph Dark's sermon. All the old bitterness and anger of his wedding-night was surging up in his soul again. What a mess had been made of his life—through no fault of his own. There were a dozen girls he might have had; some of them were in the church that night. He looked at them all and decided that, after all, he'd rather have Joscelyn. Just as things were—Joscelyn with that glorious sweep of red-gold hair over her pale, proud face. If she were not his, at least she was no other man's. Nor could be. *She* could never divorce *him*. Hugh ground his teeth in savage triumph. Frank Dark should never get her—never!

Big Sam, with Little Sam sitting across from him, gazing at the buxom Widow Terlizzick like, Big Sam vowed to himself, an intoxicated dog, did not hear much of the sermon either. Which was a pity because it was a remarkably good sermon—brilliant, eloquent, scholarly. Joseph Dark's listeners sat spellbound. He played skilfully on their emotions—perhaps a shade too skilfully—and they responded as a harp responds to the wind. They felt caught away from sordid things to hill-tops of vision and splendour; life, for the time being at least, became a thing of beauty to be beautifully lived; and few there were who did not feel a throb of glad conviction when the speaker, leaning earnestly over the desk and addressing individually every member of his audience, said thrillingly:

"And never, even in your darkest and most terrible moments, forget that the world belongs to God," closing the Bible, as he spoke with a thunderclap of victory.

Of the few was Stanton Grundy. He smiled sardonically as he went out.

"The devil has a corner or two yet," he said to Uncle Pippin.

"Gosh, but that was a sermon though," said Uncle Pippin admiringly.

"He can preach," conceded Grundy grudgingly. "I wonder how much of it he believes himself."

Which was unfair to Joseph Dark, who believed every word he preached—while he was preaching it, at all events—and surely could not be justly blamed because Robina Dark had, all unasked, given him the heart that should have belonged only to her liege lord, Stanton Grundy.

"Frank Dark's got terrible fat," said Aunt Rachel as she and Joscelyn walked home. "He's following in the footsteps of his father. *He* weighed three hundred and fifty-two pounds afore he died. I mind him well."

Joscelyn writhed. Aunt Rachel had always possessed the knack of making everything she mentioned supremely ridiculous. Joscelyn's romantic love for Frank Dark was dead—dead past any possibility of a resurrection. It had died as suddenly as it had been born, there in the porch of Bay Silver Church. But she could have wished, for her own sake, to be able to look upon the corpse with some reverence—some pity—some saving wish that it could have been otherwise. It was dreadful to have to mock herself over dead love—to hear others mocking. Dreadful to think of having wasted on Frank Dark the years that should have been given to bearing Hugh's children and building a home for him and for them at Treewoofe. Dreadful to think that all the passion and devotion and high renunciation of those processional years had been squandered on a man who had simply become a person likely to "weigh three hundred and fifty-two pounds before he died." Joscelyn would have laughed at herself except for the fact that she knew if she began to laugh she would never be able to stop. All the world would laugh at her if it knew. Even the tall, wind-writhen lombardies against the moonlit clouds above William Y.'s place, seemed to be pointing derisive fingers at her. She hated the stars that twinkled at her—the chilly, foolish night-wind that whined mockingly—the round hill shoulders over the bay that were shaking with merriment. What was Aunt Rachel saying? Something about Penny Dark being more conceited than ever since he had got Aunt Becky's bottle of Jordan water.

"He needn't imagine he's got the only one in the clan."

Joscelyn felt that she wanted to do something very cruel. She wanted to make some one else feel a little of the pain and humiliation she was enduring.

"Oh, but he has, Aunt Rachel. I spilled your bottle of Jordan water long ago and filled it up with water from the barn pump. That's what you've been worshipping all these years!"

II

One grey November evening Gay carried home a letter from Noel. When the postmaster had handed it out to her, her heart had given a suffocating bound, as it would do, she thought, if she were buried underground and Noel walked by her grave. It was a long time since she had had a letter from him. A long time since she had seen him—not since that bitter night at the Silver Slipper. She did not even hear much about him—her clan were surprisingly considerate in regard to that. Almost too considerate. Their avoidance of all reference to Noel was too pointed. Gay knew what it meant when everybody stopped talking as she entered a room. It hurt her—or her pride. For she had still some pride left in which she tried pitifully to wrap herself from what she thought was the half-pitying, half-contemptuous gaze of her little world. She felt as if every one must be watching her to see how she took it—watching her around corners—behind window-blinds—across the church.

And she had still a tormenting secret hope that all would come right yet. Noel *must* have loved her. It couldn't have been all pretence. He was just bewitched by Nan's daring and "differentness" and bold coquetry—by the way she could use her eyes. What if—Gay caught her breath as she hurried along—what if this letter were to tell her he had come to his senses—what if it were asking her to forgive him and take him back? Why else should he have written at all?

Gay flitted home like a little shadow through the melancholy moonlight of the late autumn night. The distant hills were cold and eerie in the chill radiance. The sea moaned hollowly down on the beach. A lonely wind was looking for something and moaning pitifully because it could not find it. It was a dead world—everything was dead—youth, hope and love were dead. But if Noel's letter only said what it might say there would be an immediate resurrection. Spring would come back even in grey November and her poor, cold, dead, little heart would beat again. If Noel would only come back to her. She did not care how much he had hurt her—how rottenly he had used her—if he would only come back. Her pride was only for the world. She had no pride as far as Noel was concerned. Only a dreadful longing to have him back.

She went to her room, when she reached Maywood, and laid the letter on the table. Then sat down and looked at it. She was afraid to open it. She dared not open it yet—she would let herself hope a little longer. She thought of that evening in June when she had gone from Aunt Becky's levee to read Noel's letter among the ferns in the shadowy hollow of that little wayside nook. There had been no fear then. How could a few short months have made such a difference in anybody's life? She wondered dumbly if she could possibly ever have been the happy girl of the lovely apple-blossom-time. Then a whole universe of wonder had been hers, with the Milky Way for a lover's path. Now it had shrunk to a little room where a pale girl sat staring with piteous dilated eyes at a letter she was afraid to open.

She recalled the first time she had got a letter from Noel—all the "first times." The first time they had met—the first time she had danced with him—the first time he had called her "Gay"— the first time his smooth, flushed cheek had rested against hers— the first time she had poked her fingers through a little gold curl falling down on his forehead and saw it glistening on her hand like a ring of troth—the first time he had said, "I love you."

And then the first time she had doubted him—such a little, little doubt like a tiny stone thrown into a pool. The ripples had widened and widened until they touched the farthest shores of mistrust. And now she could not open her letter.

"I won't be such a coward any longer," said Gay passionately. She snatched it up and opened it. For a few minutes she looked at it. Then she laid it down and looked around her. The room was just the same. It seemed indecent that it should be just the same. She walked a little unsteadily to the open window and sat down on a chair.

Noel had asked her to release him from his engagement. He was "very sorry" but it would be foolish "to let a boyish mistake ruin three lives." He had "thought he loved her" but now he "realized that he had not known then what love was." There was a good deal more of this—Noel had so many apologies and excuses that Gay didn't bother to read them all. What did they matter? She knew what was in the letter now.

She sat at her window all night. She could not sleep and she did not want to sleep. It would be so terrible to awake and remember again. There was nothing in the world but cold, pale moonlight. Would she ever forget that dreadful white, unpitying moon above the waiting woods—the mournful sound of the wind rustling the dead leaves on the trees, this chilly November night? There was nothing left for her in life—nothing—nothing. It was just as the Moon Man had warned her—she had been too happy.

She thought the night would never end. Yet when the trees began to shiver in the wind of dawn she shrank from it. She could not bear this dawn—all other dawns she could bear but not this one. And it was such a wonderful dawn—a thing of crimson and gold and quivering splendour—of flames and wings and mystery—such a dawn as should break only over a happy world on a happy morning for happy people. It was an insult to her misery.

"I could live through this morning if there were to be no more mornings," thought Gay drearily. Those interminable mornings, stretching before her, year after year, year after year, till she was old and lean and faded and bitter like Mercy Penhallow. The very thought of them made Gay feel desperate. She shivered.

"Will I ever get used to pain?" she thought.

Gay told her mother quite calmly that afternoon that she had broken her engagement with Noel. Mrs Howard wisely said very little and less wisely made Gay's favourite cake with spice frosting for supper. It did not heal Gay's broken heart; it only made Gay hate spice cake for the rest of her life.

Mercy recommended fresh air and an iron tonic. William Y. said he hoped Noel Gibson would get enough of that little wasp of a Nan before she was through with him.

"Remember you're a Penhallow. They don't wear their hearts on their sleeves," cautioned Cousin Mahala kindly. Gay looked at her with sick eyes. She had gone on smiling, that day, before the clan until she could smile no more. But she did not mind Cousin Mahala seeing into her soul. Cousin Mahala *understood*.

"Cousin Mahala, *how* can I go on living? Just tell me how— that's all I want to know now. Because I *have* to live, it seems."

Cousin Mahala shook her head.

"I can't—nobody can. And you'd only think me heartless and unfeeling if I told you you'd get over this. But I will tell you something I've never told any one before. Do you see that little field over there between Drowned John's farm and the shore road? Well, I lay there among the clover all night, thirty years ago, agonizing because Dale Penhallow didn't want me. I didn't see how I was to go on living either. And now I never pass that field without thanking my lucky stars he didn't."

Gay shrank into herself. After all, Cousin Mahala didn't understand. Nobody understood.

Nobody but Roger. Roger came along that evening to find Gay huddled on the veranda steps in the twilight, feeling like some poor little cat freezing before a merciless locked door. She looked up at him with her terrible, tortured young eyes, over the fur of her collar as he sat down beside here, her face one little, white, pinched note of pain—the face that was meant for laughter.

"Gay—my poor little Gay," he cried. "What have they been doing to you?"

Gay laid her tired head down on his shoulder.

"Roger," she whispered, "will you take me for a drive in your car? A *fast* drive—I don't care how fast—a long drive—I don't care how long—right through the sunset if you like—and *don't talk to me.*"

They had their long and fast drive—so fast that they nearly ran over Uncle Pippin at the turn of the Indian Spring road. He skipped nimbly out of their way and looked after them, chuckling.

"So Roger's out for the rebound," he said. "He always was a cool sort of devil. Knew how to wait."

But Uncle Pippin didn't understand either. Roger just then was feeling that it would be a delightful sensation to find Noel Gibson's throat between his fingers. And Gay wasn't feeling anything. She was numb. But that was better than suffering. She seemed to leave pain behind her as she swooped along the road, the lights flashing on dark woods and tossing trees and frosted ferns and alluring dunes—on—on—on through the night—across the world—not having to talk—not having to smile—conscious only of the sweep of free, cold wind in her face and Roger's dark strength beside her at the wheel. This big, quiet, gentle Roger, with his softly luminous eyes and his slim brown hands. It seemed the most natural thing in the world that he should be there beside her. When they went back—when they stopped—pain would run to meet her again. But this relief was blessed. If they need only never stop—if they could go on and on like this forever—over the hills—down into the valleys of night—along the windy shores of starlit rivers—past the curls of foam on long, shadowy beaches, in the beautiful darkness that was like a cool draught for a fevered soul to drink! If only they need never turn back!

III

Pennycuik Dark was on his way to propose to Margaret Penhallow. Though he had made up his mind to do it in September, it was not done yet. Every morning Penny thought he would go up to Denzil's that evening and have done with it. But every evening he found an excuse to defer it. He might never have gone at all had it not been for the gravy stains on the table-cloth. Penny, who was as neat as one of his own cats, could not endure a mussy table-cloth. Old Aunt Ruth was getting inexcusably careless. It was high time the house had a proper mistress.

"I'll go this evening and get it over," said Penny desperately.

He dressed and shaved as for a solemn rite, wondering uneasily what it would be like to have some one there in the room, watching him shave.

"It may be all right when a fellow gets used to it," sighed poor Penny.

He walked up to Denzil's—no use wasting gas on a two-mile errand—wondering what the people he met would say if they knew what he was out for. Mrs Jim Penhallow's great flock of snowy geese in a dun, wet November field—white as snow in the autumnal twilight—hissed at him as he passed. Penny reflected that he might as well buy a goose for the wedding-supper from

Mrs Jim as not. She might let him have it a bit cheaper, since they were first cousins.

At Denzil's gate he paused. It was not too late yet to back out. He might still return home a free man. But the gravy stains! And the jug! Penny lifted the gate latch firmly. The Rubicon was crossed.

"By ginger, this makes me feel queer," thought Penny. He found he was perspiring.

The amazing, the ununderstandable thing was that Margaret did not jump at him. When she had finally disentangled his meaning—for Penny went all to pieces at the crucial moment—forgot every word of the speech he had so carefully composed and rehearsed and floundered terribly—realizing that Pennycuik Dark was actually proposing marriage to her, she asked rather primly for time to consider it. This flabbergasted Penny. He, who had not had the least doubt that he would go home an engaged man, found himself going home nothing of the sort. He was so indignant that he wished he had never mentioned the matter to her. Gracious Peter, suppose she wouldn't have him after all! Ridicule would be his portion all the rest of his life. And she had wanted a week to make up her mind—to make up her mind whether or no to marry *him*, Pennycuik Dark! Did any one ever know the like?

Margaret really passed as disagreeable a week as Penny did. One day she thought she would marry Penny; the next she thought she couldn't. In spite of her desire for marriage in the abstract she found that in the concrete, as represented by little dapper Penny Dark, it was not wholly desirable. It would have amazed Penny, who had no small opinion of his own good looks, had he known that Margaret thought his bodily presence contemptible and his chubby pimply little face positively ugly—and worse than ugly, rather ridiculous. To wake up every morning and see that face beside you. To listen to his funny vulgar stories and his great haw-haws over them! To hear him yelling to Baal if he had a hangnail. To think it a joke, as he still did, when he stuck out his foot and tripped somebody up. To be always called "Mar'gret."

Then she didn't like his fussy, lace-trimmed house. Too many jigarees on it. So different from little grey Whispering Winds, veiled in trees. Margaret felt positive anguish when she realized that marriage meant the surrender of all the mystery and music and magic that was Whispering Winds. She would be too far away from it even for occasional visits. She could never again nourish a dear, absurd little hope that it might sometime be hers.

And she must give up certain imaginary love affairs with imaginary lovers, such as she had been fond of dreaming. She felt that it would be wrong, when she was married, to dream those romantic love-affairs. She must "keep her only" to Penny then. And she knew he would never consent to her adopting a baby. He detested children.

But there were certain advantages. She would be a wedded wife with a home and social standing such as she had never possessed. Nobody would ever say to her again, "Not married yet—well—well?" She would have a car of her own to ride in—or her husband's own. Margaret reminded herself very sensibly that she could not expect to have a man made for her. She knew most of the clan would think she was in luck to get Penny. Yet, as she worked all that week at Sally Y.'s nasturtium-coloured chiffon dress, watching it grow to a thing of flame and loveliness under her fingers, she "swithered," as she expressed it. She just couldn't make up her mind to marry Penny, somehow. Finally she remembered that she would certainly have no chance of Aunt Becky's jug if she stayed an old maid. That tipped the balance. She sat down and wrote a note to Penny. Determined to infuse a little sentiment into her acceptance, she merely sent him a copy of some Bible verse—Ruth's immortal reply to Naomi. At first Penny didn't know what the deuce it meant. Then he concluded that she had accepted him. He and Second Peter looked at each other with an air of making up their minds to the inevitable.

He went up to see Margaret, trying to feel that it was the happiest day of his life. He thought it his duty to kiss her and he did. Neither enjoyed it.

"I s'pose there isn't any particular hurry about getting married," he said. "It's a cold time of year. Better wait till spring."

Margaret agreed almost too willingly. She had had her white night after she had mailed her letter to Penny. She went to Whispering Winds and walked about it until midnight to recover her serenity. But she was now resigned to being Mrs Pennycuik Dark. And she could have the winter to plan her trousseau. She would have a nice one. She had never had pretty clothes. Life, as far back as she could look, had been as dull and colourless in clothes as in everything else. She would have a wedding-dress of frost-grey silk with silvery stockings. She had never had a pair of silk stockings in her life.

Altogether Margaret was much more contented than Penny, who when he went home had to brew himself a jorum of hot, bitter tea before he could look his position squarely in the face. Sadly he admitted that he was not as happy as he ought to be.

"Things," Penny gloomily told the two Peters, "will never be the same again."

The affair surprised the clan but was generally approved. "The jug's responsible for that," said Dandy Dark when he heard of it.

Margaret suddenly found herself of considerable importance. Penny was well-off; she was doing well for herself. She rather enjoyed this in a shy way, but Penny writhed when people congratulated him. He thought they had their tongues in their cheeks. The story went that when Stanton Grundy said to Penny, "I hear you're engaged," Penny had turned all colours and said feebly, "Well, it's not—not an engagement exactly—more like—like an experiment." But nobody knows to this day whether Penny really said it or not. The general opinion is that Stanton Grundy made it up.

The affair made less of a sensation than it might have, had it not coincided with Gresham Dark's discovery that his wife, after eighteen childless years, was going to present him with an heir. Gresham, who belonged to the excitable Spanish branch, quite lost his head over it. He rushed around, buttonholing people at church and auctions to tell them about it. The women of the clan could have killed him but the men chuckled.

"I suppose you can't blame *that* on the jug," said Uncle Pippin.

IV

Early in December Frank Dark's engagement to Mrs Katherine Muir was announced in the local papers. It surprised nobody; all had seen in what quarter the wind was setting from the first week after Frank's arrival home. Frank, they thought, had feathered his nest well. Kate was a cut or two socially above what he had any right to expect. Her face was rather the worse for wear and she was a bit bossy. But she had the cash. That was what Frank was after. Of Kate's wisdom they had a poorer opinion. She was, it was thought, taking a risk. But Frank was not going west again. He was going to buy a farm—with Kate's money?—and settle down among his clan. He would likely go pretty straight, surrounded by such a cloud of witnesses. To be sure, on the day he married his plump widow, it was easy to see he was three sheets in the wind. But public opinion excused him. A man must have some courage, even if it were only Dutch courage, to tackle Kate.

It was reported that he was trying to get Treewoofe. Some said Hugh refused to sell and had snubbed Frank cruelly; others had it that he was considering the offer. Kate had always had a fancy for Treewoofe.

Joscelyn heard all the rumours with many others. She had not seen Frank since that night in Bay Silver Church, but gossip soon informed her that he was after Kate. Well, what did it matter? She had always despised Kate Muir. It was nothing to her whom this new Frank, red-nosed and puffy-eyed, married. But when she heard that he was going to buy Treewoofe a fresh agony possessed her. Frank at Treewoofe! Black, moustached little Kate mistress of Treewoofe! Joscelyn fled to her room to face the thought and found it could not be faced.

It had been a hard day for her. Her mother and Aunt Rachel had bickered almost continually, owing to Aunt Rachel's having upset her stomach eating something she should not. Aunt Rachel had been "on a diet" ever since the night Joscelyn had told her about the Jordan water. She had fretted so over it that she grew ill and Roger had been called in. Joscelyn hated herself for having told Aunt Rachel—poor Aunt Rachel who had so little to make life worth living. She would have bitten her tongue out if that would have unsaid the fatal words. Nothing could unsay them; stricken Aunt Rachel took the bottle off the parlour mantel and buried it in the garden; then she proceeded to develop "stomach trouble," and Joscelyn soon had plenty of other reasons for wishing she had held her tongue. Aunt Rachel's stomach became the pivot about which all the meals revolved; they could not have this and they could not have that because "poor Rachel" could not eat it. If they had it "poor Rachel" could not resist the temptation and calamity followed. The previous evening company had come to tea and something extra had to be provided. Mrs Clifford had warned Rachel that the cheese soufflé would not agree with her stomach and Rachel had responded pettishly that she guessed it was her own stomach. To-day was the consequence and Joscelyn had to set her teeth to endure it—as a sort of penance because it was all her fault. But this news about Treewoofe was unbearable.

She looked up at it, lying in its mysterious silence of moonlit snow fields, with flying shadows from the passing clouds of the windy night sweeping over it, so that it now became almost invisible in the silver loveliness of the winter landscape, and again loomed suddenly forth at her on its white eerie hill in that cold ghostly moonlight. Was Hugh there? Was he going to sell Treewoofe? Was he going to get a divorce and marry Pauline Dark? The silence around her seemed verily to shriek these questions at her. And there was no answer.

It had been a hard autumn and winter for Joscelyn. She felt

indescribably poorer. Life had tricked her—betrayed her—mocked her. And when her romantic infatuation, as she now bitterly saw it, had vanished, her old feeling for Hugh had come back. All at once he was dear—so dear. Not that she held any hope that matters could ever be put right between them. Hugh, she was sure, hated her now, if he did not actually despise her. Besides, he was going to go to the States for a divorce and would marry Pauline. Everybody said so.

Joscelyn was racked with jealousy. She hated the very sight of Pauline. She felt that Pauline already pictured herself as Hugh's wife and mistress of Treewoofe. She remembered how she had seen Hugh and Pauline talking together at Aunt Becky's funeral and looking up at Treewoofe. But it was still more dreadful to think of Frank and Kate being there. That was desecration. As long as Hugh was at Treewoofe, even with Pauline, Joscelyn would not feel so helplessly bereft. Every day and night she looked up at Treewoofe, loving and craving it the more intensely that she dared not let herself love and crave Hugh. She saw it on stormy days, with swirls of snow blowing around it—under frosty sunsets when its light burned like jewels over the rose tints of the snowy fields—on mild afternoons when the grey rain wrapped it like a cloak—in the pale gold and misty silver of early, windless mornings. Always it was there, her home—her real and only home—luring, repellent, scornful, desirable by turns. Her home from which she must always be an exile through her own folly. Pauline would be there—or fat, giggling Kate. Joscelyn gritted her strong white teeth. A mad impulse assailed her. Suppose she went to Hugh—now—when he was sitting alone in that lonely house with the winter wind blowing around it—and flung herself at his feet—asked him to forgive her—to take her back—humiliated herself in the very dust? No, she could never do that. She might if she had any hope he still cared. But she knew he didn't. He was in love with Pauline now—everybody said so—Pauline with her slim darkness and her long velvety eyes. She, Joscelyn, was a woman without love—without a home—without roots. She must spend the rest of her life forever beating with futile hands at closed doors. An old line of poetry, read long ago and forgotten for years, flickered back into memory:

Exceeding comfortless and worn and old
For a dream's sake.

Yes, that had been written for her. "For a dream's sake." And now the dream was over.

"Joscelyn," wailed Aunt Rachel from the hall, "I wish you'd fill the hot-water bottle and bring it up and lay it acrost my stomach. If that don't help you'll have to phone for Roger. And I suppose he'll be off joy-riding with Gay Penhallow. It's off with the old love and on with the new mighty easy nowadays. People don't seem to have any deep feelings any more. Aunty But's just been in on her way to Gresham's. They've sent for her three times already on false alarms, but she guesses this is genuine. She says Gresham was yelling over the phone as if 'twas him was having the baby 'stead of his wife. She says she knows for a fact that Aunt Becky's jug is to be raffled off. Dandy got stewed at Billy Dark's silver wedding and let it out. Raffling's immoral and oughter be stopped by law."

"Dandy didn't get drunk at the wedding," said Joscelyn wearily. "He took an overdose of painkiller to cure a stomach-ache before he went and it made him act very queerly; but he kept fast hold on his secrets, Aunt Rachel."

"It's awful what stories get around," sighed Aunt Rachel. "And Aunty But says Mar'gret Penhallow's getting a lot of silly, fashionable clo'es to be married in. Mar'gret wants taking down a peg or two, and if my stomach was what is used to be"—Aunt Rachel gave a hollow groan—"I'd go and do it. But somehow I can't get up much pep nowadays—living on slops."

V

Likely Gay was "joy-riding" with Roger the night Aunt Rachel's stomach was acting up. If not, it was a safe wager that Roger was talking to her in the living-room at Maywood, with a driftwood fire dreaming dreams of fairy colours in the grate and a maddeningly complacent mother painstakingly effacing herself as soon as he came. Gay, who couldn't bear to be alone with herself, did not know what she would have done through that terrible autumn and winter without Roger.

By night she was still given over to torture but by day she had achieved self-command. The clan had decided that she hadn't cared so much for Noel Gibson after all. They thought she had taken it pretty well. Gay knew they were watching her to see how she did take it and she held her head up before the world. She would not give all those heartless gossipers food for talk. She would not let them think she knew of their whispers and their curious eyes. She did not laugh very much—she who had always been a girl of the merriest silver laughter—and Stanton Grundy said to himself, as he looked at her in church, "The bloom's gone," and, old cynic though he was, thought he would enjoy "booting" Noel Gibson. Some of the clan thought Gay was "improved" since certain little airs and graces had been dropped. All in all, they did not talk or think about her nearly as much as sensitive little Gay thought they were doing. They had their own lives to live and their own loves and hates and ambitions to suffer and scheme and plan for. And, anyway, Roger could be trusted to handle the situation.

At first, when they went riding, Gay wanted to go in silence— silence in which a hurt heart could find some strength to bear its pain. But one night she said suddenly,

"Talk to me, Roger. Don't ask me to talk—I can't—but just talk to me."

Roger, to his own surprise, found that he could. He had never talked much to Gay before. He had always felt that he could talk of nothing that would interest her. There had been such a gap between her youth and his maturity. But the gap had disappeared. Roger found himself telling her things he had never told anybody. He had never talked of his experiences overseas to any one but he found himself relating them to Gay. At first Gay only listened; then, insensibly, she began to talk, too. She took to reading the newspapers—which worried Mrs Howard, who was afraid Gay was getting "strong-minded." But Gay only wanted to learn more about the things Roger talked of, so that he would not think her an empty-headed goose. She had, without realizing it, come a long, long way from the tortured little creature who had lain under the birches, that September night, and cried her heart out. No longer an isolated, selfish unit, she had become one with her kind. She had realized what some one had called "the infinite sadness of living" and the realization had made a woman of her. Her April days were ended.

There was a sad peace in knowing nothing could ever happen to her again—that life held nothing for her but Roger's friendship. But she would always have that; and with it she could face existence. How splendid Roger was! She had never half appreciated him before. Tender—strong—unselfish. Seeing the best in everybody. He told her things about the clan she had never known before—not the petty gossip everybody knew or the secret scandals Aunt Becky and her ilk knew—but noble things and kindly things and simple, wholesome things that made Gay feel she came of a pretty decent stock, after all, and must live up to the traditions of it. It was amazing how good people really were. Even her own Darks and Penhallows whom she had laughed at or disliked. Who would have supposed that Mercy Penhallow, malicious Mercy who was afraid to be out after dark—perhaps for fear of the ghosts of reputations she had slain—could have been a perfect heroine during the terrible Spanish flu epidemic? Or that William Y., who held the mortgage on Leonard Stanley's farm, should, when Leonard died, leaving a wife and eight children, have gone to Mrs Leonard—pompously, because William Y. couldn't help being pompous—and torn the mortgage to pieces before her eyes? Or that shrinking little Mrs Artemas Dark, seeing that big bully of a Rob Griscom at the harbour cruelly beating his dog one day, had flown through the gate, snatched the whip from the thunderstruck Griscom, and whipped him around and around his own house until he had fallen on his knees before her and begged for mercy?

And—Gay thought it suddenly one evening before the driftwood fire—what nice dimples Roger had in his thin cheeks when he smiled!

Still, Gay had her bad hours—hours when her heart ached fiercely for her lost happiness—hours when she wanted nothing but Noel. If she could only wake and find it all a dream—if she could only feel his arms about her again and hear him saying he loved her and her only! She wanted to be happy again. Not just this dull resignation with the moonlight of friendship to show the narrow path of life. She wanted love and full sunshine and— Noel. Everything was summed up in Noel. And Noel was with Nan.

Gay saw nothing of Nan now. Mrs Alpheus had found herself no longer able to endure the dullness of Indian Spring and had taken an apartment in town. She never saw Noel either. She wondered when he and Nan would be married and how she could get out of going to the wedding. Nan would invite her, she was sure of that. Nan who had told her so confidently that she was going to take Noel from her. And Gay had been so sure she couldn't. Oh, poor little fool!

"Life isn't fair," said Gay, her lips quivering. For an hour she would be nothing but little, jilted, heartbroken Gay again, only wanting Noel. If he would only come back to her! If he would only find out how selfish and vain and—and—empty Nan was! Nan couldn't love anybody—not really. Of course she loved Noel after a fashion—nobody could help loving Noel—but never, never as Gay loved him.

There came an evening at the end of a blustery March day

440

when Mercy Penhallow told Mrs Howard that Mrs Alpheus had told her that Noel and Nan would be married in June. There was to be a clan church wedding with bridesmaids in mauve taffeta, tulle hats of mauve and pink, and corsage bouquets of pink sweet peas. Nan had everything planned out to the smallest detail. Also her house. She was even, so Mercy said, going to have sheets in her guest-room to match her guests' hair—nile-green for red hair, orchid for brunettes, pale blue for golden hair. And all the furniture was to be extremely modern.

"I expect she's even got the nursery planned out," said Mercy sarcastically.

Mrs Howard did not tell Gay about the nile-green and orchid sheets or the mauve and pink bridesmaids but she did tell her of the wedding. Gay took it quietly, her eyes growing a little larger in her small white face. Then she went up to her room and shut the door.

Why had she kept hoping—hoping? She must have been hoping, else this would not twist her heart-strings so. She took a bundle of Noel's letters out of her desk. She had never been able to burn them before but she must do it now. Here they all were— the ones he had written her first on top—fat, bulging letters. They grew thinner and thinner. The later ones were pitifully thin. Still, they were from Noel. Something of his dear personality was in them. *Could* she burn them? An old verse came into her head—a verse from a sentimental poem in an old faded scrapbook of her mother's. There had been a time when Gay had thought it so lovely and sweet and sad. She quoted it now about Noel's letters, feeling that it was very appropriate.

"Yes—yes," said poor Gay trembling,

Yes, the flames the link shall sever
Their red tongues will never tell,
When I've crossed the mystic river
They will keep my secret well.

She laid Noel's first letter in the grate and held a lighted match to it. The little flames began to eat it greedily. Gay dropped the match and covered her face. She couldn't bear to look at it. She *couldn't* burn those dear letters. It was too much to ask of herself. She snatched up the rest of them, her body racked by painful little sobs, and hurried them back into her desk. They were all she had left. Nobody could blame her for keeping them.

She sat at her window for awhile before she went to bed. A red, red sun was sinking between two young spruces in Drowned John's hill pasture. After it disappeared there came the unearthly loveliness of a calm blue winter twilight over snow. A weird moon with a cloud-ribbed face was rising over the sad, dark harbour. Winter birches with stars in their hair were tossing all around the house. There was a strange charm about the evening. She wished Roger could see it with her. He loved evenings like this. There had been a little snow that day, following on the heels of the mad galloping March wind, and the hedge of young firs to the left of the house were white with it. Something about them made her think of the apple blossoms on the day of Aunt Becky's levee. How happy she had been then. And it had all gone with the apple blossoms.

"I feel so old," said Gay, looking particularly young and piteous.

VI

Little Brian Dark was alone in his kitchen loft one night in late March, looking out on a landscape that was black and ugly in the ugliest time of year—when the winter whiteness has gone, leaving only the bare bones of the world exposed to view. There was a cold, yellow strip of sky in the west under a sullen, cloudy sky, hanging over frozen fields. The trees looked as if they could never live again.

Brian, as usual, was lonely and hungry and tired. As long

as the light lasted he had consoled himself by looking at the gorgeous pictures of good things to eat in the advertising pages of a pile of old magazines under the eaves. What curly, delicious strips of bacon—what tempting muffins—what mouth-melting cakes with icing! Were there really people in the world—perhaps little boys—who ate such delicious things?

The lamp in the Dollar living-room was out but a light burned in the little room upstairs looking out on the kitchen roof. Brian knew that Lennie Dollar slept there; he had envied Lennie all winter because he had such a warm cosy little room to sleep in. Often during the past winter Brian had wished he could snuggle in there, too. The loft was always cold, but it had been colder this winter than ever because in the preceding autumn Brian had accidentally broken one of the window-panes and Uncle Duncan and Aunt Alethea were so angry with him because of his carelessness that they would not replace it. Brian had stuffed an old sweater in it but that did not keep all the extra cold out.

Yet Brian was not so entirely friendless as he had been. There was Cricket. One little white blossom of love had begun to bloom in the arid desert of his unwelcome existence. Cricket would soon come now. He pulled out the old sweater before he lay down on his bed, so that Cricket could get in.

He lay there expectantly, listening to the eerie sounds the spruce trees made outside in the dark. It was time Cricket came. Surely Cricket would come. Surely nothing had happened to Cricket. Brian lived in daily terror that something would happen to Cricket.

Cricket had been coming every night for three weeks. He had been there alone one night, very lonely and unhappy as usual. Aunt Alethea had been angry with him and had sent him supperless to bed. He looked out of the window. The sky was sharp and brilliant, the stars cold and bright. He was such a little fellow to be all alone in a great, lonely world. He had prayed to his dead mother in heaven for food and comfort. He was afraid that God, even a young God, might be too busy looking after more important things to bother about him, but Mother would have time. Brian knew a little about his mother now. One day he had met the old Moon Man on his ceaseless quest and the Moon Man had stopped and beckoned to him. Brian's knees knocked together as he obeyed. He did not dare disobey, although he went in such terror of the Moon Man. And then he found the Moon Man was looking down at him with gentle, kind eyes.

"Little Brian Dark, why are you so frightened of me?" asked the Moon Man. "Have they been telling you false, cruel things about me?"

Brian nodded. He could not speak but he knew now the things *were* false.

"Don't believe them any longer," said the Moon Man. "I would hurt nothing, much less a child. Laura Dark's little child. I knew your mother well. She was a sweet thing and life hurt her terribly. Life is cruel to us all but it was doubly cruel to her. She loved you so much, Brian."

Brian's heart swelled. This was wonderful. He had often wondered if his mother had loved him. He had been afraid she couldn't, when he was such a disgrace to her.

"She loved you," went on the Moon Man dreamily. "She used to kiss your little face and your little feet and your little hands when nobody saw her—nobody but the poor crazy old Moon Man. And she took such good care of you. There wasn't any baby taken such good care of, not even the rich folks' babies that came through a golden ring."

"But I hadn't any right to be born," said Brian. He had heard that so often.

The Moon Man looked at him curiously.

"Who knows? *I* don't think Edgley Dark had any right to be born when his mother hated and despised his father. But the clan thinks that is all right. It's a strange world, Brian. Good-night. I cannot stay longer. I have a tryst to keep—she's rising yonder over that dark hill, my beautiful Queen Moon. We all must have something to love. I have the best thing of all—the silver Lady of the skies. Margaret Penhallow has a little grey house down yonder—foolish Margaret who is going to marry and desert her dream. Chris Penhallow loves his violin. He's given it up just now for the sake of an old shard but he'll go back to it. Roger Dark and Murray Dark, foolisher still, loving mortal women, disdaining the wisdom of the moon. But not so foolish as if they didn't love anything. What have you to love, Brian?"

"Nothing." Brian felt the tears coming into his eyes.

The Moon Man shook his head.

"Bad—very bad. Get something to love quick—or the devil will get hold of you."

"Mr Conway says there isn't any devil," said Brian.

"Not the devil of the Darks and Penhallows—no, there's no such devil as that. You needn't be afraid of the clan devil, Brian. But get something to love, child, or else God help you. Goodnight. I'm glad I've met you."

Brian was glad, too, although he didn't understand more than half the Moon Man had said. Not only because one fear, at least, had gone out of his life but because he knew that his mother had loved him—and had taken good care of him. That seemed wonderful to Brian, who could not remember any one taking care of him in his life. It must be very sweet to be taken care of.

So he had prayed to his mother, thinking that perhaps she might be able to take a little care of him yet if she knew he needed it so much. Then he had lain down on his poor bed, forgetting to stuff the sweater in the window. Presently there was a little scramble on the roof of the porch outside the loft, a dark little body and two moon-like eyes for a moment poised on the sill against the dim starlight—then a leap to the floor—the pad of tiny paws—a soft furry thing nestling to him—a silken tongue licking his cheek—a little body purring like a small dynamo. Cricket had come.

Brian gathered the little creature in his arms in rapture. He loved cats and Aunt Alethea would not have one around the place. Now he had a kitten of his own—a dear striped grey thing after his own heart, as he discovered when the dawn came. The kitten stayed with him all night but at the first hint of daylight it was off. Brian thought sadly he would never see it again. But every night since then it had come. Brian had no idea where it came from. It did not belong to the Dollars and there was no other house near. He believed his mother had sent it. She was still taking care of him.

Brian loved the little cat passionately and knew it loved him. It purred so ecstatically when he petted it. What comfort and companionship he found in it! He was no longer afraid of the rats. They never dared come out when Cricket was there. And he was no longer lonely. He saved bits from his own scanty rations for Cricket, who was thin and evidently got none too much food, although occasionally he would bring a mouse in his own little jaws and eat it daintily on the loft floor. How Cricket enjoyed those morsels and how Brian enjoyed seeing him enjoy them, licking his small chops after them as if to salvage every ghost of flavour. Brian was desperately afraid his aunt would find out about Cricket. Suppose Cricket were to come in the day? But Cricket never came by day. Just at night he came to bring a message of love to a lonely child who had no friends.

And this night, too, Cricket came, just as Brian was beginning to feel really frightened that he was not coming.

"Darling Cricket," Brian reached under his flat chaff pillow and drew out the bit of meat he had saved from his dinner. Hungry as he was himself, he never thought of eating it. He listened with a heart full of happiness to Cricket crunching it in the darkness and fell asleep with the kitten cuddled on his breast.

VII

It was spring again and Gay Penhallow was walking over a road she had walked with Noel a year ago—and remembering it. Calmly remembering it! Gay had reached the stage where she remembered these things calmly, as things that had happened long ago to somebody who was a quite different person. Some of the old sweetness had come back into life. One couldn't be altogether hopeless in spring. She was actually enjoying the charm of the May evening; she was conscious of the fact that she had on a very becoming new dress of young-leaf green with a little scarlet sweater. She wondered if Roger would like it.

All the familiar things that had once made life sweet were beginning to make it sweet again. Yet there was always that little heartache under it all. A year ago she and Noel had walked down this road on just such an evening. There had been a misty new moon, just as to-night; there had been the same gay little wind in the tree-tops and the same little smoky shadows under the young, white, wild cherry trees. And their steps and hearts had beaten time together and Gay had been thrilled with a rapture she would know no more.

She saw old Erasmus Dark whitewashing the trunks of his apple trees as she passed by his orchard, and envied him a little— done with all passions of life. Drowned John, Uncle Pippin and Stanton Grundy were talking at the latter's gate as she went by. Gay smiled at Uncle Pippin, whom she liked, and the radiance of it fell alike over Drowned John, whom she liked only moderately, and on Stanton Grundy, whom she did not like at all because he always seemed to be so cynically sceptical of the existence of things that were pure and lovely and of good report. She did not know that Grundy's glance followed her admiringly.

"An eyeful, eh—an eyeful," he remarked, nudging Uncle Pippin.

Drowned John nodded agreement. A thoroughbred, every inch of her. Showed her knees too much, of course. But at any rate knees that could be shown. Not like Virginia Powell's knees—knocks that affronted the daylight.

When Roger's car flashed past them and picked up Gay at the curve of the road, the three weather-beaten old farmers smiled quite sympathetically.

"Looks as if that would be a match yet," said Grundy.

"Fine—fine—except—isn't he a *little* too old for her?" asked Uncle Pippin anxiously.

"A husband older than herself would be a good thing for Gay," said Drowned John.

"If she marries Roger, will it be for love or loneliness?" queried Grundy dryly.

"Love," said Drowned John, with an air of knowing all about it. "She's in love with Roger now, whether she knows it or not."

"I reckon she *can* love," said Grundy. "Some women can love and some can't, you know—just as some can cook and some can't."

"Well, it's a good thing kissing never goes out of fashion," said Uncle Pippin.

Roger thought Gay looked like a slim green dryad as she stood against the trees at the curve in the road. In spite of the new moon and the shadows and the faint stars, she made him think of morning. There was always something of the dawn about her; her very hair seemed to laugh; the little rosy lobes of her ears looked like unfolded apple blossoms. And she was gazing at him with just the very eyes a dryad should have.

"Hop in, Gay," he ordered laconically. Gay hopped, thinking what a delightful voice Roger had, even when he spoke curtly.

"Going anywhere in particular?"

"No. I just came out for a walk to escape Mrs Toynbee. She was at Maywood for supper and I nearly died of her."

"It's only female mosquitoes that bite," said Roger cheerfully. "Where'll we go?"

"The shore road and step on the juice," laughed Gay.

The shore road. Had Gay forgotten the last time they went along it? They whirled past the blueberry barrens and the maple clearings, past the Silver Slipper and the big empty hotel, on down to where the dunes lay, darkly soft against a silvery sea. Roger stopped his car and they sat in silence for awhile—one of those silences Gay loved. It was so easy to be silent with Roger.

There had never been any silence with Noel—Noel was too much of a talker to like silence.

The moon had gone down and the world lay in the starlight. Starlight is a strange thing and not to be taken as a matter of course. Roger suddenly fell under its magic and did something he hadn't seen himself doing for a long time yet.

"Gay," he said coolly, "I always do one wild thing every spring. I'm going to do this spring's tonight. I'm going to ask you to marry me."

Gay flushed beautifully—then turned very white.

"Oh, Roger—must you?" she said.

"Yes. I must. I can't stand this any longer. Either you've got to marry me, Gay—or we must stop—all this."

"All this." All their jolly drives and talks together. All the vivid companionship that had helped her through the otherwise unbearable months behind. Gay felt desperately that she could not lose it. She was so afraid of life. It is dreadful and unnatural to be afraid of life in youth. But it had played her such a trick. She must have some one to help her face it again. She didn't want to marry any one, but if she had to, it might as well be Roger. He needed some one to take care of him—he worked so hard.

"You know I don't—love you, Roger," she whispered. "Not in *that* way."

"Yes, I know. That makes no difference," said Roger mendaciously.

"Then—" Gay drew a long sigh—"then I'll marry you, Roger,—whenever you please."

"Thank you, dear," said Roger in a strangely quiet voice. Inside he was a seething volcano of joy and exultation. She would be his—his at last. He'd soon teach her to forget that popinjay. Love him. She'd love him fast enough—he'd see to that, when the time came. Gay, darling adorable little Gay was his, with her wind-blown curls and her marigold eyes and the slim little feet that were made for dancing. Roger could have knelt and kissed those little feet. But he did not even kiss her lips. Only her little hands

449

when he lifted her from the car at the end of their drive. Roger was wise—the time for kisses had not come yet. Gay was glad he did not kiss her. Even yet her lips seemed to belong to Noel. She went up to her room very quietly and sat for a long time behind her white curtains. She felt a little tired but content. Only she wished she could just find herself married to Roger without any preliminaries. The clan would be so odiously pleased. Their complacency would be hard to bear. What was it Mercy had said to her one day lately—"You'll find Roger will be the best for keeps?" No doubt he would be, but Gay knew if Roger and Noel were standing there before her, hers for the taking, to which one she would turn. Yet Roger, knowing this, still wanted to marry her.

Gay did one foolish secret thing before she went to sleep. She took the little rose-bowl, where the last rose leaves had been dropped on the night she was engaged to Noel, and went down with it to the gate at the side of the garden. The field before her was Artemas Dark's and the garden behind her was her mother's. But this wee green corner was hers; she dug out a hole under the trees with a trowel and buried the little rose-jar, patting the earth on the grave tenderly. All her childhood and girlhood were in it—all the happiness she had ever known. No matter what life held for her with Roger, there would be no more rose leaves for the little Wedgewood jar. It was sacred to something that was dead.

VIII

Penny and Margaret were not married yet. It was to have been in the spring; but when spring came Penny thought they'd better put it off to the fall. There were some alterations to make in the house; a new porch should be built and a hardwood floor laid in the dining-room. Margaret was very willing. She was no more eager for the happy day than Penny was.

In reality Penny was a rather miserable man. At times he fairly oozed dejection.

"Dash it," he informed the two Peters gloomily, "I've lost my enthusiasm."

He didn't want to break up his old habits—his comfortable ways of life. As for Aunt Ruth, certainly she had her faults. But he was used to them; it would be easier to put up with them than to get used to Margaret's new virtues. There wasn't really any danger of his dying in the night. He was good for twenty years yet.

He began to have horrible nightmares, in which he really found himself married—sewed up fast and hopelessly. It was an infernal sensation. He began to lose weight and a hunted look came into his eyes. Margaret was quite unconscious of this but the clan at large were not so blind, and bets were exchanged at the blacksmith's forge as to whether Penny's affair would ever come to a climax or not. The odds were against it, the general opinion being that Penny was simply stringing Margaret along until the matter of the jug should be decided.

"*Then* he'll squirm out of it some way, slick and clever," said Stanton Grundy. "Penny's nobody's fool."

Penny, however, felt like a fool. And when the incident of the merry-go-round occurred he felt more keenly than ever that Margaret would never do for a wife.

The merry-go-round affair did make considerable of a stir. More people than Penny were scandalized. It was certainly an odd thing for a woman of Margaret's age to do. Had she no dignity? No sense of the fitness of things? No realization that she was a Penhallow.

The merry-go-round was in the park in town. Margaret found herself looking wistfully at it one evening when Penny had taken her in for a drive and had gone to park his car before they settled down to listen to the band concert. Neither he nor Margaret cared for band concerts but hang it, a fellow had to do something to pass the time when he took his girl out.

Margaret had hankered all her life for a ride on the merry-go-round. There was something about it that fascinated her. She thought it would be delightful to mount one of those gay little horses and spin madly round and round. But she had never really thought of doing it. It was only a bright impossible dream.

Then she saw little Brian Dark looking at it longingly. Mr Conway had brought Brian in and had gone off and left him. He did not mind giving the kid a drive but he had no money to waste on him, by gosh. Brian thought it would be a wonderful thing to have a ride on the merry-go-round. His little face was so wistful that Margaret smiled at him and said,

"Would you like a ride, Brian?"

"Oh, yes," whispered Brian. "But I haven't any money."

"Here's the dime," said Margaret. "Take it and have a good ride."

For a moment Brian was radiant. Then his face clouded over.

"Thank you," he stammered, "but—I guess—I don't know—I guess I'm a little scared to go alone," he concluded desperately.

Margaret could never quite understand and explain just what did come over her. The inhibitions of years fell away.

"Come with me. I'll go with you," she said.

And that was how Penny, returning a moment later, saw a sight that paralysed him with horror. Margaret—*his* Margaret—spinning furiously about on the merry-go-round—up and down—round and round—riding for dear life and *riding astride*. Her hat had fallen off and her loosened hair blew wildly round her face. Penny gave an agonized yelp but Margaret neither heard nor heeded. She was having the time of her life—she was—why, she was drunk or exactly like it, Penny thought in disgust. Her eyes were shining, her face was flushed. When the ride was ended Margaret wouldn't get off. She paid for herself and Brian for another ride—and then another. At the end of the third her senses returned to her and she got off dazedly. It did not need Penny's expression to make her thoroughly ashamed of herself.

"Oh, Penny—I'm sorry—I don't know what got into me," she

gasped.

"You made a nice exhibition of yourself," said Penny coldly.

"I know—I know—but oh—" for a moment that graceless exultation swept over Margaret again—"Oh, Penny, it was glorious. Why don't you try it yourself?"

"No, thank you." Penny was very dignified all the rest of the evening, and he snubbed Margaret on the way home. Margaret took it meekly, recognizing his right and his just grievance. But she was not so meek when Mrs Denzil tackled her a few days later about it. They had an actual fight over it. Margaret was by no means as unassertive as she used to be. Sometimes she spoke her mind with astonishing vim. Getting engaged, Mrs Denzil told her, seemed to have gone to her head. Denzil soon settled them. He wasn't going to have any ructions among his womenfolk. He told Margaret she'd better mind her P's and Q's or she wouldn't get Penny after all. This did not alarm Margaret quite as much as Denzil expected. There were times when Margaret, in spite of her trousseau dresses and silk stockings, and the glamour of being Mrs, almost wished she had never promised to marry Penny— times when she wondered if it were not possible somehow to escape marrying him. She always concluded rather sadly that it wasn't. Nobody would believe anything but that Penny had thrown her over and Margaret couldn't face *that*. It would be too humiliating. She must go through with it.

Penny, however, had made up his mind after the merry-go-round affair that Margaret would never suit him—not with that wild strain in her. Where on earth did she get it? There was no Spanish blood in *her*. But how to get out of it? *That* was the difficulty. The whole clan would cry shame on him if he threw Margaret over. And Dandy would never give him the jug. If he could only induce Margaret to throw *him* over. Ah, there was an idea now! But it would be no easy matter—no easy matter. Penny had what he considered a veritable inspiration. He would get drunk—ay, that was it. He would get drunk and go drunk to the church garden-party at Bay Silver. Margaret would be so disgusted that she would turn him down. He knew her strict temperance principles. Hadn't he heard her recite at a concert long ago. "Lips that touch liquor shall never touch mine"? He would shock her till she was blue round the gills, by gad he would. Of course there would be a bit of scandal but he could soon live it down. Lots of other men in the clan got stewed now and then. He did not think it would seriously impair his chances for the jug. Aunt Becky had said "addicted to drinking." You couldn't be thought an addict on the ground of one spree. It was over twenty-five years since he had been drunk before and an election had been to blame for that. He had been pretty offensive on that occasion. A prim old maid like Margaret wouldn't stand for it. Penny chuckled. He was as good as free.

Everybody was at the garden-party when Penny arrived there. Nan and Noel were there; their wedding, which was to have been in June, had been put off till September. Gay and Roger were there. You had to go to your own church garden-party, even though you would much rather be away for a long moonlit spin together. Gay achieved a careless, impudent little nod for Nan and Noel, though her heart seemed to turn over in her breast at sight of them. Joscelyn was there—and Hugh. Frank and Kate were there, though the women thought Kate would be better at home in her condition. But people had no shame nowadays. The two Sams were there, carefully avoiding each other. Big Sam came to get a square feed, but when he saw Little Sam treating the Widow Terlizzick to hot-dogs and ice-cream it spoiled the party for him.

A cog had slipped in Penny's plans. Most of the clan perceived with a tolerant smile that Penny was more or less lit up, but he was not actually drunk. He had only got as far as the sentimental stage when it was suddenly revealed to him that he was really desperately in love with Margaret. By gad, she was a fine little woman—and he was mad about her. He would go and tell her so. Had he ever thought of jilting her? Never! He hunted out some cloves and set out for Bay Silver, the ardent lover at last.

Margaret had visited Whispering Winds before coming to the party. She went there as often as she could now, because she knew that she would never see it again once she was married to Penny. That night she had hung an old iron pot on a tree and filled it with water for the birds. The little garden was very sweet, with the perfume of young wild ferns growing along the sagging fence. The peace and dignity and beauty of it seemed to envelop her like a charm. She wanted to stay there forever, alone with the happy thoughts that came to her among its flowers and grasses. Tears came into her eyes. She loathed the sparkle of Penny's ring on her hand. It was a diamond—Penny liked to do things handsomely and he was not mean—and Margaret had once thought it would be a wonderful thing to have a diamond engagement-ring. But now it was only a fetter.

Margaret was surprised when Penny rushed to meet her on the church grounds. She had a dreadful feeling that he was going to kiss her right there before everybody; and although he did not actually do it, it was certain she had a narrow escape. Margaret was so innocent that she really never suspected Penny's condition; but she was sure something queer had come over him. He was squeezing her hand—he was gazing at her adoringly—he was—yes, he was actually calling her "Little One."

"Little One," he was saying, "I had begun to think you were never coming."

Margaret let Penny carry her off for a walk through the graveyard. He insisted on walking with his arm around her waist, which made her feel terribly self-conscious. From the bottom of the graveyard there was a very fine view of the gulf and the Rose River valley with the moon rising over it.

"What a lovely moon," said Margaret desperately, because she had to say something. What *had* got into Penny?

"Oh, damn the moon," said Penny, aggrieved because Margaret was not so responsive as he thought she ought to be.

Margaret was shocked. She knew men swore but surely not in the presence of ladies they were engaged to. Penny might at least wait until they were married.

Penny made haste to apologize.

"I never could see much sense in admiring the moon," he explained, "but I only said that because I want you to think about *me* and not about the moon. Forgive me, Little One. I won't say naughty words again before my own sweetest."

"We—we ought to get back to the grounds," said Margaret confusedly. Really, this love-making which was so attractive in fancy, was nothing more or less than dreadful in reality. "We won't get a good seat if we are late."

"I don't care where I sit as long as I sit with you, my darling," said Penny.

Penny sat with his arm around Margaret all through the programme, oblivious to the giggles of the young fry and the amused grins of the oldsters. He squeezed Margaret's hand at all the sentimental passages in the songs, and he told her she had the finest pair of legs in the clan, by gad, she had!

Margaret, who had always secretly thought her slender, well-shaped legs rather nice, nevertheless belonged to a generation that did not discuss legs. She was embarrassed and tucked her legs blushingly out of sight under the plank she sat on. To turn the conversation into safer channels, she told Penny that Nigel Penhallow had called to see her on his recent visit from New York and had told her he wouldn't be surprised if that old *Pilgrim's Progress* Aunt Becky had given her, turned out to be of some value. It was a very old edition and in fair condition. He had offered to find out just what it was worth. Margaret wondered if she hadn't better let him. Penny advised against selling it.

"I've enough for our comfort, Little One, and"—Penny was on the verge of tears by now—"when I'm gone, Mar'gret, there'll be enough to keep you in decent widowhood."

Margaret had not yet accustomed herself to the thought of being Penny's wife. The idea of being his widow overcame her. She went home very unhappy. Penny had almost wept when he kissed her good-night. And, having heard some one ask her if her sore throat were better, he could not leave her until she had promised to tie a stocking round her throat when she went to bed. If he cared as much as this for her she must be faithful to him.

BLINDLY WISE

"That damn' jug will be the death of some of us yet," said Uncle Pippin viciously.

For it had come out that the reason Walter Dark's pig was where it should not have been that particular afternoon, was because Walter was having a spat in his yard with Palmer Penhallow about who should get the jug. They were so hot about it that Walter did not notice before it was too late that his pig had got out of his pen at the barn and was scooting down the lane to the road. When Walter did see it and started in pursuit, the pig was already out on the King's Highway and before Walter could even yell, the whole thing happened.

Young Prince Dark and Milton Granger were spinning up the road in Prince's motor-cycle. Hugh Dark was coming down the road in his car, on his way home from a political convention where it had been as good as decided that he was to be his party's candidate at the forthcoming Provincial election. It had been one of Hugh's ambitions for years but he felt no elation over its realization. He was not thinking of it at all as he drove moodily along through the amber haze of the warm July afternoon, past sunny old pastures and rose-sweet lanes, friendly gardens full of wine-hued hollyhocks, misty river shores, old stone dykes under the dark magic of the spruce woods, and windy hills where the fir trees were blowing gaily and the tang of the sea met him. All the beauty of the world around him suggested only thoughts of Joscelyn. Suppose he were going home to Treewoofe to tell *her* of the honour that had come to him. Suppose when he got out at his gate Joscelyn were meeting him with the wind of the hill ruffling her red-gold curls, eager to know what had happened at the convention—ready to console or congratulate, as the event required. It would be worth while then. But now—dust and ashes.

At this moment everything happened at once. Walter Dark's pig had reached the road. Prince Dark, tearing onward at his usual headlong rate, struck it before he could turn or slow down. Prince and Granger were both thrown out by the impact, Prince flying clean across the ditch against the fence and Granger being hurled like a stone into the ditch itself. The pig lay calmly, too dead to tell what he thought about it, and the motor-cycle shot blindly across the road. Hugh swerved sharply to avoid it. His car skidded in a circle. Everything suddenly became doubly clear. All the colours of the landscape took on an incredible vividness and brilliancy. Also the whole affair seemed to take an interminable time, during which he lived over all the emotions of his life and loved and hated and despaired for an eternity. Then the car went over the edge of the little ravine that skirted the road, just as Walter's belated yell rent the air and the group of men before the blacksmith's forge awoke to the fact that a tragedy had been enacted before their eyes.

Wild confusion followed for a space. Uncle Pippin frantically implored them to keep their heads. The conscious Prince and the unconscious Granger were picked up and carried in, the latter with an ear almost sliced off. Hugh's car was upside down in the ditch with Hugh still clutching the wheel. When he was eventually extricated he gasped Joscelyn's name twice before relapsing into complete unconsciousness. By the time the three victims had been taken to the hospital and Walter Dark had sadly dragged his dead pig home on a stone boat, uneasily speculating whether Prince Dark could sue him for damages or whether he had a case against Prince for killing a valuable pig, the news of the accident had spread to Bay Silver in a garbled fashion that left every one in doubt as to who was killed and who were maimed for life, and Joscelyn was walking up and down her room in a frenzy of suspense and dread. What really had happened? Was Hugh badly hurt or—she would not let herself even think the word. And she could not go to him. He would not want her. He had no need of her. She meant nothing to him—she who had once meant so much. She could not even telephone to find out the truth about the affair. Any one—every one else—could make inquiries but not she. Meanwhile she would go mad; she could not endure it; she had been a fool and an idiot, but even fools and idiots can suffer. Once she paused with clenched hands and looked at Treewoofe. The day had been cloudy by times but now the sun suddenly came out and performed its usual miracle. The hill swam in loveliness and Treewoofe—her home—her *home*— shone on it like a jewel. Was Hugh there—dead—suffering? And she could not go to him! Perhaps Pauline was there!

"If I think things like this I'll lose my senses," moaned Joscelyn. "Oh, God, dear God, I know I was a fool. But haven't You any pity for fools? There are so many of us."

Joscelyn had to endure as best she could until the evening. And yet, amid all her agony, she was conscious of an exultation that she had this to be in anguish over. Anguish was not so dreadful as the emptiness that had been her life of late. Then Uncle Pippin called and told them the truth. Things were not so bad after all. Prince and Hugh were not seriously hurt. Prince was already home and Hugh was still in the hospital, suffering from slight concussion, but would be all right in a few days. Young Granger was the worst; he had nearly lost an ear and was still unconscious, but the doctors thought he would recover and meanwhile they had sewed on his ear.

"I hope it will cure Prince of that habit of reckless driving," said Uncle Pippin, shaking his head, "but I dunno's anything will do that. He was swearing dreadful when we picked him up; I rebuked him. I says, 'Any one that's been as near the pearly gates as you was two minutes ago hadn't ought to swear like that,' but he just kept on. He damned that poor pig up and down and all the universe thrown in."

"I didn't like the way the wind sobbed last night," said Aunt Rachel, shaking her head. "I knew sorrow was a-coming. This proves it."

"But sorrow hasn't come—Hugh wasn't badly hurt," cried Joscelyn involuntarily. She was so suddenly light-hearted in her release from torture that she hardly knew what she was saying.

"What about poor young Granger in the hospital, with his ear off?" said Aunt Rachel reproachfully.

"And the pig?" said Uncle Pippin. "It was sorrow enough for the pig."

II

Joscelyn, coming home across lots from an errand to the harbour, paused for a moment at the little gate in Simon Dark's pasture that opened on the side road leading down to Bay Silver. It was a windy, dark grey night, cold for August, with more than a hint of nearing autumn in it. Between the gusts of wind the air was full of the low continuous thunder of the sea. Low in the west was a single strip of brilliant primrose against which the spire of a church stood up blackly. Above it was the dark sullen beauty of the heavy storm-clouds. Everywhere, on the hills and along the roads, trees were tossing haglike in the wind. A group of them overhanging the gate was like a weird cluster of witches weaving unholy spells.

The summer—another summer—was almost over; asters and goldenrod were blooming along the red roads; goldfinches were eating the cosmos and sunflower seeds in the gardens; and in a little over a month the matter of the jug would be decided. Clan interest was again being keenly worked up over it. Dandy had kept his mouth shut immovably and nobody knew anything more about it than at the start.

But Joscelyn cared nothing who got the jug. She was glad to be alone with the night—especially this kind of a night. It was in keeping with her own stormy mood. She liked to hear the wild night wind whistling in the reeds of the swamp in the corner of the pasture—she liked to hear its sweep in the trees above her.

She had been tempest-tossed all day. In such stress she was accustomed to think that peace was all she asked or desired. But now she faced the thought that she wanted much—much more. She wanted womanhood and wifehood—she wanted Hugh and Treewoofe—she wanted everything she had wanted before her madness came upon her.

Everything beautiful had gone out of her life. She had lived for years in a fool's paradise of consecration to a great passion. Now that she had been rudely made wise, life was so unbelievably poor—thin—barren—so bitterly empty. If Frank had never come home she could have gone on loving him. But she could not love the tubby, middle-aged husband of Kate and the prospective father of Kate's baby. Life, with all its fineness and vulgarity, its colour and drabness, its frenzy and its peace, seemed to have passed her by utterly and to be laughing at her over its shoulder.

Nothing was talked of in the clan just now but weddings— Nan and Noel, Gay and Roger, Penny and Margaret, Little Sam and the Widow Terlizzick—even Donna and Peter. For Peter was home again, and report said he had come for Donna and would have her in Drowned John's very teeth. As Uncle Pippin said, Cupid was busy. Amid all this chatter of marrying and giving in marriage, Joscelyn felt like a nonentity—and nobody, least of all a Penhallow with Spanish blood in her, likes to feel like a nonentity.

It was not quite dark yet—not too dark to see Treewoofe. The hill had been austere all that day, under the low, flying grey clouds. Now it was withdrawn and remote. One solitary light bloomed on it through the stormy dusk. Was Hugh there— alone? Suppose he did really love Pauline and wanted to be free? The thought of Pauline was like a poison. Pauline had gone to see him when he was in the hospital. But so had every other Dark and Penhallow in the clan—except Joscelyn and her mother and aunt.

Sometimes, as now, Joscelyn felt that if she could not discover the answer to certain questions that tortured her she would go wholly mad.

She did not see Mrs Conrad Dark until they were fairly face to face over the gate. Joscelyn started a little as she recognized the tall, dark, forbidding woman before her. Then she stood very still. She had not seen Mrs Conrad for a long while. Now, even in the gloom, she could recognize that hooded look of hers as she brooded her venom.

"So?" said Mrs Conrad tragically. Stanton Grundy had once said that Mrs Conrad always spoke tragically, even if she only asked you to pass the pepper. But now she had a fitting setting for her tragic tone and a fitting object. She leaned across the gate and peered into Joscelyn's face. They were both tall women—Joscelyn a little the latter. People had once said that the main reason Mrs Conrad didn't like Joscelyn was that she didn't want a daughter-in-law she would have to look up to.

"So it's you—Joscelyn Penhallow. H'm—very sleek—very handsome—not quite so young as you once were."

Convention fell away from Joscelyn. She felt as if she and Mrs Conrad were alone in some strange world where nothing but realities mattered.

"Mrs Dark," she said slowly, "why have you always hated me—not just since—since I married Hugh—but before it?"

"Because I knew you didn't love Hugh enough," answered Mrs Conrad fiercely. "I hated you on your wedding-night because you didn't deserve your happiness. I knew you would play fast and loose with him in some way. Do you know there hasn't been a night since your wedding that I haven't prayed for evil to come on you. And yet—if you'd go back to him and make him happy—I'd—I'd forgive you. Even you."

"Go back to him. But does he want me back? Doesn't he—doesn't he love Pauline?"

"Pauline! I wish he did. *She* wouldn't have broken his heart—she wouldn't have made him a laughing-stock. I used to pray he would love her. But she wasn't pretty enough. Men have such a cursed hankering for good looks. *You* had him fast—snared in the gold of your hair. Even yet—even yet. When he was fainting on the road down there, after the accident that might have killed him—he called for you—you who had left him and shamed him—it was you he wanted when he thought he was dying."

A fierce pang of joy stabbed through Joscelyn. But she would not let Mrs Conrad suspect it.

"Isn't he going to sell Treewoofe?"

"Sell Treewoofe! Sometimes I'm afraid he will—and go God knows where—my dearest son."

Something gave way in Mrs Conrad. Joscelyn's apparent immobility maddened her. She let loose all the suppressed hatred of years. She shouted—she cried—she raved—she leaned across the gate and tried to shake Joscelyn. In short she made such a show of herself that all the rest of her life she went meekly and humbly before Joscelyn, remembering it. Uncle Pippin, ambling along the side road from a neighbourly call, heard her and paused in dismay. Two women fighting—two women of the clan—they must be of the clan, for nobody but Darks and Penhallows lived just around there. It must be Mrs Sim Dark and Mrs Junius Penhallow. They were always bickering, though he could not recollect that they had ever made such a violent scene as this in public before. What if Stanton Grundy should hear of it? It must be put a stop to. Little Uncle Pippin valiantly trotted up to the gate and attempted to put a stop to it.

"Now, now," he said. "This is most unseemly!"

Just then he discovered that it was Joscelyn Dark and her mother-in-law. Uncle Pippin felt that he had rushed in where both angels and fools might fear to tread.

"I—I beg your pardon," he said feebly, "I just thought it was some one fighting over Aunt Becky's jug again."

It was quite unthinkable that Joscelyn and Mrs Conrad could be rowing over the jug. Since it couldn't be the jug it must be Hugh, and Uncle Pippin, who was not lacking in sense of a kind—as he put it himself, he knew how many beans made five—

understood that this was no place for a nice man.

"Pippin," said Mrs Conrad, rather breathlessly but still very tragically, "go home and thank the good Lord He made you a fool. Only fools are happy in this world."

Uncle Pippin went. And if he did not thank the Lord for being a fool he did at least thank Him devoutly that he still had the use of his legs. He paused when he got to the main road to wipe the perspiration from his brow.

"A reckless woman that—a very reckless woman," said Uncle Pippin sadly.

III

Nan was in the room before Gay had heard any sound. She had never been to Maywood since the night of the dance at the Silver Slipper—Gay had never met her alone since then. Occasionally they met at clan affairs, where Nan had always greeted Gay affectionately and mockingly and Gay had been cool and aloof. The clan thought Gay handled the situation very well. They were proud of her.

Gay looked up in amazement and anger from her seat by the window. What was Nan doing here? How dared she walk into one's room like that, unannounced, uninvited? Nan, smiling and insolent, in a yellow frock with a string of amber beads on her neck and long dangling amber earrings, with her blood-red mouth and her perfumed hair and her sly green eyes. What business had Nan here?

"Has she come," thought Gay, "to ask me to be her bridesmaid? She would be quite capable of it."

"You don't look overjoyed to see me, honey," said Nan, coolly depositing herself on Gay's bed and proceeding to light a cigarette. Gay reflected rather absently that Nan was wearing that ring she was so fond of—a ring that Gay always hated—with a pale-pink stone cabachon, looking exactly as if a lump of flesh were sticking through the ring. The next moment Gay felt an odd sensation tingling over her. Where was Noel's diamond? And what was Nan saying?

"And yet I've come to tell you something you'll be glad to hear. I've broken my engagement with Noel. Sent him packing, in short. You can have him after all, Gay."

Long after she had spoken, the words seemed to Gay to be vibrating in the atmosphere. It seemed to Gay a long, long time before she heard herself saying coolly,

"Do you think I want him now?"

"Yes, I think you do," said Nan insolently. She could make any tone—any movement—insolent. "Yes, in spite of that big diamond of Roger's"—ah, Gay knew very well Nan had been jealous of that diamond—"and in spite of the new bungalow going up at Bay Silver, I think you want Noel as badly as you ever did. Well, you're quite welcome to him, dear. I just wanted to show you I could get him. Do you remember telling me I couldn't?"

Yes, Gay remembered. She sat very still because she was afraid if she moved an eyelash she would cry. Cry, before Nan! This girl who had flung Noel Gibson aside like a worn-out toy.

"Of course it will give the clan the tummy-ache," said Nan. "Their ideas about engagements date back to the Neolithic. Even Mother! Although in her heart she's glad, too. She wants me to marry Fred Margoldsby at home, you know. I daresay I will. The Margoldsby dollars will last longer than love. I really was a little bit in love with Noel. But he's getting fat, Gay—he really is. He's got the beginnings of a corporation. Fancy him at forty. And he had got into such a habit of telling me his troubles."

Gay suddenly realized that this was true. It struck her that Noel had always had a good many troubles to tell. And she remembered as suddenly that he had never seemed much interested in *her* troubles. But she wished Nan would stop talking and go away. She wanted to be alone.

Nan was talking airily on.

"So I'm going to Halifax for a visit. Mother, of course, won't leave till she knows who is to get that potty old jug. Do you ever think, Gay, that if Aunt Becky—God rest her soul—hadn't left that jug as she did, you'd probably have been married to Noel by now?"

Gay *had* thought of it often—thought of it bitterly, rebelliously, passionately. She was thinking it again now, but with a curious feeling of detachment, as if the Gay who might have been married to Noel were some other person altogether. If only Nan would go!

Nan was going. She got up and flung another gratuitous piece of advice insolently to Gay.

"So, Gay dear, just tell your middle-aged beau that you don't want a consolation prize after all and warm up the cold soup with Noel."

Really, Nan could be very odious when she liked. Yet somehow she didn't hate her as before. She felt very indifferent to her. She found herself looking at her with cool, appraising eyes, seeing her as she had never seen her before. An empty, selfish little creature, who had always to be amused like a child. A girl who said "hell" because she thought it would shock her poor old decent clan. A girl who thought she was doing something very clever when she publicly powdered her nose with the unconcern of a cat washing its face in the gaze of thousands. A girl who posed as a sophisticate before her country cousins but who was really more provincial than they were, knowing nothing of real life or real love or real emotion of any kind. Gay wondered, as she looked, how she could ever have hated this girl—ever been jealous of her. She was not worth hating. Gay spoke at last. She stood up and looked levelly at Nan. There was contempt in her quiet voice.

"I suppose you came here to hurt me, Nan. You haven't—you can never hurt me again. You've lost the power. I think I even feel a little sorry for you. You've always been a taker, Nan. All through your life you've taken whatever you wanted. But you've never been a giver—you couldn't be because you've nothing to give. Neither love nor truth nor understanding nor kindness nor loyalty. Just taking all the time and giving nothing—oh, it has made you very poor. So poor that nobody need envy you."

Nan shrugged her shoulders.

"Please omit flowers," she said. But her subtle air of triumph had left her. She went out with an uneasy feeling that Gay had had the best of it.

Left alone, Gay sat down by her window again. Everything seemed different—changed. She wished this hadn't happened. It had unsettled her. She had been so contented before Nan came—even happy. Thinking of the new bungalow Roger was building for their home.

"I want to build a house for *you*," he had said, his eyes looking deep into hers with a look that was like a kiss. "A house that will be a home to come to when I'm tired—on a little hill so that we'll have a view, but not a hill like Treewoofe—too high above all the rest of the world. A house with *you* in it, Gay, to welcome me."

They had planned it together. The clan overwhelmed them with floods of advice but they took none of it. It was to have one window that faced the sea and another that looked on the dreamy, over-harbour hills. And a quaint little eyebrow window in the roof.

They would be able to look through their open dining-room door into the heart of a blooming apple tree in its season—a hill of white blossom against the blue sky—to eat supper there and see the moonrise behind it. There was a clump of cool, white birches at one corner. A spruce bush behind it where dear little brown owls lived. Gay had been so interested in everything. Her bathroom was to be mauve and pale yellow. She would have window-boxes of nasturtiums and petunias and Kenilworth ivy. She was thinking about nice linen—nice little teacups. The wedding was to be in late October. The clan had really behaved beautifully—although Gay knew what they were saying behind her back.

And now everything was tangled up again. Gay walked late that night, in the old Maywood garden that lay fragrant and velvety under the enchantment of a waning moon. The ghost of a lost happiness came and mocked her. Noel was free again. And Gay knew that what Nan had said was true. She *did* want him—with all her heart she wanted him still—and she had to marry Roger in October.

IV

Peter Penhallow was finding out the fun of really trying to get something. After a year in Amazonian jungles, where, when his temper had cooled, he spent most of his time longing to hear Donna's exquisite laugh again, he had come home to make it up with her. Never doubting that he would find her as ready and eager to "make up" as he was. Peter knew very little about women and still less about a woman who was the daughter of Drowned John. He arrived Saturday night, much to the surprise of his family, who had supposed him still in South America, and had promptly telephoned Donna—or tried to. Old Jonas answered the phone and said all the folks were away—he didn't know where.

Peter chewed his nails in frenzy until next morning, when he saw Donna across the church. His darling—unchanged—with the mournful shadows under her eyes and her dark, cloud-like hair. What a pair of fools they had been to quarrel over nothing! How they would be laughing over it presently!

Donna got the shock of her life when she saw Peter looking at her across the church. Outwardly she took it so coolly that Virginia, who was watching her anxiously, threw her eyes up at the ceiling in relief.

Donna had hated Peter furiously for over a year and it seemed now that she hated him more than ever. After the first startled glance she would not look at him again. When church came out he strode across the green to meet her—exultantly, triumphantly, masterfully. That was where he made a fatal mistake! If he had been a little timid—a little less cocksure—if he had shown himself a repentant, ashamed Peter, creeping back humbly for pardon, Donna, in spite of her hate, might have flung herself on his neck before everybody. But to come like this—as if they had parted yesterday—as if he had not behaved outrageously to her when they *had* parted—as if he had not ignored her existence for a year, sending never a word or message—expressing no contrition—coming smiling towards her as if he expected her to be grateful to him for forgiving *her*—which was exactly what Peter *did* expect—no, it was really too much. Donna, after one level, contemptuous glance, turned her back on Peter and walked away.

Peter looked rather foolish. Some boys standing near giggled. Virginia swept after Donna to help her through this ordeal. And, "Don't be so—emotional," was all the thanks she got.

Drowned John wanted to swear but couldn't, realizing thankfully that in little over a month more the affair of the jug would be settled and free speech once more be possible. Finally Peter turned away and went home, lost in wonder at himself for putting up with all this just to get a woman.

Peter's next attempt was to stalk down to Drowned John's, walk into the house without knocking, and demand Donna. Drowned John raved, stamped and played the heavy parent to perfection—yet still—will it be believed?—did not swear. Peter would have cared little for Drowned John if he could have seen Donna but not a glimpse could he get of her. He went home, defeated, asking himself for the hundredth time why he endured this sort of thing. It was really an obsession. Donna wasn't worth it—no feminine creature in the world was worth it. But he meant to have her for all that. He was not going to endure another such year as he had endured among the upper reaches of the Amazon. Sooner would he knock Donna over the head and carry her off bodily. It never occurred to Peter that all he had to do was to ask forgiveness for that night at the west gate. Nor, had it occurred to him, would he have done it. It had been all Donna's fault. *He* was forgiving *her*—most magnanimously, without a word of reproach, and yet she seemed to expect him to crawl on all fours for her.

Eventually, finding it impossible to obtain speech with Donna, Peter wrote her a letter—probably the worst letter that was ever written in the world for such a purpose. Donna got it herself at the post-office and, although she had never seen Peter's large, black, untidy handwriting before, knew at once that it had come from him. She carried it home and sat down before it in her room. She thought she ought to return it to him unopened. Virginia would advise that, she was sure. But if she did, she knew she would spend the rest of her life wondering what had been in it.

Eventually she opened it. It was a blunt epistle. There was no word of repentance—or even of love in it. Peter told her he was leaving in a week's time for South Africa, where he meant to spend four years photographing lions in their native haunts. Would she come with him or would she not?

This take-it-or-leave-it epistle infuriated Donna, when one "darling" or even an X for a kiss might have melted her into a forgiveness that hadn't been asked for. Before her rage could cool she had torn the letter four times across, put it in an envelope and directed it to Peter.

"I'll *never* forgive him," she said through set teeth. It was a comfort to articulate the words. It made her feel more sure of herself. In her heart she was afraid she *might* forgive him. She dared not leave the letter lying on her table all night, lest her resolution fail her, so she went down and gave it to old Jonas to mail on his way to town. Then, the thing being irrevocable, she went to her father and told him she was going away to train as a nurse, whether he was willing or not. Drowned John, who was thoroughly fed up with having a sulky thunderstorm at table and hearth for a year, told her she could go and be dinged to her. Whatever theological difference there may be between "damn" and "ding," there was none whatever in Drowned John's meaning or intonation.

As for Peter, when he got back his torn letter, he gave himself up to hate for a time and hated everything and everybody, living or dead. So matters stood until the night Dandy Dark's house burned down.

V

The old Moon Man went singing softly through the quiet September night, under a silvery harvest moon. He went along by the dim ghostly shore of the Indian Spring river, past friendly old fields where the wind purred like a big cat, through woods where the trees were talking about him, along lanes where there was a strippling of moonlight on the narrow grassy path and over hills where he paused to listen to eternity. He was very happy and he pitied the poor folks asleep in the houses as he went by. They did not know what they were missing.

It was he who first saw that Dandy Dark's house, perched on the shoulder of a small wooded hill where the road turned down to Bay Silver, was on fire. The flames were already bursting out of the roof of the ell when the Moon Man thundered on the door and a drowsy hired boy shuffled down from the kitchen chamber to demand what was up. The Moon Man told him and then strode calmly off. The fire was no longer any concern of his. He was not going to lose another minute of this beautiful night for it. Behind him he left alarm and confusion. Dandy Dark was away—nobody knew where. Dandy had taken to staying out late at nights, though as yet nobody knew of it except his wife. But the clan at large knew that something had come over Dandy in the past few weeks. He was changed. Unsociable, uneasy, irritable, absent-minded. Some put it down to the fact that the date for the jug decision was drawing near and argued that the decision must be in Dandy's hands, since he was so manifestly uncomfortable about it. Either that, or something had happened to the jug.

Nobody dared ask Dandy about it; he positively snapped now if any one referred to the jug. But everybody more or less was beginning to feel uneasy, too. And now Dandy's house was burning. The hired boy had yelled down the hall for Mrs Dandy, had roused a neighbour on the phone and had dashed to the barn for ladders. In an incredibly short time a crowd had gathered, but from the first it was manifest that the house was doomed. They had got out most of the furniture and were grimly watching the spectacle when Dandy arrived home.

"Good Gosh," cried Dandy, "where is the jug?"

Incredible as it may seem, nobody had thought about the jug. Everybody stared at each other. There was no one to ask. Mrs Dandy, when the hired boy roused her, had promptly run out of the front door in her night-dress and fainted in a corner of the garden. Foolish Mrs Dandy was noted for doing things like that. She had been carried over to Penny Dark's house on the next farm and was being attended to there.

"Doesn't *any one* know anything about the jug?" howled Dandy, losing his head completely and running wildly about, clawing over the stuff that had been saved from his blazing roof-tree.

"Where was it kept?" shouted somebody.

"In the spare-room closet," moaned Dandy.

Nothing had been saved from the spare room. It was far down the upstairs hall in the ell and the hall had been too full of smoke to reach it.

Peter was standing among the crowd. He had been among the first to arrive and had worked heroically. And now they had not saved the jug. The jug Donna wanted so much—the old jug Aunt Becky had told him tales of in his childhood—the jug that had ruined his elopement and wrecked his hopes. Peter snatched a reeking coat that was hanging on the fence, flung it over his head and dashed into the house. He must save that jug for Donna.

Every one yelled after him and then went mad. The yard was filled with dancing, shouting frantic figures, among which

473

suddenly appeared a raving maniac of a boy from Penny Dark's who gasped out a horrifying question. Where was Donna Dark? She had been staying all night with Mrs Dandy—she had been sleeping in the spare room—was she safe?

Some women fainted with a better excuse than Mrs Dandy. Some went shrieking about for Donna. The men gazed at each other and then at the burning house. They shook their heads. It was a madman's attempt to enter that house now. Peter would be burned to death, trying to save Donna—for nobody now doubted it was Donna he had gone to save. He must have heard what the boy was saying before any one else did.

Peter had gone up the blazing staircase three steps at a time, ready to plunge into the inferno of smoke and flame that had been the hall, when he stumbled and almost fell over the unconscious form of a woman lying on the floor at the head of the stairs.

Good God, who was it? She must be rescued, jug or no jug. He picked her up and turned back with a feeling of regret. No hope of the jug now. Poor Donna would be bitterly disappointed. He stumbled down the stairs and out of the door into the seething crowd. The yells and shouts changed suddenly to hurrahs. Peter was a hero. Eager hands took his slim white burden from him. Drowned John, who had just driven in, having heard of the fire but not of Donna's danger until he arrived there—was shaking his hand and sobbing, with tears running down his face.

"God bless you, Peter—you saved her—God bless you for saving Donna—my poor little motherless girl—" Drowned John was almost maudlin—people had to lead him away and calm him down, while Peter stood very still and tried to realize that it was Donna whom he had carried out of Dandy Dark's burning house. Donna!

"She kem up to-day to help me make the baked damson preserve," sobbed Mrs Dandy on the kitchen lounge at Penny Dark's. "I never did or could seem able to bake damsons so as to please Dandy. Donna knew how—Dandy's mother taught her 'fore she died—so I asked her if she'd come up and do 'em for me. They're all burned up now. It looked like rain at supper-time and Dandy was away—he's always away now, it seems to me—so I told Donna she might as well stay all night. Oh, dearie me, to think what might have happened!"

"The jug's gone, though," said William Y. gloomily.

"The jug? It ain't broken?" cried Mrs Dandy shrilly.

"It's burned up with all the rest of the spare-room things."

"Oh, no, it ain't." Mrs Dandy looked very sly and cunning. "When I put Donna to sleep in the spare room I took the jug in its box outen the closet and took it down to my own room. I didn't know what Dandy might of said to me if I'd left that jug in the same room with *anybody*. Folks say I'm silly but I'm not so silly as that. And when I heard Tyler yelling fire I grabbed holt of that box first thing along with the old teapot with the broken spout I keep my bit of money in, and run out with them and dropped them over the fence into the burdocks in the back yard. I reckon you'll find them there."

Find them there they did, much to everybody's relief. Donna had come to her senses and had been taken to the hospital, and everybody went home through the pale-yellow, windy dawn, telling tales about the fire. One of the funniest was that of Penny Dark, who, summoned to the telephone from his bed, had lost his head and torn over to Dandy's place in his pyjamas. Worse still, in trying to climb over the picket fence back of Dandy's barn, he had slipped and the waist cord of his pyjamas had caught on a picket. There poor Penny had hung, yelping piteously, until some one had heard him above all the din and rescued him. Most people thought it served him right for wearing pyjamas. It had been suspected for several years that he did but nobody ever was really sure, for old Aunt Ruth had kept his secret well.

"And Happy Dark is home," said Sim Dark. "Walked in last night after his mother had gone to bed, ate the supper she'd left, and then went to sleep in his own room. *She* didn't know it till he come down to breakfast this morning. Said he'd met an old crony in Singapore who gave him an old Charlottetown paper to read. It was the one where that fool reporter had writ up the story of the jug. Happy said he thought he might as well come home and see what his chances were for it. His mother's so uplifted she can hardly talk. Just sits and looks at him."

But among all the events of that night, the really tragic one was not talked over at the clan breakfast-tables because it was not known until several days later. Christopher Dark, drunk, as usual, had run in at the kitchen door of the burning building unseen of anybody, and had been killed by a falling beam. People supposed he must have been making a crazy effort to save the jug. The clan was properly stirred up over the dreadful end of poor Chris, but under all their horror was a calm conviction that everything was for the best. One disgrace to the clan was ended.

Murray Dark looked at his house proudly when he came home from the funeral.

"We'll soon have a mistress for you now," he said.

Donna sent for Peter as soon as she was allowed to see anybody, and begged him to forgive her. She knew now that he really did love her, in spite of everything, or he would never have dashed into that blazing house to save her. Peter did not undeceive her. He remembered that he had once heard Stanton Grundy say that life would be unbearable if we didn't believe a few lies. The deception sat lightly on Peter's conscience, for he knew that if he had dreamed for a moment that Donna was, or even might be, in that doomed house he would have gone through it from cellar to attic for her.

"But no more eloping," said Donna. "I'll marry you in the open, in spite of Father's teeth."

Drowned John, however, showed no teeth. He told Donna that since Peter had saved her life he deserved to get her and she could go and photograph lions in Africa with his blessing. The first time Peter went to Drowned John's after Donna came home, Drowned John shook hands genially with him and took him out to see his favourite pig. Peter concluded that, after all, Drowned John was a great old boy.

"Well, here's congratulations," said Roger, meeting Peter coming beamingly out of the west gate.

"Thanks. And I hear you're to be congratulated, too."

Roger's face hardened.

"I don't know. Are congratulations in order if you are going to marry a girl who is in love with another man?"

"So? It's that way still?"

"Still."

"And you *are* going to marry her?"

"I am. Congratulate me now if you dare."

VI

Joscelyn Dark wakened one September morning, knowing that something was going to happen that day. She had received some sign in her sleep. She sat up and looked out of her window. The sunlight of dawn was striking on Treewoofe, although the lower slopes were still in shadow. Around it golden grain fields lay in the beauty of harvesting. The air was rose and silver and crystal. The house seemed to beckon to her. All at once she knew what was to happen that day. She would go to Hugh and ask him if he could forgive her.

She had wanted to go ever since the night she had met Mrs Conrad, but she had not been able to summon up enough courage. And now, in some mysterious way, the courage had come. She would learn the truth. Whatever it might be, sweet or bitter, it would be more bearable than this intolerable suspense.

She could not go before evening. The day seemed long; it hated to go out; it lingered on the red roads, on the tops of the silver dunes, on the red ploughed summer fallow on the shoulder of Treewoofe. Not until it had really gone and the full moon was shining over the Treewoofe birches did Joscelyn dare to set out. Her mother and Aunt Rachel had gone to prayer-meeting, so that there was no one to question her. Old Miller Dark shortly overtook her in his buggy and offered her a "lift," which Joscelyn accepted because she knew it would offend poor old Miller if she refused. In her high rapt mood she did not want to see or ride with any one. Old Miller was in a great good humour; he had just about finished his history of the clan. Meant to have it published in book form, and would she subscribe for a copy? Joscelyn said she would take two; she wondered if old Miller had put anything about her and Hugh in it. He was quite capable of it.

Joscelyn got out at William Y.'s gate. Old Miller supposed she was going to see the William Y.'s and she let him think so. But as soon as he had disappeared around the wooded curve she walked up the Three Hills road to Treewoofe. The air was keen and frosty; the waves far down on the bay quivered as if they were tipsy with moonlight; it was just such another night as her wedding-night had been, eleven years ago. What a fool she had been? Hugh could never forgive her. She was seized with a spasm of panic and was on the point of turning and running madly down the hill.

But Treewoofe was close to her—dear frustrated Treewoofe. She trembled with longing as she looked at it. She pulled herself together and walked across the yard. There was a light in the kitchen but no answer came to her repeated knocks. She felt heart-sick. She could not go back without *knowing*. With a shaking hand she lifted the latch and went in. She crossed the kitchen and opened the door into the hall. Hugh was sitting there, alone, by the ashes of his desolate fireplace. In the light that fell over his face from the kitchen she saw the stark amazement on it as he stood up.

"Hugh," cried Joscelyn desperately—she must speak first, for who knew what he might say?—"I've come back. I was a fool—a fool. Can you forgive me? Do you still want me?"

There was a silence that seemed endless to Joscelyn. She shivered. The hall was very cold. It had been so long since there had been a fire in it. The whole house was cold. There was no welcome in it for her. She had alienated it.

After what seemed an eternity Hugh came towards her. His hungry eyes burned into hers.

"Why do you want to come back? Don't you still—love *him*?"

Joscelyn shuddered.

"No—no." She could say nothing more.

Again Hugh was silent. His heart was pounding with a wild exultation in his breast. She had come back to him—his again—not Frank Dark's—his, his only. She was standing there in the moonlight where she had mocked him so long ago. Asking his forgiveness and his love. He had only to put out his hand—draw her to his breast.

Hugh Dark was his mother's son. He crushed back the mad words of passion that rushed to his lips. He spoke coldly—sternly.

"Go back to Bay Silver—and put on your wedding-dress and veil. Come back to me in it as you went away—come as a bride to her bridegroom. Then—I may listen to you."

Proud Joscelyn went humbly. She would have done anything—anything that Hugh commanded. Never had she loved him as she loved him standing there, tall and dark and stern in the moonlit hall of Treewoofe. She would have crawled to him on all fours and kissed his feet had he so commanded. She went back to Bay Silver—she went to the garret and got the box that contained her wedding-dress and veil. She put them on, like a woman in a trance obeying the compulsion of some stronger will than her own.

"Thank God, I'm still beautiful," she whispered.

Then she walked back to Treewoofe, glimmering by in the silver of moonlight and the shimmer of satin.

Uncle Pippin, who was always where nobody expected him to be, thought she was a ghost when he saw her. The excited yelp he emitted might have been heard for a mile. Uncle Pippin didn't approve of it. Well-behaved young women didn't go strolling about on moonlit nights, wearing wedding-clothes. It couldn't be the jug that made Joscelyn do this. So Uncle Pippin fell back on the Spanish blood. A bad business that. Really, nothing but queer things had happened since Aunt Becky died. He sat in his buggy and stared after her until she disappeared. Then he drove home with badly shaken nerves.

Joscelyn had not even noticed Uncle Pippin. She went on, past the graveyard where her father lay, up the Three Hills road. For a wonder, no one else saw her. Nobody ever believed Uncle Pippin had seen her. The poor old man was getting dotty. Imagining things to make himself important.

The lights of beautiful Treewoofe were twinkling through the tall slender birches when she came back. Every room was lighted up to flash a welcome to her—its mistress for whom it had waited so long. She and Treewoofe were good friends again. The front door was open—and goblins of firelight were dancing in the hall beyond it. The mirror over the mantel was turned face outward again, and Hugh was waiting for her by the fire he had kindled. As she paused entreatingly in the doorway, he came forward and led her over the threshold by one of her cold hands. A wedding-ring was lying on the dusty mantel, where it had lain for many years. Hugh took it up and put it on her finger.

"Joscelyn," he cried suddenly. "Oh, Joscelyn—*my* Joscelyn!"

VII

Margaret had made many wedding-dresses for other people with vicarious thrills and dreams but she made her own very prosaically. Her wedding-day was finally fixed for the first of October. That would give them time for a bridal trip to points on the mainland before the date appointed for the final disposal of Aunt Becky's jug. Neither she nor Penny felt any elation over the affair. In truth, as the fatal time drew near, Penny grew absolutely desperate. At first he thought he would ask Margaret to postpone the wedding again—until after the puzzle of the jug was solved. That would not affect his chances materially. Then Penny threw up his head. That would be dishonourable. He would break the engagement before, if break it he must. Ay, that would be nobler. Penny felt a fine glow of victorious satisfaction with himself.

He went up to Denzil's, one evening, firmly resolved. No more shilly-shallying. Jug or no jug, he would be a free man. He had known yesterday that he could not go through with it. Margaret had told him that his watch was wrong. It always infuriated Penny to be told his watch was wrong. It was not the first time Margaret had offended in a similar fashion. And he was in for marrying a woman like that. What a devilish predicament!

Margaret had evidently been crying. And Margaret was not one of those fortunate women who can cry without their noses turning red. Penny wondered testily why a woman who was engaged to *him* should be crying. Then he thought she might suspect his real feelings on the matter and be weeping over them. Penny felt his heart softening—after all—no, this would never do. He must not be hen-hearted now. This was his last chance. He mopped his brow.

"Mar'gret," he said pleadingly, "do you think we'd better go through with it after all?"

"Go through—with what?" asked Margaret.

"With—with getting married."

"Don't you want to marry me?" said Margaret, a sudden gleam coming into her eyes. It terrified Penny.

"No," he said bluntly.

Margaret stood up and drew a long breath.

"Oh, I'm so thankful—so thankful," she said softly.

Penny stared at her with a dawning sense of outrage. This was the last thing he had expected.

"Thankful—thankful? What the hell are you thankful for?"

Margaret was too uplifted to mind his profanity

"Oh, Penny, I didn't want to marry you either. I was only going through with it because I didn't want to disappoint you. You don't know how happy it makes me to find out that you don't care."

Penny looked rather dour. It was one thing to explain to a

woman that you didn't see your way clear to marrying her after all. It was quite another to find her so elated about it.

"I only asked you out of pity, anyhow, Mar'gret," he said.

Margaret smiled. The Griscom showed there Penny's great-grandmother had been a Griscom.

"That isn't a sporting thing to say," she murmured gently. "And would you mind—very much—remembering that my name is Margaret—*not* Mar'gret. Here is your ring—and I've something rather important to attend to this evening."

Thus coolly dismissed, Penny went—stiffly, rigidly, neither with handshake, bow, nor backward glance.

Penny was huffed.

The important thing which Margaret had to do was to write a letter. She had not been crying because she was going to marry Penny exactly—she had been crying because suddenly, unbelievably, magically, a darling dream could have come true if she did not have to get married. And now that the marriage was off, the dream *could* come true. The letter was to Nigel Penhallow.

When it was written Margaret felt curiously young again, as if life had suddenly folded back for thirty years. She slipped away in the September moonlight to visit Whispering Winds. It would be hers—dear friendly Whispering Winds. All the lovesome things in its garden would be tended and loved. The little house should be whitewashed twice every year so that it would always be white as a pearl. She would be there in cool, exquisite mornings—in grey, sweet evenings—there to hear little winds crying to her in the night. It would be so deliciously quiet; nobody could ever open her door without knocking. She would be alone with her dreams. She could cry and laugh and—and—*swear* when she wanted to. And she would adopt a baby. A baby with dimples and sweet, perfumed creases and blue eyes and golden curls. There must be such a baby somewhere, just waiting to be cuddled.

She looked lovingly at the trees that were to be hers. Whispering Winds belonged to its trees and its trees to it. One little birch grew close to it in one of its angles. A willow hovered over it protectingly. A maple peeped around a corner. Little bushy spruces crouched under its windows. Dear Whispering Winds. And dear Aunt Becky who had made it all possible. Margaret prayed that night to be forgiven for the sin of ingratitude.

No one in the clan could find out just why the engagement had been broken off. It was inconceivable that Margaret could have done it, although for some reason best known to himself Penny had taken up and was nursing an aggrieved attitude.

"These mysteries will drive me distracted," groaned Uncle Pippin, "but I'll bet that fiendish jug was at the bottom of it somehow."

The clan were astounded when they heard Margaret had bought old Aunt Louisa's cottage from Richard Dark, still more astounded when they found she had sold the *Pilgrim's Progress* Aunt Becky had given her to a New York collector for a fabulous sum. Actually ten thousand dollars. It was a first edition and would have been worth thirty thousand if it had been in first-class condition. It was plain to be seen now why she had thrown Penny over so heartlessly. Penny himself chewed some bitter cuds of reflection. Who would ever have dreamed that any one would be crazy enough to pay ten thousand dollars for an old book like that? Ten thousand dollars! Ten thousand dollars! But it was too late. Neither he nor the clan ever really forgave Margaret—not for selling the book but for getting it from Aunt Becky in the first place. What right had she to it more than anybody else? Denzil was especially grouchy. He thought Margaret should have gone on living with him and used her money to help educate his family.

"Throwing it away on a house you don't need," he said bitterly. "You'd show more sense if you put what it cost you away for a rainy day."

"Umbrellas have been invented since that proverb," said Margaret blithely.

VIII

Gay was lingering by the gate, watching a big red moon rising behind a fringe of little dark elfin spruces over Drowned John's hill pasture to the east of her. Behind her, through the trees around Maywood, was visible a great, fresh, soft, empty, windy yellow sky of sunset. A little ghost of laughter drifted to her from the hill road. There was, it seemed, still laughter in the world. She was alone and she was glad of it. Just now life was bearable only when she was alone.

For weeks Gay had been dully unhappy—restless—indifferent. The new house no longer thrilled her; everything was tarnished. She wished drearily that she could go away—or die—or at least cease to exist. Life was too perplexing. She could not help thinking of Noel all the time. What was he doing—thinking— feeling? Was he very unhappy? Or was he—wiser? If she only knew the answers to those questions! She would never know them. And in little over a month she had to marry Roger.

She was still there when Noel came. Now that she was not waiting for him—now that she was going to marry Roger—he came. When she lifted her head he was standing before her. Looking like a movie star—handsome and—and—*dapper!* Yes, dapper, just like little Penny Dark. In twenty years' time he would be just like Penny Dark. Gay's head spun around and she wondered if she were going crazy.

"Noel!" she gasped.

"Yes—it's Noel." He came close and took her hand. She looked at him. Had he grown shorter? No, it was only that she had grown used to looking up at Roger. Noel's hair *was* too curly—what had Nan said once about the tongs? Oh, what had got into her? Why was she thinking such absurd things—now at this wonderful moment when Noel had come back to her?

Noel was leaning over the gate, talking rapidly—telling her he had never really cared for Nan. Nan had chased him—hunted him down—he had been bewitched temporarily—he had never

484

really loved any one but her, Gay. Would she forgive him! And take him back?

Noel had evidently very little doubt that he would be forgiven. He had, Gay found herself thinking, quite a bit of confidence in his own powers of attraction. He put his arms about her shoulders and drew her close to him. For long months she had longed to feel his arms about her so—his lips on hers—his face pressed to her cheek. And now that it had come about, Gay found herself laughing—shaking with laughter. A bit hysterical perhaps—but Noel did not know that. He released her abruptly and stepped back a pace in amazement and chagrin.

"You're—so—so—funny!" gasped poor Gay.

"I'm sorry," said Noel stiffly. This was not at all what he had looked for.

Gay forced herself to stop laughing and looked at Noel. The old enchantment had gone. She saw him as she had never seen him before—as her clan had always seen him. A handsome fellow, who thought every girl who looked at him fell in love with him; shallow, selfish. Was this what she had supposed she loved? Love! She had known nothing about it till this very moment, when she realized that it was Roger she loved. Roger who was a *man*! This Noel was only a boy. And he would never be anything but a boy, if he lived to a hundred—with a boy's fickle heart, a boy's vanity, a boy's emptiness. She had fancied herself in love with him once—fancied herself heart-broken when he jilted her—and now—

"Why, it's all ancient history," she thought in amazement.

As soon as she could speak she told Noel to run away. Her voice still shook and Noel thought she was still laughing at him. He went off in high dudgeon. It was a new and very wholesome experience for Noel Gibson to be laughed at. It did him no end of good. He was never quite so self-assured again.

Gay stood by the gate for a long while, trying to adjust herself. The sky faded out into darkness and the moonshine bathed her. Passing breaths of autumn wind sent showers of silvery golden leaves all over her. She loved the night—she loved everything. She felt as if she had been born again. How lucky Noel had come back. If he hadn't come back she might always have fancied she cared—might never have seen the fathomless difference between him and Roger. To come back so soon—so shamelessly. Hadn't he *any* depth? Couldn't he care really for anybody? But he had come—and his coming had set her free from phantom fetters.

"I suppose if it were not for the jug I'd still be engaged to him—perhaps married to him."

She shuddered. How dreadful that would be—how dreadful it would be to be married to any one but Roger! It was simply impossible even to *imagine* being married to any one but Roger. God bless Aunt Becky!

Still she had an odd but fleeting sense of loss and futility. All that passion and pain for nothing. It hurt her that it should seem so foolish now. It hurt her to realize that she had only been in love with love. The clan had been right—so right. That stung a little. It isn't really nice to be forced to agree with your family that you have been a little fool.

But she knew she did not care how right they had been. She was *glad* they had been right. Oh, it was good to feel vivid and interested and alive again—as she hadn't felt for so long. All the lost colour and laughter of life seemed to have returned. The time of apple-blossom love was over. Nothing could bring it back. It was the time of roses now—the deep, rich roses of the love of womanhood. Those months of suffering had made a woman of Gay. She lifted up her arms in rapture as if to caress the night— the beautiful silvery September night.

"Let me brush the moonlight off you," somebody said—a dear somebody with a dear, dear voice.

"Oh, Roger!" Gay turned and threw herself into his arms. Her face was lifted to his—her arms went about his neck of their own accord—for the first time Roger felt his kiss returned.

He held her off and looked at her—as if he could never have enough of looking at her. She was an exquisite thing in the moonlight, with her brilliant eyes and her wind-ruffled hair.

"Gay! You love me!" he said incredulously.

"It will take me a whole lifetime to tell you how much—and I never knew it till an hour ago," whispered Gay. "You won't mind how silly I've been, will you, Roger? You'll find out—in time—how wise I am at last."

Roger met the Moon Man on the way home.

"One *does* get the moon sometimes," Roger told him.

IX

Little Brian Dark was prowling about the roads, looking for some of his Uncle Duncan's young cattle which had broken out of their pasture. His uncle had told him not to come home until he found them, and he could get no trace of them. Rain was brewing and it was a very dark and cold and melancholy October night. A fog had blotted out the end of the harbour road; a ghostly sail or two drifted down the darkening bay. Brian felt horribly alone in the world. His heart swelled as he passed happy homes and saw more fortunate children through lighted, cheery kitchen windows. Once he saw a boy about his own age standing by his mother's side. The mother put her arm about him and kissed him fondly. Brian choked back a sob.

"I wonder," he thought wistfully, "what it would be like to be loved."

Now and then through an open door he caught delicious smells of suppers cooking. He was very hungry, for he had not had his supper. And very tired, for he had been picking potatoes all day. But he dared not go home without the young cattle.

Sim Dark, of whom he inquired timidly, told him he had seen some young beasts down on the shore road leading to Little Friday Cove. Sim felt an impulse of pity for young Brian as he drove away. The child looked as if he didn't get half enough to eat. And that thin sweater was not enough for a cold fall night.

The Duncan Darks ought to be ashamed of themselves. After which, Sim went home to his excellent supper and well-dressed family and forgot all about Brian.

Brian trudged down the long grassy road to Little Friday Cove. It was getting very dark, and he was frightened. Little Sam's light gleamed cheerily through the blur of rain that was beginning to fall. Brian went to the house and asked him if he had seen the calves. Little Sam had not, but he made Brian go in and have supper with him. Brian knew he ought not to go in, with the calves yet unfound, but the smell of Little Sam's chowder was too tempting. And it was so warm and cosy in Little Sam's living-room. Besides, he liked Little Sam. Little Sam had once taken him out for a row one evening when the gulf had been like rippled satin and there was a little new moon in the west. It was one of the few beautiful memories in Brian's life.

"We're in for a rain," said Little Sam, ladling out the chowder generously. "My shin's been aching scandalously for two days." Little Sam sighed. "I'm beginning to feel my years," he said.

By the time supper was over, the rain was pouring down. Little Sam insisted that Brian stay all night with him.

"It ain't fit for you to go out a night like this. Listen to that wind getting up. Stay here where you're comfortable and have a look round in the morning for your calves. Likely you'll find 'em over in Jake Harmer's wood-lot. His fences are disgraceful."

Brian yielded. He was afraid to go home in the dark. And it was so warm and pleasant here. To be sure, he thought uneasily of Cricket. But if Cricket came he would likely just curl up on Brian's bed and be quite comfortable. No harm would come to him.

Brian spent the pleasantest evening he had known for a long time, sitting by Little Sam's blazing fire, petting Mustard—who was a very nice old cat, though not to be compared to Cricket—and listening to Little Sam's hair-raising ghost stories. It did not occur to Little Sam that he should not tell ghost stories to Brian. It was a long time since he had had anybody to listen to his tales.

Little Sam had already spent many lonely evenings this fall. He dreaded another winter like the last. But he did not mention Big Sam. The Sams had at last given up talking about one another. Little Sam only pointed Aurora proudly out to Brian and asked him if he didn't think her pretty. Brian did think so. There was something in the white, poised figure that made him think of music in moonlight and coral clouds in a morning sky and all the bits of remembered beauty that sometimes—when he wasn't too tired and hungry—made a harmony in his soul.

It was a long time before Brian could sleep, curled up in the bunk that had once been Big Sam's. The wind roared at the window and the rain streamed down on the rocks outside. The wind was offshore and the waves were not high, but they made a strange, sobbing, lonely sound. Brian wondered if his aunt and uncle would be very cross with him for staying away and if Cricket would miss him.

When he finally fell asleep he had a dreadful dream. He was standing alone on a great, far-reaching plain of moonlit snow. Right before him was a huge creature—a creature like the wolf in the pictures of Red Riding Hood, but ten times bigger than any wolf could be, with snarling, slavering jaws and malignant, flaming eyes. Such hate—such hellish hate—looked out of those eyes that Brian screamed with terror and wakened.

The room was filled with a dim greyness of dawn. Little Sam was still snoring peacefully, with Mustard curled up on his stomach. The wind and rain had ceased and a peep from the window showed Brian a world wrapped in grey fog. But the horror of his dream was still on him. Somehow—he could not have told how or why—he felt sure it had something to do with Cricket. Softly he slipped out of bed and into his ragged clothes— softly slipped out of the house and latched the door behind him. An hour later he reached home. Nobody was up. There was a strange car in the garage. Brian tiptoed across the kitchen and climbed the ladder to the loft. His heart was beating painfully. He prayed desperately that he might find Cricket there, warm and furry and purring.

What Brian saw was his Uncle Duncan asleep on his bed. There was no sign of Cricket anywhere. Brian sat down on the floor, with a sick feeling coming over him. He knew what must have happened—what had happened once before. Visitors had come—more visitors than there were beds for.

His uncle had given up his own bed and come to the loft.

Had Cricket come? And if so, had he gone away safely? Brian was asking these questions of himself over and over when his uncle awoke, stretched, sat up, and looked at him.

"Find the cattle?" he said.

"No-o-o, but Little Sam says he thinks they're in Jake Harmer's wood-lot. I'll go right away and get them."

Brian's voice shook beyond control but it was not with fear about the cattle. What—oh, what was the truth about Cricket?

Duncan Dark yawned.

"You'd better. And where'd that cat come from that woke me up pawing at my face? You bin having cats here, youngster?"

"No-o-o, only one—it came sometimes at nights," gasped Brian. It seemed that his very soul grew cold within him.

"Well, it won't come again. I wrung its neck. Now, you hustle off after them cows. You've plenty of time before breakfast."

Later on, Brian found the poor dead body of his little pet among the burdocks under the window. Brian felt that his heart was breaking as he gathered Cricket up in his arms and tried to close the glazed eyes. He felt so helpless—so alone. The only thing that loved him in the world was dead—murdered. Never again would he hear the pad-pad of little feet on the porch roof—never again would a soft paw touch his face in the darkness—never again would a purring thing snuggle against him lovingly. There was no God. Not even a young careless God could have let a thing like this happen.

When night came Brian felt that he could not—*could not*—go to his bed in the loft. He could not lie there alone, waiting for Cricket, who could never come again—Cricket lying cold and stiff in the little grave Brian had dug for him under the wild cherry tree. In his despair the child rushed away from the house and along the twilit road. He hardly knew where he was going. By some blind instinct rather than design, his feet bore him to the Rose River graveyard and his mother's neglected grave. He cast himself down upon it, sobbing terribly.

"Oh, Mother—Mother. I wish I was dead—with you. Mother—Mother—take me—I can't live any longer—I can't—I can't. *Please,* Mother."

Margaret Penhallow stood looking down at him. She had been down to Artemas Dark with a dress for May Dark and had taken a short cut through the graveyard on her way back, walking slowly because she rather enjoyed being in this dreamy spot where so many of her kindred slept and where the crisp, frosty west wind was blowing over old graves. Was this poor Laura Dark's boy? And what was his trouble?

She bent down and touched him gently.

"Brian,—what is the matter, dear?"

Brian started convulsively and got up, shrinking into himself. His painful little sobs ceased.

"Brian,—tell me, dear."

Brian had thought he could never tell anybody. But Margaret's soft grey-blue eyes were so tender and pitiful. He found himself telling her. He sobbed out the story of poor Cricket.

"It was all I had to love—and nobody but Cricket ever loved me."

Margaret stood very still for a few moments, patting Brian's head. In those few moments the dream of the golden-haired baby vanished for ever from her heart. She knew what she must do— what she *wanted* to do.

"Brian, would you like to come and live with me—down at Whispering Winds? I'm moving there next week. You will be *my* little boy—and I will love you—I loved your mother, dear, when we were girls together."

Brian stopped sobbing and looked at her incredulously.

491

"Oh, Miss Penhallow—do you mean it? Can I really live with you? And will—will Uncle Duncan let me?"

"Yes, I do mean it. And I don't think there's much doubt that your uncle will be glad to get—to let you come to me. Don't cry any more, dear. Run right home—it's too cold for you to be here like this. Next week we'll arrange it all. And will you call me Aunt Margaret?"

"Oh, Aunt Margaret,"—Brian caught her hand—her pretty slender hand that had so kindly touched his hair—"I—I—oh, I'm afraid you won't love me when you know all about me. I'm—I'm not good, Aunt Margaret. Aunt Alethea says so. And she's—she's right. I didn't want to go to church, Aunt Margaret, because my clothes were so shabby. I know that was wicked. And I—I had such dreadful thoughts when Uncle Duncan told me he'd killed Cricket. Oh, Aunt Margaret, I wouldn't want you to be disappointed in me when you found out I wasn't a good boy."

Margaret smiled and put her arm around him. How thin his poor little body was.

"We'll both be bad and wicked together then, Brian. Come, dear, I'll walk part of the way home with you. You're cold—you're shivering. You shouldn't be out without a jacket on a night like this."

They went over the graveyard, past Aunt Becky's grave and gleaming monument and down the road, hand in hand. They were both suddenly very happy. They knew they belonged to each other. Brian fell asleep that night with tears on his lashes for poor Cricket but with a warm feeling of being lapped round with love—such as he had never known before. Margaret lay blissfully awake. Whispering Winds was hers and a little lonely creature to love and cherish. She asked for nothing more—not even for Aunt Becky's jug.

FINALLY, BRETHREN

The clan had hardly got its second wind after the reconciliation of Hugh and Joscelyn when the last day of October loomed near— the day when it should be known who was to get Aunt Becky's jug. The earlier excitement, which had waned a little, especially in view of all the approaching weddings—"a lot of marrying this year," as Uncle Pippin said—blazed up again fiercely, coupled with anxious speculations as to what had caused the change in Dandy.

For Dandy was changed. Nobody could deny that. He had become furtive, morose, unfriendly, absent-minded. He snapped at people. He went to church regularly but he never lingered to talk with folks after the service. Assemblies at the blacksmith's forge knew him not. Town on Saturday knew him not. Some thought it was because of the fire but the majority refused that opinion. Dandy had lost practically nothing by the fire except his spare-room furniture. He was well insured and had an old house on his lower farm to move into temporarily. It must be something connected with the jug. Did Dandy really have to decide who was to get it and was afraid of the consequences?

"Looks like a man with something on his conscience," said Stanton Grundy.

"Can't be that," said Uncle Pippin. "Dandy never had any conscience, to speak of."

"Then he must have nervous prostration," said Grundy.

"I shouldn't wonder," agreed Uncle Pippin. "Having that jug for a whole year and mebbe having to settle who's to get it 'd be hard on anybody's nerves."

"Do you suppose," suggested Sim Dark horribly, "that Mrs Dandy has smashed the jug?"

The tension grew as the last of October approached. Drowned John and Titus Dark both reflected that, jug or no jug, they could let themselves go in another week. William Y. had bought a new mahogany table in Charlottetown, and gossip said he meant it as a stand for the jug. Old Miller Dark was holding the final chapter of his history open until he could include the lucky name. Chris Penhallow was looking lovingly at his dear neglected fiddle. Mrs Allan Dark, whose spirit and determination had so far kept her alive, reflected with a tired sigh that she could die in peace after the thirty-first of October.

"And here's Edith going to have a baby that very week," wailed Mrs Sim Dark.

It was just like Edith to have a baby at such an inconvenient time. Really, her mother thought vexedly, she might have planned things better than that.

The day came at last. A grey day with a grey wind. Autumn groves that had been an enchantment of gold and spruce-green were leaflessly grey now. Red-ribbed fields on the Treewoofe hill testified to many a glad day's work on Hugh's part. A great pyramid of pumpkins shone goldenly in Homer Penhallow's yard. The gulf was dark blue and the pasture fields adream.

Everybody was at Dandy's, except poor Mrs Sim—Edith had run true to form—and the Jim Trents, who were quarantined for measles and were at home bitterly wondering if they had served God for naught. Dandy's bull-dog, Alphonso, sat on his haunches at the front door as if he never expected to do anything but sit.

"On the whole, you are the ugliest brute I ever saw," Peter told him—which didn't hurt the dog's feelings any. He simply made a blood-curdling sound that gave Mrs Toynbee a spasm.

"Going to give us anything to eat, Dandy?" whispered Uncle Pippin.

"The wife has prepared refreshments, I believe," said Dandy nervously. He didn't think anybody would have much appetite after they heard what he had to say.

Murray Dark sat and watched Thora as usual—with this

difference: that he was wondering how soon it would be decent to begin courting her. If Chris had died a natural death Murray would have waited only three months. But as things were, he thought he'd better make it six. Margaret wore an exceedingly pretty grey silk dress—it had been intended for her wedding one—and looked so young and dainty and happy that Penny felt another dreadful qualm and Stanton Grundy wondered if it mightn't be wise to marry again after all. There must be a good bit of that ten thousand left, in spite of her foolish purchase of that tumbledown little place and all the new furniture they said she had put in it. Stanton determined to think it over. Eventually he decided not to. Which was just as well because Margaret had no longer any hankerings for marriage. She had Whispering Winds and Brian and she was perfectly happy. She no longer even cared about the jug.

Donna still cared a little, but not so greatly. After all, you could not take a jug like that to Africa. She was thinking more of the wedding-breakfast and the decorations of the church. For Peter, who was one of the born wanderers of the earth, found himself roped in for a conventional wedding with all the fuss and frills possible. Drowned John was determined on it. He loved a big colourful wedding, in keeping with the traditions of the clan. He had been cheated out of it on Donna's hurried war bridal with Barry but by—goodness, he wasn't going to be cheated out of it the second time. And thank heaven decent dresses were in again! Donna's wedding-dress, Drowned John decided, should sweep the floor. Donna didn't care. Where she was going with Peter she would wear nothing but knickerbockers. Luckily Drowned John knew nothing of this. It would have seemed more outrageous to him than the lions.

Roger sat and worshipped Gay openly and shamelessly—her shining hair, her marigold eyes, the charming gestures of her wonderful hands. He looked so happy that he made some of them feel a bit uneasy, as if it were flying in the face of Providence.

Nan was there, darting the mockery of her green eyes over

everything, although she rather avoided looking at Gay. Thomas Ashley and his wife, of Halifax, were there, though the clan thought they hadn't any business to be. They were no relations, although they were visiting the William Y.'s. Nobody, looking at Thomas' moon face, pursy old mouth and tortoise-shell glasses would have dreamed that he came there fired by a romantic memory. He wanted to see Mrs Clifford Penhallow again. He had been wildly in love with her when he was young and, as his wife knew bitterly, had never wholly got over it. Thomas was looking furtively at all the women in the room. Mrs Clifford had not come yet. He wondered who the grim, homely woman under the mantelpiece was.

Hugh and Joscelyn were there, although Joscelyn would rather have been home, painting the woodwork in the spare room at Treewoofe. Rachel Penhallow was there, as happy as it was possible for her to be. Penny Dark had heard that her bottle of Jordan water had been spilled and he promptly sent her his, glad to get the absurd thing out of the house. Rachel had gone off her milk diet at once. Kate and Frank and their baby were there. The baby cried a great deal and Stanton Grundy glared at it. Tempest Dark was there. Lawson and Naomi Dark were there. Naomi looked a little older and tireder and more hopeless. David Dark was there, comfortably sure that Dandy, at any rate, would not ask him to open with prayer. Uncle Pippin was there, wondering why, in spite of all the repressed excitement, everything seemed a little flat. Not much like Aunt Becky's levees. Uncle Pippin decided it was because every one was too polite. Things weren't interesting when people were too polite. Aunt Becky had never been too polite. That was why her levees had been so interesting.

II

The crucial moment had arrived. Dandy had come in and stood before the stove, his back to the mantelpiece. He was deathly pale and it was observed that his hands were trembling. The strain suddenly became almost unbearable. Artemas Dark tried to steady his nerves by counting the roses on the wallpaper. Rachel Penhallow immediately had a feeling that something was going to happen. Mrs Howard reflected with a gasp that the windows in that house couldn't have been opened for a hundred years. Why had Mrs Dandy put such a roaring fire in the stove, even on a chilly October day? But she was always a little mad, anyway.

Dandy had once looked forward to this moment, when, clothed with authority, he should stand up before them all and announce Aunt Becky's decision. And now he wished himself dead. He turned suddenly on Percy Dark.

"Would you mind stopping that everlasting drumming on the table?" he asked irritably.

Percy jumped and stopped. He started to say something but Drowned John nudged him fiercely.

"Dry up," said Drowned John.

Percy dried up.

"Come, come, Dandy," said William Y. impatiently. "Step on the juice. We've had enough of suspense. Tell us who's to get it and have it over."

"I—I can't," said Dandy, moistening his lips.

"Can't *what?*"

"Can't tell you who's to get the jug. I—I—don't know. Nobody ever will know—now."

"Look here, Dandy—" William Y. rose threateningly. "What does this mean?"

"It means"—the worst was out and Dandy had a little more courage—"I've lost the letter Aunt Becky gave me—the letter with the name in it. There *was* a name in it—she told me so much."

"Lost it! Where did you lose it?"

"I'm—not sure," hesitated the wretched Dandy. "That is—I'm almost sure it fell into the pig-pen. I always carried it round in a folder in my breast pocket. I never let it out of my possession. One day, some two months ago, I was up in the barn loft forking down straw. You know the flooring is just poles—there was gaps between them. I took off my coat when I got warm working and put it on again when I finished. When I went back to the house I—I missed the folder. I hunted everywhere—*everywhere.* It must have fallen into the pig-pen—the pig-pen is right under the loft, and the pigs must have et it altogether, letter and folder and all."

For a few minutes everybody said nothing very rapidly. Then—

"Damn it!" exploded Drowned John. All the repression of months was in his ejaculation. Everybody forgave him. Titus Dark looked envious. He had got so out of the habit of swearing he was afraid he could never get into it again. Even his horses had learned to understand a milder vocabulary. And a fat lot of good it had done!

Tom Dark remembered he had seen a black cat run across the road on his way to Dandy's. William Y. looked around on the circle of outraged faces. This was what you might call a hellish discovery. The situation demanded careful handling and he felt that he, William Y., was the man to handle it.

"Are you sure you had it in your pocket when you went up into the loft—sure it hadn't dropped out before?"

"Almost sure," stammered the miserable Dandy, who couldn't feel sure even of his own name just then. "I searched everywhere. It's been wearing me to a shadow. The wife said to pray about it. Dang it, I've prayed till I was black in the face."

"And you've no idea what name was in the envelope?"

It seemed incredible that Dandy didn't know *that.*

"I ain't got the least idea," said Dandy. "It was sealed—I never saw so much sealing-wax on the back of any letter. And Aunt Becky made me swear I wouldn't tamper with it."

Drowned John determined to take a hand. William Y. wasn't going to be let run things.

"We'll have to draw lots for it," he said.

"That isn't a Christian way to decide it," said William Y.

"Anybody got any other suggestion?"

"Let's vote who's to have it—secret ballot," said Junius Penhallow.

"With everybody putting his own name in the ballot," remarked William Y., with a smile of icy contempt for such a suggestion. "No; *I'll* tell you what should be done—"

"Here's the Moon Man running across the yard," interrupted Uncle Pippin. "He seems in a mighty hurry."

Those who could look out of the window did so. They saw the Moon Man with his long black coat streaming out behind him in the wind like the mantle of a prophet of old. In a few seconds he had reached the house, crossed the hall, and was standing breathlessly in the doorway of the room. The whole clan realized that the Moon Man had one of his really crazy fits on.

"I heard the devil cackling as I came down by the barn," said the Moon Man. "He was in glee over this unholy gathering where envy and all uncharitableness prevail."

His look scorched everybody and left them feeling like cinders.

"It has been revealed to me what I should do."

The Moon Man strode to the table between the two windows— he snatched up Aunt Becky's jug—he hurled it furiously at the mantelpiece. Roger, realizing before any one else, but just too late, what the Moon Man meant to do, sprang up and caught at his arm. He could not save the jug but he deflected slightly the Moon Man's aim. The jug hurtled through the air at Lawson Dark. And Lawson Dark, who had not stood or walked for eleven years, saw it coming and sprang to his feet to avoid it. The jug struck him squarely on the head, crashed like an egg-shell, slid off against the stove, and fell on the floor in hundreds of tiny fragments. Harriet Dark perhaps turned over in her grave. Possibly Aunt Becky did, too. But Lawson Dark, with blood trickling from a cut on his forehead, had turned dazedly to his wife.

"Naomi!" he cried, holding out his hands to her. "Oh, Naomi."

III

"Don't it beat hell?" said Sim Dark.

"And we won't ever know who should have had the pieces," said William Y. disconsolately, as they lingered in the yard, after Roger had taken charge of Lawson and carried him and Naomi off home.

The clan were not inclined to discuss what had happened to Lawson. It savoured too strongly of something miraculous and unclan-like. The jug was a safer topic—now.

"That doesn't matter much," said David Dark. "There's thousands of 'em—they could never be stuck together."

"Anyhow, if anybody had got it I reckon he'd never have got home alive," said Stanton Grundy. Tom Dark, who had never cried in his life, was crying because he hadn't got the jug. His wife dragged him hastily off to his car to hide his shame. Joscelyn and Hugh went away together very silently, thinking only of the look on Naomi Dark's face when Lawson had turned to her with his glad cry of recognition. Mrs Alpheus was furious with both the Moon Man and Dandy. Something—she wasn't quite clear what—ought to be done to both of them. Homer Penhallow and Palmer Dark passed each other without recognition. It was very satisfying to be enemies again. Life had been so darned dull when they had to be friendly. David and Percy Dark nodded shamefacedly to each other and mentioned the weather. The graveyard fracas was forgotten.

"It's a funny world," sighed Uncle Pippin.

"Let's laugh at it then," said Stanton Grundy.

Old Thomas Ashley was not happy. Somebody had come up to him on the veranda and said archly, "Don't *dare* to say you don't know *me*." He stared at her in silence. It was the grim lady who had sat under the mantelpiece. No, he didn't know her—and yet—

"I'm Mavis Dark," she said more archly still.

"Mavis Dark! Impossible!" exclaimed Thomas Ashley.

"Oh, *have* I changed so much?" said Mrs Clifford poutingly. "Don't you remember that summer you were here?"

Thomas Ashley looked at her. The skin which had been creamy in youth was yellow now—the smooth cheeks were wrinkled—the smooth neck wattled. The sleek, black hair had turned grey—the gracious curves had vanished.

"But—but—you were beautiful then," stammered poor old Thomas.

"You've changed a little yourself," Mrs Clifford reminded him acidly.

Thomas Ashley went away, lamenting a lost dream. He wished he had never heard of the old Dark jug. But his plump, pretty little wife was not ill-pleased. The ghostly rival of thirty years was laid at last. God bless Aunt Becky's jug!

Tempest Dark, his eyes alight with good-humoured mockery, had decided that he would keep on living. He had found a job that would give him bread and discovered that existence was possible even without Winnifred.

"After all, life's worth living when a comedy like this is played out," he reflected.

"Dang it, I believe there *is* something in prayer after all," said Dandy, when the last car had driven away.

IV

Winter was coming on apace; November wore away. At Treewoofe Hugh and Joscelyn kept glowing fires in every room and laughed at the winds that swirled up from the gulf. Peter and Donna were on their way to Africa. Roger and Gay were not yet home from their honeymoon. Margaret and Brian were nested in Whispering Winds. And one cold evening poor, lonely, hungry Big Sam set out for a walk around the shore to the lighthouse on Bay Silver Point. It was a long walk and he had various rheumatic spots about his anatomy, but there would be some cronies at the lighthouse and Big Sam thought an evening of social intercourse would be better for his nerves than playing tit-tat-o, right hand against the left, at home. These short days and long, early-falling evenings were depressing, he admitted. And the Wilkins' shanty was draughty. Perhaps Happy Dark would be at the lighthouse, with his ringing tales of life in the tropic seas. And maybe the lighthouse-keeper's wife might even give them a bite of lunch. But he would not let his thoughts dwell on Little Sam's suet puddings and chowders and hot biscuits. That way madness lay.

There had been a skim of snow that morning, melting into dampness as the sun rose for an hour or two of watery brightness before shrouding himself in clouds. The brief day had grown cold and raw as it wore on and now land and sea lay wrapped in a grey, brooding stillness. Far away Big Sam heard a train-whistle blow distinctly. The Old Lady of the Gulf moaned now and then. A storm was coming up but Big Sam was not afraid of storms. He would come home by the river road; the tide would be too high on his return to come by the Hole-in-the-Wall.

As a matter of fact, when he reached the long red headland known as the Hole-in-the-Wall, he blankly realized that the tide was already ahead of him. There was no getting around it. He could not climb its steep rugged sides; and to go back to where a road led down to the shore meant a lot of extra walking.

A daring inspiration came to Big Sam. Since he could not get around the Hole-in-the-Wall, could he go through it? Nobody ever had gone through it. But there had to be a first time for anything. It was certainly bigger than last year. Nothing venture, nothing win.

The Hole-in-the-Wall had begun with a tiny opening through the relatively thin side of the headland. Every year it grew a little larger as the yielding sandstone crumbled under wave and frost. It was a fair size now. Big Sam was small and thin. He reckoned if he could get his head through, the rest of him could follow.

He lay down and cautiously began squirming through. It was tighter than he had thought. The sides seemed suddenly very thick. All at once Big Sam decided that he was not cut out for a pioneer. He would go back out to the road. He tried to. He could not move. Somehow his coat had got ruckled up around his shoulders and jammed him tight. Vainly he twisted and writhed and tugged. The big rock seemed to hold him as in a grip of iron. The more he struggled the tighter he seemed to get wedged in. Finally he lay still with a cold sweat of horror breaking over him. His head was through the Hole-in-the-Wall. His shoulders were tight in it. His legs—where *were* his legs? There was no sensation in them, but they were probably hanging down the rock wall on the hinder side.

What a position to be in! On a lonely shore on a fast-darkening November night with a storm coming up. He would never live through it. He would die of heart-failure before morning, like old Captain Jobby who tried to climb through a gate when he was drunk, and stuck there.

Nobody could see him and it was no use to yell. Before him, as behind him, was nothing but a curving, shadowy cove bounded by another headland. No house, no human being in sight. Nevertheless, Big Sam yelled with what little breath he had left.

"Wouldn't you just as soon sing as make that noise?" queried Little Sam, sticking his head around the huge boulder that screened him.

Big Sam stared at the familiar spidery nose and huge moustache. Of all the men in River and Cove to catch him in this predicament, that it should be Little Sam! What the devil was he doing, squatted here a mile away from home on such a night?

"I wasn't aimin' to sing, not being afflicted as some folks are," said Big Sam sarcastically. "I was just trying to fill my lungs with air."

"Why don't you come all the way through?" jeered Little Sam, coming around the boulder.

"'Cause I can't, and you know it," said Big Sam savagely. "Look here, Samuel Dark, you and I ain't friends but I'm a human being, ain't I?"

"There are times when I can see a distant resemblance to one in you," acknowledged Little Sam, sitting calmly down on a jut of the boulder.

"Well, then, in the name of humanity help me out of this."

"I dunno's I can," said Little Sam dubiously. "Seems to me the only way'd be to yank you back by the legs and I can't git round the cape to do that."

"If you can get a good grip on my shoulders or my coat you can yank me out this way. It only wants a good pull. I can't get my arms free to help myself."

"And I dunno's I will," went on Little Sam as if he had not been interrupted.

"You—dunno's—you—*will*! D'ye mean to say you'll leave me here to die a night like this? Well, Sam Dark—"

"No; I ain't aiming to do that. It'll be your own fault if you're left here. But you've got to show some signs of sense if I'm going to pull you out. Will you come home and behave yourself if I do?"

"If you want me to come home you know all you've got to do," snapped Big Sam. "Shoot out your Roarer."

"Aurorer stays," said Little Sam briefly.

"Then I stay, too." Big Sam imitated Little Sam's brevity—partly because he had very little breath to use for talking at all.

Little Sam took out his pipe and proceeded to light it.

"I'll give you a few minutes to reflect 'fore I go. I don't aim to stay long here in the damp. I dunno how a little wizened critter like you'll stand it all night. Anyhow, you'll have some feeling after this for the poor camel trying to get through the needle's eye."

"Call yourself a Christian?" sneered Big Sam.

"Don't be peevish now. This ain't a question of religion—this is a question of common sense," retorted Little Sam.

Big Sam made a terrific effort to free himself but not even a tremor of the grim red headland was produced thereby.

"You'll bust a blood-vessel in one of them spasms," warned

Little Sam. "You'd orter to see yourself with your red whiskers sticking out of that hole. And I s'pose the rest of you's sticking out of the other side. Beautiful rear view if any one comes along. Not that any one likely will, this time o' night. But if you're still alive in the morning I'm going to get Prince Dark to take a snap of your hind legs. Be sensible, Sammy. I've got pea soup for supper—hot pea soup."

"Take your pea soup to hell," said Big Sam.

Followed a lot of silence. Big Sam was thinking. He knew where his extremities were now, for the cold was nipping them like a weasel. The rock around him was hard as iron. It was beginning to rain and the wind was rising. Already the showers of spray were spuming up from the beach. By morning he would be dead or gibbering.

But it was bitter to knuckle under to Little Sam and that white-limbed hussy on the clock shelf. Big Sam tried to pluck a little honour from the jaws of defeat.

"If I come back, will you promise not to marry that fat widow?"

Little Sam concealed all evidence of triumph.

"I ain't promising nothing—but I ain't marrying *any* widow, fat *or* lean."

"I s'pose that means she wouldn't have you."

"She didn't get the chance to have me or not have me. I ain't contracting any alliance with the House of Terlizzick, maid *or* widow. Well, I'm for home and pea soup. Coming, Sammy?"

Big Sam emitted a sigh, partly of exhaustion, partly of surrender. Life was too complicated. He was beaten.

"Pull me out of this damn' hole," he said sourly, "and I don't care how many naked weemen you have round."

"One's enough," said Little Sam.

He got a grip somehow of Big Sam's coat over his shoulders and tugged manfully. Big Sam howled. He was sure his legs were being torn off at the hips. Then he found that they were still attached to his body, standing on the rock beside Little Sam.

"Wring your whiskers out and hurry," said Little Sam. "I'm

afraid that pea soup'll be scorched. It's sitting on the back of the stove."

<h1 style="text-align:center">V</h1>

This was comfort now—with the cold rain beating down outside and the gulf beginning to bellow. The stove was purring a lyric of beech and maple, and Mustard was licking her beautiful family under it.

Big Sam drew a long breath of satisfaction. There were many things to be talked over with Little Sam—incidents they could discuss with the calm detachment of those who lived on the fringe of the clan only. What name had really been in the envelope Dandy's pig had eaten. The uncanny miracle of Lawson Dark's restoration. The fact that Joscelyn Dark had got over her long fit of the sulks. The wedding of Peter and Donna and all the expense Drowned John must have gone to. All the things that had or had not happened in the clan because of Aunt Becky's jug. And some amazing yarn of Walter Dark's black cat that had fallen into a gallon of gasoline and come out white.

Really the pea soup was sublime.

After all, them earrings rather became Little Sam. Balanced the moustache, so to speak. And Aurorer—but what was the matter with Aurorer?

"What you bin doing with that old heathen graven immidge of yours?" demanded Big Sam, setting down half drunk his cup of militant tea with a thud.

"Give her a coat of bronze paint," said Little Sam proudly. "Looks real tasty, don't it? Knew you'd be sneaking home some of these long-come-shorts and thought I'd show you I could be consid'rate of your principles."

"Then you can scrape it off again," said Big Sam firmly. "Think I'm going to have an unclothed nigger sitting up there? If I've gotter be looking at a naked woman day in and day out, I want a white one for decency's sake."

THE END

OTHER BOOKS TO EXPLORE BY
L. M. MONTGOMERY

THE ANNE OF GREEN GABLES SERIES
Anne of Green Gables
Anne of Avonlea
Anne of the Island
Anne's House of Dreams
Rainbow Valley
Rilla of Ingleside
Anne of Windy Poplars
Anne of Ingleside
Chronicles of Avonlea
Further Chronicles of Avonlea
The Anne of Green Gables Poetry Book - Selected Poems from
    Anne and Her Friends

THE STORY GIRL SERIES
The Story Girl
The Golden Road

THE EMILY STARR SERIES
Emily of New Moon
Emily Climbs
Emily's Quest

PAT OF SILVER BUSH SERIES
Pat of Silver Bush
Mistress Pat

OTHER BOOKS TO EXPLORE BY
L. M. MONTGOMERY

NOVELS
Kilmeny of the Orchard
The Blue Castle
A Tangled Web
Magic for Marigold
Jane of Lantern Hill

POETRY
The Watchman & Other Poems

AUTOBIOGRAPHY
The Alpine Path: The Story of My Career

COLLECTIONS
The Anne of Green Gables Collection - Volumes 1-3
  (Anne of Green Gables, Anne of Avonlea and Anne of the Island)
The Emily Starr Series
  (Emily of New Moon, Emily Climbs and Emily's Quest)
The Story Girl & The Golden Road
Pat of Silver Bush & Mistress Pat
The Blue Castle & A Tangled Web
Magic for Marigold & Jane of Lantern Hill
Lucy Maud Montgomery Short Stories, 1896 to 1901
Lucy Maud Montgomery Short Stories, 1902 to 1903
Lucy Maud Montgomery Short Stories, 1904
Lucy Maud Montgomery Short Stories, 1905 to 1906
Lucy Maud Montgomery Short Stories, 1907 to 1908
Lucy Maud Montgomery Short Stories, 1909 to 1922